Sunset Over Earth

By
D. R. Wales

Contents

Miner's Blues

The Harpies

The Sunk'n Norwegian

Dim Sun

The Passenger

The Goose Chase Begins

The Nightmare

The Root of All Evil

The Forbidden System

Plentiful Fields

Of Freezers and Leaks

Confessions

Race Against the Clock

A Grave to Hide In

Fallout

Echoes in Time and Space

Limping Forward

Hot to Hell

Breaking the Bank

The Guild

Augmented Realities

Holding the Baby

Infiltration

The Wait

Recovery

Fish in a Barrel

Left at Albuquerque

The Exquisite Torture of Dinner Small Talk

Now What?

What Do We Do with a Returning Captain?

Bon Voyage

Countdown

Hatches, Matches & Dispatches

Unwelcoming Committee

A History of Eris

Sparring

This Could Be Heaven

Parting of Ways

Sunset Over Earth

Loose Ends

Miner's Blues

"Weapons at my command," Hannah called as she started to tap away on the holo-console of her chair.

Laura flopped back against her chair. "Are you sure? Don't you think it would be better to let Jon do the aiming," she said, knowing that her captain wasn't going to listen one bit. She never did. "Cracking an asteroid is a little different to fighter combat."

Hannah smiled as she completed her string of commands. "I am sure, I've been doing this sort of thing for years. Load a mining charge and ready the cutting beams." With a final bit of flair, she locked in her target location. "Relax; in a few minutes we'll be swimming in platinum, palladium and whatever the hell biotite is."

At the helm, Emily placed her head on the console.

Jon's avatar materialised next to the Captain's Chair. He opened his mouth to explain what biotite was, but Laura shook her head. With a small shrug, he simply went back to monitoring the systems of the *Sigyn*.

"Okay, Em, just keep us where we are and this pinata won't be around for much longer."

The holographic viewscreen showed the asteroid lazily spinning through space. There was nothing particularly interesting about it, just one of thousands of a similar size in the belt. But after a poor run, Hannah was eager to make some money from prospecting.

As she tapped the console to execute her commands, the screen showed the charge heading for the asteroid, where it slammed into a fissure near the edge as planned. It failed to detonate, causing the asteroid to start a drunken wobble.

"Huh, must have been a dud," she said. "Remind me not to buy charges from Taylor again."

"If, I may Captain," Jon said politely. "You bought them from Singh and Sons." He paused for a moment. "It didn't arm. I believe I did warn you about them."

While Hannah gave her AI a narrow look, Laura took it upon herself to finish the job. A precision hit from a cutting beam was enough to detonate the charge. On the screen, beams lanced out to chop the remains into bitesize chunks. Of course, the image was completely generated by the visual systems; the beams were invisible, but humans tended to get upset if they couldn't see them.

"Maybe this won't be a bust after all," Hannah announced with a smile. "Have Annie get the Bumbles on the gather."

"Really?" Emily asked, looking to Laura. "Are we really going to call the new drones 'Bumbles'?"

With a pitying look, Laura just shook her head. After a few runs, her new crewmate would learn to simply ignore the oddities. And if she was really lucky, in a few runs she'd have served her punishment. Laura was unlikely to ever be in that situation. That said, there were worse places to be: debtors' prison; working in a brothel; childminding.

A line of drones moved away from the ship, their gravity manipulators armed, ready to start gathering the precious rock. They had, in accordance with their nickname, been painted black and yellow, like rotund bumblebees, flitting from flower to flower to collect nectar.

"Got a ship on the extreme edge of my sensors," Jon said.

"I see it," Laura replied. "Coming in this general direction, trying to look casual." She shook her head. "No IFF, but it has to be a MC enforcer from the emission profile. We need to leave."

Hannah sat upright in her chair. "Stealth?"

"They know we're here," Emily replied. "Stealth won't stand up to an intense scan."

"How much have we got?"

"About 7%," Jon answered. "Most of its low grade, low value."

Emily started to tap on her console. "Drones are coming back in. I'm securing hatches and readying for a Hop."

"No, I'm not losing the haul."

"In case you didn't hear," Laura replied, calmly and in a sweetly condescending tone, "that is a Mining Commission enforcer. Assuming it's only a *Gypsum*-class recon, we'd only be slightly outgunned."

"We have papers," she replied, knowing fine well they were fake. While they would fool most of the miserable prospectors that would try to muscle in on a haul, the Commission wouldn't even consider them. The fines alone would be crippling without having to try to bail the *Sigyn* out of the impound.

Suddenly, the solution came to her. "The cloaking device."

Jon closed his eyes and took a deep, simulated breath, as Laura and Emily looked at each other.

"Ten says we freeze rather than suffocate," Laura said, offering her hand.

Emily shook it. "Done."

"Oh, come on, it only fried the power once," Hannah shot back, a touch annoyed that her own crew were rebelling against her plan. "Annie is certain the new distributor coils mean it is perfectly safe."

"If you need me, I'm going into dumb-mode and saving my higher functions," Jon said before his avatar vanished.

Even the AI was mutinying. That was just what she needed.

At least she could rely on Annie to follow orders and do what needed to be done. You could always rely on an engineer to get things done.

No sooner had Hannah tapped the command to bring the clocking device, a very much non-standard piece of hardware for a *Van Ransselaer*-class, online, the comm-link to the engine room burst into life.

After several seconds of what could only be described as indecipherable exclamations of alarm, there was a long pause. "You want the cloak? Are you half-daft, woman?"

Hannah chewed her lip. "Is that a problem?"

"Oh, no, no really. Just making sure you're aware of what you're asking for," Annie replied. "Laura, put me down for ten that the heat sinks' cook us."

It was official; the entire crew was against her. Well, Kelly hadn't voiced any opinion, but that was a very cold comfort considering she was likely in the Sickbay and not hearing any of the exchanges. There were times Hannah wondered how she ever managed to keep her captaincy without a mutiny.

Well, just the one mutiny, but that hadn't had any real force behind it and had been stopped with a bottle of wine. It was mostly in good fun. Usually.

The Bridge lights dropped and the hum and thrum of the ship died away to near silence. The gravity started to dip as power was diverted away from the gravity generator plates in the deck to feed the exceedingly hungry cloaking device.

"Status of our friend?" Hannah asked.

Laura had to tap a few times on her console to get it to respond. "Scanning the area, which suggests they can't see us, but they're moving in on where they likely saw our ghost."

Emily was already working on it, using a gentle thruster burn to move the *Sigyn* a few hundred metres away. The Commission ship slowed, but soon turned towards the asteroid remains. After another series of scans, the ship dropped a small location marker, turned its IFF back on, and started to head out of the belt.

Allowing the minutes to tick by, just in case the ship came back, hoping to catch whoever had been mining in the area, Hannah sat drumming her fingers, much to her crew's annoyance.

"Target the beacon and disable it," she said eventually. "I'm taking the cloak offline."

Despite the highly illegal action of tampering with equipment belonging to one of the Commissions, no one objected. The crew of the *Sigyn* were used to illegal actions and slipping through the narrow loopholes of the law, where they could.

As the cloaking device powered down, the bubble of warped space that bent all electromagnetic wavelengths around it dissipating, a highly charged pulse fried the beacon as it drifted lazily through space. Almost immediately, the drones were out again, feverishly gobbling up the fractured asteroid.

Cutting beams lashed out occasionally to remove useless rock, but otherwise, the ship sat quietly, her holds filling up with material that would hopefully save the entire run.

Jon reappeared. "Cargo bays three, four and five are full."

"Oh, welcome back to the land of higher brain function," Hannah replied, leaning on her elbow, pursing her lips slightly. "Remind me again why I installed you?"

"Because when you first tested that heap of junk, you fried your previous AI's neural net." He shook his head sadly, having seen the reports of the damage that had been done to Patrick, his predecessor. From a high functioning AI with all the emotional intelligence of a well-rounded human and super-intelligence, he was reduced to what amounted to a blue-screen of death. There had been nothing left to save.

Hannah looked at her lap for a moment. "Yes, well, he was rather annoying and thought he knew better than to shut down," she replied. "You've been a joy these last four years."

He wasn't exactly pleased with what he knew was a thin compliment.

"Let's get all hatches secured and get away from here before our friend comes back," she said. "Warp to the edge of the system then plot a slipstream course to the rendezvous."

Emily's jaw clenched slightly as she plotted a course for the warp drive. "It'll only take six hops to get to the rendezvous with the *Sheba*," she replied. "We'll still be on time, but much less likely to die if we try arriving at the same time."

"True, but slipstream is more fuel efficient."

"We get free fuel," Laura replied, although she knew the battle was lost before it had even begun.

"True, but it takes so long to skim a star and I'd have to surrender some to the *Sheba* or pay to take from her reserves," she said. As such, saving fuel was the best way to reduce the loss of income from the *Sheba*'s mistress. "And Helen doesn't even give me discount."

The ship lurched slightly as the warp drive came online, pulling the ship into a bubble of subspace to bypass the very annoying and normally infallible Special Relativity. While better than crawling about at relativistic speeds, it would still take years to get between star systems at warp.

Emily wasn't ready to give up yet. "Would it not be preferable to lose money rather than be scattered across lightyears of space if we're forced out of slip-space by the *Sheba*'s wake?"

Slipstream travel was the fastest and least expensive way to traverse the galaxy. It was, however, exceptionally dangerous for small ships. Slightly contrary to normal motion, larger objects moved with greater ease through slip-space, but created large wakes. Normally, it wasn't a problem, but if a small ship was attempting to pass close to a larger one, the wake would disrupt its slip-shields, pushing parts of the ship back into normal space.

The outcome was considered similar to what happens if the lid was left off a blender.

"We'll be fine," Hannah replied with confidence.

It took half an hour of stony silence for the *Sigyn* to reach the outer edge of the solar system where it was safer to enter slip-space. With no further objections, the ship shuddered as it tore through the fabric of space-time to enter slip-space.

Propelled along by the strange tidal forces of slip-space, the *Sigyn* travelled like a ship down a river, it's slip-shields keeping them safe and moving the way they wished to go as Jon made millions of subtle adjustments a second to fight nature's desire to force them back to normal space. The currents of exotic energy that flowed between large gravity wells objected to having normal matter riding them.

An alarm started to ping away in an unalarming way.

"I'm detecting a wake," Jon said calmly, but with a slight hint of self-satisfaction.

"We detect wakes all the time," Hannah replied, "is there a problem with your ability to perform the calculations to avoid it?"

Before he could answer, the subdued alarm became more alarming.

"From the adjustments I'm having to make, I'd say it's from a ship heading to roughly our destination," he said. "It's big enough to force us out if we don't stay ahead of it."

Hannah wondered if she was cursed. The chances that the *Sheba* was going to arrive at the same time as they were was astronomically small, yet was apparently going to happen. "Then by all means, please keep us ahead of it."

The alarm stepped its cries up a notch as the deck started to shudder slightly. Several other alarms began to shout for attention; the shuddering was a sign that the slip-shield emitters were started to get feedback as they changed output rapidly.

Pressing the comm calmly, Hannah decided to seek some advice. "Annie, are you monitoring what's going on."

What came back was incomprehensible, aside from the occasional expletive, before there was a short pause. "Aye, well, I reckon she'll hold together for…" there was a pause as she was probably consulting a reading, "about thirty seconds, then we all die horribly."

"Jon?"

"Twenty-seven, twenty-six, twenty-five –"

"Well, this is just great," Laura said over the din.

Emily shrugged. "I told you so."

Without warning, the shuddering eased off and the alarms started to go quiet. As the crew tried to figure out if it was because they were dead, the ship returned to normal space at a dead stop, intact and undamaged.

Hannah smiled. "See, no –"

The whole ship lurched to port violently as a particularly piercing alarm screamed for a few moments.

"I took the liberty of moving us," Jon said flatly. "Thought it best to; *Sheba*'s manoeuvring options were somewhat limited as she came back into normal space. The message coming from her is," he pondered how to phrase it, "blue to say the least."

With a nod, Hannah stood. "Take us in to dock."

The Harpies

She hadn't even made it off *Sigyn* before the summon had been sent. Feeling like a naughty schoolgirl being made to go to the headmaster's office, Hannah made her way to the Aviary where the most senior officers met away from the rest of the crew.

Contained within would be the Harpies. The name had originally been meant as an insult, but it had been turned into a mantle of pride.

The lights were down low as Hannah crept in and took her place at the table.

"We were starting to wonder if you were going to join us," Helen said as the lights came up to reveal the rest were already standing at their places. She always enjoyed a bit of theatre when in the mood – usually a foul one.

"The lift was a bit slow. Might want to look at that; give it a bit of oil, some TLC."

Hannah looked at her four sisters. Helen was looking at her sternly, as usual. Harry and Holly looked at the table, avoiding eye contact. Heather smiled weakly, her eyes pleading with her sister to keep her jokes to herself, just for once.

"So, just how close did we get to ramming you this time?" Helen asked. She knew the answer, but she had a point to prove.

"You wouldn't have hit me," she replied. "There was, oh, about three thousand metres between us."

Harry looked up. "That is an acceptable exit space for both ships."

"Thank you, Harriet." Helen's tone made it clear she was not going to tolerate comments. Harry fizzed for a moment, before looking away again.

"Well, at least you managed to buy the new converters for *Frigg*, *Idunn* and *Sif*."

Hannah smiled. "I brought back some pretty valuable ore that should help us bring in some cash."

"We'll get to that mess in a moment. Where are the converters?"

"I can explain –"

"You can explain that, for the fifth month running, your ship is the only functioning one we have?" Helen asked as she slammed her hand onto the table. "For God's sake, Hannah, we can't carry on like this."

She drew herself up. "They were fake."

Her sisters all looked at one another for a moment. "We had it on good authority that they were suitable," Holly replied. "My distributer said the dealer was legit."

A tiny victory had been won. It wasn't much, but that was what she was willing to take at the moment and hope everything else would be forgotten. "They were Mk Is dressed up as Mk IVs."

Heather closed her eyes and shook her head. "If we'd used them, there is a very good chance they'd have overloaded. The ships would have been stranded or destroyed." The idea that someone had either knowingly tried to damage their operation or hadn't verified the seller properly was worrying. It was becoming hard enough to find aftermarket parts without drawing attention.

"Annie checked them thoroughly," Hannah continued to press her point home.

"Fine, good job," Helen admitted, grudgingly.

Holly looked to her older sister. "There is the matter of the second meeting that was set up, however."

"Yes, I was getting to that." Things instantly were not going as well as hoped.

"Why didn't you get to Anderson's, Hannah?"

"Well, I made a very valiant effort to get to that mobile junk heap" she replied, looking each of them in the eye. "Sadly, I had to make an unscheduled emergency stop at Yukon Outpost. A small crew welfare emergency."

Holly called up a spreadsheet on the table's holographic display. It showed a series of transactions from *Sigyn*'s account that Hannah used for business purposes. "Hm, yes, one that we paid the docking fee for. You also made a large payment to a chop shop and back paid from your personal account."

"Oh?"

"Hannah, please," Heather started before Helen cut her off with a glare.

For what felt like an eternity, Hannah looked at her sisters. Helen was trying to set her on fire with her stare, which Holly was trying to match, but it came off as comical. Harry just looked like she didn't want to be there, leaving Heather as her only ally.

Nothing new there.

"I got a discount using a business account, and I paid it all back."

"Doing your dolly up," Helen said sharply. "Instead of getting the goods we needed."

"She is not a dolly and I don't own her," she shot back.

"Maybe we should discuss this later."

"Stop defending her, Heather," Helen replied. She braced herself against the table and looked down to gather her thoughts. "Sheba?"

A hologram of a regal looking woman appeared beside Helen. "Yes, Commodore?"

"Commodore, is it?" Hannah asked, her anger starting to really bubble. "You are the eldest of us by three minutes and now you want to climb above us?"

"What is the state of my *little* sister's finances?" Helen continued, ignoring the remarks.

Sheba looked pointedly at Hannah. She disliked being ordered about, which only seemed to happen when Helen was taking issue with something Hannah had done. "Her personal account is virtually empty. Between it and a few shares and bonds, she has less than two thousand goldcoin to her name."

"What about her assets?"

"Currently, she has the ore in *Sigyn*'s hold, plus a few other bits of cargo," the AI answered, having demanded the information from Jon, who was forced to comply. "Other than that, she has the ship itself."

Seeing where it was going, Hannah decided there was only one other thing she had. Lifting herself up slightly, she wiggled then walked herself two steps to the side on her hands. When she dropped, the table now came to a little below her chin. Staring up at Helen, she lifted her artificial legs up, one at a time, and slammed them onto the table.

"Oh yes," Sheba said, lifting her nose slightly. "I'd forgotten about those. Two lower legs, including knee joints, custom made."

"Helen, you have made your point," Harry said, still unable to look at the proceedings.

Looking at the legs, still with the boots on, Helen just shook her head. "They're worthless."

"Put them away in storage," Hannah replied, "since we're all identical, if any of you lose a leg, you'll have a spare to hand. Or should that be 'to foot'?"

Sheba whispered to Helen, having run through the calculations of the worth of the ore, minus costs, to figure out how much would still be owed from the botched run. She took no pleasure in having to arbitrate the quintuplets' fighting. They might look identical, the leg issue non-withstanding, but they certainly were very different people.

"Put your legs back on," Helen said finally. "You'll not be paid for your services this time."

"What? We have an agreement that I get paid for doing your jobs."

"You did. Considering you seem to have no money, I'm curious about where you are laundering it from through us? I should call the taxman myself."

She looked to her other sisters. "Are you okay with this? I bought my ship by myself, I run it by myself and I help keep your ships going. You have bled me dry running around trying to keep this rust bucket afloat and I asked for nothing but to be paid like any other contractor. You have withheld my pay for the last four runs over nothing."

Holly shook her head and braced herself against the table. "You haven't actually completed the last four jobs to spec, why should we pay?"

Snatching her legs from the table, Hannah put them under her arm and started to march towards the door.

Heather started to follow her. "Hannah, let me help you."

"Let her go," Helen called after her. "If she wants to make a spectacle of herself, let her."

With her head held high, as if it was the most normal thing in the universe for a woman to be walking around with her legs under her arm, Hannah headed back to her ship.

Harry didn't know what she'd done to have earned the hellish task before her. She tried to keep out of trouble at work, did as she was told and still, she was being sent into the lion's den to negotiate.

She stood outside the bare metal door, wondering if it was better to go in or go back with her tail between her legs.

No, she had to do it. Heather would be too emotional about it all and only get herself in trouble, Holly would make things worse by being an accountant and Helen would demand obedience. She'd demand obedience from a feral cat and be surprised when it didn't work.

She pushed the bell and waited.

When the door opened, she stepped in, put one hand out defensively and held the large bar of chocolate she'd brought where it could be seen in the other. "Hannah, I've come to bargain," she said, quickly, seeing there was a leg ready to be launched at her like a javelin.

The leg was lowered, but not put down. "That had better be the offering to open negotiations and not the only thing you brought."

Harry smiled and relaxed a little. She pulled a roll of toffees from her pocket and tossed them over. "Will that do as an offering?"

"For now," she replied, opening three toffees and stuffing them in her mouth.

The room was a tip, as normal. Alongside the various items of clothing scattered about the floor, there were magazines, books, mugs, batteries and pieces of paper on most surfaces. In amongst it all were the various certificates, medals and mounted badges that Hannah had earned as a fighter pilot before moving into commercial flying, with a few illegal slants on it. Hidden in the debris were a few pictures; one of the five sisters as children with their parents; one of Hannah when she graduated flight school, smart in her uniform; a number from various times of her and Ali.

Those were the ones she looked happiest in.

She looked at her sister, sat on a basic, metal-framed chair, the lower parts of her trouser legs flapping. She looked tired and slightly beaten.

"So, what's the deal?" she slurred, chewing away on the toffees.

"Holly has found another, more reputable dealer for the converters," Harry replied as she took a seat. "One we've used before. Helen has asked me to go with you."

Hannah laughed, bitterly. "Asked or demanded?"

She sighed; it had been an order, but she wasn't willing to admit it. "She and Holly are worried about your reliability; Helen thinks you're holding out on us, using money you aren't declaring as well as laundering illegal funds through the company account. They get the fact Ali's treatment cost a fortune, but that was your money to spend. We all understand why you're doing it."

"Oh, so Ali was a worthy cause but Kelly isn't?"

Harry rubbed the bridge of her nose. "Hannah, I understand she's been mistreated, but right now, she is a lobotomised sex-doll playing at nurses and maids. She barely meets the requirements for being a synth, let alone sentient, and you are risking a lot to repair her. And if you are laundering money, you're putting us at risk too. You can't save everyone."

Sliding off the chair, Hannah marched over and snatched the bar of chocolate from her sister. "So, I should have just left her on the trash heap I found her on and let that bastard that cut her up go unchallenged?"

With a shrug, Harry wished she hadn't started the conversation. It wasn't the first time and it wouldn't be the last that Kelly would be a contentious topic of conversation. Personally, she liked the synth, but it would take years and a fortune to return her to her original design. And as long as she looked the way she did, she was going to draw the wrong sort of attention.

"I guess Mum and Dad shouldn't have bothered getting me legs," she continued. "If Dad hadn't had to work longer hours to pay them off, he might still be alive."

"Hannah —"

"Or better yet," she carried on, "if they had given me away when I was born deformed, Grandad might have been slightly more forgiving of Dad and supported the rest of you more."

A heavy, unpleasant silence filled the room between the sisters. Their family situation had always been difficult and while no one had ever blamed Hannah for their troubles, their mother's father had been very vocal on the fact his daughter and son-in-law could only have children by artificial means. Hannah's disability had been chalked up to an issue in the process.

"Where does the Fuhrer wish me to take you?" Hannah asked after having eaten half the bar of chocolate at a sickeningly fast pace.

"Don't call her that," Harry chided. "We're to go to Heimdall."

The rest of the chocolate vanished. "I'll stay here, you can take the ship," she said through a mouthful, rubbing melting chocolate and saliva from her chin. "I am not going anywhere near there."

"Your ship is the only one, aside from *The Queen of Sheba*, with a worthwhile functioning FTL drive," she replied. "And you know the *Sheba* isn't permitted to enter most systems due to her size."

Hannah just shook her head. "No, the crew will listen to you. In fact, wear my clothes and they won't even be able to tell the difference. I am not going where there are Purists of any denomination, even if they are just 'passing through'. I will not go anywhere near them, their space or their narrow, brutal views."

While Harry shared her sister's hatred of Purists, although to nowhere near the same level, going to the Heimdall system wasn't a guarantee of meeting any. It was far from their space and few of the extreme ones could stand being surrounded by the very things they preached against. But Heimdall was a popular place for them to preach.

"If you stand down, even for one journey, Helen will see it as you breaking contract," she cautioned. "She'll either put you out or fine you what little you actually have. And you know she'll give Vic command if she decided to commandeer *Sigyn*." It was a lie, but sometimes it was the only way to get Hannah to do something for her own good.

She threw her hands up. "Why does my own sister hate me?"

"Please, look at it from her point of view; she has a massive operation to run, most of her ships aren't flying and times are tough. We are running a hair's breadth from bankruptcy."

"Maybe I should cut her off at the knees and let her see things from my point of view."

Harry's temper finally bubbled over. "Yes, we get it, you've got no legs. Give it a bloody rest."

Both women looked at the laps for a few minutes, neither knowing what to say.

"I'm sorry," Hannah whispered.

"I'm sorry, too," Harry replied.

Hannah looked at her photographs for a moment. "I'm sorry, it's," she rubbed at her nose, "it's seven years tomorrow."

Closing her eyes, Harry cursed herself for forgetting. She then cursed Helen for either forgetting or not caring. There were times she wondered if they had all been sequenced from the same common embryo.

She looked at her sister and smiled weakly. "I'm so sorry." Crossing the small room, she hugged and held her. After saying her goodbyes, Harry left.

Kelly appeared from the bedroom where she'd been waiting after finishing cleaning. With limited tasks as a nurse and a strong urge to serve, she generally took on the role of janitor and engineering assistant.

"Thank you," she said quietly. "For sticking up for me."

Hannah smiled and shrugged. "Part of the ship, part of the crew. I'm sorry you had to hear that."

"Nothing new," she replied as she started to tidy up the discarded clothes. "You actually putting things away would be new, though."

"Hm, seems your sarcasm is starting to grow in. How are you getting on with the new intestines?"

Holding a t-shirt, Kelly stopped to consider the question. "It's so strange having any again. I feel bloated and uncomfortable, but it's better than having to either vomit or open my abdomen up to empty my stomach if I eat anything."

Hannah had to agree with that. When she'd found Kelly two years previously, pretty much her entire insides had been removed to allow her frame to be made slenderer than would be natural on a human. It seemed that her owner had removed almost everything that wasn't useful for sex, including her personality. When she'd started to become boring, he'd told her to wait in a dumpster, hoping she'd be junked before anyone noticed and reported the act.

Sometimes, rummaging in bins was a lifesaver.

"Well, I imagine it'll take time to get used to them," she replied. "I'm sorry that I couldn't afford to fix that waspish waist and get you a full digestive system. Next time."

"Perhaps it's better you don't," she replied, looking at the door where Harry had exited. "At least, not for now." She paused and frowned. "I hope that is not a comment about my personality."

Hannah chuckled. "Of course not. You're sweet and fluffy, like a cute little bumblebee."

A warm smile appeared on her face and for a fleeting moment, she appeared almost completely human. But it passed in a flash, leaving her with the slightly wax-work emulation of a human woman.

It was going to cost millions to get Kelly back to a physical point where she could pass for a normal human, as her model of synthetic was meant to do. It would likely take years of therapy to slowly restore her emotional intelligence without causing her a nervous breakdown and rampancy. Not being able to process her abuse was all that stopped her trying to self-terminate, but that meant she couldn't be truly free.

However much it cost, however long it took, Hannah considered it worth it. Especially in those human moments that appeared.

Kelly continued to sort the laundry, oblivious to what her captain was thinking. She stopped and frowned a little. "You should put your legs back on; you risk damaging your skin wandering about without them."

"Yes, Mother."

The Sunk'n Norwegian

Hannah could have been looking in a mirror as she stood looking at Harry. Dressed in identical clothes, not even a close inspection could tell them apart. Unfortunately, the clothes weren't her idea of comfortable. Or suitable for business.

"Why are we dressing like you on a date?" she asked. "Well, at least you going to a date," she added, rolling her eyes slightly.

"Because this is the best way to distract merchants is to look sexy," Harry replied with a self-assured nod. "And by looking sexy, they assume we're dumb and it makes them easier to trick. And you know fine well I don't date."

Looking at the white low-cut vest top and black leather bolero jacket her sister was wearing, Hannah did not feel in the least bit happier. "Perhaps it would be easier if we just went naked? These trousers are skin tight and they make your ass look like a small planet."

Harry crossed her arms, which did little to help her case. "And your ass looks better?"

"It's a peach."

"We have the same flat ass."

"Come on, can't we go in looking like proper ship captains?"

"You mean your normal 'Rogue Trader' look?" Harry asked as she tied her hair back into a tight ponytail.

"Smart trousers, a nice shirt and a captain's vest or jacket," she replied, doing the same. "Hell, I'd even, at a push, go with a smart dress. We're meant to be doing business, not going partying with the local pimps. I feel like a piece of meat."

Harry smiled. "But a very sexy piece of meat." She leant back a little on her heels. "If we were to update our relationship from sisters to clones, would it be incest or masturbation?"

With a taught smile, Hannah stepped around her sister and headed for the door. "It's been so long since I've been anywhere with you without Helen's claws in your back, I'd forgotten what a deviant you are."

They left Hannah's cabin and made their way to the engine room to find Annie, passing along the utilitarian corridors, each step they took in sync.

"Here's your cover ID," Harry said. "Arm out so I can load it."

Hannah held her arm out, pulling her sleeve up to reveal the implant on the inside of her wrist. Harry held a small data stick over it until it beeped. "Does Three-Minute-Advantage know you're using forged IDs again?"

"Where do you think I got them from? Your name is, for the moment, Olive."

Not a name she felt overly pleased with, but cover was cover. However, she wasn't done complaining about the clothes. "Does this sort of thing actually work?" she asked, running a thumb around her waistband to get it to sit right. "I find clever talking works better."

"You? Talk clever to a merchant?"

She tried to look innocent and failed miserably. "Fine, I prefer to blackmail them or stick a gun in their vitals. It's not like I've ever shot any of them."

Harry smiled triumphantly. "And that's why we need fake IDs."

When they arrived in the engine room, Annie stood looking at them for a heartbeat. "Jon? How much whisky did I drink last night?"

Jon appeared beside her, towering over the petite engineer. "Only half a bottle; rather light for you on a Wednesday night."

"Are you ready to go?" the sisters asked in perfect unison.

"Don't do that," Annie replied. "It's creepy enough you look the same without you dressing identically and speaking like linked bots."

The sisters looked at each other, before slowly turning back to smile at Annie, their heads tilting in unison. "We're not creepy."

Lifting a wrench, Annie pointed it at them threateningly. "I said; don't do that."

"Fine."

"We."

"Won't."

Annie stood looking at them. "I don't care that one of you is my captain, I will visit violence on you both. And why are you both dressed like slutty backing dancers?"

"I told you," Hannah said immediately, shattering the illusion. "Please, can't we just go as professionals. If you want a piece of meat to distract the seller, I'm sure Annie will undo a few more buttons on her overalls."

Clutching the neck of her overalls, Annie looked scandalised, despite the fact they were unbuttoned to the waist, revealing a grubby, fitted t-shirt underneath. "Indeed I will not. I could lose my certification by bringing the Guild into disrepute through inappropriately dressing. We're taking Kelly, can't you ask her to play sexy?"

"I'm not going to humiliate her like that," Hannah replied.

"Better than taking the risk of getting yourself propositioned by dressing like that," Jon said, half turning away from the sight.

Smiling thinly at Hannah's glare, Harry simply shrugged. "If people can't control themselves around two attractive women, then they'll deserve the fatal shot I'll give them in the face."

"I think I like you better when Helen has you beaten into submission."

Jon looked to Annie. "This is a terrible idea."

She nodded. "Yup, but at least you aren't going to be stuck with them. Do I get to be captain if they don't come back?"

The hum in the room died down as the ship dropped out of warp, having arrived at its destination.

For nearly a century, *The Sunk'n Norwegian* had served as an independent spaceport in a very low orbit of the gas giant Heimdall VII. *The Norwegian* had originally been one of the largest ships ever built, an Oblivion-Class Super Fleet Carrier called *Pride*.

The Oblivion-Class had been built by the Restoration with the purpose of being able to deliver an entire battlefleet into a system in one go. Fleet Carriers had previously been used only to bring in small ships, such as frigates, destroyers and gunboats that risked being destroyed in slipstream by the larger vessels.

Only three were built. Each was a hundred kilometres long, shaped like a cigar and able to deploy and support an entire fleet of capital ships and fighters on operation for years on end. They were less starships than they were starbases with a slipstream drive.

After the defeat of the Restoration, marked by the destruction of the *Oblivion* when she'd been rammed by explosive laden carriers, the *Pride* had ended up trapped in Heimdall VII. The attempt to escape the same fate as her sister ship had not gone to plan due to a panicked miscalculation that had dropped the ship into the upper atmosphere of the planet.

Abandoned for less than a year, an enterprising business man claimed the ship and turned her into a port. His plan for luxury accommodation mixed with affordable housing, plazas, schools and spaces for independent traders and workshops never happened. Dying shortly after securing his prize, his younger brother turned the *Pride* into a den of sin.

Gambling, brothels, indentured servant markets, illegal augmentations, smuggling and unregulated businesses reigned supreme, as long as they paid their fees. Mercenaries often operated from *The Norwegian* because it was outside of all law enforcement jurisdiction.

Repairs were infrequent, so the entire structure looked rundown and scummy, which was how most people who frequented liked it. It was also one of the few places were people of all faiths, politics and persuasions mixed freely.

Hannah had been a few times, but not for many years. Once, the allure of cheap thrills and cheaper drinks had drawn her, but the risk of encountering Purists, particularly those that were sympathetic to the Restoration Remnant, had soured the place. Harry wasn't so fussy and had often made trips when she had a ship to take her.

Sigyn touched down in one of the less desirable docking bays, the sort where a crew could come back to find their ship on blocks with vulgar graffiti all over it. It was, however, free for up to three days, which was preferable to the extortionate rates charged in the secure bays, which often weren't that secure, but attracted a higher class of criminal. They usually left calling cards and a fruit basket after stripping a ship to the support frame.

"So, where is our converter dealer?" Hannah asked as she clattered down the ramp, trying to get used to her stupid costume.

"Washington Square," Harry replied. "About twenty kilometres away and eighty metres up. Cabs are this way," she added, pointing to a collection of what looked like multi-person coffins that were perhaps once yellow.

They couldn't get the door to open on the first one, so moved to the second. The seats were badly worn and being held together with large bands of silver tape.

Eyeing it balefully, Hannah tutted as she gingerly got in. "I remember when I could afford to come in the business docks."

Annie shrugged as she dumped her tool bag into the cab. "This is an upgrade for me," she said cheerily. "I used to have to come in the tradesmen's entrance." Jumping into one of the rear seats, she immediately produced a screwdriver and started tightening a number of screws holding the seat together.

Once the four women were in and the door closed, the virtual driver came online.

"Welcome to *The Sunk'n Norwegian*, your one stop for everything you could ever want," the badly synthesised male voice announced. "I am Cab Charlie-4590, but you can call me Charlie. Before we take off, please state your names, reason for visit and anticipated duration for security purposes."

"Hi Charlie, I'm Liz Peterson and this is my sister Olive," Harry said sweetly. "We are here to do a little shopping along with our friends, Annie…" she turned in her seat to face Annie and whispered; "are you still a MacNeil?"

Bristling slightly, Annie huffed. "Indeed I am not. I've completed several degrees since; I'm a MacLennan."

"Sorry," she replied, knowing how touchy members of the Scottish Guild were when it came to their degrees. "Annie Clan-MacLennan."

Kelly leant forward when it became clear Harry had no idea of what was appropriate here as she didn't know how Hannah had registered her. "And Kelly."

Harry gave Hannah a peculiar look that would be followed by a rather pointed question at some point in the future when there were fewer ears listening. "We'll be here three days at most," she said, while still looking at her sister. "Free parking."

"Absolutely the right decision," Charlie replied cheerily. "Now, there are a number of items that require licences on the station. If you have any unlicensed items, you can either purchase one or leave items with me; I'll be your cab for the duration of your stay."

As they trundled along one of the cab tunnels, Charlie chatted away, completely oblivious to the fact no one was listening. He pointed out places of interest, landmarks (mostly hull dents) and offered exciting shopping locations.

By the time the cab set down in Washington Square, Annie had been employed to find a mute button, but had sadly failed.

Washington Square was a large collection of buildings that had once been maintenance sheds in a destroyer bay with more recent constructs nestled in between. The Square occupied most of the port wall, with a similar area a hundred-

and-fifty metres 'above' on the opposite wall of the bay. Cabs flitted between the areas, or passed through, using the access ways as shortcuts.

The first thing the group got to see was the security point; a doorway with a number of armed mercenaries lounging around and two official looking men behind a desk with a bored looking woman lurking nearby.

With her best swagger, Harry approached the officials and smiled. Without a word, she presented her wrist for scanning. It was only when Hannah appeared that they lifted a scanner. Most people were checked using their DNA, but identical twins caused problems. As such, all multiple-birth children and clones were required to use an implant or genetic ID card as identification. The implants were meant to be tamper proof, but it was relatively easy for those that knew what they were doing to unlock them.

One of the men nodded the sisters on, while the other checked Annie's identity.

Hannah held her breath as she walked through the door scanner. Sometimes her legs sent the damned things crazy, but others ignored them. She was lucky this time.

Despite having put her tool bag on the conveyer scanner, Annie ran afoul of the door. She marched back to the end of the conveyer and started to rummage in her pockets, of which there were many, to draw out more tools. After that, she pulled several small devices from her boots, a torch and spirit level from somewhere inside her overalls, and finally a handful of washers she had apparently been storing in her bra.

When it went off again, she trudged back, pulled a fork and knife from her hair, which promptly unfurled to cascade the full length of her back like a shampoo commercial, and placed them in the scanner as well.

"I can't take you anywhere, can I?" Hannah asked as Annie started to replace her tools and bits and pieces where they had come from.

"How do you carry all that?" Harry added.

She smiled. "I'm Scottish," she replied, as though that was a suitable explanation, while she finished pinning her hair back up. Seeing this wasn't an acceptable reply, she shrugged and added: "You need to learn more than just your discipline degrees to earn the right to be Scottish."

Hannah rolled her eyes, but decided it wasn't worth trying to pry into the secrets of one of the most affluent, mysterious and desired guilds in the galaxy. Harry took the cue and started to head for the shop.

It was then they realised that Kelly had yet to join them. She was still being held at the desk by the two officials, who seemed to be rather concerned about her specs.

Smiling innocently, Kelly fluttered her eyelashes. "Is there a problem?"

"Says here you are a 'Cybus Mk XIV Erica-Louise'," one of the men said, looking at his tablet. "You don't look like a Mk XIV Erica-Louise."

Despite wearing baggy clothing to mask her outline, it was still going to be obvious to anyone that had a picture of a stock model that she was not a stock model. "Oh, I know. I've had some work done," she replied, leaning towards the desk, placing her hands together on the edge. "Are my updates not on that little tablet?"

The female official sighed loudly, grabbed her coffee and disappeared for her break.

"Oh look, there they are," the other replied. "Oh my."

The smile faltered so slightly as Kelly's right eye twitched. "Yes, well, some of them weren't my smartest ideas ever."

Seeing there were no military grade changes or the usual suspicious upgrades that suggested weapons, smuggling or voids for transporting stolen goods (the list of changes was woefully incomplete), they waved her through.

"You okay?" Hannah asked quietly.

She twitched again. "I'm fine."

The group made their way through the moderately busy streets as people milled about, looking for places to shop, merchants peddled their wares from ramshackle stalls and sign holders tried to direct potential customers. The people were of all races, although some had been so heavily modified it was difficult to tell what they might have been. A cat-girl was twirling her tail suggestively at a man that was almost certainly more machine then human while her companion, who had either had her ears sculpted to look like an elf or a Vulcan, twirled a sign of a brothel known as "The Menagerie". Dressed in their snowy robes, two Purist monks were trying to hand out leaflets to save people from the sins of excessive surgery, cybernetics and gene modification by embracing the pure human form as it had been on Ancient Earth. They might as well have been handing out 'morning after' pills in a fertility clinic.

Hannah had spotted the monks, put her head down, and ploughed on through the crowd. When they were out of sight, she stopped beside a quiet stall and took several deep breaths. Several people looked at her curiously until the others formed a defensive shield about her.

"It's okay," Harry said softly, "they're just preachers and I'm certain they aren't Remnant."

"I don't care," she replied, reciting one of her calming mantras in her head. "They are Purists, they are all the same and I can't forgive them, any of them, for what they did."

Kelly stepped in, gently pushing Harry aside. "Look at me. You are safe, this place is safe. I have you. Come on, say it with me."

"I'm safe, this place is safe and you have me," Hannah repeated quietly, over and over for several minutes as Kelly kept her gaze held and repeated the mantra with her. Her reactions weren't normally nearly so bad, but with the time of year, the mere sight was enough to induce some panic.

Without a word, she stood up straight and started to head towards the shop again as though nothing had happened. No one said anything to her about it; they didn't think it would help and had no idea what to say anyway.

Harry leant into Annie. "Kelly's pretty good with her," she said.

"Aye," she replied. "She was a private nurse providing palliative care to her first owner. Still got most of her medical knowledge, but she's really good with anxiety."

The shop they were looking for was larger than the others around it, taking up an entire block and rising three storeys high above the mostly single storey buildings. A large neon sign declared the shop was called "Bit's and Bob's". Much of the building appeared to be stores.

Inside, the place was like a jumble sale. Boxes and crates sat on the floor with parts stacked on top of them, half dismantled objects lay forgotten on benches. Men and women in grease and oil-stained overalls worked on a few parts and mostly ignored the newcomers.

A rotund man in his later years waddled over to them, wiping his thick fingers on a cloth that should have been binned decades ago. He sniffed and coughed. "I help you?" he asked.

"We're here to see Devadas," Harry said sweetly. "Tell him it's the Harpies."

The man nodded. "Mmhmm," he replied, both in acknowledgement of the request and in appreciation of the collection of ladies before him. Without another word, he waddled off towards a door at the back of the shop marked "Private".

"Seriously?" Hannah enquired. "That's how we are announcing ourselves now?"

Before more could be said, the burly man stuck his head through the door and nodded for them to follow.

The back room was considerably nicer; everything was clean, neat and tidy, with only the finest items on display in cases. Sat on a plush semi-circular couch, behind a table, was a well-dressed man in a sand-coloured suit.

Harry trotted over to him as he stood up and stepped around the table. She launched herself the last step, grabbing his head to pull him into a passionate kiss. Hannah pulled the scrunchy from her hair and pinged it at her sister in annoyance.

After longer than was seemly, Devadas came up for air. "Well, that was quite the welcome," he said, stroking Harry's face gently. "Oh, I know you said your sisters were identical, but I had no idea you meant inseparably identical."

With a forced smile, Hannah ignored the comment. "When you said you'd used the dealer before, did you mean for business or just pleasure?"

Devadas let Harry go and came over to Hannah. "Apologies, Captain, I have been incredibly rude." He bowed deeply. "I am Devadas Kumar-Khan, owner of this humble establishment. I believe you are in need of some Smith & Kalstein Spiral Converters, Mk IV?"

"Yes."

He winced slightly at the terse reply, but simply nodded. "I'm afraid I can't fulfil the order. But I do have one pair and plenty of damaged ones that could make a few goods ones," he added hastily when he saw Hannah's eyes narrow.

"Annie, check them, please," she said. "I'm going back to the ship to change out of these stupid clothes."

Dim Sun

Harry was a little surprised to see Hannah waiting for her in the shop when she emerged from Devadas' private rooms nearly three hours later. She'd changed into a pair of sensible cargo trousers, thrown her old bomber jacket with her squad badges on and tied her hair into a lopsided plait that came over one shoulder and the strap of a satchel over the other.

"I hate you," she said curtly, but without any malice.

"Where'd you park your fighter, fly-girl?" Harry asked with a cheeky smile, pinching Hannah's cheek before being brushed away. "I'm starving; come on, there's a great Chinese restaurant nearby."

Without a word of complaint, Hannah fell into step with her. "Aww, does your boyfriend not feed you?"

"He's not my boyfriend."

"Aww, does your cuddle buddy not feed you?"

Harry stopped and looked at her sister incredulously. "Cuddle buddy? What are you? Twelve? And it's not like that at all; Devi is someone whose company I enjoy."

"And his dick."

"And his tongue," she added with a flick of her tongue, enjoying seeing Hannah squirm slightly at the discussion of her sex life. "It's particularly interesting if he's recently had a curry –"

Hannah immediately walked off, having no desire to hear anymore. They continued in silence until they arrived at a small shopfront with an ornate sign showing a Chinese style dragon. The writing was purely in Cantonese.

Despite the fact the human race had proliferated across the galaxy and long left behind the traditional stomping grounds of races and cultures, many had survived, mostly intact; others not so much. With people often mixing with people like them, it had ensured the survival of many cultures, long after it had been expected humans would become almost homogenous. In some cases, such as the Scottish Guild, anyone could become associated with a culture, if they followed the rules and traditions.

A number of heads came up and turned to look as they arrived, suspicion and curiosity etched on most faces. Fortunately, thanks to a series of small implants, both Hannah and Harry were able to switch to conversing with the staff in flawless, accent-less Cantonese. This dispelled the questioning looks as the diners returned to their meals and conversations, satisfied the newcomers were going to be suitably respectful and understanding of acceptable customs.

The ordered fried beef ho fan for the table, char-sui buns, fried squid, pork and prawn dumplings, char-sui cheung fun and beef, ginger and spring onion buns with a pot of jasmine tea. Aside from to speak to the staff, they reverted to English to talk.

"Dare I ask what price Devi wants for the converters?" Hannah asked as she lifted her cup of tea.

"He wanted two-fifty for the pair, plus ten for each of the junk ones we wanted," Harry replied as she opened the packet containing her chopsticks. "Annie called me once she'd confirmed how many she wanted. Got the lot for two-three-five."

The ho fan arrived. Hannah immediately dove into fill her bowl first. It had been a long time since she'd had Chinese food and the mix of spices and fried beef smelt good.

Harry, meanwhile, had lifted a bun as the bamboo steamer was placed on the table.

"Did you manage to get back and forth okay?" she asked, not referring to the Purist monk incident directly.

She nodded. "Yeah, I don't know what happened earlier. I guess I'm just a little on edge, but I managed to walk past them without incident."

They ate in silence for a few minutes. Hannah looked at the tv screens around the restaurant, currently showing a cooking show where the host was making a fish soup of some sort. When Harry's implant buzzed, she watched as she answered a message with a coy smile and immediately knew what was going on. The holoimage was one way, obscuring what was on it to anyone else; she wanted privacy.

"I'm guessing you are planning to see a few people while we're here," she said, wrestling a slippery cheung fun into her bowl with her chopsticks. It started to split, spilling some of the contents.

Harry shrugged. "Yeah, a few."

Placing her chopsticks down, Hannah tapped her wrist to call up her calendar. With a few taps, she pulled up Harry's calendar on the blue tinted hologram projected from her wrist and playfully flicked through it.

"Eight people over two and a half days?" she asked. "And looking at the names and addresses, a fair few prostitutes. Seems you have more than one type of dim sum on your agenda."

Swiping her hand across Hannah's wrist, Harry closed the hologram and glowered. "For your information, Helios is the best masseuse I've ever come across. And if you ask if it has a happy ending, I will throw tea over you."

Holding her hands up in surrender, Hannah kept quiet on that comment.

"And Felicity is a beauty therapist."

"But you plan on shagging the rest?"

Popping a piece of squid in her mouth, Harry shrugged. "Yup."

Hannah shook her head as she piled more ho fan into her bowl. She wasn't disgusted by her sister's exploits, but she did pity her slightly. Jumping for person to person, paying for attention, but trying to keep it quiet from the others; that wasn't any way to live.

"You're judging me."

"Of course not," she replied. "Come on, we are one messed up group of sisters. We have the Fuhrer –"

"Don't call her that."

"— the accountant that is sleeping with the XO, the same one that is after my ship," she continued while stuffing beef and noodles into her mouth, "the overly nice and nervous put-upon geologist, the nymphomaniac and me. Little old me; a widow, who has a few issues and no –"

"Legs."

"Cash."

They sat quietly for a moment. Harry poked at her food, picking at bits of it while Hannah continued to eat at a ferocious rate.

Harry broke the silence. "Perhaps you should look at getting back out there?"

"Offering me one of your booked slots?"

She huffed slightly. "No. I mean, there are plenty of dating apps. You could look at joining online social clubs, or even try mixing more with the *Sheba*'s crew. There's even apps for veterans to meet others even just for someone that understands."

Hannah snorted a laugh. "Yeah, so I can sit with someone and reminisce about 'the war' and compare medals, swap stories and have synchronised flashbacks?" She lifted a bun, bit into it and used it to point accusingly at her sister. "What makes you think I haven't put myself out there?"

Realising she was touching a nerve, Harry relented and moved on to ask what Annie and Kelly were getting up to now the converters had been dealt with. They'd gone on a joint shopping trip to look at one of the few common interests they had; machine parts.

The bill arrived and they split it, leaving a tip and taking the mints with them as they got up to leave.

With a brief goodbye, they parted ways. Hannah watched as Harry almost skipped into the crowd and vanished off to her next rendezvous. This left Hannah to go somewhere she was pretty sure she'd be safe and could make some money at the same time.

Following a map on her implant, she made her way to the nearby casino district. On the way, she passed a number of small shops with outrageous claims they could make a person a fortune without much hassle. She imagined most of them were either fronts for smugglers or chop-shops. Some people refused to take cloned tissue or cybernetics on principle or for religious reasons, so there was always a market for organ donation. Willing or not, on occasion.

As she passed one, a man stepped not quite into her path. "Hello, Miss. I noticed you looking at a few of my competitors; I can offer you some excellent deals the others can't with exceptional pay-outs."

With time to kill and nothing better to do, she decided to see just what these deals were. Not that she had any intention of partaking. "Oh, like what?"

"Three million krone for a nine-month contract. Fifty percent up front, all expenses covered and fifty percent on successful delivery," he said, pulling a leaflet from his waistcoat pocket.

"Delivery of what?" She also noted the pay was in the local currency; it was probably considerably less when converted into standard goldcoin.

"The baby," he replied as though it was blindingly obvious. "Surrogacy is a very lucrative business if the surrogate is willing to wave all rights and be discreet. Are you okay, Miss?"

Hannah shook her head to clear it a little bit, forcing an unpleasant memory out. "I, ehm, no, I can't," she babbled before settling on a suitable lie. "I don't have the equipment."

The man made a silent 'oh', realising he'd was about to potentially lose a sale. "Well, I do also deal in donations. Kidneys, lungs, liver, marrow, blood, eyes. All donations come with a fixed price, good after care and if necessary, a suitable, if low-grade, replacement."

It had been a terrible idea to engage with the man, so Hannah continued lying to get herself out of yet another sticky situation. "Oh, I'm sorry, I can't. The naval docs did a good job putting me back together after the accident, but at my last insurance physical, the examining doc took one look at my scan, screamed and vomited. And put me into the highest bracket of special cover," she said. "I mean, they aren't even sure where some of my vital organs are, only that they are in there somewhere." It wasn't uncommon for a person's insides to look like a bad imitation of what Picasso might have painted, especially the poor.

Looking decidedly green, the man made an excuse about hearing someone in the shop calling him and ran off.

She soon found herself at one of the sleazier casinos. It had bright signs declaring all sorts of deals that looked really good, until you remembered the house always wins. Or at least, nearly always.

Inside, the place was trying to be art deco, but everything just looked tired. It was clean, but a little bit worn, the colours a little too faded, much like the career losers that huddled around the holo-roulette tables, clustered about the virtual craps and clutched at their cards.

"Good afternoon, Miss," one of the cashiers said warmly. Compared to the rest of the place, she was a ray of sunshine and vibrancy. "Can I be of assistance?"

"Yes, I'd like to get five hundred's worth of chips, please."

"Cash, bank transfer or credit?"

Where many fell into the trap was taking the casino credit. They'd quote a fantastic near zero interest rate on it, not mentioning that that was for the day you took it out. After that, the interest rate spiralled and money could be reclaimed in all sorts of ways, often in organs if the person had no material possessions. The behaviour was illegal in most systems, but here, it was the way of things.

"Bank transfer," she replied. "Sinclair, Alison Joanna," she added, holding her implant out ready for the scanner.

The scanner read her credentials, chirped happily as it accessed the accounts in the name of Alison Joanna Sinclair and displayed the various options. The cashier's eyes bulged slightly at the number of accounts and the quantities in them. Why keep an account with three goldcoin in it when there is a similar one with a hundred thousand goldcoin?

Hannah selected an account, transferred the money and received her five hundred chips. With a polite thanks to the cashier, she slid them into a cup, which she put in her satchel, and headed for the holo-roulette.

As a rule, holo-roulette was a bad choice for honest players; the house would often tweak the programmed odds on the fly to prevent large pay outs. For cheats, it was even more dangerous if they were foolish and greedy. Most cheaters would place a massive bet on one number and then use all manner of devices to force the wheel to give them a win.

With years of experience, Hannah was far savvier. First things first, play a little without cheating at all. Second, identify any other cheats, report them to security and claim any bounties the casino offered. Third, keep the cheating infrequent and only on short odds. Fourth, first sign of trouble, play straight until it looked safe to leave.

After watching for a few spins, Hannah placed her first chip down on the same number as a man that was clearly cheating. On hitting the table, the chip turned the same colour of brown as her jacket and the dealer acknowledged she was now playing.

"Lucky number twelve," she said to the cheat. "My birthday."

He smiled. "Well, hopefully it will be your lucky day." With a wink he placed a few more chips onto twelve.

The dealer spun the wheel once all the bets were in. The ball quickly bounced into twelve on the holographic wheel.

"Oh my God, I never win," Hannah said in fake surprise as she collected her winnings. She placed a few chips on number ranges and on two random numbers after placing her original chip back in her cup. The wins this time were much smaller, but they were skimmed off as well.

After a few minutes of middling success, in which she still came out ahead by quite some way, she wandered away. She'd made sure to lose on her last few spins so her exit appeared to be her cutting her losses.

Immediately, she approached a man that was built like a barn in a security uniform. Behind him was a poster announcing that turning in a confirmed cheater was worth one hundred chips, plus additional at the duty manager's discretion.

"Guy in the denim vest, roulette table two," she said quietly, pretending to be looking for something in her bag. "Winning a lot and fiddling with something in his pocket."

The security man slid a finger along his jacket sleeve to open the holo-interface. He scanned the man in question and immediately the display went red. Naturally, the casino kept tabs on everyone in the place and records of any previous issues.

"Damn, who let him in again," he muttered as he fished about in his pocket. Pulling out two hundred chips, held in neat little columns, he sat them on the ledge behind him. "Thanks, Miss. Enjoy."

As he trudged away, Hannah snatched the chips and ferreted them away in her bag. Before anyone could take note of her and draw conclusions, she vanished into the forest of fruit machines. A grass could not expect to make friends with other players.

Despite the fact she was pretty good at figuring when a machine was going to give the jackpot, she sat at the first one she liked the look of: it was one of the really old style, simple ones. Winning too much would suddenly look suspicious. This was for some fun before moving on to the next place.

Sadly, luck wasn't on her side in the manner she'd hoped for. On what she planned to be her last spin, based on the fact she was sure the machine was getting ready to favour a jackpot, she hit the jackpot.

A cascade of chips flooded into the collection tray, drawing immediate attention. Suddenly the quiet corner had become a hive of activity as she tried to scoop her winnings into her satchel. It was by no means a large jackpot, but large enough to draw the vultures looking to grab any chip that escaped. At one time, Hannah would have been threatening anyone that came near trying to steal her horde; today she grabbed as much as she could, leaving the few that fell to whoever could get them.

Trying not to look guilty, and failing somewhat, she made her way over to the cashiers. She went to a young man that barely looked old enough to gamble himself.

"I think I won," she said almost apologetically as she tipped her satchel out onto the counter, using her body to stop the chips rolling onto the floor. In amongst them were the few things she kept in the bag: a notebook and pen; a little pack of tissues; lip balm; a nail file; a collection of emergency items.

It was these items that were key.

Hannah had found many men were still terrified, bewildered or just embarrassed by the sight of the contents of a woman's handbag, usually expecting all sorts of nonsense to be in them. It made anything that might lurk in a handbag ideal as the cover for other, more illicit, items.

As hoped, the young man's eyes bulged and he looked away as she apologised for the mess and started to place the satchel contents back in the bag. The poor boy was none the wiser that she had just shown him her own cheating equipment.

Without much ado, he swept the chips into an automated counter and made no comment over the fact the money was divided into two accounts with two completely different names on them, both accessible by the same set of credentials.

Hannah left the casino having managed to win nearly five million goldcoin; that would cover her lost pay, and a little bit more. She just had to not arouse suspicion and have any casino enforcers question her winnings.

The Passenger

Kelly stood looking down at the empty eyes of the synth, remembering when she'd last looked exactly like her. It was a little jarring to see and yet she couldn't stop herself looking at the rather plain and unremarkable woman she'd once been. A picture of exquisite, plain, ordinary beauty.

"Remind you of someone?" the elderly shopkeeper asked as he shuffled over.

She smiled weakly. "I looked like that, a long time ago."

He looked between the two, peering closely at them. "My goodness, yes, I can see the resemblance." He paused for a moment, looking at Kelly. "I'm guessing that your transformation was not entirely your idea?"

"No," she replied. "I was a private nurse; my owner was terminally ill. When he died, his son sold me to one of his friends, who kept me for," she searched for a polite turn of phrase, "other reasons."

The old man nodded sagely. It was a story he'd heard all too often and wondered at the way humans treated their synthetic offspring.

"My new ow-, I mean, my friend, my friends are trying to undo the damage. Physically, at least."

"Well, I'd offer to sell you this shell, but I'm afraid she's been sold."

Kelly smiled and shrugged. "I can't afford a whole new body. But thank you for the kind gesture."

Annie appeared from nowhere, a large smile on her face and something in her hands. "Look what I found; this should work to help restore your sense of smell."

Under the slightly questioning look of the shopkeeper, Kelly would have blushed if she had been able to process embarrassment as an emotion. Fortunately, in this situation, her neural net flagged it as something to be ignored; she was aware she should be embarrassed, but it provoked almost no reaction. "Gagging on cheap cologne was not considered beneficial," she explained.

As Annie returned to her gleeful dive through the shop and the shopkeeper went to serve a customer that had just arrived, Kelly went to have a look at some of the trinkets. While most of the parts were neatly stored and displayed, there was a collection of shelves with what was basically interesting looking scrap.

Some of the parts were insignia taken from old ships, others were bits and pieces that had been found in items sold to the shop that were almost worthless. She picked through them, wondering where they'd come from and if they had ever meant anything to anyone.

A little metal and plastic stick caught her eye. It was roughly the size of her thumb, the metal dulled with age and the plastic looking a bit worse for wear. Written on one of the largest faces was "USSF-017" and on the other was "Stanley" in large letters.

"What you got there?" Annie asked.

Kelly jumped slightly and gave the little engineer a half-hearted glare. "I'm lucky I don't have a heart, otherwise it would have stopped."

With a chuckle, Annie shrugged. "Aye, I'm glad I don't have one either; arteries would have been clogged up years ago thanks to my traditional diet. If you want that, I'll cover you."

"Thank you," she replied, before pondering what Annie meant; having conducted her last physical, she was well aware of the fact she did have a heart, it was her own original organic one, and it was in pretty good health.

When Annie approached the counter with her basket of parts, the shopkeeper excused himself from his other customer, and came over. He put all of her parts through the till, but stopped when he lifted the sensor suite that would restore Kelly's near non-existent sense of smell.

"Since you're buying so much, I'll let you have it," he said with a lopsided smile. "Don't thank me; it'll need some work to get it going and might not even function with her architecture. Not even sure what it came from."

Annie nodded and placed the little stick on the counter. It was put through for a single goldcoin to round the total out to a neat, whole number.

"Come on, we'd best get back to the ship," she said to Kelly as she handed her a bag to carry. "Kinda hope the Captain's found us a job to run on our way back."

They had barely made it out into the street when the other customer from the shop jumped into their path. He held his hands up as he did so, hoping he wouldn't be pre-emptively attacked if they thought he planned to mug them.

"Ladies, good day," he said in a friendly tone, "I didn't mean to eavesdrop, but I heard you have a ship that is not currently under contract. It just so happens; I am without a ship and would be willing to pay for the inconvenience of being transported to several systems for academic research."

The two women looked at each other for a moment. The man seemed friendly enough and was unthreatening in stature; he certainly looked like an academic, but perhaps one that spent more time in the field than at a desk. He was almost dashing.

"Are you a Purist?" Annie asked.

"Would it be a problem if I was?" he asked, looking a little less confident than he had.

She shrugged. "Keep it to yourself, and no, no really," she said. "Talk about it, and the captain will dump you at the first spaceport. Get really up in her face with it and she'll space you."

For a moment, there was a flicker of something on his face, which he tried to cover by running a hand through his hair. "Dr Casper Mendoza," he said with a small bow. "Antiquarian, historian and occasional treasure hunter."

Kelly held her hand out. "Kelly," she replied. "Nurse. And janitor, I suppose."

"Annie Clan-MacLennan," she said taking his hand firmly. "Supreme Master Engineer, Novice Harris Tweed Weaver, Journeyman Distiller and all my other degrees."

Casper looked suitably impressed by the list of degrees Annie had amassed, although it was common for those in the Scottish Guild to learn a lot of low-level degrees to move up the Clan system. It was also only the tip of the iceberg of her degrees.

"So, Doctor, what are you looking for?" she asked, taking the lead towards the taxi after arranging to meet Hannah there.

He smiled warmly. "Ancient debris," he replied. "I've been following up some fragments that survived The Great Collapse that suggest a ship called the *Livingstone* might still be out there," he said, clearly pleased someone wanted to know what he was researching. "From what I can gather, it was a colony ship launched from Earth in 2050."

She stopped dead. "Seriously? But that would mean it would have been floating about for... well, I've no idea."

"Perhaps ten to twelve thousand years," he replied. "If the computer memory is intact, it might be possible to circumvent the Armageddon Protocol and find out where the Sol system is."

"That could be quite valuable," Kelly said, pondering the idea of being able to find Earth. Although its location had been erased from every computer system and a complex virus imbedded in all modern operating systems made sure it stayed that way, an older computer might just work. Humans were oddly attached to a place most of them now believed to be a myth.

They walked on for a few minutes before Annie spoke again. "Not to be rude, but what sort of budget are you thinking of spending?"

"Well, I'm sure your Captain will be reasonable," he replied, "but I am well-funded by my department and a number of private individuals."

Hannah was standing leaning against Charlie the cab when they arrived. She looked mildly happier than when they'd last seen her and considerably more comfortable in her own clothes.

"Ah, you must be the Captain. Dr Casper Mendoza." He expended his hand and gave Hannah a firm shake. His face went slightly pale as he caught sight of one of her badges.

She frowned slightly and followed his gaze. He was looking at her last squadron badge and her Commonwealth Wing Commander insignia below it. Few people made the connection these days, but there had been a short time when anyone who knew anything about the Battle of Hafan and saw her badges would instantly start asking questions.

"Captain Hannah le Conservatrice," she said by way of introduction. "Something wrong?"

Casper shook his head slightly as he regained his senses. "Sorry, I," he faltered for a moment, blinking in rapid bursts, "I was there. I, ehm, I saw Abertawe City burn as I got out on a transport." He bit his lip for a second. "I also saw the *Monitor* going down."

A tight smile came to Hannah's lips. She'd had a front row seat to the destruction of the bridge of the Remnant flagship and its subsequent uncontrolled landing on the moon of Morgannwg. And yet, something rankled her that she couldn't quite put her finger on. Perhaps it was because few would ever admit to being at that bloodbath of a battle.

"You have business for me?" she asked, moving away from the past.

"Oh, yes," he replied, passing a tablet over with a list. "There's quite a few there, but I can make this worth your while. Academic research," he added, hoping she'd understand his desire to visit the systems.

She scrolled through the list of systems to give herself time to think. Casper seemed reasonable enough and looked respectable, perhaps a little bit too respectable for her ship. But something just felt wrong about him. Her instincts were usually good, but after her little incident, she was still a bit frazzled. And Hafan was a very painful subject.

"Five platinumcoins," she said, knowing no one would be stupid enough to pay that. You could by a better ship than *Sigyn* for that, if considerably smaller.

"Three."

"Half now, half on completion, plus a share of any material findings."

"Done."

A small alarm was going off in her head now. She was definitely going to have to Google him before they took off. Still, that money would cover the backlogged pay from her sisters, get Kelly mostly fixed and leave some in the bank. She called up her account and held her arm out.

After a few taps on his tablet, Casper swiped it over her wrist and transferred one and a half platinumcoins, or 1.5 billion goldcoins, into her account.

"Excellent," she said with a smile. "We leave in two days; I still have some business to conduct here."

"Of course, Captain," he replied. "And thank you."

Hannah had barely made it to her cabin before her screen was beeping with an incoming message. She was not in the least bit surprised.

"Hello, Helen," she said, feigning mild surprise mockingly, "to what do I owe the pleasure of a call?"

"Can't I simply call to check in on my sister?"

Had she said almost anything else, it might have been believable. "I'm guessing someone noticed the large sum of money entering my *personal* account and you are in the process of syphoning it away."

Helen winced and pulled a sour face. "Well, there are various things that you need to pay for."

"And after I've given you such good service for free lately?"

Again, a wince and sour look. "Yes, well, results get pay. Given your poor performance, it should cover some of the penalties."

"No," she replied, bracing herself in front of the screen. "All of it. Based on the amount you've failed to pay me, any debt you care to dream up is wiped and there will be over six hundred million goldcoin left."

Helen's face went blank for a moment as she appeared to be looking at something off screen. "Not quite. We can't just let you go until the other ships are operational. And Holly has recalculated the ship's value based on some of the modifications we've just found out about that means your insurance premiums with us need evaluated." She smiled slightly. "Such as a military grade cloak."

With a few nods, Hannah stepped back from the screen. "Fine. Empty the account. I'm terminating my contract with you."

"You can't."

"Read Paragraph Four, Section One, Subsection Eight, Line Two," she replied. With a great deal of satisfaction, she watched as Helen went a delightful shade of beetroot. "I'll bring Harry back in a few days. Depending on how much is in my account will determine if I go my own way and if you get the converters Annie is repairing."

For a moment, it looked like Helen might have been about to explode in rage. Drawing a sharp breath through her nose, she managed to, just, keep a lid on it, although the pulsating vein on her forehead was still in danger of spraying the walls red. "For all that you hate Grandad, you are bloody well like him."

"Oh, I'm much worse," she replied before cutting the link. She dropped into a chair and kicked at the table.

Money had always been a horrible thing in the family. Her grandfather had run a seemingly successful mining business in the *Sheba*, but when he'd died four years previously and given it to the sisters, minus Hannah, they'd found he'd been running up debts and using money he syphoned from "charities" he ran. Holly had had a real time trying to balance the books and get them back into profit, but with years of poor maintenance and little investment, it was proving near impossible.

Despite her initial fury at being disinherited due to bigotry, Hannah had quickly been grateful the old bastard had given her one goldcoin in his will. She'd already bought *Sigyn* and been running a small profit, on top of her savings from her military pension and Ali's life insurance, although that had only finally been paid in full the previous year.

Keeping that money away from Helen, who would have almost certainly wormed it out of her with promises of shares and repayment, had made things much harder. The account attached to the *Sheba* was monitored closely, but Holly was aware of her accounts. Fortunately, for the sake of family peace, she only looked at the ones in Hannah's name.

That said, she'd already pumped vast amounts of money into the business through shareholdings and fake companies she "owned" for tax purposes in various different sectors.

Reasonably wealthy and she could barely spend a goldcoin without someone trying to raid her accounts. What was the point?

She'd have to speak to Harry when she got back. No doubt her activities were being interrupted by their sister demanding action be taken.

Across the station, Hannah couldn't have been more right about Harry's situation.

Kelly sat in her cabin looking at Stanley, the little trinket she'd bought. She had no idea what it might be for and if it was actually meant to do anything. For all she knew, it was just a fancy name tag belonging to a pet or a ship.

"Jon?"

"Yes," he replied as his avatar appeared, "what's up?"

"Do you have any idea what this is?" she asked, holding Stanley up for him to see. Of course, he could see it where it had been sitting with the internal sensors and his eyes were fake. It was a completely pointless, but completely human, action.

Naturally, as his programme dictated, Jon moved his head about to examine the object, though it made no difference to his ability to analyse it.

"It looks like a memory stick."

She nodded. "Like a portable hard drive?"

"Of a sort," he replied. "It's very old. In fact, if the markings are correct, it's pre-Unity." He looked at it for a moment and sighed. "Sadly, most, if not all of the data on it is probably corrupt."

Closing her hand around the little device, Kelly wondered even more what it had been for and who had owned it. Had it held cherished childhood memories, work data or photos of loved ones? Maybe it had been a mission recorder from some ancient ship.

"I can try to read it, if you like?"

"Can you?"

Jon smiled weakly. "I can try."

It was a gamble to attempt it. Most of the ancient protocols still existed and could be accessed to talk to the exceptionally dumb systems of the past. The issue was the Armageddon Protocol could potentially infect and destroy any data that might pertain to Earth. Then there was the risk of viruses; a few ancient and normally harmless viruses had mutated on encountering an AI and done considerable damage.

Kelly placed Stanley on the reader port that sat at the back of her desk. Immediately the malleable little tendrils snaked out to look for a way into the device. One pushed the metal to one side, which swivelled to reveal a rectangular port.

Like wild animals scenting a kill, the tendrils struck, grabbing the port and spreading over it. She always found it unnerving to watch; any time she needed work on her neural net, it was tendrils like that snaking over her skull, invading her brain. It made her skin crawl.

"Are you okay?" Jon asked.

"I think I'm having an emotional response," she replied.

"Should I call Annie?"

"No," she replied quickly. "It's okay. If it becomes too much, I'll let you know."

He nodded, not completely convinced by her assurances. Emotional responses in neural nets that were meant to suppress them was either a sign of increasing sentience or rampancy. For her sake, and for that of the crew, he hoped it was her naturally healing and moving towards increased sentience.

For a few minutes, they stood looking at Stanley, as if that would help.

"I'm sorry, almost everything has degraded," Jon said after a little while. "I have a few poor-quality images, some fragmented text documents and one video."

"Can I see?"

The images showed a few distorted images of space, nothing that could be used to identify locations, and one of ten people floating in a mess. The people all wore identical uniforms and were smiling. Behind them was a banner that proclaimed "Happy 2065".

"The *USS Stanley* was a United States Space Force vessel launched in 2059," Jon said, reading the text fragment he was displaying on a screen. "She was a *Venture*-class deep space frigate. Her last recorded mission was to find a ship that had gone missing sometime after it had launched in the 2050s."

Kelly looked at the text. "I can understand most of the words, but the sentences don't make sense. It's like really bad Shakespeare."

He chuckled. "Old Modern English is quite different from Modern English."

The tendrils released Stanley and retreated into their home.

"What about the video?" she asked.

Jon played it, although most of it was static. Even the clear bits didn't really mean much as the man, the *Stanley*'s Captain, was speaking in Old Modern English and had a drawling accent. He translated what he could.

"...culations were off by almost a lightyear. With no way to restart their warp drive, they must have accelerated to relativistic speeds using their ion engines," he said before the image broke up again for a few seconds. "Never find them now. God rest their souls."

"Was the ship ever found?" she asked.

With a shrug, Jon shutdown the media. "I doubt it. Once at near lightspeed, there would be no easy way to find or catch it. Deep space vessels used cryo-sleep for the crews back then. The crew would have died in their sleep when their nutrients ran out."

She lifted the little device and looked at it for a moment. It had a ring on it to allow it to be clipped onto something; taking an old necklace, she attached the drive to it and put it around her neck.

"What happened to the *Stanley*?"

"I'm afraid I don't know," he replied. "I've checked the net and there is no record of either ship."

The Goose Chase Begins

With a great deal of willpower, Hannah tried not to look at the time. She failed almost immediately and tutted loudly at the fact there was less than two hours before she was going to have to pay for the privilege of being parked.

Harry hadn't come back yet and wasn't picking up calls. Part of her was a little worried her sister might be in trouble, but none of the security services had come across her and there were no demands for ransom. She was probably having far too much fun.

The past day had been quite boring; Emily and Laura had taken their turn to go sightseeing and shopping, so Hannah had been left guarding the ship. Casper had bored her a few times in the mess with his accomplishments, until Annie had taken it upon herself to entertain him. Or perhaps entertain herself with him.

Leaning against Charlie, she contemplated leaving and dismissed it. She liked Harry too much and couldn't stand the bitching from the others if she left her.

A commotion started to stir in the distance. People were shouting in annoyance as someone or something forced its way through the crowd. Following the initial commotion was a second, more obvious one. A man, head and shoulders above most of the crowd, was pushing through, chasing the invisible first person.

But whoever it was, was coming her way.

Then the message appeared: *Start the car!*

Hannah had barely managed to get the door open when Harry, dressed only in her underwear and carrying the rest of her clothes under her arm, burst from the crowd, charged towards Charlie, hair flying about her like a wild mane, and threw herself in.

The door had barely closed when the giant of a man threw himself against it. He was roaring incoherently, but phrases like; "kill you", "if I see you again" and "cost a fortune" could just be heard.

He jumped back when Charlie started to lift-off, but continued to rant and rave, fists in the air.

Harry was sprawled on the seat, panting and sweating as she tried to get her breath back.

"I take it he objected to you having fun with his partner?" Hannah said coolly.

"Nah," she replied in between breaths. "He doesn't mind me and Nora having sex. He often joins in," she continued. "What Jimmy does object to is the fact I accidentally lifted a bottle of his very expensive wine."

"You ran through the streets in your bra and knickers because you drank a bottle of wine?"

She grimaced. "Oh, we didn't open it, but there's no way he can sell it now."

Hannah didn't even want to think about the implications. With most people, they'd then go on to explain it had been used in some innocent way, but with

Harry.... She was certain that bottle had gone somewhere that would make it undrinkable for most.

"Charlie, take us back."

"What?"

With a smile, Hannah tapped her nose.

Jimmy was still standing when Charlie touched down again. He was breathing like an enraged bull, but didn't step forward when Hannah got out. Harry was cowering her seat.

"Jimmy? Hannah," she said, holding her hand out. He took it reluctantly, glaring over her at Harry. "I believe there was an incident involving some wine?"

"I came home to find a bottle of Château Picard up to the shoulder –"

"I don't need the details of where it went," she replied, praying Harry had only been licking it. "I'll buy it."

Jimmy frowned. "Well, okay."

Much to her surprise and disgust, he gingerly drew the bottle out of a pocket in his jacket and held it out. "The price is two-fifty. Excuse the ruined label; someone got it wet."

Hannah called her account up on her wrist and made the purchase. She took out a tissue and took the bottle by the base. Judging by the state of the peeling label, it had been submerged in water. Without further ado, she went back to Charlie and handed it to Harry, who immediately clutched it to her chest.

"Hey, Harry? You're welcome to come visit any time," Jimmy called. "But if you touch my wine again, I'll shove it so far up your –"

The door closed and cut off exactly which orifice the bottle would be inserted into, not that Harry would mind which. Charlie, who had passed no comment on the whole affair, lifted off once more to head back to the dock.

"Thank you," Harry said meekly.

"Don't," she replied. "Just promise I will never see that bottle again."

She nodded. "Just so you know, I thought it was white and put it in a bucket of cold water. That's what ruined it."

"Put your clothes on."

"How did you afford it?" she asked as she wriggled into her trousers.

Hannah told her about her winnings at the casino and the job she'd taken on. While losing a quarter of a million goldcoin on a bottle of sullied wine had not been factored in, it was hardly a crippling blow. It was actually not too bad for a vintage wine, some of which would sell for tens of millions.

"So, are we going back to the *Sheba*?" Harry asked, flopping back into her seat.

"Just to drop off the converters, then I'm back out."

They sat in silence for the rest of the short trip. So far, only the money Hannah expected to be taken had vanished from her account, but that didn't mean Helen wasn't going to have Holly take it later. She'd needed a base to work from, but the *Sheba* had been bad for business.

"I hope you had a most enjoyable visit," Charlie said warmly as he landed. "Remember to like me on social media and fill out a feedback form so others can benefit from your experience."

"Thanks, I will do," Hannah lied. She rarely bothered with feedback.

She had barely managed to get onto the ship when Casper appeared, Annie following him like a puppy.

"Ah, Captain. Oh, there's two of you?" he said, spotting Harry.

"My sister," Hannah replied. "What can I help you with?"

He passed her a tablet with a map on it. "It appears one of my target sites is on route to your base vessel. Could we stop on the way? I estimate it will take no more than six or seven hours to scan –"

"Sure," she replied, passing the tablet back.

Barely breaking her stride, she continued on towards the Bridge, Harry following her. It didn't take long to get to the centre of the ship where Emily and Laura were already completing the necessary checks for lift-off.

Hannah flopped into her chair and immediately felt better. The Bridge was off limits to passengers (Harry counted as crew), so she always felt it was a safe space from unwanted attention, more so than her cabin.

"Has Dr Mendoza given you a list of stops on the way back?" she asked.

Emily turned in her seat. "Yeah. A few of those systems are not exactly well travelled."

A slight smile started to come to Hannah's features. "Hm, that could mean there will be things to discover and less people to stop us taking them."

Laura shook her head. "Or more pirates."

"Plot a course to the nearest system on the list," she replied, ignoring the remark. "Let's get away from this hole."

Tapping away on her console, Emily plotted the course out of the bowels of *The Sunk'n Norwegian* and to the outer edge of the system. The first system, Clutha, was within a single Hop. She was slightly surprised when Hannah accepted that as the way to go.

As the ship shuddered slightly, passing through the upper atmosphere of the planet, Hannah got up to get a coffee from the replicator. She really couldn't be bothered now with the whole thing, despite the big pay-out. But a contract was a contract.

Harry caught her eye and mouthed: "Are you okay?"

She shrugged and went back to the centre seat. The apathy would pass in time. Right now, her biggest worry was the Hop. No matter how often she was told, no matter how often Jon and Annie showed her stability readouts, every Hop felt like she was taking negative G.

By the time *Sigyn* had reached a safe distance to Hop, she was taking deep breaths as subtly as she could. It wasn't normally this bad, but given the events of the past few days, she wasn't overly surprised.

The Hop Drive, a colloquial name for the Azhikelyamov-Mashayekhi Forced Space-Time Burrowing Engine, worked on a simple principle. The engine created a type of exotic particles called Cochrane particles which pulled the ship into an otherwise inaccessible domain to bypass normal space. Exactly how, what that domain was or how the ship returned to normal space was completely unknown, lost in the Great Collapse.

When activated, the effects from the crew's point of view would be instantaneous. Small ships, single person pods and fighters would experience almost no time passage. Larger ships would 'lose' a tiny amount of time, milliseconds to a second at most. Massive ships, the few that had survived the process, had been known to lose years.

Hannah had never been that interested in the science of the Hop Drive, but had always found it disconcerting. Events in her life had made that disconcertion worse.

"We have arrived in Clutha," Emily announced. "Plotting a search pattern based on Dr Mendoza's data." She tapped away on her console. "Should take us about six and a half hours to cover all the ground."

Jon appeared. "I can cover this, if you want to get some rest?"

Laura looked askingly at Hannah, who simply nodded before standing up. She'd barely taken a step when it was just her and Harry left.

"Do you want to talk about it?"

Hannah shook her head. "No, not really."

"I'm here if you want to talk about anything."

She bit back a vicious remark. What did Harry know of anything that was troubling her? In the space of six hours, she'd lost half of those under her command, a twenty-year relationship was destroyed and she'd been retired on medical grounds. Her life had ended and she'd been left to pick up the pieces herself for the last seven years.

"I'm fine," she replied tersely. She'd clasped her hands together, her left thumb stroking the flesh between her right thumb and index finger to keep herself from biting her nails. "I just need a good sleep and I'll be right as rain."

Harry grabbed her wrist as Hannah turned to leave. She froze, instantly regretting her action. The look she was getting was not one she'd seen very often, but it was a strange calm that washed over Hannah shortly before her Naval training kicked in and she kicked someone's ass clean across the galaxy.

The look softened. Twisting her wrist, she took Harry's hand rather than trying to break free. "I'm fine."

Annie rolled onto her side as she heard hushed voices. She recognised Casper's voice, but couldn't hear anything distinct. The other voice was male and commanding.

Moments later, he appeared and slipped back into the bed beside her, pulling her close.

"Sorry, my Head of Department looking for an update," he said. "He always manages to pick the worst times to call."

They lay together a while in comfortable silence.

She stretched and rolled over him to leave the bed. He rolled onto his side, propped up on his arm, to watch as she grabbed her scattered clothes.

"You know, you really are much better looking out of those overalls," he said with an appreciative grin. "Why don't you stay a bit longer?"

"I'd love to," she replied. "But I have work to do." She stopped dressing for a moment, giving Casper a questioning look. "Wait. Are you saying I'm not good looking when dressed?"

Raising his hands defensively, he sat up to keep balance. "Ah, no, that's not what I said. I said you look better out of your clothes. Those overalls don't do much for your rather fine figure."

Annie pulled her t-shirt on and swaggered over to the bed. She pulled him into a kiss. "Nice save. Now, I have to get on." Pulling up her overalls, she fastened them and started for the door.

"Can I see you again?"

"Oh, I'm sure I'll be back," she replied, grinning over her shoulder.

Stepping out of the door, she nearly walked straight into Hannah as she passed. The two did an awkward little avoidance dance to come to a halt, face to face.

"Captain, how's it going?" she asked.

"Good, good," Hannah replied, nodding. "Having fun with the good Doctor, were we?" she added with a coy smile.

As warmth spread over her face, Annie knew she was probably bright red. "Oh, you know, just comparing notes on various common interests."

Jon materialised at this point as well. "Hm, yes, that's one way of putting it. Does that mean my services are not required tonight?"

Annie went crimson.

"You know something," Hannah said, "I'm actually less surprised at you, somehow, having sex with the computer than I am you having sex with a flesh and blood man." She smiled a little more as Jon also started to blush. "I hope you haven't installed a hard-light emitter in your cabin; the cost of running something like that will come out your pay."

"Tha mi duilich, chan eil mi a' tuigsinn Beurla," she replied in Gaelic. "Tìoriadh."

As Annie darted away, Hannah looked at Jon questioningly. "What did she say?"

He shrugged. "Gaelic is a protected language," he replied. "I'm forbidden to translate it without authorisation of a Member of the Scottish Guild. You'll have to ask a Member or take a degree from the Guild to learn it."

With an exasperated tut, she turned on her heel. "Well, I'm off to bed. Shout if anything exciting comes up."

"Hannah."

She stopped dead. Jon always called her "Captain".

"If you should wish my services, I'd be happy to oblige."

"If you never mention that again, I won't have Stevie lobotomise you when we get to the *Sheba*," she replied without turning. She started again towards her cabin, muttering about the state of her crew.

The Nightmare

The sun beamed down on the rolling, grassy knolls of the park, warming the ground and people stretched out on it. Children ran around, chasing balls and each other. A group of model makers sailed boats on the lake, the water sparkling like a liquid diamond.

Hannah felt content, her head resting on Ali's shoulder as the couple enjoyed being able to just be together without work getting in the way. It was, of course, likely to only be a short reprieve: the fleet was due to move out within the week, meaning she'd be back in her bunk with the rest of the Wing.

It would, hopefully, be her last tour. The Remnant had been in full retreat after their crushing defeat at Arcturus. Once a peace had been signed, Hannah could get a nice desk job or perhaps teach at the Academy. They could finally live together all the time, rather than having to make do with when she wasn't on deployment.

Ali gave her a squeeze, prompting her to roll slightly to look into those warm hazel eyes she'd fallen in love with as a giddy teenager. The eyes were the same as ever, full of warmth and kindness, even if the face had changed from that of a handsome young man into a gorgeous woman.

Their relationship had never floundered with Ali's transition, but it had alienated them from both their families. Ali's parents were staunch Limited Interventionists, believing that the human body should be left as it is as far as possible. Being born in the wrong body did not constitute a reason for medical intervention. And while Hannah's parents had been completely unfazed by their daughter's relationship, her mother's family had seen it as more reason to pretend she and her sisters didn't exist.

"I don't suppose you can go AWOL?" Ali asked.

"Oh? Are you going to run off and leave your patients while we fly off into the sunset?"

Pushing a strand of hair out of her eyes, Ali smiled at Hannah. They joked often about just running away from their lives to live off-grid, but it was nothing but a fun fantasy.

"Wing Commander Sinclair?" a voice said behind them.

"Yes?" Hannah replied, looking up at the young man. Immediately, she knew it was bad news. Giving Ali a peck on the cheek, she got up and took a few steps away with the Corporal. He handed her a message. She opened the envelope, but it burst into flames and she dropped it immediately on instinct.

Everything was suddenly on fire. The trees were burning like torches as the sky turned black, choked with smoke and ash. Fighters and emergency shuttles whizzed through the clouds, the glow of their engines adding to the hellish landscape. Charred grass crunched under her feet as she took a few steps back. Her dress had been replaced with her flight suit.

Turning to where Ali had been lying, there was nothing but more scotched land.

She ran.

The outcome was a forgone conclusion, but she couldn't help herself. Despite hours in the cockpit, hours in battle, she ran as fast as she could towards the hospital.

Where once had been a ten-storey block stood a burning, crumbling mass of twisted concrete, metal and carnage. Outside were piles of bodies where the Purifiers had either rounded up their victims for execution or where they'd dumped those they'd found and killed inside.

After nearly six years of war, Hannah had seen a lot of battlefields, but this one made her physically sick. Men, women and children had been butchered simply because they were "impure"; they're genetics had been altered, cybernetics had been added beyond what would be lifesaving, or their life saved using cloned tissues. Nothing had mattered to the Remnant; such people were just abominations to them that had to be culled. It was nothing more than a twisted, petty act of revenge by a beaten band of lunatics.

And somewhere, in the mess of human wreckage, was Ali.

Hannah woke, screaming and thrashing in her bed, panic coursing through every fibre of her being. She flailed at the wall by the bed, unsure of how to get out of it in the dark, before tumbling out onto the floor in a tangle of sheets.

"Hannah, it's okay, you're on *Sigyn*," Jon urged as he appeared, bringing the lights up gently. "You are okay, you are safe."

She cried something incoherent at him before wrapping her head in her arms and dissolving into a mess of hyperventilation and sobbing.

Kelly, who Jon had alerted, burst into the cabin and made her way into the bedroom. In an act of extreme rudeness that she would never normally consider, she walked straight through Jon, ignoring him completely.

"Hannah, you are going to be okay," she said. "Remember your breathing; in through the nose," she continued before loudly breathing in, "and out through the mouth."

For several minutes she tried to get a response, but nothing much seemed to be working. Hannah slumped against the bed and appeared to have gone back to sleep. Seeing little else to be done, Kelly lifted her back into bed, tucked her in and motioned for Jon to follow her.

"What was that?" he asked as they stepped into the living area.

"I'm not sure," she confessed, "but I think it might have been a night terror. They're pretty rare in adults." This was not a condition she had knowledge of, beyond that it would pass and the sufferer would likely have no idea of what happened when they woke.

Jon nodded dumbly. "So, what do we do?"

She frowned at him. "You're the one with the entire Internet at his fingertips; you tell me."

While it was true that he had access to the Internet and everything in it, the problem with that was finding anything of use. While his neural net was designed to be able to cope with high volume requests and multitasking, there were limits to what he could achieve. His advantages came at the cost of poor intuition compared to humans and synthetics like Kelly.

Seeing that there wasn't going to be any big breakthrough, Kelly managed to smile weakly. "I'm sorry I walked through you," she said softly, fiddling with her nightie absently.

"Thank you, but I understand and it's okay," he replied. Normally, a degrading act like that would make him quite irate, but it hadn't been done with malice or as a snub. In fact, he was pretty sure if he'd had a body, Kelly would simply have pushed him aside.

"Kelly?" a small voice called from the bedroom.

Like a concerned parent, she immediately made her way in to see what was going on. Hannah was sitting up, bleary eyed and confused.

"Why are you in my cabin?" she asked, more with confusion than annoyance or accusation.

"You may have had a night terror," she said, sitting on the edge of the bed. "Jon panicked and called me."

She looked more confused now. "A night terror?"

"I'll explain in the morning." She gently stroked her hair and smiled softly. "You should try to get some more sleep."

Hannah nodded. "In a little bit," she replied. "Would you stay?"

Without a word, she shuffled further on to the bed and sat with her back against the wall. It wasn't the first time that she'd been asked to stay, although, it was usually only a nightmare that triggered the request. It was this, however, that had led to the persistent rumour that she was just Hannah's dolly.

Sitting against the headboard, Hannah hugged herself and listened to the gentle humming of the ship.

"You really should wear your legs in bed," Kelly said softly as she stifled a yawn. Unlike Jon, who didn't ever need to sleep, she needed the same amount as a human to keep her neural net healthy.

Wrinkling her nose, Hannah shook her head. "I don't like the feel of them in bed." Yawning, she wriggled to settle down. Kelly moved to join her. While Hannah normally slept close to the wall, she moved to the other side of the double bed to avoid feeling trapped.

As she rolled to face the door, the pain of missing Ali stabbed at her. She blinked a few tears away before quickly falling asleep.

When Hannah woke the next morning, she felt terrible, but didn't really remember what had happened the night before. Bleary-eyed and bursting for the toilet, she swung herself to the edge of the bed and put her legs on. The artificial flesh automatically clung to her thighs and blended in so perfectly, no one would ever know they weren't an organic part of her.

As she emerged from the en-suite, she decided breakfast was the first order of the day. In fact, she was almost certain she could already smell it. Bacon, possibly sausage, definitely eggs, scrambled with milk. And coffee, that unmistakable waft of pure get-up-and-go, caffeine loaded, wonder-bean juice.

Staggering in a haze of sleepiness and hungriness, it was a few seconds before she realised the reason she could smell food was because it was actually cooking.

"Good morning," Kelly said with a smile as she tipped bacon from a pan onto a waiting plate.

Hannah suddenly felt very exposed. She was wearing nothing but a pair of pants and an ancient t-shirt, which she tugged at for a moment in a futile effort to stretch it to make it a short dress. As the blurriness cleared and she saw it was Kelly, she relaxed a little and continued to the little table on the far side of the room.

"Morning," she replied. It was yet to be determined if it could be classed as good. It was looking positive, but looks could be deceiving. "Ehm, not to be rude, but why are you making me breakfast?"

Kelly brought the two plates over and sat them at the table. "You don't remember what happened last night?"

Frantically, Hannah tried to remember what had happened the night before. Had she finally gone over the edge? Was this the morning after the night before with Kelly?

No.

No, she was absolutely certain she had not done anything regretful in that sense. Vague memories of being awake came to her and the brief discussion.

"I remember something happened," she replied. "I woke and you told me I'd had a night terror, or something like that?"

Kelly explained what had happened as they both started into their breakfasts. "You were," she paused, searching for the right word, "unsettled. You woke me a few times and you were muttering in your sleep."

Pushing a piece of sausage about the plate, Hannah slumped into her seat. "I think I was dreaming a lot."

They ate in silence. It was starting to grow oppressive for Hannah, although Kelly appeared completely oblivious to it. After years of struggling to eat food and fearing to do so, she was enjoying being able to eat, at least vaguely normally.

"Kelly, there's something I have to tell you."

She looked up; her face blank.

"I… I actually have probably most – no, I have more than enough of the money needed to fix your body," Hannah said, feeling completely disgraced. "A lot's been tied up in funds and I've been trying to avoid letting Helen know I have it."

"I know."

"You know?"

A frown flickered across Kelly's face before she went back to her normal gentle smile. "Yes. You told me, last year." She chewed on a piece of toast, unintentionally drawing the torture out. "You were drunk at the time. It was the time you drank three bottles of wine, vomited and I had to put you in the shower."

If the deck had opened up and blown her into space, Hannah would have died grateful for having escaped the misery. Sadly, it didn't and she was left feeling exposed and thoroughly monstrous.

Reaching over the table, Kelly lifted her chin with a soft touch. "What happened to me is not your problem to fix," she said. "You've given me a home, a job and most importantly, you're my friend." Her smile brightened slightly as real warmth flowed into it. "And I can eat without having to vomit."

This managed to draw a slight giggle from Hannah. "That is the really critical thing, right there: food."

Sitting back again, Kelly sighed slightly. "I appreciate what you're trying to do, but I don't want to just shut down and go back to how I was before."

Jerking back, Hannah sat with her mouth open for a second. "You don't?"

Plucking at the sleeve of her nightie, she looked at the table. "When I was sold, the first thing he did was shunt my higher functions," she said. She looked up, her eyes slightly glazed. "He used me for a few months, shut me down and I woke up like this. I'm not that Kelly anymore and I never can be. I need to find out who I am through a slow change, becoming exactly who I want to be."

Hannah shook her head slightly. "Okay, I can understand that, but I could at least fix the critical things. Give you a more natural waist and organs so you can get all your energy from food rather than needing a wall socket." She rubbed her nose. "And perhaps undo some of the more distracting changes."

Kelly looked down at herself and shrugged. She wasn't too overly concerned about some of her features, but once her personality was restored, or at least expanded, her opinion might change. Or develop, since she didn't think she had much of one at the moment.

They sat for a while in comfortable silence before Kelly tidied up the breakfast dishes. She placed them straight into the replicator which disassembled them.

"Do you think Ali would have been happier if she'd used a Rep to transition?" she asked, dragging Hannah from her thoughts.

It seemed a slightly odd question to ask; Ali had been dead for nearly five years before she'd met Kelly, so they'd never met. After a moment's hesitation, she realised that she was trying to evaluate the option of a quick transformation.

"We talked about it," she replied. "After we married and got away from her parents, we planned to save up the money. Unfortunately, life isn't nice like that, so we went the old school route."

She sat back in her seat and chewed her lip slightly. "I thought it would be better to get it over and done with, but Ali actually thought it better she transitioned slowly, more for my sake."

Kelly tilted her head like an inquisitive bird. "She believed you would struggle with a rapid change?"

The silence was deafening. Hannah had always known Ali identified as a woman and was sure she was fine with that. Yet, there had been times when she'd woken in the night, wondering who the person next to her was. And after the last major surgery, she'd found herself in the horrible situation of not finding her new wife as physically attractive as she had her husband. It had taken a few months for her to really come around, but she'd loved Ali too much and their marriage had survived.

With a great deal more tact than most people would display, Kelly said nothing and started to tidy up. There wasn't much lying around the place, but enough to look unbecoming of a ship's captain.

"Thank you," she said softly, getting up from the table.

"You're welcome," Kelly replied with a warm smile. "But please, try to keep this place tidy."

The Root of All Evil

Sigyn's trip back to the *Sheba* had been uneventful, with nothing but some vaguely interesting rocks found during the system scan. Despite the quiet journey, and the considerable crew chatter about their big pay day, the tension had become unbearable.

Hannah lounged in her seat, frowning into the middle distance as they dropped into normal space. She wasn't sure if she would have been more annoyed if Helen had robbed her blind, but as it was, she hadn't. She'd had days to do it, so was unlikely to take all the money now.

Swooping in, *Sigyn* gently came to rest in the docking cradle on *Sheba*'s hull, becoming almost indistinguishable from the massive mining vessel. Only the difference in colours gave away the fact they were separate entities.

Once the docking procedure was complete and the airlock connected, Hannah made her way towards the Aviary to see what fresh hell would be waiting, Harry following her. She hadn't even set foot on the *Sheba* when her back was up.

Vic stood waiting for her, smiling politely in that sickeningly pleasant way he always did. What Holly saw in him, aside from his good looks, pleasant demeanour, wit, charm and other significant assets, Hannah didn't know. She was certain he was after her ship, even though he'd already been given *Sif* as Holly was often too busy to command her personally. Add to that he was the *Sheba*'s Executive Officer, making him Helen's right-hand man, just set Hannah's ire off.

"Welcome back, Captains," he said politely. "I trust you had a pleasant journey?"

"Right up until I got here," Hannah replied, sweeping past him without so much as a passing glance.

Harry gave him an apologetic smile. She was amazed that the man never snapped, never complained and just rolled with the thinly veiled insults.

"Were you able to secure the parts we need?" he asked, following a few steps behind the sisters.

"Yes," Hannah replied tersely.

He relaxed slightly. "Thank goodness for that. Thank you so much for your help; it'll be good to be able to get out and about with *Sif* again. You must be looking forward to getting out with *Frigg*, eh Harry?"

She nodded. "Oh yes, I can't wait to be free again."

They entered a lift, at which Hannah had hoped they'd escape Vic. Unfortunately, he stepped in too. He stood a respectful distance away, yet it felt like he was doing that only to cover something up.

He followed them out of the lift when it stopped, but headed for the Bridge instead of the Aviary, for which she was grateful. How Holly could stand him was beyond her.

"Do you always have to be such a bitch to him?" Harry asked once he was out of sight.

"I don't like him," she replied, as though that justified and explained everything.

Harry blocked her path. "No, you don't like that he got dealt a better hand in life. Come on, you've seen the pictures of what he was like as a child; the fact his parents could afford to get him a Rep is no reason to hate him."

She bristled slightly. "Perhaps not, but he comes from an exceedingly privileged family, yet acts like he's one of us."

"We come from a privileged family," Harry replied, rolling her eyes. "We own a mining company."

Hannah pushed past her. "I have a right to dislike whoever I wish," she replied. "And he wants my ship, I know he does."

They continued in silence to the Aviary.

Helen, Holly and Heather were waiting for them. Harry quickly moved to her place, nodding subserviently to Helen, giving Holly a weak smile and a much warmer one to Heather as she gently touched her shoulder.

"I trust you had a profitable journey?" Helen asked, not even bothering to keep the bitter tone from her voice.

"I believe it was rather profitable for you as well," Hannah replied. "And there is more money to come after the job is complete: I might, just, stay associated with you that long and let you have your cut."

Holly was shaking her head ever so slightly.

It was too little too late as Helen leant forward on the table. "Oh, might you? You are forgetting that you took that contract while in contract with us; you owe us the cut, even if you leave now."

Looking like a surprised goldfish, Hannah blinked a few times. "Sod off. I can use the escape clause to leave when I want, how I want."

"Oh, I don't think so," she replied, "that requires a shareholder majority to let it be invoked."

Hannah was nearly shaking. How dare her sister keep her leashed like a dog to a failing business and expect to be thanked for being robbed. Better judgement failed miserably and she played her ace-in-the-hole.

"I am the shareholders."

All the colour drained from Holly's face and appeared to be leaching into Helen's as she went purple. In fact, Hannah was sure she could just make out that she was now shaking.

"In fact," she continued, "I believe that I own one-hundred-and-four percent of the business after my last round of share buying."

Somehow, Helen managed to go an even deeper shade of incandescent rage as she turned to face Holly.

"We needed more money," she replied, unable to meet her sister's furious glare. "It's still better than nine months ago; she owned almost two-hundred percent. Had we managed to keep the ships running, we'd have been able to pay enough dividends to be back in black."

"How does she own anything?" Helen asked through gritted teeth.

All of the joy at getting on over her sisters evaporated for Hannah. She hadn't realised just how bad things were. Guilt started to well, but not enough to sway her from her course. It was too late, anyway.

"Through various investment companies," she replied. "I mean, come on, didn't you think some of the people investing in you sounded, well, suspect?"

Heather sighed a little. "It's true. I asked my old colleagues and uni friends about some of the companies claiming to specialise in mining. Some they had encountered, but most were unknown. Their theory was the companies were linked and either trying to prop us up out of kindness, or stage a silent takeover."

Holly nodded. "I checked with Companies House," she replied. "A few nom de plomes, but most were easy if you know Hannah. Sinclair Sediment Inc.; The Sisters Investments; Vulcan Alloy Enterprises; the Jupiter Mining Corporation Ltd.?"

A deadly silence filled the room. With a curt wave, Helen dismissed her sisters and stood, glaring, at Hannah until the door closed.

Now alone, she seemed to sag, leaning on the table heavily as she shook her head. "So, I guess this is it? I should have seen this coming."

"Seen what?"

"That you'd take this away from us."

Hannah rolled her eyes. "I don't want it."

Helen wasn't listening. "You know something, Grandad kept you out his will because he was convinced of this, that you'd just try to take the whole damned lot."

"How do you know that?"

She looked up, guiltily. "I was his lawyer; I updated his will when he required it."

"Money has always been an ugly, evil thing for this family," she replied, trying to keep the hurt at the betrayal from her voice. To have been disinherited was painful; to have it confirmed that her grandfather had thought her a money-grabber stung; to find out that her own sister had put that into legally binding documents was a knife in the gut.

"You know what your problem is?" she started.

"Oh, here we go," Helen replied as she pushed off the table.

"You and I are too alike. We are both stubborn, self-important and unwilling to ask for help," she continued. "You just dismissed our younger sisters like they were staff. And I let you do it. This should have been a family conversation."

She expected fury.

She got acceptance.

"You're right," Helen replied. Knowing the other three were likely at the door listening, she called them in and immediately apologised. Hannah followed suit. Why they put up with being treated like second class sisters was beyond either of them.

They all left the table and went to sit in the lounge section of the Aviary. The simple act of changing location altered the dynamic and for the first time in years, Hannah saw Helen actually smile and look relaxed. Not completely, but just enough.

"Okay, I know its poor form to talk money," Harry said as she kicked her boots off and curled up on a couch, "but how did you manage to get so much money?"

Hannah chuckled. "Well, most of the companies I own are using other people's money. You'd be surprised how easy it is to bamboozle people into investing."

"And do they actually get anything back?" Heather asked.

"Of course." She looked to Holly and smiled. "My accountant makes sure of that."

The other three looked at their very guilty sister. She shrugged a little, but offered no defence to the fact she'd been well aware of Hannah's fortune.

They moved on to less controversial topics. After a few drinks, it was like they were teenagers again, thick as thieves and having a good gossip. The old wounds would take time to heal, but at least they could, just maybe, start to do so.

Castor was fairly certain he was going to be sacked. It was his first day on the *Glorious Purity of the Soul* and he was late for his first summons. The corridors all looked the same; stark, sterile white and filled with crew in the dark grey uniforms of the Navy or crisp white robes of the Purifiers.

Hitching his robe up, he moved a little quicker. Running would be frowned upon, as it suggested panic, tardiness, or unprofessional conduct.

He nearly missed the door, which looked like every other door along the corridor. Straightening his robes, standing up a little taller, he pressed the door chime and waited for what would be an inevitable beating.

A soft voice called him in. It had to be a servant; a Purifier-General wouldn't sound so gentle.

Stepping into the room, he froze before averting his eyes to look at the floor. He was definitely going to die today.

"Are you okay?" the soft voice asked.

"Apologies, Purifier-General, I thought you asked me to come in," he replied rapidly. "I was unaware you were indisposed."

Dido smiled gently at the young man. He barely looked old enough to shave, let alone serve the Purifiers. No doubt the sight of a naked woman tending a room full of plants was enough to freak him out completely.

"No need to apologise," she replied. "Would you prefer it if I put a robe on?"

Castor's eyes bulged. It had to be a test of some sort. Would she take offense if he asked her to cover up, or would he be charged with indecency for asking her to remain unclothed.

"I'll put a robe on," she said, seeing he was struggling to answer.

He looked up to watch her walk to the back of the room, her hips swaying, to collect a pure white robe. She turned slightly side on before lifting it over her head and slowly wiggled into it. If he hadn't known better, he would have suspected she was doing it on purpose.

"So, you are my new aide," she said, walking back to him. "Do you garden?"

"I have some basic botanical training, Ma'am."

She huffed ever so slightly. "Please, you don't have to call me Ma'am."

"As you wish, Purifier-General Dido."

The slight twitch about her eyes suggested he was disappointing her already. All of his training wasn't helping in the slightest and that scared him more than anything. And he'd been pretty terrified before arriving.

"When we are alone, you can address me as an equal," she replied. "And my name is pronounced the ancient way; Dee-do, not Die-do. Now, what is your name?"

"It's Castor," he replied. Surely, she already knew that?

"A pleasure, Castor," she replied, holding her delicate hand out to him. He hesitated for a moment, before taking it.

She turned and drifted back to one of the many containers, lifting a mister. "Come on, there is work to be done," she said, nodding to the plants. "Will you check my messages while I give these little lovelies their morning feed?"

This was more the sort of work he'd trained for. Master Thomas had spent hours extolling the virtues of service, but had never once mentioned gardening. Then again, it appeared Dido was not an ordinary Purifier-General. He'd expected a battle-hardened woman, probably in her later years, that would be gruff, commanding and demanding. A beautiful young-looking woman was about as far from what he'd anticipated, especially given her reputation.

"There's a priority message from Purifier-Seeker Alphonso," he said, feeling a mix of exhilaration and terror at reading a message marked "Security One". "He says one of his agents is making progress on Project Africa."

Dido stopped misting. "Do you know anything about Project Africa?" she asked as she placed the mister down and drifted over.

He shook his head.

"Reply, telling Alphonso to contact me the instant he knows more," she continued. "Project Africa will ensure we can save the human race by regaining our original, pure form so we can continue to evolve as nature intended."

The explanation didn't really clear anything up, but he was too afraid to ask further questions. Security One clearance was so far above what he should be looking at, he was terrified he'd get altitude sickness just thinking about it. He couldn't understand why he, a mere Purifier-Adept, would be serving as an aide to one of the most respected Purifiers in the galaxy.

"Any other messages?" Dido asked, still hovering about him.

"Mostly reports from Purifiers in the field," he replied. "The unrest on Drozana Station has settled down with few casualties, but the people of Plentiful Fields continue to resist our teachings."

She frowned lightly, a sadness crossing her face. Pressing a button on the console, she opened her direct line to the ship's bridge. "Admiral Green, set course for Plentiful Fields and ready the Marines for action."

"As you command," was the only response.

"Come, Caster, we must ensure we are ready." She took a deep breath before smiling weakly at him. "I hope not to have to use violence, but I fear blood shed is inevitable."

The Forbidden System

"Are you sure these coordinates are right?" Hannah asked as she looked at the tablet. "Because if they are, that's not good."

Casper looked pensive for a moment. "Well, they were on the list when I hired you and they are correct." He wrung his hands as he considered the issue. "Will that be a problem?"

After a thought, she shrugged. "No, I guess not." She sat back in her chair, trying to appear far more nonchalant that she felt. How come Emily hadn't said anything? "Can you tell me exactly what we've spent the last six weeks looking for?"

Tapping away on his tablet, he called up a small holographic image of what looked like a metal cigar with three sets of four large pods around it, clustered at the middle. At one end was a large ion engine and what appeared to be a primitive warp drive.

"This is the *EECV Livingstone*, a very early deep space colony vessel," he said, gesturing to the image. "Or at least, my colleagues think this is what it probably looked like. It's from back when humanity thought colonising planets was a smart thing to do."

After some success and a lot of uninhabitable worlds that killed the colonists, humanity had taken to building stations and megastructures to live on. Terraforming had come later, allowing totally barren worlds to be reshaped to Earth standard. Only a few hundred planets had ever been colonised, despite humanity's unrelenting conquest of the stars.

Hannah nodded, although it did little to cover the fact she didn't much care and was concerned about not getting her money. Mostly due to being dead.

"Final payment before we arrive."

With a slight frown and pursing of his lips, Casper tapped away on his tablet and authorised the transfer of funds.

"First sign of trouble, we bug out," she added. "That place is haunted and I can't fight ghosts."

With a snort, he sat back and shook his head. "Ghosts?" he replied, folding his arms. "There's no such thing as ghosts. Nothing but superstition and rot. Next you'll be telling me you believe in the Eris myth."

She had no desire to argue the point. It was true she had no idea why the system they were hurtling towards was quarantined on pain of death. Although, if the stories were right, no one was enforcing the penalty from the outside particularly zealously.

"So, how did a colony ship get lost?" she asked, heading to the replicator. "Want anything?"

"Green tea, please," he replied, relaxing as they moved onto a topic he knew more about. "It's quite simple, really. They missed their target. As far as we can tell, it happened from time to time."

She was surprised that anyone could miss a solar system; they were rather large and not exactly prone to erratic movements. Sipping her Earl Grey tea, she pondered what it must have been like, living on Earth at the dawn of interstellar travel. Limited to one planet or crawling about at a snail's pace, AI that wasn't smart enough to talk back like a smart-arse, simple problems and simple needs. Frankly, it sounded awful.

"Well, I suppose I can let you on the Bridge when we arrive," she said, standing up from the table again. "We'll be there in about nine hours; I'm sure you can amuse yourself until then."

He blushed and tried to hide in his tea.

With a satisfied smile, Hannah left the mess and headed for her cabin. Normally she'd have gone to the Bridge, but having a chill and some sleep now would be critical if she planned to stay on duty as long as they were in the Exclusion Zone.

When she arrived back at her cabin, she was slightly surprised to see that Kelly hadn't been in to tidy up yet. Feeling a little guilty, she made a vain attempt at picking up her discarded clothes from the floor. They were laid to rest on the back of a chair, making the floor look a little better if not the rest of the place.

Mess dealt with, sort of, she curled up on the couch and indulged in her guilty pleasure; a silly little farming simulator aimed at children. For an hour, she watered a range of crops; corn, cabbage, wheat, pumpkin, beetroot and apple trees. Animals had buckets of feed supplied to troughs, eliciting happy faces and little speech bubbles with hearts in them. Gathering some eggs, she gave them to one of her virtual friends who needed some to complete a challenge.

She'd been playing, on and off, for years. Before it, there had been other simple simulation or puzzle games she'd played in bed as a child or in her bunk between duty shifts. It had been the one thing she'd shared with virtually no one; it had been her secret pleasure and that was the way it was going to stay.

Her back popped in several places as she stretched. One of the horrors of getting older was the weird noises the body made. At least she hadn't reached the stage of groaning when she got out of bed. Well, except when she was hungover, but that was a different situation altogether.

The past few weeks she'd slept peacefully, lost in deep, dreamless sleep that had left her refreshed. Hopefully, she'd manage the same again, ready for whatever fresh horrors would be thrown at the crew on arrival at their destination.

It felt like her head had barely touched the pillow before her alarm was going. She felt only marginally better than when she'd gone to sleep. Coffee would solve that.

Armed with what could be classed as a small bucket of coffee, she returned to the Bridge, feeling like she'd never been away. Such days were good when nothing was going on, but sucked when charging towards what could be certain death. Or worse; fines from all the governments of the galaxy for breaching the Exclusion

Zone. And there were a lot of governments that would be looking for a piece of her hide.

"Have you two been here the whole time?" she asked as she dropped into her chair, careful not to spill the scalding java about herself.

"Of course not," Laura replied. "We took turns on short shifts. Dare I ask why we are heading towards the Exclusion Zone?"

Emily smiled and put her knitting back into the drawer on the side of her console. "Bet it's for something ridiculous, like the Holy Grail."

"Maybe the Golden Fleece?"

"Nope, I've got it: Elvis's Rhinestone Jumpsuit," Emily chuckled.

Hannah snorted loudly. "How about a crew that respects the captain?" she offered. "What are you knitting this time?"

"Scarf for Hubby," she replied. "It gets cold down in Ore Processing."

Hannah imagined it probably did when you stopped working for a quickie most days. It was that behaviour that had landed Emily on *Sigyn*. While she didn't mind her knitting while on duty if nothing was going on, it might have been better to focus considering where they were going.

"We've entered the Exclusion Zone," Jon reported as he appeared. "No signs of any other ships, satellites or drones."

Despite the fact the environmental controls were working perfectly, holding the temperature at a constant and comfortable level, she felt a chill run down her spine. She'd been here once before, as a Flight Lieutenant, on a patrol to investigate a rumour that the Remnant were using one of the systems as a staging ground.

"I'm detecting a very faint radio signal coming from one of the systems," Jon said. "It fits the parameters of Dr Mendoza's search."

"Call him up to the Bridge," Hannah said as she fidgeted in her chair. "Take us in and keep an eye out for anything."

The feeling that something was watching them, that something was waiting to pounce, that something would go horribly wrong grew, weaving its tendrils around the Bridge and the crew. Casper's arrival made them jump, loosening the grip of fear for a moment. It grew tighter almost immediately.

"The signal is coming from somewhere in orbit of the fourth planet," Jon announced as he pulled an image of the planet in question onto the viewscreen. The large, rocky world was deep orange in appearance, drifting lazily through space.

Casper stepped forward, looking at the screen. "Is that…?"

Hannah cast him a sidelong look. "Welcome to Gallifrey, Doctor."

The Exclusion Zone was not unique in the sense of being a no-go area of the galaxy. Thousands of planets had been quarantined for various reasons, usually to protect non-sapient indigenous life or to stop humans being infected with lethal diseases.

What made it unique was the size and the fact no one knew why it existed. Seven solar systems in close (relatively speaking) proximity had been cordoned off since at least the Collapse. The Peacekeeper Order, United Systems Alliance Navy and the Commonwealth Navy patrolled the area around it, keeping potential travellers away.

Naturally, since no reason was known for why it was off limits, rumours were rife. They always fell into three categories: The Unity, the pan-galactic government of the Golden Era before the Collapse, had used one of the systems as a homeworld after Earth had been abandoned, leaving it full of highly advanced technology; The Unity had been experimenting in the systems and whatever they had been doing went wrong, forcing them to abandon and quarantine them for safety; the only other technologically advanced life in the galaxy, beside humanity, either lived there or had lived there in the past and it was being covered up.

All Hannah knew was that many ships that went into the Exclusion Zone turned up elsewhere in the galaxy with most of the crew dead or wishing they were for the short time they survived before their cellular structure disintegrated – parts of them aged massively at random.

And of all the systems, Gallifrey's system was the one said to be most cursed.

Rumour, again, surrounded why the planet was named as such. Those of the alien cover up persuasion believed the civilisation that had lived there, or did, had developed time travel and a way to cheat death, much like the Time Lords that lived on the fictitious namesake. Given the Unity's extreme power at its height, those who favoured the second homeworld theory likened the Unified Council to all powerful beings who could all but control time and the fate of the universe.

The system appeared empty, the planet nothing but a barren world. Whatever had happened would likely remain forever a mystery.

"I'm detecting a single ship," Jon said in hushed tones. "It's orbiting the planet, very low power signature, a few million clicks ahead of us. IFF identifies her as the *Livingstone*."

Casper stumbled and half fell into a seat at an auxiliary console, muttering to himself.

"Take us in," Hannah ordered. "If anything moves in this system, get us out of here." She got up and went to Casper. "Will there be a way to get in?"

He blinked a few times, confused and a little dazed. "Wha-? Oh, yes, yes," he replied. "There should be several airlocks along the hull. I believe the main one will be near the middle of the ship, as will the main power umbilical point."

Jon nodded, having located the spot.

"We should have a suit in your size," she said, returning to her chair.

"What?"

"Well, don't you want to see what's in there?" she asked. "I assume that's why you hired my ship? As for the suit, God knows what horrible diseases might be lurking."

"Air is likely a bigger issue," Jon said, rolling his eyes slightly.

She ignored the comment. "ETA?"

"Four minutes," Laura replied. "It'll take a few minutes to position the docking clamps, umbilical and airlock."

"Em, get your glad rags on, we're going to take a walk."

Emily sagged for a moment before dragging herself from her seat.

"Jon, get your Mini-You ready and have Kelly and Annie suit up too."

Rolling his head back, Jon let out a groan. The Mini-Jon, a small drone that he could pilot to access off-ship systems, was, quite frankly, offensive to his sensibilities. From a hatch at the back of the Bridge appeared a two-foot tall, squat dustbin. Hannah had drawn a lopsided grinning face on it as well as, for some bizarre reason, a bowtie.

"Laura, you're in charge," she called over her shoulder as she half dragged Casper from his stunned slump.

"Well, duh," she muttered, being the only person left on the ship.

Hannah made her way down to the airlock located at the very bottom of the ship, Casper practically tripping over himself as he tried to keep up. She pretended not to notice the look that passed between him and Annie when she joined them.

In the airlock, she grabbed her old flight suit. For a moment, she just stood holding it, remembering times gone by. It denoted her last flying rank of Wing Commander; she'd been promoted to a desk job for a short time before being discharged and the suit was never updated.

The one downside with the flight suit over the EV suits was the fact it was almost skin tight. She quickly threw her jacket, t-shirt and jeans off, and dragged the suit on as fast as she could. Back in the day, that had taken a few seconds. Now, it was a slower, less flattering affair.

With a few passing years, a few extra pounds had gone on. While no one would call her fat, far from it, she wasn't the skinny girl she had been.

"Do you need a hand?" Kelly asked quietly. "Or perhaps some butter?"

"Funny."

"You could just use an EV suit."

"I'll not be beaten by a jumpsuit," she replied as she managed to tug it on. Immediately she regretted wearing it; she'd have to take it off in her cabin to avoid exposing more of herself than she'd like. She placed on the outer protection layers and performed her pre-use checks.

Helmets went on and the door to the ship closed. A decontamination cycle ran, flagging up all sorts of heat warnings briefly on the HUDs. Using the wrist mounted interface, Hannah had the outer door open.

A burst of escaping air buffeted them as the pressure equalised.

Expecting to drop on to the deck, Hannah nearly flipped head over heels as she passed through the airlock door into a zero-gravity corridor. The grav-boots kicked in and she landed with a soft thud on the wall.

"Any idea of which way to go?" she asked Casper when they had assembled.

"The Bridge should be up at the front," he replied, projecting a small holographic map. A section right at the very front of the cigar-shaped body was highlighted in red.

Kelly peered at the map. "Why would they put the most important control centre in the most vulnerable place?"

Annie gave a short, sarcastic laugh. "Seems they hadn't figured out how stupid that was, yet."

They started to walk along the corridor, only the lights from their suit torches illuminating the way. Every twenty feet, they stepped through open bulkhead doors, only passing junctions on a few occasions.

"The pods are pre-fab buildings," Casper said to no one in particular. "The ship would drop them from low altitude before returning to a stable orbit. The crew would position them to form the colony hub and expand from there."

It took almost half an hour for them to walk to the Bridge. The *Livingstone* dwarfed *Sigyn*, which was a reasonable size for a modest freighter at nearly 180 metres long; *Livingstone* was at least twelve times that length.

The doors to the Bridge were closed. A dead interface sat on the wall to the right. Casper immediately started to look for an access point or manual override. Kelly simply got a grip of one door and used her enormous strength to slide it open.

Everyone piled in.

Annie immediately started to search the various consoles for any that might control power distribution. With the two ships connected, it would be possible to divert power to bring the dormant systems back online.

Light flickered around the room, consoles started to boot up the operating systems and screens flickered into life.

"I'll see if I can take a copy of the computer core," Mini-Jon said as he hovered around the consoles. "I won't link in directly in case I corrupt the data."

"I doubt anything much has survived the past ten thousand years," Hannah replied as she looked around. "I can't imagine old hard drives were as good as they are now."

"Actually," Annie replied from her station, "it hasn't been thousands of years for the ship. According to the logs I can access, time dilation due to relativistic speeds mean less than four centuries have passed on board."

Hannah nodded. She understood the concept of relativity and time dilation, but it always amazed her how it worked. In a universe when faster-than-light travel existed, there was little need to really know about time dilation. How could time actually move at different rates for different things because of speed?

Unable to resist the temptation, she moved to the centre seat. The Captain's Chair was on a slightly raised dais in the centre of the Bridge, a solitary sentinel surrounded by the workstations of underlings.

Just as she was about to park her rear, Casper clenched his fists a few times before shakily pointing at the console he was at. "We're not alone," he said.

She flew over to the console, roughly pushing him out of the way. Looking over the readout, she was immediately confused that it wasn't a tactical, navigation or sensor console. In fact, it wasn't even taking readings from outside the ship; it was an internal readout.

Then she saw it.

Two life signs.

"Jesus Christ, there are people still alive on this ship."

"It's been four hundred years and there's no heat or oxygen recycling," Emily replied. "I'm no biologist, but surely people need that to live?"

Casper had slid back into the console as Hannah muttered an apology for pushing him. "They are in cryo-stasis," he said. "An exceptionally primitive way to put a person into hibernation. Even so, to have survived…" he tailed off as he read the logs.

"Oh," he muttered, trying to wipe his face, forgetting his helmet was in the way. "The computer," he continued, "it… it selected those with the best chance of survival."

Hannah, Annie and Emily all looked at each other in confusion.

"It turned off their life support one by one, killing a colonist to extend the life of another," Kelly said from her commandeered station. "Seems to have been an emergency protocol."

The Bridge was silent as everyone considered the ramifications of what they'd just learnt. It was mass murder, in effect. Had the colonists known that might be their fate? Was it really possible that ancient humans had been so brutal in their thinking, so relentless in their pursuit of new land?

"We need to get them out," Casper said.

"And then what?" Hannah asked. "We can't take them on to *Sigyn* in case they catch something from us, or we get something from them."

"We can't leave them to die."

Kelly coughed politely. "I'm sure I can run some scans and create suitable inoculations. Anyway, the logs show the ship was sterilised after the crew went into stasis, so you lot should be perfectly safe."

They all looked at each other, wondering who'd be first to take their helmet off and risk it. After a few glances, they all silently decided it was safest to keep themselves sealed away.

"Jon, how are you getting on with the computer?" Hannah asked.

The dustbin Mini-Jon turned. "Oh, just bloody peachy. It's like talking to a petulant child. And the download speeds? It'll be hours and hours before I've got a full copy. Broadband, my arse; total misnomer, right there."

"Let's go find the human popsicles, shall we?" she replied.

The stasis chambers were incredibly grim.

Row after row of clear fronted coffins, proudly displaying the desiccated remains of the poor sods that had been identified as less likely to survive than someone else. The nutrient paste that had fed directly into a surgically placed port on each colonists' stomach had turned out to be the critical component. When it had been stopped and saved for another, the occupant simply starved to death in their sleep. After that, the other supplies were cut off and the body left to rot.

Emily had had to go back to the Bridge. She'd nearly vomited when she saw the first body and started to freak out.

Hannah had seen enough bodies to be unfazed by them individually, but the sheer number, contained in glass and metal tubes was disturbing. At any moment, she expected one to move and all of them to start banging on the lid, moaning to get out. Asking why they'd been left to die.

They found the two tubes in the fifth large room they entered, not far apart from each other. A man and a woman, both looked quite young and in reasonable condition. Their faces were partially obscured by masks that provided air, but their naked bodies were mostly visible. Various straps and life-sustaining devices covered their modesty.

Kelly found a computer nearby and started to access their files.

"Huh, we're in luck," she said. "The tubes have been monitoring their vitals and bacterial, viral and fungal cultures. Their DNA is also in the database, so I can whip up something to protect them from you lot."

"Are they carrying anything nasty?" Annie asked, peering in at the young woman. She wrinkled her nose slightly as she tried to get a decent look at her and all the primitive tech.

"No," Kelly replied as she took notes on her suit computer. "You, however, would likely kill her in a few weeks. He might, just, survive."

Hannah joined Annie in peering at the woman. "Can we take the pods back to the ship?"

"No, that would kill them."

"How long until we can get them out?"

Kelly shrugged. "A few hours, maybe? I'm a doctor, not a fortune-teller."

Hannah and Annie shared a puzzled look. "Are you okay?"

"I'm… yes, I'm fine," she replied. "Sorry, this is actually really difficult. I can't make much sense of the language, so I'm relying heavily the medical terms and pictures."

Saying nothing, Hannah smiled, nodded and moved away towards the man. She'd noticed that Kelly tended to be more human when she was dealing with medical matters. It probably meant that the last remnants of her original personality were linked to her medical knowledge, colouring it. At least, she hoped that was the case and it wasn't rampancy. Once they'd got the two popsicles off ice, she'd have Annie double check her.

When Hannah found the man, she immediately took a step back. He was big, squashed into his tube in what had to be an exceptionally uncomfortable position. The man was a mountain of muscle, even after four centuries of only having stasis muscle preservation techniques.

She tried to peer down the tube to see if the rest of him was as impressive, but everything of interest was hidden.

"A guy that looks like that is usually compensating," Annie quipped, having had the same idea when she'd found him initially.

"Is that why you're taken with our cargo?" she asked, nodding to Casper. He was too busy trying to watch over Kelly's shoulder, avoiding her pointed shrugs to get space to work, to notice the comment.

Annie blushed heavily and muttered something in Gaelic. Something rather crude.

"I need to pop back to the ship to get the drugs they need," Kelly said as she headed for the door. "It'll take a few hours to synthesise, and I think, emphasis on think, it'll take at least twelve hours to get them defrosted."

Hannah nodded. "I'll go make sure Em hasn't passed out between here and the Bridge."

Casper tagged along as Annie went with Kelly. He stumbled along silently a step or so behind Hannah.

"I thought you'd be more excited," she said as they left the stasis chambers.

"What? Oh? Yes," he replied absently. "I'm sorry, I never expected to find an ancient ship, let alone two ancients. Imagine what they can tell us of the past? Oh God, we might be able to find Earth."

She was less hopeful on that front. The Armageddon Protocol was designed to continually wipe references to Earth's location in AIs and computers. They were unlikely to find anything useful.

"I remember agreeing to me getting a share of any profit from this little adventure," she said. "Dare I ask what something like this is worth?"

Casper flailed slightly. "Worth? This is priceless. We are standing in a cultural artefact; you can't put a price on that. Imagine trying to sell Stonehenge, the Coliseum, the Taj Mahal, the Declaration of Independence?"

Hannah decided not to burst his bubble by pointing out that a great many cultural artefacts had been sold and were still being sold. Sadly, Roddenberry's Great Space Bird of the Galaxy had gone extinct with the Unity, assuming it had ever found a safe place to roost amongst humanity.

He started to babble excitedly about how much could be learnt from such an ancient ship; the cultural norms of the 21st Century, the languages, concepts of beauty, attitudes towards all sorts of things. Even just knowing what it was like to face the reality of death from minor ailments like heart disease, cancer and AIDs because quick cures had yet to be invented.

It was the most excited he'd seemed about the whole venture. That bothered her, but she just couldn't figure out why. Maybe it was just that she wasn't as excited about it. Even if the ship revealed all sorts of secrets, there would still be a huge hole in history; it had spent thousands of years travelling at near light speed with no updates on the state of the universe.

Plentiful Fields

Castor struggled up the hill, his legs aching terribly. He gripped his right hip as he tried to keep the aching in the joint at bay, but it only let the pain in his knee and left foot come through. Worse, he was being weighed down by the heavy flak vest he was wearing over his robes and the helmet that was slowly trying to cook his brain.

Mingled in with the sweet smell of flowers, trees and grass was the acrid stench of smoke. Struggling to breathe was not helping him with the climb up the gentle slope. Part of him was glad that his infirmity kept him from the front lines, but at the same time, he wanted nothing more than to help drive forward the ideals of absolute purism.

Dido was sitting by herself, clad in her combat armour, but with her helmet stowed. Blood and dirt clung to the armour, here and there; none of the blood was her own. She was staring out over the grassy fields to the little village of Strawberry, now smouldering away.

She snapped her head towards him as he came closer. Tension left her as she realised it was him. He noticed that a small, wrist mounted disruptor had deployed, but now slithered back into the armour from whence it came.

"You startled me," she said with a slight smile.

"I'm sorry," he replied, standing a safe distance away. It was only then he realised he'd been holding his breath when she'd turned.

Another smile and she shook her head. "Don't be. Please sit. You don't look at all well."

With all the grace of an arthritic old man, Castor levered himself down, trying his best not to make grunts and groans. His joints were burning now, making his legs stiff and uncooperative.

"Are you hurt?" she asked, reaching out to help him down.

"No, no," he replied, accepting the hand without even thinking. "When I was little, the Plague Bringers attacked my home. I was lucky, so the doctors told me," he said with a bitter smile. He gave her a pathetic shrug. "I didn't die."

Taking several deep breaths, he sat back and tried to stretch his legs out into a position that wasn't uncomfortable. The vest kept getting in the way, digging into the ground behind him and into his thighs.

"You can take that off, we should be quite safe," Dido said, nodding to the vest.

Looking down at the burnt village, he looked back at her. Forgetting himself, his look questioned why she still wore her armour if it was safe.

She caught the look and giggled. "I would take mine off, but I'm not wearing much under it and you didn't seem too comfortable last time."

Castor babbled for a second, his tongue as uncooperative as his legs. "No, no, if you prefer. Don't take any notice of me. I'm, eh, just a little unused to, well, you know?"

He blushed heavily, waiting for the inevitable questions, jokes or puzzled looks. While not an ugly young man, he was no oil painting either. Add to that his infirmity and he wasn't exactly a master of romance.

But she said nothing. She simply stood up, flicked her wrists together and the armour started to dismantle and retreat into bands on her wrists, around her neck and waist. Under the armour was a skin tight suit. Sitting again, she sighed contently and stroked the grass.

"It's been too long since I sat on real grass on a planet," she mused. "I could sit here forever."

"I'd rather leave as soon as possible," he replied, looking at a small stone he'd lifted. It was cold, smooth on one side, but rough and sharp on the other. He threw it; it sailed in a shallow arc down the hill, crashing into a larger rock before tumbling helplessly through the grass.

"Why?"

Looking at the ground, he sighed. "This used to be my home."

Dido nodded. "Ah," she said. "Now it makes sense. Were you drafted?"

"No, I volunteered to serve," he replied, looking at the horizon. "When the Restoration came to stop the plague, I saw you only wanted to help. I begged my father not to join the Resistance, but he was too wrapped up in the lies."

"Was this your village?"

"No, I'm from Blueberry," he replied. "But I knew people from here. I saw people I played with as a child being taken to the prison camp on my way here. If they recognised me, they didn't show any sign of it. I'm just another White Robe to them."

She placed her hand gently on his shoulder. "I'm so sorry. I wish it hadn't gone this way, but what they did…."

Castor nodded. He understood well enough that what was happening here had to happen. The Resistance had bombed several food stores and the dwellings of Restoration colonists. They'd killed non-combatants. They'd killed children, even babes in arms.

And for what? The right to butcher themselves with gene therapy, cybernetics and Replicants? No one could afford anything like that here, there wasn't even the facilities to perform such acts. All they had done was kill for their pride.

Most would be put in prison or to work for a time once they had been tried. After that they would be sent to other settlements in the Restoration.

"Do you have any family left here?" she asked, snapping him from his thoughts.

"Father died," he replied matter-of-factly. "Blew himself up trying to make a bomb. That's when I joined the Purifiers. My mother and sister were transported; I tried writing, but they only reply with the word 'traitor'. I don't know where my brother is; he'd already left to go to university when the Sagittarian Uprising started."

He glanced at her, the first time since he'd sat down. She was looking at him with a sad smile, clearly appraising him. Sat on the grass, without any armour on, she looked so vulnerable and harmless. It was easy to forget what she was.

Looking down again quickly as he remembered himself, cursing his foolishness for having looked upon her for as long as he had. Perhaps he'd join his father in a few heartbeats.

"My father died, too," she replied. "He was in command of the *Monitor of Purity* at Hafan."

The comm-unit on her collar chirped. "Dido, go ahead."

"Purifier-General, we've managed to corner a guerrilla unit south-west of Strawberry," the voice on the other end said. "They want to talk to the person in command to discuss a surrender."

"Understood, I'm on my way."

She stood up and deployed her armour again. Castor watched as she was once more coated with nano-fibres and armour. Even clad in the weaponised suit of nano-tech, she still looked too soft and gentle to be a Purifier-General.

An armoured hand was offered to him. Taking it, he pulled himself up, wincing as he moved. With effort, he managed not to grunt, gasp or growl through the pain. For a moment, he thought she was going to offer to carry him. Despite the pain, he was glad she didn't shame him by offering.

Together they started slowly down the hill towards the village.

Most of the buildings had been wood and stone constructions, quaint little blocks where a family had lived. Now they were ruins, skeletons lying in the dust, killed by their owners in an act of futile defiance. The few defenders that hadn't died in the suicidal act of denial had been shipped off for treatment.

Castor paused as he passed a house that had once had a rose garden in front of it, a vegetable patch to the side. He remembered a girl he'd gone with to dances a few times, before she'd dumped him when he'd expressed his desire to join the Purifiers. Nothing more than a teenage love affair of hand-holding, chaste kisses and awkward moments.

A small, cloth doll lay on the ground. It had to have been dropped by a small child, probably a little girl. Perhaps it was a daughter of the girl he'd known?

He picked it up and gently smoothed the stringy hair back from her face. Aside from a bit of dirt, the little doll looked intact, her dress scruffy by design. Becoming aware of the fact Dido was watching him, he slipped the doll into his robes.

Catching up to her, he looked at the question etched in her piqued eyebrow. "It would have been cruel to leave her," he replied as though it was the most natural thing in the world for a grown man to think a homemade doll needed saving.

"It would," she agreed.

Leaving behind nothing but charred buildings and dust, the pair headed south-west. Not far off stood a collection of sturdy buildings with tiny figures surrounding them. Despite struggling to keep a decent pace, Dido didn't leave Castor behind.

"General," a squat Major said as they arrived. He waved them in behind the mobile shield to give his report without fear of being shot at. "We have about a dozen armed men holed up in the building. They want to talk to you."

She nodded slowly, scanning the building and surrounding land. The marines had taken up sound positions to cover all of the exits while not exposing themselves to unnecessary danger.

"Armaments?"

"Older particle rifles, but they still pack a punch," the Major replied. "Possibly boobytraps inside; the place is a maze of rooms and corridors. Scans show they are clustered around a central room, which makes me suspicious."

"It's a central storage building," Castor said. He flushed slightly when the Major glared at him, but Dido was giving him a curiously encouraging look. "The surrounding villages bring produce and take what they require. Each has its own entrance and series of storerooms, with a central room used for county meetings."

Taking a small step back, Dido folded her arms. "Weaknesses?"

He shrugged. "It's a store. The walls are thin if they aren't loadbearing. Fire from personal weapons will just pass through the outer structure: some of the inner store walls are near bomb-proof."

"Hopefully this won't end in blood," she replied, looking at the store.

The Major snorted.

"You can't go in there," Castor said, much to his own surprise as everyone else's. "It's a last-ditch tactic; lure you in and commit suicide, taking you out in the process. Some may hide in the stronger parts in hopes of surviving and making a run for it in the chaos."

"Well," the Major announced as he slammed his hands together, "that sorts it. Orbital strike. Nice, neat and final."

Dido gave him a cold look and rolled her eyes slightly. "They're farmers," she said, wondering how the man had ever made it as far as he had. "Dropping bombs on them from a starship might not endear their surviving kith and kin to us."

The Major stood mildly aghast, quite clearly desperate to ask why that would matter. He did have just enough sense not to ask a Purifier-General to explain herself; that was a good way to get demoted or posted to a backwater colony on latrine duty.

Instead, he dipped his head slightly in submission. "Orders, Ma'am?"

Castor watched as Dido proceeded to issue a series of orders to have them men spread themselves out in a very particular way. He could understand covering the doors, but some of the other positions were beyond his limited tactical knowledge.

"Let me go in," he said, creating a wave of surprise. Mostly from himself. "Some of them might know me, or of me. I might be able to talk them down; appeal to their better natures as one of them."

He could see his argument wasn't gaining much traction; rolling eyes, questioningly raised eyebrows and scowls.

"You do realise they will probably just shoot you?" she asked.

"Better me than you."

"No," she replied, a little too forcefully. "That is not how this works."

"One missile…"

"Major, if you suggest orbital bombardment of a shed again, I will see to it that you spend the rest of your life polishing missiles."

Castor wasn't ready to let it go yet. Farmers they might be, but most of the farmers he knew had become quite skilled guerrillas and far more cunning than their demeanour and actions would suggest. That was what made them fatally dangerous.

"I'm going in to negotiate one of them coming out to discuss a ceasefire," he announced. "That is far better than anyone else going in."

Before he could be stopped, possessed by a great need to be useful, he strode as best he could towards the store. The door wasn't locked, grimly holding on with a single hinge, so that it nearly came off in his hand.

"Hello? I am Purifier-Adept Castor," he called into the dimly lit corridor beyond. "I have come to negotiate on behalf of Purifier-General Dido. I'd appreciate it if you didn't shoot."

Dido groaned slightly.

Moving slowly, looking out for all the normal traps, he moved deeper into the store, heading for the centre. There were a few unsophisticated traps; tripwires attached to farming implements for the most part. It worried him that they were so easy to spot.

"Stop right there, White Robe," a rough voice called from somewhere to his right. "Hands where I can see them."

"I don't know where you are, so I don't know if I'm going to put them in the right place," he replied sheepishly, immediately feeling a total fool. This had been a spectacularly, horrifyingly terrible idea.

Instead of being shot, there was a spate of hushed conversation around him. Several men, ranging from his own age to a man that was past his prime, shuffled into view. It wasn't all of them, he knew that much, but enough to make a show of something near trust.

"We said we'd only talk to the leader," the old man said, his rifle aimed casually at the floor.

"Surely you didn't expect someone who had made it to Purifier-General to simply waltz into your lair?" he asked, trying to keep his voice firm. Why hadn't he gone for a piss before undertaking this suicidal adventure?

The men looked at one another for a moment. "Fair point," the leader replied. "You seem familiar."

"I used to be called Faruk," Castor said, trying to appear relaxed. "My family are from Blueberry."

One of the men took a step closer. "You hung about with Lilly, back when you were a teenager, yeah? Yeah, I remember you."

"Tomo, it's nice to see you again."

"Shut your trap, White Robe," another said, lifting his rifle with the intention of using the butt. Tomo put his arm in the way and just shook his head.

"Remnant killed her; you know that?" Tomo asked. "Her man tried to keep what was theirs, she got in the way and died. You work for a bunch of killers, murderers, thieves. You aren't one of us."

Castor nodded a few times as memories of Lilly flooded. "And if they hadn't brought the medication, how many of you would still be alive?" He gave them a moment to digest it. "None, or at least not enough. And where was the Alliance? The Peacekeepers? Or the Hospital – surely it was exactly their sort of work?"

Several of the men moved uncomfortably, but not enough to have been swayed. The rest just looked annoyed, suggesting he'd pushed it too far. Luck was running out and he had no idea of how to drag himself out of the rather large hole he'd dug and was starting to furnish.

He watched, detached from the whole ugly affair, as the leader lifted his rifle. Tomo started to protest, but no one was even listening anymore.

"We said the leader, not a lacky."

With reflexes borne of self-preservation, Castor did what was probably the only action that could save his life. His knees buckled and he dropped like a sack of tatties, seconds before a bolt of exotic particles ripped through the space he'd occupied.

Dropping to the ground had a second lifesaving effect; the room was instantly filled with weapons fire from outside. Chaos erupted as the farmers tried to flee to protection while trying to fire back at enemies they couldn't see.

As Castor looked up, hoping to slither away, he found the lead farmer standing over him, ready for a second shot. There was no possibility of him missing, bar some sort of divine intervention.

Intervention arrived, although it wasn't divine.

The man was hit in the chest and collapsed. A pair of hands grabbed at Castor. Before he could register what was going on, he'd been flung over a pair of armoured shoulders and was being carried swiftly out of the line of fire.

Bolts of energy slammed into an invisible shield, flaring only millimetres from his face. Through the flashes, he could see the men he'd just tried to save being gunned down. Tomo had thrown his weapon down and was lying on the ground, hoping to wait it out. The wall behind him collapsed under the extreme fire, crushing him.

Out in the open and away from the firefight, which was rapidly winding down, Castor was unceremoniously dumped on the grass. He sat up and watched as the marines continued to fire indiscriminately at the store; slowly, a bit at a time, it folded in on itself.

Dido sat down next to him, her helmet retracting back into her collar. "Well, that could have gone better."

"I had to try," he replied weakly. "I probably couldn't have done any worse."

"But you tried to do the right thing," she said as the lighter walls of the store collapsed completely, leaving just the solid partial structure. "But next time, please don't walk into hell; I might not be about to drag your ass back out."

They sat in silence for a while as the marines picked through the rubble, looking for survivors, traps and anything worth taking.

"I think it's best I go back to the ship," he said. He'd felt his connection to his home slipping away for months, but now it was gone. The hope that coming back would reaffirm the connection had been obliterated; the place was agonising now. Everyone he'd known and cared about was gone – dead or transported.

Standing, Dido offered him a hand. "I think so. I'll walk you to the shuttle after I've spoken with the Major."

He nodded. It was pretty obvious he'd be reassigned after this epic mess. The fact people had just died hadn't even entered his head fully.

Of Freezers and Leaks

Hannah stepped into the stasis chamber room. The place was no less horrifying than it had been the first time. Rows of bodies watched her; their heads seemed to silently turn to watch her pass. Even though she knew it was her imagination, she couldn't shake the feeling.

"If you plan on asking 'how long', I don't know," Kelly shouted irritably from somewhere in the room. "I've administered the drugs and managed not to kill them. Just."

She found her standing beside the tube holding the muscular man, tapping away on a tablet as she compared readouts from the wall. For a moment, Kelly looked completely human, complete with interesting little ticks and quirks coming through as she worked, the glow of the console picking out the little changing creases and wrinkles of her expressions.

"The big guy is taking it far better than the girl did," she continued without looking up. "Her heart nearly gave out, but she's stable now. She might need further treatment later, but for now, she'll live."

With a light touch, Hannah placed her hand on Kelly's shoulder and smiled. "Have you slept? Eaten anything?"

"Yes."

A few empty wrappers were sitting on the floor, discarded carelessly. With the all clear on the disease front, they'd been able to ditch their suits, except for the gravity boots to counter the lack of artificial gravity.

"Candy bars don't count," she replied. "Not with the guts you've got."

Kelly took a sharp intake of breath and pursed her lips slightly. "Hannah, I'm busy."

Mouth open to make a retort, Hannah just stood for a moment. Clearing her throat, she took a step back. "As soon as you're done, Annie is going to give you a full check-up."

"I'm fine," she said, head dropping. "Look, I have two patients that are dying and I'm trying to save them with something with all the sophistication of a homicidal potato. It's like this sodding computer wants them to die."

Hannah just stood for a few seconds that seemed to stretch into forever. "Anything I can do to help?" she asked, weakly.

"Console over there," Kelly replied, pointing to one near the centre of the corridor through the tubes, "See if you can get the girl's tube to the defrosting room. There should be an automatic transport system."

Not waiting to be told twice, she went to the console. Most of it was made up of pictures with writing underneath. While many of the words were familiar, some of the phrases seemed cumbersome; it was like the whole thing had been written by Shakespeare.

The console showed two viable tubes; one was blue, the other green. Making the assumption that green was good, she tapped on it. More Shakespearean script that seemed to be asking if she wanted to start the thawing out process. She pressed "Yes" and hoped it was going to do the right thing.

Whirring and grinding filled the room. She jogged to the tube just in time to see it retract into the bank it was attached to. It moved down, leaving an opening where it had been.

Following a series of illuminated signs, she made her way to the deck below. The room they led her to was in darkness until she walked in. Sitting in the centre was the tube, horizontal on a platform.

"Dost thou wish to commence the process of awakening from cryogenically induced slumber on this vessel?" the computer asked.

"I doeth?" she replied, hoping it would have a clue what she meant.

A screen on the wall started to display screeds of text that shot past too quickly to read while there were an alarming number of beeps and chimes. The text vanished to be replaced with a countdown reading nine hours and forty-three minutes.

Above her, the ceiling opened as the second tube was lowered next to the first by an arm. Again, the computer asked, in its most formal tone, if she wanted to awaken the occupant.

Kelly strode in, tapping away on her tablet. She immediately went to one of the consoles and started to compare the readings. Hannah watched as she tapped away on both, lost in her work. Her face became an ever-changing mix of expressions, rolling from one to another with the odd snort, sigh or grunt.

A loud hiss made her jump as the first tube seal broke. The arm in the ceiling appeared again to lift the top half of the tube away, leaving the woman inside exposed to the air for the first time in around four hundred years, at least, from her point of view.

Taking a series of tools from a drawer, Kelly started to examine the young woman. Using a light, she tested pupil reactions; a small hammer tested reflexes, which drew a small frown from the synth; she probed around the site of the stomach tube. All the time, she took notes.

"Should we take her mask off?" Hannah asked.

"No, she'll suffocate if you do," she replied. "The tube is regulating her air supply; it'll tell us when her body will be able to breathe unassisted."

She moved onto the man as the arm lifted the cover from his tube. Repeating the process, she frowned less, but still chewed her lip ever so slightly.

Hannah had to marvel at the sheer size of the man. Anyone she'd ever met that looked like him either had a prosthetic body, cybernetics or had been genetically engineered to be that muscular. He'd have had to do it the old-fashioned way by actually working out. And working out a lot at that.

"Does his file say why he's so big?" she asked, curious as to why someone would go to all the effort of building so much muscle. Even in the 21st Century manual labour had been all but eliminated by machines.

Kelly blinked a few times. "Oh, he was the ship's fitness instructor," she replied. "He's clearly good at his job."

With a coy smile, Kelly shook her head. "I'm going to start taking their stomach tubes out. If you plan on staying, you'll need to get scrubs on and make yourself useful. But I'll warn you, it's probably going to be unpleasant."

"I've seen my share of war wounds," she replied, the slight smile on her face fading as those wounds came back to her. An urge to vomit climbed, but she swallowed and her stomach settled.

Kelly left the room to collect the tools she'd brought with her from *Sigyn*, fearing the only tools on the *Livingstone* were likely to be hacksaws and bale twine for sealing wounds.

Hannah followed some wall mounted pictures that seemed the right way to go to get scrubs. In a small room, she found cupboards of scrubs in sealed bags. Or at least, they had been sealed; most of the plastic had decayed or gone brittle, splitting and exposing the contents.

A set of scrubs from *Sigyn* were presented to her. She smiled and started to change, washed her hands and prepared for surgery. With the hairnet and facemask on, she looked almost like a real doctor.

In the next room, where the tubes had moved to for the surgery, Kelly had already started to prepare the woman.

"Do we know her name?" Hannah asked as she stood, feeling like a spare part.

"Dr Aisha Tehrani," she replied, checking the readouts on the tube again before slowly pressing a few buttons. "She's a British-Iranian biologist. Her job was to study the changes in the colonists as part of the long-term survivability studies being conducted and that of any life found on the target world. Twenty-nine years old, unmarried, identified as straight, two sisters and parents were on Earth when she left." She paused to look up at Hannah. "Can you bring four of those black caps over?"

The black caps were small and in sealed bags. Kelly had to have had them made on *Sigyn* and brought them with her.

Putting her tablet down, Kelly placed her thumb and forefinger on the bridge of her nose, through her mask, as though she was going to stop a sneeze. With a quick, sharp movement, there was a gentle crack, not unlike that of a broken nose being put back in place. She twitched her nose a few times.

"What the hell was that?" Hannah asked, stopping in her tracks.

"Oh, I just turned my sense of smell off," she replied as though she'd taken a piece of jewellery off. "Annie bought a module that she thought would be compatible and installed it. Turns out it was from a dog; took quite a bit of work to recalibrate it."

Shaking her head, Hannah frowned. "Wait, you can smell as well as a dog?"

"Oh, no. It would have to be calibrated again," she replied. "And after a few minutes of being able to smell like that, I'd never do it again," she added with a shudder.

She continued to prepare her patients, wiping them down to ensure there was less chance of infection. Laying out her tools, she double checked everything before preparing to make a start.

"So, who is he?" Hannah asked, still feeling like an extra.

Kelly looked up. "The beefcake? Carlisle Chesterton III, goes by Carl. Thirty-three-year-old American fitness instructor and physiotherapist. Unmarried, straight, three brothers, played for the Patriots for three seasons before an injury forced him to stop playing."

"Playing what?"

"No idea," she replied. "Right, I'm ready to start on Dr Tehrani. Can you hold this light, please?"

With a deft touch, Kelly started to make an incision into Aisha's abdomen. Hannah watched as she skilfully worked her way around the original surgery marks, keeping the damage to a minimum. While it would have been easier to remove the tube, the risk of stomach juices escaping or infection getting in were too great. So far, there was little to be squeamish about.

"Can you open two of the cap bags please?" she asked. "I'm going to disconnect the feeding tube, cap it, then remove it from her stomach and cap the other end. This might smell a bit."

Braced for, well, she wasn't quite sure, Hannah watched as Kelly unclipped the thin feed tube from the port. For a moment, there wasn't really any smell at all and she wondered what the fuss was all about.

Then it hit her.

Clamping a hand to her mouth, Hannah fought down the urge to vomit as the stench of partially digested nutrient paste and stomach juices clawed at her nose. She retched and realised she was not going to keep her stomach contents down.

Almost tripping herself, she turned and ran for the washroom, praying she'd make it to a sink before she lost control.

She made it to the sink.

She didn't get her mask off.

Kelly stood looking at her handiwork and smiled. Both ports had been removed successfully, but she'd not healed the scars. Those could be removed later, if the patients wished. Some people preferred to keep scars; others would want them gone.

After the quick surgery, she'd removed the various other tubes and wires. The only thing tethering Aisha and Carl to their tubes were the breathing masks, which were still in the process of weening them off artificial respiration.

She headed through to the washroom to find Hannah was sitting on the floor looking positively miserable. Had she turned her sense of smell back on, she'd have been greeted with the tang of vomit.

"You okay?" she asked softly.

Hannah managed to smile a bit. "I didn't get the mask off."

She'd changed out of her scrubs and washed up, but she looked ashen and kept looking down at her feet. After a moment she pushed herself up and half leant against the wall.

Taking off her kit, Kelly washed up, then went to check on her third patient.

"It's okay, most people don't cope well with the smell of bowels during surgery," she said, smiling at her downcast captain. Then she realised that it probably wasn't the smell. It was the memory of the last time Hannah would have smelt it.

Gently, she lifted her face. "I'm sorry," she said softly.

When Hannah put her hand on her hand, she assumed it was to take it off her face. Instead, she gave her a lopsided smile and slowly stroked it with her thumb. Something in her eyes seemed to sparkle a little bit.

Kelly felt something.

That wasn't right; emotions were meant to be flagged as there, but not felt. How could she be *feeling* something warm and heavy, yet light.

The computer beeped that the two tubes had returned to the main room and were awaiting attention. Hannah dropped her hand, coughed slightly and looked at her feet again. The two women took a step apart, unable to look at the other before going to check on their patients again.

"Will you be okay looking after this pair?" Hannah asked, still not quite managing to look at Kelly. "I'd best get back and make sure the place isn't on fire."

"Yeah, I'll be fine."

"As soon as you can move them, get them on *Sigyn*."

Hannah left and headed back towards the airlock. She needed a shower and a stiff drink after that little episode. And perhaps something to eat, since her lunch was now in a waste system.

"Jon," she said as she stepped through the airlock. "Jon? Jon? Are you listening?"

He appeared, looking mildly confused. "Captain, hi, you roared?"

She frowned and gave him a sidelong look. "I wouldn't say I roared. Are you okay? You don't normally take three tellings."

With what on a human would have been a put-on smile, he simply shrugged a little. "I guess I was a little distracted with all the new information. Do you have any idea how long it's been since I've had so much new information to look at?"

She didn't, and wasn't overly fussed about guessing.

"Did you know the Covfefe system is named after a Tweet by the 45th US President that people believe he was trying to spell 'kerfuffle'?" he asked, his eyes wide and little more glazed than normal. "Someone called it that because they didn't realise it was a typo by an incompetent fool and thought it was a word."

He suddenly froze, his eyes moving from side to side as they often did when he was assessing new data. "Oh. Oh no."

"Let me guess," she replied, no longer in the mood for jokes and factoids, "JFK was shot by the Queen of England armed with weaponised bagpipes because he was Hitler in disguise?"

With a puzzled look, Jon went to say something, but stopped. "No, I'm detecting a signal being sent from inside the ship." He swallowed nervously. "It's a Remnant signal. And England was ruled by the Scottish royal family at that point, so there was no Queen of England, strictly speaking."

Hannah's eyes widened to the point they were ready to roll out her head, ignoring his historical babble. "What? How long has that –? Never mind, block it." She started to march along the corridor. "Where did it come from?"

Jon swallowed nervously.

"Where?"

"Annie's cabin," he said quickly. "Dr Mendoza is with her."

She continued to march along the corridor, stopping only to grab a pistol from a weapons locker. Jon hurried along behind her, babbling apologies for not having detected the transmission, having no idea how long it had been broadcasting and that he deserved to be punished for being so careless.

Hannah didn't hear him.

She arrived at the door to Annie's cabin. "Open the door."

"You might want to call in first, I think they might be –"

"Open it."

The door slid open and Hannah moved in. She gripped the pistol in both hands, her sidearm training flooding back to her. Despite knowing almost exactly where they were, she swept around the living room before moving to the bedroom.

Annie and Casper were on the bed, stripped to their waists, clearly intent on going further until they had been interrupted.

"Hannah, what the hell?" Annie cried.

"Annie, get away from him."

"What is going on?"

"He's a Remnant spy."

Annie was up immediately, backing away from the bed, pulling her overalls back on and zipping them to the throat. She crossed her arms over her chest and moved behind Hannah. "Cas?" she asked, her voice shaking nearly as much as she was.

Casper held his hands up and rolled into a sitting position. "I'm going to reach into my jacket pocket, pull out my comm and throw it towards you. Please shoot it," he mouthed and mimed, hoping they'd understand.

Taking out the comm, he tossed it to the deck where Hannah shot it. The device fizzed and crackled before sitting gently smoking.

"It's true," he said softly, placing his hands on his head.

Annie flew from the room.

"I had no choice," he said, looking up at Hannah.

"Sure, you didn't."

"They have my family," he said, tears starting to form, a look of panicked mania growing. "I really am Dr Casper Mendoza, everything I said about my work is true. I'm from Plentiful Fields. The Remnant took it 'under their protection' years ago after a pandemic. The killed my stepdad, sent my mum and sister to a work camp and I've no idea what they did to my brother." He rocked back and forward on the bed a few times, looking at the floor before looking up again. "They abducted me and forced me to work for them. They said they'd kill my mum and sister."

Hannah didn't lower her aim. She'd heard sob stories before. Spies were often well trained to spin convincing lies. And then the pieces fell into place; she hadn't taken to him for a very good reason.

"You said you were on Morgannwg," she said slowly. "That you saw Abertawe burn and the *Monitor* fall from the last shuttle: that's not possible. The last shuttle had left the system half an hour before I sent the *Monitor* to its grave."

He nodded. "I know. I got it wrong, hoping you'd notice and ask me later. The two Purists on the *Norwegian* were watching me. That comm has been monitoring everything I've said. Every word, every sound," he added, coming to a devastating realisation; he'd had to carry that with him everywhere.

"Give me one good reason to not blow your brains out?"

"Annie deserves first refusal on that," he replied.

The pistol lowered. She could see what Annie might like about him; he seemed sweet, even if he was an enemy spy. All she cared about was that he seemed genuine.

"Get up," she said, waving towards the door. "Slowly. I'm going to lock you in your cabin."

Offering no resistance, he got up, pulling his shirt on. As he went to get his jacket, Hannah shook her head, so he left it. He moved slowly, edging round the room to get to the door without giving a reason to be shot.

He'd barely made it through the door when Annie struck. A straight right slammed into his jaw and poleaxed him.

Hannah grabbed Annie and pulled her away as she launched several vicious kicks into his chest and stomach. He'd made no effort to block or stop her, taking the beating in as dignified a manner as anyone possibly could.

"I'm going to kill him," she snarled as Hannah dumped her on the couch. Although she was a good deal shorter, she was naturally more solidly built, making her harder to manhandle than anticipated. Her pure fury didn't make things easier, either.

"Hey, calm down."

"Piss off," she shot back. "Why didn't you say anything, you bastard? How could I have let you into my bed?"

Casper got shakily to his feet. "What was I meant to say? 'Hey honey, was that good for you? By the way, I'm a spy'? I never meant to trick you. I..." He looked at the ground and took several deep breaths. "I really do like you. I really like you," he said as the tears started again and his lip quivered. It was both touching and pathetic.

"And I *was* falling for you."

That struck him far harder than the punch or kicks. He just started to crumple and shrink in on himself, crushed by the knowledge that he'd violated someone that loved him. With the simple omission of truth, he'd damned himself.

Jon, who up to this point had been standing like an unneeded mannequin at a fashion show, stepped forward. "I'll stay here if you want to take him."

Hannah gave Annie a hug before she strode over to Casper. She pushed him roughly through the door and into the corridor. He didn't resist as he walked in a dreamlike state back to his own cabin.

She shoved him in and locked the door, setting it to only open on her command. She'd question him later, but first she had to check on Annie. By the time she got back to her cabin, Annie was curled up on the couch looking into the middle distance and Jon was doing his best carboard cut-out impression.

And there was almost certainly a Remnant fleet preparing to get underway to come and take the *Livingstone* from them by force.

Confessions

Hannah sat opposite Casper, staring at him. Part of her, a quite considerable part, wanted to blow him out an airlock and leave the system as soon as possible. It had been effortless to get a story out of him.

He'd been working in Abertawe for the University of Essex, following up on stories of ancient caverns below the city containing pre-Collapse artefacts. The stories had been nothing but that, but he'd still been writing his report when the Remnant had attacked.

The shuttle he'd boarded had been damaged and picked up by a fleeing Remnant frigate. Fearing he'd be executed or sent to a labour camp, Casper had told them who he was, hoping to prove he was a citizen. He still felt the shame at his cowardice and panic, but there was little he could do about it now.

Unfortunately, the Purifier-Paladin assigned to watch over him, a surprisingly young woman for such a high rank, had asked too many questions and realised just how useful he might be. In less than an hour, armed with only the answers to some seemingly innocuous questions, she'd located his mother and sister, learnt of his research and exactly how to twist the knife to make him dance.

After that, he'd spent nearly two years being trained as a spy while continuing to work at the University, under the ever-watchful eye of the undercover Purifier-Seeker Alphonso.

She looked at him and let out a low sigh. "How long until the fleet gets here?"

"I don't know."

"How many ships? What classes?"

"I don't know."

"What battlegroup? Which fleet? Who is the commander?" she asked, leaning forward.

"I don't know."

"Well, what do you bloody well know?"

She threw herself to her feet and prowled around the room, desperate for an answer. Normally, she'd have simply called a few friends and let the Navy or the Peacekeepers look after the Remnant. Calling in from the Exclusion Zone? From Gallifrey? She'd probably be told she was getting what she deserved.

"Do you have any idea what is at stake here?" she asked when he didn't answer.

His eyes narrowed slightly. "Not at all," he replied with a taught, unpleasant smile. "It's not like I've had seven years of being reminded of what was going to happen to me."

There was no point shouting at him; he was a victim as much as anyone else. Hannah rubbed the bridge of her nose as she tried to think of anything he'd said that might be of any use at all.

"This Purifier-Seeker Alphonso, he's your handler?" she asked, sitting down again, trying to take a relaxed air.

Casper flexed his jaw a few times. No one had offered him ice for the punch.

"Generally, no, he has one of his minions make direct contact with instructions, but he is the one I report to." He sat back and crossed his arms for a moment, before leaning forward again, rubbing the back of his neck. "He knows I'm here, on this ship."

The room started to spin and fall away, sucked into an unwelcome blackhole. Hannah just sat, blinking slowly as her brain tried to calmly plot what to do, whilst also experiencing a catastrophic meltdown.

There was nowhere to run, nowhere to hide.

"He knows exactly what this ship is called, it's ID? The lot?"

He nodded, slowly at first, but quicker as the horror of what he'd done started to sink in. The Remnant might be reviled in many parts of the galaxy, but there were enough people willing to make a quick buck to deal with them. And more than a few undercover agents and spies that would easily find out where *Sigyn* was at any given moment.

"Do you have any idea what you've done?" she asked, gritting her teeth. She wasn't going to have a panic attack in front of, what was effectively, a prisoner. The urge to run was becoming overwhelming; she could just hold it off for now, but it would be a delaying tactic at most. She ran through all the possibilities of places to go, as if the handful of hellholes might give her some hope. Even the Guilds, The Alliance, Commonwealth and Peacekeepers might turn her over to avoid another war, or would take everything for their own ends.

"Yes," he whispered. "I never thought we'd find anything, or that it would be just debris." He took a deep breath and closed his eyes. "I'm sorry."

Hannah snapped her head up to glare at him. "Sorry?" she replied. "You're sorry? Oh, woopty-do, you're sorry for completely ruining my life and that of my crew." She snapped her fingers at him until he looked at her. "By saving your own ass, you have killed everyone on this ship. Probably on my sisters' ship as well. Do you know that's hundreds of people, by the way?"

"And what do you think will happen to me, hm?" he asked, a flicker of fire in his eyes.

She looked blankly at him for a moment before shrugging, pulling a slightly disgusted face at him. "What do I care? Promote you, hang you, use you for a good time; all the same thing to me."

Casper held her stare. "You don't mean that."

"I do."

"No," he replied, shaking his head without breaking the stare. "You're not like that."

She was on him, her pistol pressed roughly unto the underside of his jaw and her knee lodged firmly in his stomach. "Try me," she hissed, twisting the pistol to hurt him. "I'll blow your brain to kingdom come."

He shifted slightly under her; it was immediately apparent that he had the advantage of height, weight and she was off balance. If he'd wanted to, he could have rolled her; she very much doubted he had the strength to throw her from their current positions without losing his head.

"If you were going to, you would have already," he said as best he could with a pistol barrel trying to get into his mouth through his throat.

For a long time, Hannah just looked at him.

She got off him, flapped impotently and kicked a chair over as she let out the scream she'd been holding in. He was right. She'd fired a lot of shots from fighters that had happened to kill people, but she'd never looked a person in the face and ended their life. Warning shots were as close as she'd come to that on a few occasions.

"Hey, it's okay."

Reacting on instinct, she struck out at Casper as he approached her. A few movements and he was on his back, groaning, while she stood, completely unaware of what she'd done.

Taking a few stumbling steps, she left and locked him in again. By the door, she slumped to the floor and immediately burst into tears, the pistol discarded beside her.

Kelly sat in the small Engineering Lab, which was basically a glorified cupboard where Annie kept her prized possessions: her tools. The walls were lined with cupboards, toolboxes, lockers and trunks; all full of just about every type of tool known to man, including cooking utensils. There were signs promising pain for anyone that didn't return, lost or broke borrowed tools; some were quite graphic.

She'd gone to check if she was okay, having heard from Hannah what had happened. Approximately ten seconds after entering, Annie had had her seated and plugged in to the diagnostic equipment. Keeping busy was what was keeping her together. Kelly only wished it wasn't by working on her.

"So, you've been emotional," Annie said by way of both explanation for the check-up and for the sake of talking about something. "Have you been feeling anything?"

"Well, maybe," she replied. Her attention was focused more on the little tendrils that were creeping around the nape of her neck, penetrating the small port at the base of her skull that would allow them direct access to her neural net. She'd been designed to intentionally not be able to feel anything in that port, yet she was certain she could feel them wriggling in it.

Annie appeared in front of her, smiled and took her hands. "It's okay, try not to think about them."

Easy for her to say; she wasn't being violated on the most basic level. Then again, was that how she felt about Casper? He'd lied to her while they'd been sleeping together, so perhaps she understood the concept, if not the actual sensation of having your brain invaded.

She smiled back, hoping to put Annie at ease, more than through any feeling of comfort.

Too desperate for any distraction from her own problems, Annie didn't even notice the fake smile. She went back over to her console and pulled it over so Kelly could see, if she wanted to.

"Okay, let's have a look and see... Oh," she said, tapping away on the console. "Hm, okay. Tha sin inntinneach. Ehm?"

"What?" Kelly asked, unable to move her head too much with the metallic rope jammed into the back of it. "What? Annie, what is it? What's wrong?"

Annie crouched in front of her in an effort to be comforting again.

It didn't help.

"Kelly, you're evolving."

She blinked a few times. "Evolving? Into what?"

"Well, your neural net is evolving," she explained. "Pathways are forming that bypass the emotional shunt, allowing you to experience emotions and emotions from recent memories."

A few more blinks, this time a little faster. "Am I going rampant?" she asked, almost in a whisper.

"Opposite," Annie replied. "You're naturally moving towards full sentience. But, before you celebrate, there are potential complications to consider."

Kelly sat, barely listening to what she was being told. She'd heard talk of synths that had become sentient, even read a few books on the matter, but never imagined it would happen to her naturally. Millions of questions, hopes and fears flashed through her mind. The main one was: what now?

"I'm sorry, what did you say?" she asked, shaking her head the little bit that she could to clear it.

Annie smiled weakly. "You have to decide what you want to do. If you want to go down this route, there is a risk of emotional trauma later," she said. Looking at the floor for a moment, she paused. "At the moment, you will still be unable to process the emotions of old memories, but that may come in time."

Her eyes widened a little. "You mean, I'll," she swallowed and sniffed, "have to process ten years of being raped almost daily? Of being held captive? Treated like a toy, a thing?"

"Possibly," Annie replied, unable to meet her gaze. "But if you have me reverse this change; it won't happen again." She looked up and chewed her lip a little. "You'd only move towards sentience by having someone plug you in and activate the various parts of your net that are currently blocked."

Kelly sat at a complete loss about what to do next. Her entire existence had been devoid of meaningful choices; she had served, she had slaved and then she had been whatever she had been. All the key moments had been offered by others or thrust on her.

"Get that bloody thing out of me," she hissed through gritted teeth. "The connector, get it out," she repeated when Annie just stared at her. "Now."

As soon as the connection was severed, she sprang from the chair and rubbed at her neck to close the port as quickly as she could. The idea of not having to plug in again sounded preferable, but what might that actually mean for her?

"How is this happening?" she asked. Everything she'd read had never given any detail on why some synths became naturally sentient and others didn't.

Annie coughed lightly and looked at a thoroughly uninteresting cabinet with something almost like longing. Probably longing to climb into it.

"Well," she said, looking to another random cabinet, "well. Good question. Very good question, aye. Have you been, well, not to be prying mind you, interested in anyone, or anything if that's the case, more than usual?"

Kelly put a hand on her hip and sucked slightly on her teeth. "Is that relevant?"

"Och, aye, very," she replied quickly. "Desire for another seems to transcend the buffers, blocks and protocols that run at the most basic level of your net. A ghost in the machine, as it were."

Catching the tone, she got what Annie was angling at. Normally keeping a reaction hidden wasn't just easy, it was actually impossible to react. Now, she could feel her face scrunching up slightly and a subtle warmth spreading across it.

"Although, it can be triggered by a group of people accepting a partial-sentient synth as, basically, human."

"I'm going to need some time to think about this," she said.

Annie nodded. "Aye, I get that, but you don't have much," she replied. "The connections are spreading and solidifying quickly. If you want me to stop it, I need to know in the next few days." She shrugged ever so slightly. "You have, maybe, two weeks before it becomes a permanent change."

It wasn't enough time.

There was too much to consider, too many other choices that would have to hang off the back of it. Did she want to be fully sentient, or moving that way, and still looking like a dolly? Did she even want to become fully sentient? Was she feeling things, or were they just delusions, some corruption of her neural net?

And she'd have to talk to Hannah about it.

But Annie wasn't finished with the news. "There are other aspects to consider," she said softly, gently touching Kelly's arm. "If you let this happen, you won't be who you were before. You might hold onto, or rediscover, interests and aspects from your original personality, but ultimately, you'll be moulded by influences as you grow."

She nodded and gently patted Annie's hand. "I was a palliative care nurse, now I'm not. I'm not that girl anymore and even if I waited, I never will be again."

With a small smile, Annie nodded, looking slightly relieved to hear that. But she had one final hurdle to throw into the way.

"One last thing; if you go ahead with letting this happen, you need to be certain if you," she paused for a moment to look at nothing again, "get involved with anyone." Rubbing her arm slightly, she continued to look away. "If… if that person broke your heart before you have finished the process, the trauma could send you rampant. And I mean axe-wielding, shrieking like a banshee, 'kill all the humans' rampant."

For the first time in a long, long time, Kelly felt fear. It crept up on her, slithering through the firing artificial neurons on her net, jamming up processes and filling them with images that made her want to run as fast as she could.

"You need to consider if you care for that person or care about them," Annie continued. "The two are quite different."

Kelly frowned as she considered the idea. Could she tell the difference when she'd been originally designed to care for someone and still followed that general directive?

"Is the time before a broken heart worth the pain?" she asked.

Annie immediately pulled a face, shrugged and sniffed loudly. "Wouldn't know, don't have a heart to break. And if I did, there would be less risk of me skinning the person that broke my heart and wearing their skin as a cape."

"That's the biggest lie I've heard since you told Laura she looked good with her hair dyed platinum blonde."

The faintest of smiles appeared for a brief moment. "She was like mutton dressed as lamb."

Kelly gently touched her arm, mimicking Annie's gentle comfort. "You know you can talk about what happened to any one of the crew. If you wanted to talk to me as your doctor, I'd keep everything in confidence if you preferred. Or we can get plastered on cheap whisky and bitch about things."

She laughed, but it was a sad splutter. "I don't drink cheap whisky, cheeky besom." She wiped her nose of the sleeve of her overalls. "Aye, that might be nice."

The door opened and Hannah flew in. "Annie, I need us out of here," she said without preamble, warning or realising what was going on in the room around her. "There is almost certainly a fleet on the way."

"Hannah, are you okay?" Kelly asked as she gently put a hand on her shoulder, concern etched on her face.

Imagining that her face was probably red and puffy, Hannah moved her head in something between a nod and a shake. "No, not really," she replied. "Are you okay? You look a little, well, off?"

"Impending doom first?" Annie asked, hoping this would quickly distract from the emotional problems. "How long have we got?"

"No idea."

With an exasperated, but unsurprised, roll of her head, she sighed dramatically. "Well, I can probably lash the warp drives together in about half an hour."

"I need a little more speed than that."

Her eyes bulged in mock surprise. "Well, the Hop Drive will need completely recalibrated, but Jon can work on that. Slipstream? With the Bumbles' I can get emitters set up on the *Livingstone* and plumbed in to our system in, oh, say, ehm, maybe three days?"

"Three days?" Hannah replied, her face falling. "I need hours, not days."

"Hannah, you're asking me to install modern systems on an antique that might not even survive the shield deploying, let alone slipstream. I've no pattern to work from to place the emitters; I don't even know if I can do it. You're asking for a miracle."

"I thought Scottish engineers were miracle workers?"

Annie threw her arms up. "Aye, there's miracles and then there's miracles. Fixing a broken computer system with tape and paperclips is not the same as water into wine. You're asking me to rebuild the universe with a bucket, two spades, a bottle of juice and some inspirational montage music. Whilst blindfolded. And drunk."

Hannah placed both hands on Annie's shoulders and smiled; it was the sort of smile that usually came before a neck was bitten. "Annie, honey; there is a Remnant fleet on the way. If they get here and we aren't moving? We. Are. Dead."

She slapped her. Not hard, but with enough force to make a point. Kelly winced.

"Oh, I had no idea we'd die if we're found here, of all places, strapped to the most prized lump of steel in the galaxy," she replied. "Jon. Jon. Jon? Jon, you useless excuse for a lightbulb, where are you?"

Jon appeared and smiled. "You roared?"

"Start calculating the settings for the Hop Drive," Annie replied as she started to gather all sorts of tools that vanished into her overalls.

He shrugged a little. "The settings are fine."

"For us and the *Livingstone*," she shot back.

"You're kidding," he replied with a jovial laugh. "Oh, God, you're not. I'll get on with it then." He vanished.

"Do you need anything?" Hannah asked, moving quickly out of the way as Annie flew around the room, seemingly without touching the floor, grabbing bits as she went.

"Everyone out of my way for now," she snapped. "I'll scream if I want anything."

Taking that, wisely, as a cue to get lost, Hannah steered Kelly out of the room and into the main engine room. They passed through it quickly to the freedom of the corridors beyond, safe from hurled tools and Scottish insults. The insults usually hurt more.

"Are you okay?" Hannah asked.

"Yes, I'm fine," Kelly replied. She smiled and gently placed her hand on Hannah's elbow, running it down her forearm a little. "Really, I'm good. My check-up confirmed no signs of rampancy or damage."

She smiled a little more for a moment, but this time it didn't reach her eyes. "But there are some things I need to think about. Nothing bad, but I need a little time to consider them."

Hannah pulled her into a hug. "As long as you are okay."

They stood awkwardly as they broke the hug, unsure of what to do next. Both started to talk at the same time, apologised and immediately spoke over the other to tell them to go first.

"I'd best check on our patients," Kelly said, chewing her lip a little. "I'll keep them sedated until we're safe."

"Good idea," she replied. "I'd best get to the, eh, the… place?"

"The Bridge?"

"Yeah, that one."

She turned to go and ploughed immediately into the door frame leading into the engine room. Staggering only slightly, she tried to recover her dignity and made her way to the Bridge. With every step, the lightness that had bubbled up dissolved under the crushing horror of facing the Remnant again.

Race Against the Clock

For thirteen hours, Hannah had sat, fidgeting, drinking too much coffee and fretting about what was going to happen. Her head hurt, her eyes were dry and sore, but she was far too wired to even contemplate sleeping.

Emily had stopped asking if she was okay or suggesting she get some rest ten hours previously. She'd left, had some sleep and come back to find her captain sitting like a dishevelled gargoyle in the middle of the Bridge.

When Jon appeared and spoke, Hannah jumped slightly, nearly spilling the remains of her stone-cold mug of coffee.

"I've picked up a little bit of comms chatter," he said softly. "A Remnant Squadron has been spotted moving in this general direction."

"Which one?"

"Not sure, but a destroyer called *Glorious Purity of the Soul* was mentioned by name."

She rested her head against the back of the chair. "Gung-ho Green," she muttered.

"Captain?"

"Admiral Jameson 'Gung-ho' Green is a fighting Admiral," she replied. "Almost every Remnant Admiral, and most others for that matter, take a carrier of some sort as a flagship. Green took a destroyer and is well known for getting in about his enemies. That man loves a knife fight."

Jon nodded a few times. "Would I be hoping too much that his nickname suggests recklessness?"

"You would. It's only because he appears gung-ho compared to the others that sit at the back of a fight. ETA?"

He shrugged. "Unknown."

"Has Annie finished with the slipstream drive yet?"

"All of the emitters are installed," he replied, bringing up a small holo-version of the two ships, *Sigyn* looking like a little beetle on the back of a cow. "It's now a matter of linking everything together and balancing the power requirements."

She looked at the hologram, pretending to understand the complex engineering on display. All she wanted to know was when they could leave. Sadly, that was something that was not going to happen.

Jon frowned briefly. "I'm detecting slipstream wakes heading this way."

"ETA?"

"Unknown."

Clenching her fists and sucking on her cheeks, Hannah took a deep breath and tried to plan her next moves. Fleeing with no reliable FTL was pointless and hiding was impossible; the stealth system and cloak couldn't conceal both ships without extreme modifications. It was at times like this she wished she'd hire more than one engineer, but given Annie's wages, she doubted she could afford one that would be worth having. And they'd probably just fight with each other all the time.

"Can we use warp?" she asked.

Emily shook her head. "The system is lashed, but I'm still trying to get the *Livingstone* warmed up. Fuel is flowing, but I think it'll take about half an hour to get it going. Our drive isn't powerful enough to move us both."

No hiding and a big rock strapped to the bottom of the ship; great.

"Annie, not wishing to pressure you, but can you give me a realistic time for slipstream and Hop?" she asked, expecting nothing but abuse. Hop was preferable because there was no wake, no emissions and no way of tracking a ship unless it appeared within sensor range.

There were a few Gaelic noises, but contemplative rather than combative. "I can get you slipstream in about an hour and a half, but I can't work on the Hop drive at the same time."

"I might be able to help," Emily said.

"I'll take it," came the reply through the comms. "Hop is at least four hours of work and no guarantee."

With a nod, Hannah dismissed Emily to Engineering. She sat at the helm, called up her profile layout, flexed her fingers and tried to remember the feel of piloting *Sigyn*. When she'd first bought the ship, she had piloted it herself; *Sigyn* could, just, be run by a single person, but worked best with at least three and the AI.

Laura gave her a sidelong look. "Still remember how to fly this ship?"

She rolled her eyes, tapped in a few commands and smiled. "I still remember how to engage ramming speed." Helpfully, there was a button for that labelled very clearly on her profile.

Time slowed to a painful crawl. Every few minutes, Hannah checked the time on her console, hoping for anything to happen. At this point, she'd even take the Remnant arriving just to end the painful waiting.

An odd feeling started to creep into her. Something about it was strangely familiar, but it took her considerable thought to place. It was the anticipation of battle; the rising excitement of getting tore into the enemy, fear of defeat and quiet melancholy of better times and paths not taken that might have led to somewhere less potentially lethal.

Instead of triggering panic, which she'd quietly feared would happen for years, it focussed her mind. Yes, *Sigyn* had been in scuffles before and had to trade blows with other ships, but never Remnant. Trading shots with pirates and overeager patrol ships was not real combat; those enemies lacked the training, discipline and tactics to pose a true threat, often squandering ship size and power advantages with stupidity.

The Remnant were trained, disciplined and frequently clever. And their ships were armed to the teeth.

"Slipstream events on the edge of the system," Jon announced as he brought up a map on the viewscreen. One by one, five tags appeared.

"One *Revenant*-class heavy destroyer, *Glorious Purity of the Soul*; two *Colorado*-class interceptor destroyers, *Slough* and *Seeker of Truth*; two *Montol*-class destroyers, *Saint Piran* and *Beast of Bodmin Moor*."

"They do pick the most ridiculous names for their ships," Laura lamented. "I mean, who the hell calls a ship *Slough*?"

On the screen, the five ships appeared to be struggling to form up after returning to normal space. It was a tactic frequently employed by the Remnant to confuse people. Every wobble was choreographed to look like it was random and disorganised so that anyone watching would be lulled into complacency.

Like a group of confused ducks, the massive ships bumbled around, making a real show of their act. Several times the elegantly crafted ships, all sweeping lines and pure white, came close enough that there would surely be collision warnings blaring on their bridges.

Hannah wasn't fooled. No one could manage a staggering entry like that without meaning to.

"Incoming hail," Jon said, breaking the tension that had been building as the chaotic ballet finished. "They are requesting a holo-call."

Getting up from the helm, Hannah stepped to the side and nodded. The Bridge in front of her was replaced by an image of the *Purity*'s Bridge, seamlessly joining the two so that a person would think they could step from one ship to another.

The contrast was immediate: *Sigyn*'s Bridge was dull with low lighting, small and compact; *Purity*'s Bridge was large, spacious, bathed in good lighting and manned by at least a dozen crew at various stations.

While Hannah stood in her baggy cargo trousers, which were a touch the worse for wear, a shapeless t-shirt and jacket covered in pockets, Green stood in a neat, crisp navy suit. He wore no medals or other decorations, just his rank and the relevant trappings of his position. Beside him stood a woman with a strikingly beautiful face, her hair cut in an odd fashion; cropped short on the right, but lengthening all the way around until the point on the left nearly touched her shoulder.

The woman, a Commander from the rank, suggesting she might be the XO, was clearly not. Her stance, the way she tugged at the uniform as though it didn't fit and chafed was unnatural for an officer. She had to be a Purifier, playing at Navy to blend in.

"Hello, I'm Captain Hannah Sinclair of the independent trade ship *Sigyn*. How may I be of assistance?"

"Admiral Jameson Green, Commander of the *Glorious Purity of the Soul*," the grizzled man replied with a polite, almost warm, smile. "And I'm actually here to see if you require assistance. This system is normally off limits."

Hannah nodded vigorously. "Of course, yes, but I have a permit granting special dispensation to recover an automated ship that strayed here. I'll send it right over."

The permit was, naturally, fake. Had any major power, other than the Remnant, set eyes on it, it would have held up for a few seconds until someone checked a database. The down side was the Remnant were unlikely to give a toss if she had a permit, let alone care if it was real.

Green frowned lightly and tilted his head slightly. "An automated ship?"

"Yes, very embarrassing, actually," she continued, rolling her eyes. "A film company were making a 21st Century flick using a model ship that they managed to lose. Eighteen months later, it starts broadcasting from here."

From the knowing smile, the few short nods, Hannah knew she was only buying minutes. It was a weak ploy, but it was better than nothing. Or the truth.

"Well, that's the most unusual reason to be here I can think of," he replied, "but I guess it's better than attracting passersby in. My squadron will move in to provide you with an escort."

"No," she replied, a little too quickly. "There are, ehm, well, stories about this system. I'm not sure having so many ships in orbit would be a good idea."

Green looked around and spoke to someone near the back of the Bridge, the audio cut so she couldn't hear what was being said. The XO continued to look uncomfortable, but seemed even more out of place as the discussions went on around the Bridge, of which she appeared to be playing no part.

"We are aware of the stories," he replied. "I'll send you coordinates of a point in the asteroid belt that should be safe. How soon can you be there?"

"Two hours."

With a quick look over his shoulder, Green accepted the timeframe. "Please, call if you require any assistance. Green out."

The hologram dissolved, leaving the Bridge dim again. Hannah moved immediately to the helm and started the slow, difficult process of trying to turn *Sigyn* with such a massive load. Every command was sluggish and needed far more power than normal; it was graceless, especially considering how long it had been since she'd flown anything. As much as she wanted to run, she had to make it look like they were complying.

"Captain, the destroyers are continuing to fan out," Jon said. "It's subtle, but I'm sure they mean to surround us before we get to the destination."

"How long?"

"One hour forty."

That left, in theory, ten minutes. The longer the warp drive took to power up, the longer they might get, but it wouldn't be long before Green came calling again.

A blip appeared on her console.

"Shutdown all active sensors, keep the weapons cold and shields up for navigation only," she said, trying to keep her voice even.

Laura tapped away on her console as the colour drained from her face. Seven blips had appeared from the planet; five moved at high speed towards the incoming destroyers, two moved slowly to take up positions on either side of *Sigyn*.

The two drones kept their distance, but they were keeping pace with *Sigyn* and following every course correction. Beyond that, nothing. No communications, no spikes in power, no attempts to throw the interlopers across the galaxy while reducing them, intentionally or not, to soup.

Hannah's main hope was that the drones would be pleased when they left. Her second hope was that the Remnant continued to just sit where they were, their own shadows perched on their shoulders.

"How long until we have slipstream?" she asked, tapping away on the console to make a minor course correction.

"Annie's running the last few safety checks before she engages the drive," Jon replied.

"We've got about ten minutes," she replied, "tell her to use as much of it as she needs; I don't want to be splattered."

She was aware, rather acutely, of the pointed look Laura was giving her, which Jon was no doubt mirroring. There were times when playing fast and loose was an acceptable risk. Right now, she'd prefer having to talk to Green to stall him than try to go to FTL too soon.

A destination had already been selected. It was an unremarkable system with plenty of places for a ship to hide. Several gas giants with thick atmospheres; asteroids with caverns and passage ways hundreds of metres, even kilometres, wide; and the star emitted high-powered flares from time to time, that if they were lucky, would blind anyone looking for them.

This was not where Hannah planned to go.

As soon as the Hop Drive was online, she was heading in a completely different direction. Untraceable and out of reach, she could safely dump the *Livingstone* somewhere secure and plan her next moves with the crew in peace.

"Green is hailing," Jon announced. "Audio only."

Hannah nodded.

"Captain, this is Admiral Green," the disembodied voice said. "We're detecting energy spikes in your slipstream drive."

Cursing under her breath, she came up with the best lie she could manage. "Yes, my engineer is checking the system in preparation for departure. I'm assuming you want to be here as little as I do?"

"Of course, but first we need to inspect your ship, your cargo and verify a few things," he replied. "All standard procedure, you understand."

Jon flashed up a map, showing that the destroyers were starting to circle again, their drones following them, but doing nothing to help or hinder. Why couldn't they just make the squadron vanish?

"Admiral, I understand completely, but given where we are, might it be better if your ships didn't move in what, may, be interpreted as a potentially threatening manner?" she said, trying to manoeuvre out of the wolf pack.

For longer than expected, silence.

"Captain, come to a complete stop and prepare to be boarded."

On the helm console, a little green light blinked on. It was perhaps the most important, most beloved and most silently worshiped light in the universe. Hannah immediately turned to point at Jon, cocking her fingers like a gun.

Jon nodded.

"Got to catch me first," she said.

In a wash of exotic particles, *Sigyn* made the jump to slip-space, dragging *Livingstone* along for the ride.

Everything shook, forcing the crew to grab whatever was in front of them for support. Slipstream was usually a pleasant, quiet affair. This ride was anything but and soon the Bridge was filled with alarms.

"Jon?"

"Sorry, it's taking time to get used to the additional mass and changes in mass distribution," he said, eyes closed as he focused on tweaking the shields to prevent the ship being shredded by tidal forces. "Until we jumped, it was impossible to fine tune the system."

The alarms stopped one by one as the shaking slowly calmed down until there was barely even a vibration through the deck.

As Hannah looked over her console, the triumphant smile faded into a light scowl.

Sigyn was a long-range variant of the *Van Rensselaer*-class, fitted with two oversized slipstream generators and a decent back-up. Normally, only one generator was needed at a time, running for about three hours before the build-up of heat from decaying exotic particle by-products would force it to shut down or burn out. The second would switch in while the first cooled, dumping the excess heat into the little bubble of normal space that surrounded the ship, from where it returned to normal space as it passed through the slip-shield. Cooldown took about two hours in slip-space, meaning *Sigyn* could travel as far as required without stopping or until out of fuel. In normal space, the generators cooled far quicker.

On the helm console, both generators were showing as active and heat was building up at an alarming rate.

"Jon, how long do we have until the generators overheat?"

Laura's head snapped towards her, eyes bulging.

"Fifty-four minutes," he replied. "The red line has been set to 93% as normal to ensure an orderly return to normal space."

"How long to cool down? Roughly."

He grimaced and shrugged slightly. "Fifteen to twenty minutes to stone cold."

It wasn't going to be enough to escape. Fifty-four minutes should equate to just over five hundred lightyears. A far cry from the two-and-a-half thousand she'd planned to travel before being able to use the Hop Drive.

Plotting a new route was the only option. By aiming for star systems rather than open space they could make use of planets and asteroids to hide or at least prevent a straight line shot at them. Aiming for systems was also considerably easier for navigation.

"How far behind us are they?"

Jon winced a little. "Holding about six minutes behind us," he replied. "Those ships can easily out pace us; they're making sure they can follow us back to normal space as soon as we drop."

Hannah started to plot new possible routes, while looking for the best way to keep ahead of the game. Most of her hope rested on the idea that the Remnant wouldn't fire on them out of fear of hitting and destroying the *Livingstone*.

Fortune was, for once, smiling on her. There were a number of systems that would be worth dropping into at slightly decreasing intervals. If they tried to overshoot a little at first, it might look like they were struggling to keep the drive cool.

"Very clever," Jon said with a smile and a small nod. "I'll make the necessary calculations and pass it on to Annie. Hopefully she can plan the more intricate parts of the Hop Drive changes during the down time."

"How long?"

"Three minutes."

Three minutes too long.

Without the stealth system or cloaking device, the only way *Sigyn* could hide was to go dark and sit behind something massive, like a planet or star.

As the *Purity*, *Saint Piran* and *Beast of Bodmin Moor* circled the system, *Sigyn* was hiding over the north pole of a super gas giant, venting heat into its thick, swirling atmosphere. The three destroyers were working their way systematically through the other planets; time was running out rapidly.

This was the third jump and the first that had posed a problem. Green had been able to anticipate their destination and arrived far sooner than previously. The only saving grace had been he'd miscalculated where they would arrive and appeared on the far side of the system.

Laura rolled her shoulders and twisted her head to the right. An alarming crack emanated from her back; she sighed and relaxed back into her chair.

"Not at all horrifying," Jon muttered.

"What?" she replied. "It's not like you've got bones or muscles."

Hannah rubbed her left eye, feeling a bit of grit in the corner. Three hours of running and not being able to do a thing about it was growing tiresome, to say the least.

"They've found us," Jon said. "Seventy seconds to intercept, ninety-three until cooling is complete."

"Get us back online. Shields?"

"Dorsal cover only," Laura replied. "The cargo is covering most of our exposed sections, but a skilled shot could get in. Anti-missile systems are similarly hindered."

There was nothing left to do as far as Hannah could see. They'd never outrun them; fighting would be painfully short; negotiation was irrelevant after having already run. Her options had been whittled away.

It was a bad idea.

Suicidal.

"Thirty seconds," Jon said. He'd taken the role of "Speaking Clock of Doom" through to an artform.

Bringing *Sigyn* round to face the much larger *Purity* wasn't easy, but with plenty of time to spare, Hannah started to charge the warp drive.

Laura looked at her, eyes wide a she saw the power distribution changing. "You're not…."

"Prepare for ramming speed," she replied with a crazed grin, borne as much from sleep deprivation as it was from excitement and impending doom.

Playing chicken with starships was a terrible idea for a great many reasons: ships were very expensive; they were quite fragile to impacts; rapid movement in tight formations could be lethal; most FTL drives disrupted local space-time as they powered up and warp did it as long as it was active.

Green, being an experienced commander and generally sensible, blinked as soon as he realised what was going on; discretion was the better part of valour. The *Purity* spun to port as fast as she could, but not quite fast enough. Sparks and shards of hull erupted along the starboard ventral side as space-time contracted and expanded at differing rates.

"Well, we didn't die," Jon said with a slightly glazed look. "That's something, but if I had real trousers, I'd need to change them."

"How much damage did we do?"

Laura snorted. "Did you do, you mean. All of that is on you."

"Superficial," he replied as the slipstream drive activated, pulling them to safety. "No damage to us and their damage will only make them angry."

A narrow escape and one that couldn't be repeated. If Green had expected it, he'd have gone to warp as well. The outcome of duelling warp drives would have had only one winner, and that was not going to be the 21st Century antique that had won round one.

They were going to have to get crafty in order to survive. Hannah's biggest fear now was that Green had been able to position the rest of his fleet in the surrounding systems to make escape impossible. He might have only arrived with his personal wolf pack, but she doubted the rest of the ships were far away.

A Grave to Hide In

Sigyn and *Livingstone* dropped back into normal space and immediately into trouble.

Four gunboats and a cruiser had been lying in wait, spread out across the system to create a net. A single gunboat was of little threat, even the four of them would be manageable, if only just. A cruiser would obliterate them. With the gunboats to corral them, *Sigyn* would have little chance of escape.

The only bit of luck was that the cruiser was twenty-one minutes out.

"Well, this is annoying," Laura announced as she flopped back in her chair. "Are we ever going to escape this lot?"

Hannah smiled and winked. "One last jump and we should, hopefully, have the Hop Drive. All we have to do is hold off the gunboats and avoid the cruiser. Jon?"

He cocked his head to one side. "The gunboats are *Goosander*-class; they'll annoy us, but we should be okay. That cruiser is the *Spectre of Eternity*, an *Eternal Heritage*-class. She won't even need her main guns to turn us to slag."

Rubbing the bridge of her nose, Hannah looked at the deckhead and growled a sigh. She'd met the *Spectre* before, but the last time it had been limping away from battle.

"Bridge, there's a bit of a problem," Annie's voice announced from seemingly nowhere. "In order to get the Hop Drive running, I'll need to take all FTL offline for about thirty minutes to do a reset."

"Yeah, next jump might be better," Hannah replied. "How long can we run slipstream for next jump? Absolute limit?"

There was a bit of muttering. "Jon, I've removed the red line. Think you can handle re-entry from the black line?"

Jon's eyes widened a little as he played with the collar of his tunic. "Yeah, sure, not a problem at all."

"I'm filled with confidence," Laura said under her breath.

One of the gunboats had managed to make its way to *Sigyn*, but had yet to open fire. It flitted back and forward; the captain clearly unsure if it was wise to take on the larger vessel without immediate support.

It made one aborted attack run, peeling off to fall back again, having either lost its nerve or perhaps as part of some obscure strategy. The others were closing, but appeared to be in no great hurry to arrive.

Hannah was in no hurry to give them a reason to move quicker. Moving in a vaguely and clumsy defensive pattern, she snaked her way away from the oncoming ships. All that was needed was some time and luck that the *Spectre* didn't arrive sooner than planned.

For the majority of the time needed to cooldown, everything was going well.

"Slipstream wake detected," Jon said. "Three vessels, I suspect."

On the viewscreen appeared another cruiser and two destroyers. While still out of range, they were much closer. Immediately, they changed course and started to bare down on *Sigyn*, looking to make the kill.

Giving up the pretence of being sluggish and wounded, Hannah's fingers flew across the console, firing thrusters and making plans for intricate manoeuvres. And promptly found out that *Sigyn* was sluggish, if not wounded. Nothing responded nearly fast enough as the massively increased inertia of dragging the *Livingstone* around killed the modest manoeuvrability.

"Jon?"

"Just a minute."

"We don't have a minute."

With a pout, he shrugged. "We'll be fine."

She didn't share his confidence. If they couldn't escape the ever-tightening net, there would be no need to worry about cooldown times.

Two of the gunboats rushed them, firing warning shots. Low powered particle beams lanced the space around *Sigyn* in an effort to herd the wallowing ship towards the newly arrived cruiser.

"Laura, use any countermeasure you have to keep them off our backs," Hannah said as she tried to dodge the fire. Normally, she hated showing her hand and all of the modifications she and Annie had installed. Now was not the time to keep one's light under a bushel.

"Aye, Captain."

The effect was immediate and what she'd feared. All of the Remnant ships accelerated, pushing their engines into overdrive to intercept them. The original cruiser was wasting its time by doing that: the high-powered burn could only be sustained for a short time; too short to reach *Sigyn* before the other ships would have crippled it anyway.

Hannah would have been doing the same thing if she was using *Sigyn*'s engines as the primary drive. With the mass of *Livingstone* in tow, going to a high-powered burn would only wear the system faster for almost no benefit.

"Slipstream in three… two…"

The ship lurched as a missile slammed into the shields, the blast being mostly deflected back into space.

"One," Jon said with a smirk.

Hannah put her head on her console. The warmth was soothing on the tension headache that was starting to grip her, along with the fact she'd not slept since… well, she wasn't actually sure when she'd last slept.

She flinched when a hand touched her shoulder.

"You okay there?" Laura asked softly.

"Just a bit worn out."

"Take a power nap," she replied. "You're no use to us half dead and trying to out manoeuvre Remnant warships."

Pushing herself up, it sounded like a reasonable idea. There was a foldout bed in her Ready Room, a tiny office off the Bridge for private discussion, calls and general hiding. Given how small the ship was, Hannah generally used her cabin as an office.

Pushing herself up, swaying ever so slightly, she staggered for the door. "Jon, where are we going and how long? Are we being followed?"

Closing his eyes for a moment, Jon consulted his sensors. "No sign of pursuit. I imagine they're struggling to get an order of transit together."

"I'm aiming for the Pergamon system," he continued, pulling up a hologram. "There's a Hot Jupiter that is extremely noisy we can hide by until Annie is finished. It's also patrolled regularly by Peacekeepers, so should give Green pause before entering."

"Wake me in about forty minutes," she replied.

The Ready Room beckoned as Hannah's eyelids started to droop and blur her vision. After a moment of scrambling with the wall hatch, the bed flopped down and she simply collapsed on to it in a dreamless sleep.

And then Jon was nagging at her.

Eyes flickering open, Hannah peered at the AI as he stood, smiling weakly. "Ugh, has it been forty minutes?"

"Yes, Captain. If you sleep longer, you'll feel worse unless you get a full rest," he replied, taking a step back. "I took the liberty of brewing you some coffee, extra strong. There's a few mints as well."

Rolling into a sitting position, she rubbed the sticky trail of drying dribble from the side of her mouth. She then wiped her hand on the bed as Jon grimaced.

Getting to her feet unsteadily, she placed a hand over her mouth, blew a puff of breath and sniffed. The mints were needed; she'd stun a horse at thirty feet.

Armed with the coffee and chewing all three mints, Hannah made her way, blinking, onto the Bridge. While still a bit tired, she was certainly feeling better than before. Setting the coffee mug into the holder on the side of the console, she consulted her implant. With a few taps, she engaged endurance mode, a standard mod from her pilot days.

Laura gave her a sidelong look with a piqued eyebrow, but said nothing.

"How are we looking?"

"Like we just crawled in after a wild night?" Laura replied with an amused snort.

"Get lost," she replied. "Jon? Jon?"

He blew out the fake breath he'd been holding. "I'm not sure we can make it," he said at last.

"What?"

Holding his hands up, he took a step back. "With our current speed, we'll overheat about three minutes too soon. If I alter the shields to push us along, they might fail."

Slipstream shields were an oddity. When in slip-space, they acted as both hull and sail for the ship. By keeping the shields "smooth", they were subjected to less stress, so the emitters didn't have to work so hard. By making the shields "billow", they caught the flow of slip-space, pushing the ship along faster, but the force increased considerably on the shields and emitters. It was this fact that made large ships faster and safer; even with smooth shields, they were so massive they caught the flow better.

"We have to get there," Hannah replied, wondering why the universe hated her so much.

Almost immediately, vibrations started to tremble through the deck. Ripples began to disturb the surface of the coffee, gently at first but growing into tiny tidal waves as the mug began to rattle.

A small warning started to ping on the helm console. Nothing serious, but it would only be the first if Jon carried on the way he was.

"All hands, brace for a rough ride," Hannah said, opening ship wide comms. She should have done that before telling Jon to go nuts, but the sheer power of the vibrations were way beyond what she'd anticipated.

The shuddering and pitching continued to get worse. Alarms were starting to appear all over the console, warning of imminent shield failures, emitter feedback exceeding recommended levels and the generators were going beyond the red line and heading straight for the black line. Beyond red, the generators would start to take damage. At black, the risk of catastrophic failure increased exponentially. *Sigyn*'s generators had a theoretical life of two-point-eight seconds beyond the black line.

"Jon, back it off."

"I can do it."

Hannah turned in her seat, wide-eyed. She realised this was a mistake as she thudded against the helm, the hard edge digging into her side.

Something was very wrong. Jon looked different, somehow. While not exactly a scruffy man, there was a neatness to the scrub of a beard he wore, his clothes looked a little sharper. His eyes were wide, staring as they moved rapidly back and forth, up and down to the point they appeared to be shaking in their sockets.

"Jon, you are going to kill us!"

He turned his head to look at her. A vacant smile started to pull onto his face as his eyes went completely white.

And just as suddenly, he looked normal again, if very confused.

Hannah and Laura were thrown against their consoles as the ship crashed out of slip-space and came to a complete stop a few thousand kilometres above Pergamon II, the Hot Jupiter sanctuary.

"My nose," Laura gurgled.

Blood was pouring from her quite clearly broken nose and had left a bright, sticky splodge on her console.

"Medical team to the Bridge," Hannah said as she got up. "Pinch your nose, just below the bone and lean forward. Breathe through your mouth slowly and don't talk or sniff." Having broken her nose several times, not that you could tell thanks to modern medicine, she was a pro at bleeding noses.

"Engine Room, Bridge; status report."

After the usual explosion of Gaelic, Annie made several exasperated noises, punctuated by the sounds of something delicate being battered by something heavy and metallic in exactly the way it shouldn't be.

"Gubbed," she replied after a few solid whacks. "All three gennies have scrammed, two adjacent emitters on the *Livingstone* have failed and at least three more are flashing amber. Half the cooling circuits have fused open from the scram shunt."

Hannah rubbed her forehead.

"I can't repair it," Annie continued. "I've no got the parts and I'd need to take the whole power grid down. I'm not even sure the gennies can be salvaged."

That meant they'd made their last slipstream jump for some time. It would cost a small fortune if the entire system had to be replaced. And it would certainly draw attention at any port they put into looking for one.

"Hop?"

"At least an hour," she replied. "It's intact, but some of the shared cooling systems need reset."

The medical team, consisting of Kelly and a triage kit, arrived on the Bridge. She immediately knelt in front of Laura, who was still blinking away tears and holding her nose as if letting go would cause it to drop off.

"You've banged that up good," she said softly. "Don't worry, you'll never know it was broken by the time I'm finished. Let's have a look."

Hannah watched as Kelly moved Laura's hands and started to gently probe the broken, bruised and puffy nose. She knew what was coming next and turned away just as the piercing scream erupted.

It had been more out of surprise at the sickening crack than pain that had Laura screaming as her nose straightened.

"Close your eyes and lean into this," Kelly said, presenting a mask to her. It would work to repair the damage, take down the swelling and heal the bruising in a few minutes. "Hold it in place until it starts to beep."

Leaving her in the capable care of the mask, she went to Hannah. "You look like crap; when did you last sleep?"

"About twenty minutes ago," she replied haughtily.

"And before that?"

The silence was all the answer Hannah could give without lying out right. "I'm fine."

"Your heartrate is up; breathing is all over the place and your right eye is twitching."

As she put her hand over her eye, she knew she'd been tricked.

"How much blood is in your coffee stream?" Kelly asked, frowning.

"I've had an acceptable amount of coffee for a woman of my age, size and disposition," she replied, which was true, if only just. At least, to avoid a lethal caffeine dose.

Kelly grabbed her arm and accessed her implant. "I told you not to use that, especially if you're drinking coffee," she snapped, shaking Hannah's arm slightly. "If you are going to insist an using that thing, I will remove it from your body and stand on it."

"It's my body and I'm not going to use the endurance module enough to get addicted or do any damage."

"I'm your doctor," she replied. "Your ass is mine when it comes to health matters. Without proper oversight, that thing is a bloody timebomb. Why the Navy didn't remove it is beyond me."

Snatching her arm back, Hannah turned the endurance mode off. "What's up with you? When did you last sleep?"

"Oh, get a room," Laura said, her voice muffled by the mask.

"Quiet, unless you want your nose spread across your face," Kelly replied lightly. "And as for you," she continued, rounding on Hannah again. "Bed."

Hannah brushed past her to return to the helm. "Until we are safe, I have a duty to keep this ship and everyone on it safe."

Kelly balled her fist and released it a few times. "Fine, but as soon as you're done trying to kill yourself, come see me for a check-up. That's a medical order; make sure she follows it, Jon."

Jon, who had been cowering by the centre seat since they'd dropped out of slipstream, nodded slowly at first before nodding so fast his head was in danger of flying off.

It was a stupid plan.

In fact, it was probably worse than trying to outrun a Remnant fleet.

It was, however, the only place Hannah could think of that they wouldn't be found.

Hafan.

After the Battle of Hafan, the system had been abandoned. Most of the mines had become unprofitable decades earlier, and after Abertawe was levelled and the shipyards devastated, the Commonwealth had simply moved out.

Hulks still littered the system, left to drift as a giant graveyard. Scavengers and Navy recovery teams had long since stripped them of the really valuable parts and of weapons. Several of *Sigyn*'s upgrades had come from there.

This was the first time Hannah had been back since the battle.

"We're not staying here, are we?" Jon asked.

"Yes," she replied. "And after your little slipstream episode, I suggest you don't annoy me or I'll have your voice changed to that of a teenage girl on helium."

Jon nodded and vanished.

Sigyn headed for the remains of a Commonwealth carrier *Killing Me Softly*. One side of the ship had been almost completely ripped open. There was a gash where a predator had sliced through to the soft internals of the fighter bays.

With care, Hannah moved them inside the corpse, entering through the wound and using the grotesquely expanded passageways to slip deep inside. A few times, wreckage had to be cleared to open the space up.

The centre of the ship was hollow; it had once been a fighter storage and maintenance bay, feeding fighters to the smaller bays at the start of a battle and giving them safe harbour after. Even small capital ships could have slipped in via the ventral bay, had the doors been open.

Once in, it would be impossible to spot the two ships as long as they kept their power down low. Not that anyone would be likely to pass by and even if they did, there was no reason to scan a decaying hulk.

For four years *Softly* had given her a place to live and now its corpse was giving her a place to hide. They hadn't detected a single ship following them over the five Hops it had taken to get to Hafan and none had ever arrived at Pergamon.

"All hands, we've arrived. Switch over to unsupported drydock protocols and get some rest."

"Ehm, Captain, remember that –"

"Yes, Jon, I know, I know," she replied irritably. Her head was thumping from lack of sleep and what was likely poisoning of some variety from the caffeine, endurance or possibly the extended Hops. They'd lost almost a minute on each jump.

Stumbling towards the door, she made her way to the Sickbay. Part of her hoped Kelly would have already gone to bed so she didn't have to endure another lecture on healthy living. And yet, she wanted to see that she was okay.

Kelly was sitting on a bed when she stumbled in.

"I'm sorry."

Hannah opened her mouth, considered what she'd just heard and tried again. "Sorry for what?"

"For arguing with you on the Bridge," she said, sheepishly. "I was worried."

"I'm sorry, too. I think we should both go to bed."

She slid off the bed and hurried over. Out of the door, they both turned in opposite directions.

"Where are you going?" Kelly asked.

"To your cabin to make sure you go to bed," she replied. "My duty as the Captain."

"Well, as Chief Medical Officer, it's my duty to see you to bed," she replied with a chuckle. "Anyway, you can barely stand."

Having none of it, Hannah simply marched off towards Kelly's cabin, expecting her to follow. "You're the only Medical Officer," she called over her shoulder.

She shrugged. "Yeah, therefore, Chief Medical Officer." She followed without further comment.

Fallout

Hannah groaned slightly as she woke, unsure of where she was or how long she'd been asleep. She didn't remember getting back to her cabin or getting into bed. In fact, she must have been so tired she'd forgotten to take her legs off. That was bad; even when she was, on occasion, too drunk to stand she always took them off. Or maybe fell out of them, she never really knew.

Rolling over with the intention to get out of bed, she found herself nose to nose with the sleeping Kelly.

With a sharp sigh, she woke and smiled sweetly. "Good morning," she said softly before becoming a little startled.

"Oh, sorry, you sat down and fell asleep instantly," she said in a hurry. "I brought you in here, hoping you'd get a better sleep in a bed than on the couch and I wasn't walking to your cabin and back."

"It's okay," Hannah replied with a chuckle. "Thank you. Just take my legs off next time."

She looked away for a moment. "Yeah, okay. Do you want into the bathroom first?"

"You go on."

Alone in the bed, Hannah looked around the small room. She was very rarely in Kelly's cabin and couldn't think of having ever been in the bedroom since she'd first shown it to her. Having expected the walls to be bare, she was surprised to see pictures, most of them paintings. Several soft toy animals sat on a chair, gawking at the newcomer to their domain with innocent interest.

Pushing herself up, she considered her surprise at the clear show of personality. Given the fact Kelly had never really shown any interests, the room was intriguing. Or was it more that in assuming she had no interests she'd selfishly never taken the time to enquire?

She reappeared a few minutes later with a towel wrapped about herself, water dripping on the floor.

"Are you okay?" Hannah asked.

Chewing her lip, Kelly refused to make eye contact. "Actually, I… I need to talk to you about that."

"Oh."

She stood for a few heartbeats. "Can I get dressed before we talk?"

"Oh, yeah, sure," Hannah replied. "I'll, eh, wait out there?"

If the bedroom had been a surprise, the living area was a complete shock.

It was richly decorated. The walls had been coloured a light blue; cushions with intricately patterned covers sat on the chairs; more art hung on the walls; a small keyboard and a small stringed instrument sat beside a desk with a pile of books, sketch pads and a hand-held games console; hobby and craft magazines sat on the coffee table.

Despite all the clutter, the place was clean and very neat. Everything had a place.

She approached a large painting that had to have been done by Kelly as it was a series of self-portraits in different styles. With a little help from her implant and Wikipedia, she managed to identify the approximate styles in use: a fair attempt at Baroque a la Rembrandt; an attempt at Post-Impressionism a la van Gogh; an unidentifiable form of Cubism attempting to capture the spirit of Picasso; a modern photorealistic painting infused with strange symbols that might have been Axel #Yolo or The Cat Strikes Back in style.

"Do you like it?"

Hannah jumped a little and staggered ever so slightly as she turned. "When did you learn to paint?" she blurted.

"In my spare time," she replied with a half shrug and lopsided smile.

"Okay. Why did you learn to paint? Or play the keyboard?"

Kelly took a deep breath and guided her bemused Captain to the couch. "That's what I wanted to talk about," she said, clasping her hands on her lap, wringing them ever so slightly.

"Hannah, I'm changing."

There was a moment of silence, during which Hannah had no idea if she was expected to say something. After it became a little unbearable, she nodded once slowly. "What are you changing?"

Kelly slumped a little. "Me," she replied. "I'm becoming sentient."

She proceeded to explain everything that Annie had told her and the little she'd learnt from reading up on the matter. Several other synths in her position had written books on the matter, which were sitting on the bookshelf with captivating titles like: "Growing a Ghost in the Shell"; "Evolution of a Synthetic Man"; "Beyond Circuits and Switches – How I Became a Woman". She'd had most for months, but hadn't really understood what they were saying until now.

"So?"

Hannah launched herself forward and pulled the startled Kelly into a hug. "I'm so happy for you," she said into her shoulder as she held her. "This is great, you get to be really you."

"Well, not quite."

She frowned as she let her go. "What do you mean?"

"Best I show you," she replied as she stood up. Tapping a few commands into a tablet, a hologram of a woman appeared. It looked like Kelly, but quite different at the same time.

The hologram looked human, rather than like a living piece of eye-candy. The exaggerated hourglass figure had become realistic, if still a definite hourglass.

Hannah got up and slowly walked around the image. "This is how you want to look?"

Kelly nodded and shrugged a little at the same time as she flushed.

"I thought you wanted to not to look like, well, a femme fatale? And a tall one at that."

She bristled a little. "What? I'm not allowed to look sexy? Anyway, I was built with a naturally curvy frame. And I've got used to my height." She gave a half shrug again, looking away. "Anyway, yeah, it's not likely to happen."

"Why?"

"Cost," she replied handing over a tablet. "I got some quotes based on what I want."

Hannah's eyes bulged as she started to read the list of components. As far as she could tell, Kelly was just about rebuilding herself from the feet up. "There's a lot of organic parts," she said, the eye-watering prices giving her slight palpitations.

"I want to be as organic as possible," she replied. "I know I'll never be truly human, but all these will make me as close to it as I can get."

Some of the modifications really were going for authenticity. Bio-synthetic skin, eyes, internal organs; all the benefits of looking and feeling like a human, and many of the drawbacks as well. As a mechanical synth, she'd last until her neural net gave out, which could be centuries; as a bio-synth, she'd only live as long as a normal human without replacements and she'd age.

"And a few mods that make me wonder if you plan to rob banks, start revolutions or become a vigilante."

At the end of what had started to feel like a never-ending list sat the sum total. "This is more than it cost me to buy *Sigyn*," she blurted before she could stop herself.

Kelly arched her eyebrows and put a hand on her hip. "You bought *Sigyn* from the Peacekeepers at an auction of confiscated goods. You got an absolute steal." She sighed and tutted. "But it is a lot of money. I can't afford it, even having it all done in stages. And that's not an option I want to go through."

Hannah frowned. "I thought that was what you wanted to do?"

"I did. Then I started to wake up and see what has been done to me and I can't stand it," she replied. "It wasn't enough for him to make me look like this, he had to make it look like I'd been worked on by a cut-price cosmetic surgeon. I could have been sculpted, but he went with implants. Obvious ones at that. I don't want to spend years being a patchwork of parts."

It was at this revelation that Hannah noticed what had really been bugging her. There was a frame with nothing in it, which at first, she'd assumed was perhaps art outside her range of vision (infrared and ultraviolet art was all the rage again). Now she realised it was a mirror that had been turned around. Kelly literally couldn't stand the sight of herself anymore.

"I can move some money about, sell some shares –"

"And then I'll be indebted to you forever."

"You'd work it off as a no interest loan."

"And be tied to the ship forever?"

This was not the response Hannah had expected, but she fought down the little bubble of annoyance. "No. If you wanted to leave, you'd still have to pay. Or I'd send the heavies."

After a second of stony silence, Kelly giggled. "Well, if you're paying, I might add a few more mods in."

"Don't push your luck."

She pouted. "I'm not bad, I'm just built that way."

"What?"

Kelly cocked her head. "Jessica Rabbit; she says similar in a film."

Hannah nodded sagely. "What?"

"I was looking at some of the data from the *Livingstone*, which included some old films. *Who Framed Roger Rabbit?* was listed. We should watch it together some time."

A coy smile spread over her face. "Oh, really?"

She nodded excitedly. "Yes, I think it'll be fun. Curl up on the couch, some popcorn, a fun film." Seeing the increasingly curious look on Hannah's face, she smiled, coughed and looked away, the merest hint of a blush coming to her cheeks.

"Right, shall we go wake the popsicles? I'm sure they're eager to get out into this brave new world."

Letting her lead the way, Hannah simply smiled.

Carl and Aisha had been kept sedated since they had been recovered. Both had been subjected to a number of therapies to get the bodies back into the land of the living, improving on the woefully primitive protocols of the *Livingstone*.

Once awake, they would still have some way to go to get back to being fully normal again. Four hundred years of nutrient paste would have taken a toll on their digestive systems, which would have to be weaned back onto solid food.

"I'm still calibrating your language modules," Jon said as Kelly started to bring them round. "I should be able to talk to them, so perhaps until I can get you both up to speed, I should do the talking."

Hannah folded her arms. "You'd better get those calibrations done quick."

With a cough, a grunt and a groan, Carl started to come round. He rolled around a little on the bed before opening his eyes. "Where am I?"

"Take it easy, you're on a ship called *Sigyn*," Jon said, sounding like a Shakespearean actor in full soliloquy. "You've just come out of a long stint in cryo."

"What's going on?" Aisha asked as she, too, woke.

Jon went through it slowly, having learnt that ancient cryogenic systems could often cause temporary confusion and mental impairment. Neither tried to get up, or possibly were so weak that they simply couldn't even try. He introduced himself, Hannah and Kelly briefly.

"Where's everyone else?" Aisha asked, her head lolling to one side for a moment.

"They didn't make it," he replied softly.

Both just blinked a little.

"Can I say 'Welcome to the World of Tomorrow' yet?" Hannah asked.

"No, you're still talking in modern," Jon replied. "You can understand them now, but I'm not done uploading your speech patterns."

"Don't confuse them more than they are," Kelly chipped in. "Hearing us will no doubt confuse the hell out of them."

Carl managed to lift his head a little to look at the two women. "Is it just me, or do they sound like they are talking like some sort of text speak rap battle?"

"Nope, they definitely sound like a bunch of bad texts," Aisha agreed.

Hannah and Kelly looked at each other and shrugged.

"Wait, did you say everyone else is dead?" she asked, the slightly glazed look she'd worn so far lifting a little.

Jon nodded and tried to appear sympathetic. "Yes, I'm afraid so. From your ship's point of view, four hundred years passed, which is considerably –"

"Four hundred years?" Carl asked, trying to push himself up shakily. "Four hundred? It was meant to be a three-year cruise."

There was an awkward silence that seemed to stretch on for four hundred years. Having just woken up from a very long sleep and still recovering, was it wise to tell them it had been quite a lot of four hundred years to everyone else?

Hannah looked at Jon. "You wanted to do the talking."

"I understand her," Carl cried, pointing at her weakly, eyes wide and a smile creeping on to his face. "I, em, can understand what she's saying now," he added lamely as Aisha gave him a slightly tired look.

Jon meanwhile looked pathetically at her. "Is it wise to say anything so soon?"

She sighed. "Chief Medical Officer, you're up."

Kelly shook her head. "I'm just a palliative care nurse."

Stepping between the two beds, Hannah knelt down to be closer to the height of the two ancient humans. She tried to smile sweetly, but it came across as a little creepy to them.

"Your ship missed target, ran out of fuel for the warp drive, so headed off at a fraction below light speed," she explained. "Do you know what that means?"

Aisha gave a tired shrug, her mind too fogged to realise what she was being told, but Carl's face went blank and grey after a few seconds of the concept sinking, very slowly, in.

"Time dilation."

"Bingo," she replied. "Due to some things I'm not going to go into, we don't actually know what year it is on your old calendar. But, based on what we can gather, you are probably about ten thousand years in your future.

"Welcome to the World of Tomorrow."

Both Kelly and Jon looked at the ceiling and pondered their life choices. Carl and Aisha looked at each other in askance. Hannah deflated somewhat that her fun welcome had dropped like a lead balloon on a high gravity world.

"So, everyone's dead?" Carl asked.

"Yes, everyone's dead."

Aisha shook her head. "What? Everyone? Peterson isn't, is he?"

"We shouldn't have let them out," Hannah muttered as she pushed herself up and stepped back.

Kelly stepped into start explaining, as simply as she could, the biological implications of what had happened to them. It could be some time before they could eat solid food (Carl nearly cried at this); they would need time to adjust as their motor function, particularly fine motor function, might not return fully for a few days; if they desired, the port scars on their abdomens could be removed completely; they had already been inoculated against all sorts of nasty modern diseases, so were perfectly safe.

This immediately attracted Aisha's interest with a barrage of questions launched. Kelly started to answer, but quickly realised it would be best left to another time.

Seeing the new passengers were going to be in the most capable hands for the moment, Hannah slipped away. She needed to speak to Annie and there was more to discuss than just the repairs she was going to undertake.

After a few initial concerns about Jon, she was almost certain that the Armageddon Protocol hidden deep in his core programming was waking up.

If it was, there was a very real chance they were in a lot of danger.

The gentle trickling of water flowed through the room, shimmering over the leaves of the assorted plants. Sage, mint and lavender filled the air, leaping playfully from a small oil heater. Along with the running water, gentle gongs and bells permeated the tranquillity.

Caster was not one for meditation, but not through lack of trying. No matter how he tried, his mind just never seemed to clear. And now with Dido sitting next to him, lost to the world, it was all but impossible.

He didn't move in case he disturbed his mistress's state of being, yet he wanted nothing more than to get up and stretch his legs. The aches had turned to tremors for a few moments, but passed in to numbness at some point.

Cracking an eye open, he found Dido looking back at him, a gently reassuring smile on her face.

"I think that's enough for now," she said softly. Putting a hand lightly on his shoulder for balance, she got to her feet and helped him up.

"I suppose we'd best go and see what Green has to say," she said, almost bored at the very idea as she stopped the ambient sound and turned the heater off. "I'm sure he'll be fired up over nothing," she continued as she lifted her robe and pulled it on.

It had been nearly a week since they'd lost the ship they'd found at Gallifrey. The fact it had slipped through their fingers was galling, but Green was taking it particularly poorly. The fact his ship had taken damage, even if it was just some dented armour, had infuriated and humiliated him beyond words.

Castor followed Dido up to the Bridge.

The Bridge was its usual hive of activity, but all the officers were focused a little too intently on their stations. Green stood in the middle of the Bridge, hewn from granite, as he stared at nothing.

"Admiral, how are we?" Dido asked softly.

"Pissed off," he replied. With a bit of a sigh, he shook his head. "My apologies, I'm just frustrated. This Captain Hannah Sinclair doesn't seem to exist beyond about five or six years ago." He shook his head as his top lip pulled back a little. "Must be a pirate that's managed to survive with her pseudonym intact that long."

Castor held out the tablet with the scant bit of information the Purifiers had managed to dredge up from the Internet. He passed it directly to Green, who scanned it and frowned.

"There's an old Commonwealth Fighter Academy picture there," he said. "Account for aging, that's almost certainly her. There's a marriage certificate to a John Alistair Sinclair, later Alison Joanna Sinclair."

Green snorted. "I'm sure that's true and not a cover identity."

Saying nothing, Castor simply took the tablet back as it was thrust at him. Arguing with an Admiral was a pointless endeavour and there was very little else to back up who they were supposedly following.

"She's clever, though," he said through slightly gritted teeth. "But she drew first blood and I intend to repay the favour."

"Once we have the ship," Dido said softly. Her voice was in stark contrast to the hard look in her eyes. "Until we have a way of going where we want to go, we might need her. If she's got half a brain, she won't have linked her ship's AI into the *Livingstone*, but I imagine it's already suffering."

She and Green continued to theorise their next steps, none of which were appealing. They'd allowed the greatest discovery of the age to slip through their fingers at the hands of a glorified freighter. Castor could see most of the Bridge crew were listening in, but trying not to look like they were doing so.

A thought struck him. It wasn't much to go with, but it might be better than nothing.

"She must have a bolthole," he said when a break in the conversation came up. "It'll be somewhere she can easily hide; the after-action reports all show her trying to hide from our ships rather than brazen it out."

Green peered at him for a moment. "We've come up short so far. How do we find a bolthole when we've the whole galaxy to consider?"

He bobbed his head in an awkward nod of acknowledgement. "Her ship is overladen, the drives struggling, so she can't have gone too far," he said, although he was absolutely certain that his superiors already knew this. It would be insulting to suggest otherwise. "She's ex-Commonwealth Navy, so her bolthole of choice could very well be a Commonwealth system that's not exactly well regarded or watched."

Dido pursed her lips. "That doesn't narrow it much in this region."

"True," he replied. "But someone must know her. Ex-comrades, retired crew. A little incentive could coax information; we know she takes on jobs, so have agents ask looking for ways to contact her about a job."

Green chuckled a little as he looked to Dido. "You always do pick smart ones."

Feeling warmth in his cheeks, Castor tried to keep the grin from his face and looked at his feet for a moment to cover his failure to do so. When he looked back up, Dido was smiling for a moment before she motioned for him to follow and made to depart the Bridge.

Echoes in Time and Space

Everything was not quite going to plan.

After a lengthy discussion with Annie about the state of what was left of the slipstream drive, Hannah had been forced to consider her options. The drive was completely ruined; generator one and the back-up were completely fried beyond repair, and two might be salvageable, if they had a working shipyard.

The cost of the repairs would be immense. To get the generators replaced would involve either breaking them down in-situ and then building the new ones in place, or, dismantling a path through the ship from one of the cargo bays. Any parts that could be scavenged would go some way to softening the blow.

If she was being honest with herself, she also wanted another look at the battlefield and, perhaps if she was feeling brave or very stupid, a touchdown in Abertawe for… well, for something.

As such, she was going to need to get something out of storage that she'd not used in a long time.

An interesting quirk of Hannah's discharge from the Navy was that her command codes had been messed up. Her Wing Commander codes had been suspended when she'd been sent for psychological evaluation; her promotion to Group Captain had not originally come with any as she was not expected to serve. However, her own Group Captain had been severely injured at Hafan and was in no state to do anything. As the duties required were only administrative, Hannah had been given codes and put to work for a few months. Bureaucracy being what it was, files were sorted in the wrong order and when she was discharged, an official found that her Wing Commander codes were dormant and since they had no record of her promotion, left it at that.

Upon learning this, having bought *Sigyn* and taken a contract moving scrap, she'd started to rummage in the supposedly locked containers. When she found out her fighter, which had been doing the rounds as a museum piece, was to be decommissioned and scrapped, she arranged to transport it.

Oddly, the records show it arrived at the Arcadia Ship-Breaker Yards, but no one could actually find it.

Since acquiring the fighter, Hannah had flown it exactly once before locking it away in its cargo bay at the aft of the ship. It had been a stupid idea to take it; too many memories. But she could hardly rock up with it five years after it was assumed scrapped.

The door into the bay was just like any other on the ship, with the exception of a "No Entry" sign on it. It was locked so that only Hannah and Annie (she could have easily hacked the door, so it was just easier to let her in) had access. Annie had set up several illicit stills in there.

It was a silly idea.

Going out into the grave she'd crawled out of in the ship she'd been buried in? Not to mention if she was spotted by anyone, lots of questions would be asked.

She placed a hand on the palm reader. She was surprised at how little it shook until she noticed her left was shaking enough for both.

Accepting the scan, the panel slid aside to reveal a key pad. In went the twelve-digit code on the third attempt. She'd had to write it down and was now struggling to read the chicken scratches and snail trails that passed as her handwriting; digital recording could be hacked and made it too easy to access.

Code in, a lever down the side of the pad popped out.

"How does Annie do this all the time?" she muttered as she started to pump the handle to prime the door. Clearly removing all the automated systems for opening was a massive oversight, even if it was serving the purpose of deterring her attempts at entry.

A solid clunk accompanied the handle locking back in place.

Stepping back, Hannah took a breath as she prepared to slide the door open. Part of her was certain she'd go in, turn around and head straight back out. Time wasted that could have been put to better use; drinking coffee, playing with her virtual farm, fantasying about some –

Hannah landed on the deck as something ploughed into her at speed. Before she could move, hands had her arms pinned and someone was lying on her to keep her from moving.

"You didn't need to tackle her," Annie said as she appeared in the corridor.

"You said we had to stop her," Kelly countered.

"Aye, as in not let her get in, not nail her to the deck."

There was a moment of silence.

"Perhaps we should take this somewhere a little less public?" Hannah said, wiggling her eyebrows in a seductive manner.

Kelly, slowly, let go and helped her up.

"I'm just going part hunting, I'll be fine," Hannah said as she slid the door open. The wall of alcohol fumes, hops, cereals, yeast, mash and sugars nearly put her on the deck again. That would explain why Annie was so eager to keep her out.

Inside, most of the closest part of the bay was filled with stills producing several different spirits and beers, barrels stacked in racks five high. In the middle was a small box that projected a sensor ghost of an empty cargo bay to any ship that tried to scan them. At the far end, under a tarpaulin, sat the CAW TX-31 Tempest that Hannah had flown.

"I didn't know we had a brewery on board," Kelly said as she stuck her head in.

"I thought we'd agreed on a whisky distillery and maybe a little bit of homebrew beer," Hannah replied, glaring at Annie. "And have you been coming and going via a wall vent?"

Annie lifted her chin. "Yes, it's easier than that bloody door. And since you were never likely to come in here, I didn't expect you to find out I've expanded the operation."

Moving from box to box, Hannah pulled random bottles to inspect what was in them. Whisky, gin, rum, vodka, cognac and at least five different styles of beer, all present and packaged for sale as rare small batch beverages.

One of them, with a rather saucy label of what could very well be her, called "Death of the Monitor", caught her eye. She'd heard Holly mention that she'd seen a bottle of it sell for an insane price for a bottle of beer. At 33% alcohol, it was probably going to be the death of the drinker if they had the whole bottle.

Behind it were other small batches of increasingly strong beer, ranging into the weird science of freeze distilling. She wasn't even sure you could class "Intercontinental Nuclear Weasel" as beer and it would certainly be lethal in anything more than shots.

"I expect my share of the profit from this," she said, placing the bottle back carefully in the box. "And the back pay."

"So, I'll be getting my wages in full?"

Hannah ran her tongue along her teeth. "Fine, but run your numbers, the real ones, through Holly. I'm not taking the beasting from the taxman over this one."

Kelly frowned as she folded her arms. "You told me we had to stop her getting to her fighter."

"No, I said into the cargo bay," Annie replied. "She'll be fine out there; I was worried about my booze. And my money."

Leaving the bickering behind, Hannah weaved through the paraphernalia to get to her fighter. She whipped the tarp off, releasing a puff of dust into the air, revealing the sleek, white fighter underneath.

The fighter looked like a white tetrahedron, sitting on three spindly legs, with a flattened fin extending from each edge of the structure. Somewhere between a shark and a crystal, the fighter looked completely unlike any other class of ship.

Pulling her helmet on, Hannah tapped at the control pad on her suit to open the hatch. What looked like a narrow bed dropped from the underside. The cockpit was a tight fit, which was why all Tempest pilots were required to be slender. Most referred to the cockpit as "the coffin".

"Can I come?" Kelly asked, having weaved her way through the homebrew. "I know there is a passenger space."

Hannah sighed a little. "It's not a passenger space, its technically for a mission specialist." She looked Kelly up and down a little. "And I'm not sure you'll fit."

"Are you saying I'm fat?" she replied, pursing her lips and frowning as she crossed her arms again.

"No, no," she said hastily. "It's more that it's claustrophobic in there and since you don't have a neural link, you won't be able to see anything. The gel layer means that there's nothing to feel, except in the most extreme of turns and twists."

Even as the puppy dog eyes came on, she was opening the hatch on the far side. It didn't open as smoothly, shuddering a few times as it dropped from lack of use. In all her sorties, Hannah had only flown with a specialist on three occasions: twice for insertion – using a fighter was a common Commonwealth tactic to sneak specialists behind enemy lines while dropships brought in decoys; and once when carrying out an escort mission – she never did find out why or what the specialist actually did in that case. Some pilots liked to tag-team as a pair, a pilot and gunner set up usually, but that wasn't her style. As such, solo interceptors tended to get the more dangerous missions as they were less valuable when only one life and one piece of hardware was at risk.

Dressed in a replicated suit, Kelly struggled onto the lowered section.

"Tuck in," Hannah said as she closed the hatch and went to get into her cockpit.

The gel layer moulded around her front as she lay down. The hatch lifted and she was pushed into another layer of gel, sandwiching her in the middle. It adjusted slightly until she felt like she was floating and could move freely.

A panel at her face lit up as the neural link between her and the fighter was established.

"Welcome back, Group Captain," a male voice said in her head. "I'm noticing a number of changes in your biometric data; nothing to worry about, aside from the caffeine addiction. I'll calibrate on your new baselines."

"Hello, Pete. How are you?"

"Oh, you know, fine for only being turned on once a month for maintenance for the past God knows how many years," he lamented. "I think the woman in the specialist bay wants to talk to you."

"You okay in there, Kelly?"

There was a muffle squeak. "Well, it's cold and dark."

"Told you," she replied, even as she asked Pete to make Kelly comfortable while the pre-start checks began.

All credit to Annie, she'd managed to keep everything in working order despite the fact the fighter was never flown. And since Pete was a "dumb" AI, there was no risk of him losing his marbles with limited contact and frequent start-up and shutdown cycles.

The fighter whipped between two lumps of shredded metal as it sped towards another hulk. Its movements were rapid, flitting back and forth like an insect. High manoeuvrability was what gave it any sort of chance at survival against other fighters and anti-aircraft weapons.

Today, however, there was nothing shooting at it, so it simply darted for fun.

Having memorised the list of materials needed; Hannah was able to let Pete scan the hulks for anything that might be a match. If they found anything, either *Sigyn* or a spacewalk would be needed; the fighter had no cargo carry facilities, beyond the ones for ammunition.

Not that it mattered so far. They'd found the square root of nothing.

"Hannah, I've scanned everything five times," Pete said coolly. "I've no issue scanning again, but we are getting to the point of insanity expecting a new result."

She sighed and came to a stop.

"You're right," she replied.

There was still plenty of fuel in the tank and she hadn't freaked out about being here yet. She was sure she wasn't going to; she'd seen ships she knew, ones where friends and comrades had served and died, and she was okay. It was just another graveyard, filled with bodies that no one came to visit.

Having said that, if the fighter had still been armed (all the weapons had been removed when it was decommissioned) she might have been tempted to blow up a few Remnant ships. For fun, but mostly out of sheer badness. Carving a giant dick into their hulls would have been immensely childish, but probably satisfying.

She'd known there would be nothing to scavenge; she'd sifted through tonnes and tonnes of material that had been salvaged by the Navy that she'd taken to reclamation facilities or dumped into stars. Her real reason for coming out was to go to Abertawe. Kelly had complicated that.

After some soul searching, she came to a decision. She headed straight for the moon of Morgannwg and Abertawe City, at least, what was left of it.

Morgannwg had been a terraformed world. Originally a barren rock, millennia previously, someone had undertaking the mammoth and frankly insane task of making it a lush garden world.

Coming in through the thick atmosphere, she could say the work had paid off. Abertawe had been reclaimed by plants; trees had started to grow wherever they could find good soil, flowers were blooming in what had been neatly mown parks and vines had snared the buildings. Another few decades and the city would have vanished completely.

The last time she'd made the journey, the city had been burning.

Circling a few times, she found a suitable park to land in near The M. Beardsmore Memorial Hospital. The arrival of the first humans in years upset a number of birds that had been sitting, happily minding their own business. In a flurry of feathers and squawking, they took to the wing and fled for safer trees.

Coming to a gentle stop, Hannah shut everything down and opened the hatch. With an awkward and ungainly wriggle, she landed on the ground. It had been a few years since she'd actually set foot on terra firma, which wasn't that odd really, but setting foot on Morgannwg was. Taking her helmet off, she took a deep breath: no smoke, no smell of death; just the smell of plants and animals.

It was nearly pleasant.

A gentle thump roused her from her thoughts. Kelly had managed to wriggle out and was now sitting on the ground where she'd landed.

"Nice re-entry," Hannah said with a smile as she offered a hand.

"Where are we?" she replied, blinking sleep away.

"Abertawe."

She nodded slowly as she took her helmet off. "I'll wait here, if you need some space."

Hannah wasn't sure how to answer that. Kelly had to know what her plan was, but was it weird to bring someone along to look for your dead spouse in a city full of the dead? No one had come back to the planet much after the attack, so, as far as she was led to believe, the dead just lay where they'd fallen.

"There'll be bodies everywhere."

"I'm a medic, I've seen bodies."

With a small smile, Hannah nodded for Kelly to join her.

They headed out of the park and immediately found skeletons, still wearing some scraps of clothing, just lying in the streets. Burnt out vehicles littered the roads, some of them containing the remains of panicked civilians who had been trying to escape the horror of war.

Most of the damage had been done when a small part of the *Monitor* had hit the outskirts, setting a raging inferno alight that had ravaged the already damaged city. Space battles normally didn't happen over planets, specifically to avoid accidental hits and gravitational anomalies, but the Battle of Hafan had been an unmitigated disaster from start to finish for both sides. The fact the dozens of ships being so close (astronomically speaking) to the planet hadn't caused massive environmental damage was only because the battle had been brief.

A small part of Hannah felt guilty; she'd destroyed the *Monitor*'s bridge, which while that hadn't felled the mighty warship, it had given the fleet a window and psychological victory. Had she, by proxy, killed all the poor sods that had been unable to evacuate?

This side of the city hadn't been burnt too badly, mostly stray ship fire or from crashing dropships. The Remnant had dropped Purifiers in what was assumed to be an attempt to take out the local leadership or the orbital defence network that would have handed the much larger Remnant fleet victory. The East End had been levelled by the firestorm.

Beardsmore Hospital looked much as it had, albeit with added foliage. The ten-storey building towered over the smaller ones that flanked it. Unlike her nightmare, there were no piles of bodies. Barricades had been left, some fallen down and a few skeletons lay at rest, but no mounds of butchered innocents. That was as far as she'd got last time before being dragged back to her fighter by two of her flight for her own safety where a medical team had sedated her.

As she walked through the remains, the distinctive marks of particle beam hits could be seen; sections of bone that were missing, scorched or slightly indented where the bone had been burnt away.

Only a weapon meant to kill would leave that sort of mark.

"Are you sure you want to do this?"

Hannah looked to Kelly. She was looking at her with real concern. It was then she realised her hands were balled in tight fists and she could feel a little dampness around her eyes.

"Yes."

They moved into the reception and on into the hospital. Ali had been working in a cancer ward; cancers were relatively easy to treat if caught early and could often be cured, but after millennia of genetic tampering, it was an extremely common ailment.

Following the signs as best they could, they arrived at the cancer department.

She had given up her seat on the evac shuttle to the mother of one of her patients. The little girl had been only nine and terrified; being the kind person she was, Ali refused her seat and had gone back to help those that had not been given evac priority. It had been a mixed blessing; the shuttle had been shot down as it left the atmosphere, burning up in seconds.

Hannah could still remember the horrifying moment when the call had come through. Although it was illegal, she'd given Ali codes to call her if needed. Being out in her fighter, the call had gone through *Killing Me Softly*'s control tower. The operator that took it had been decent enough to say nothing about the complete disregard for protocol, but that was also because the ship had been crippled and he probably had other things to worry about. Or was convinced death was coming, so didn't care.

She been trying to evade enemy fighters when Ali had told her she'd missed the shuttle and was stuck. Naturally, Hannah had said she was going to come get her, followed by declaring she'd have a military shuttle go get her. They both had known it was nonsense to suggest either course of action, but both had needed it.

Holed up in an office, Ali had spent her last few minutes going over all the things they were going to do after the battle. Hannah could retire or take a desk job on one of the core worlds. They'd defrost some sperm and eggs and finally get around to having children. A nice house in the country, or a small village, with a garden full of flowers, fruit trees and vegetables. Somewhere to grow old, grey and fat together.

She'd managed to get "I love yo-" out before she'd been shot.

A lump of dread, the size of a small planet, had formed in Hannah's stomach as she moved from door to door, checking the offices. Kelly was always a little behind her, just there quietly. She was glad she was there and that she wasn't questioning anything, morbid as the activity was.

Pushing a door that had been forced open, her worst nightmare was realised.

A pile of bones sat slumped against the wall, still half in tattered clothes and a white lab coat. The wall behind had been scorched where the beam had passed right through. A corresponding hole in the ribcage could just be made out where it was lying on the floor.

Near blinded by tears, Hannah went to the bones. She lifted the ID badge that was still clipped to the coat.

It was Ali.

She landed hard on her backside, shaking in silently violent sobs. The badge flopped to the floor as she reached for the skull. It had rolled away from the rest of the bones at some point in the intervening years.

Between the tears and shaking, she could barely focus on it. Where once there had been beautiful almond-shaped hazel eyes, full of warmth and playful undertones, were black voids. Gone was the long, dark brown hair that was always swept back from the distinctive widow's peak to cascade down the long, narrow back. The once high cheek bones looked impossibly huge and the pointed canines that they'd joked looked vampiric now looked oddly normal.

It was unmistakably Ali and yet paradoxically not. She just couldn't equate the pale lump of bone to the vibrant woman it had belonged to.

She became aware that she was being hugged. It was comforting.

Turning to face Kelly, she had no idea what to say or what to do with Ali's skull that was now resting on her lap, staring up at them both.

Kelly broke the silence with what might have been the only correct thing to say: "Do you want to bury her?"

Limping Forward

"Why do I have a feeling you are about to tell me everything is so much worse than we thought?" Hannah asked as she propped herself up against the wall of the mess.

Annie shrugged a little. "Slipstream is gone," she said, looking at the table. "And I can't even guarantee the Hop drive for long either."

Hannah gently banged her head on the wall.

"Are you saying we're stuck here?" Laura asked, leaning forward, her eyes going wide. "I really don't want to die in this hellhole. Oh, sorry," she added, looking at Hannah and cringing.

"No, not stuck, just limited in how far we should consider going."

Emily folded her arms and thumped back in her seat. "Far might be a stretch."

A painful silence filled the small mess.

Hannah couldn't help but feel it was completely, totally and utterly her fault that all of this had happened. She'd taken the job, after all. And she'd picked Hafan as the place to hide from the Remnant, which had been a bit of a stupid plan. Even after four days, they were no further forward.

Although the Hop drive itself was intact, several systems were shared with the slipstream drive as back-ups. Most of the cooling systems interacted to increase redundancy without increasing weight. Under normal operation, that was sensible for a medium sized transport that would calmly cruise about. It was proving remarkably dumb if said ship was used to outrun an entire fleet by pushing everything beyond design limits.

"Is there anything we can do to improve it? Even stripping my fighter down?"

With a shake of her head, Annie shrugged a little. "The engines on your fighter are just too small to even link into *Sigyn*."

"If we manage to get somewhere, can we afford repairs?" Laura asked.

"I'll look after that," Hannah replied.

Annie, however, wasn't finished. "Of course, with the damage to the cooling systems, that means the cloak is totally out of the question and even stealth is probably beyond us for actual practical use."

Laura frowned and pursed her lips. "But we can't use either with the cargo."

"It's staying here."

Those who had not been informed, basically everyone but Hannah, glared at her. The *Livingstone* was the ultimate payday for them. The few scraps of destroyed ancient vessels that turned up at auctions sold for enough to buy a small asteroid. The *Livingstone* might just buy a planetary system.

"Hands up for mutiny," Laura announced as she thrust both her hands in the air.

"Funny," came the terse reply. "We can barely move; trying to drag that thing along will cripple us and raise a giant red flag to every bounty hunter, merc and Remnant spy for lightyears." She couldn't quite believe she was justifying dumping cargo. For a transport captain, that was possibly the greatest sin imaginable; captains had been hanged by their crew for less. "It'll be fine here until we can safely transport it. After we find a buyer or an auction house, they can handle it."

"What about getting *Sheba* to take it?" Emily asked.

"The Remnant know about her. They'll be watching her, expecting that. Anyway, she'd never get into the system undetected."

Laura snorted. "It's a miracle we did."

Hannah tilted her head a little and shrugged. "Well, I'm just that good."

"All in favour of mutiny?"

Slamming her hand on the nearest table to draw attention did just that, but mostly because of the small yelp she let out in doing so. "This isn't a democracy, or an anarchic commune; it's a dictatorship and I dictate.

"Jon, where can we make it to that could accommodate us for repairs?"

A holographic image of the local section of the galaxy appeared. It was considerably smaller than *Sigyn*'s normal range. Several systems lit up in blue.

"And which ones are," she searched for the correct phrasing, "the path less travelled?"

Of the blue dots, only two remained as the rest went red. One was on the very edge of their range. Hannah pointed to the other one and not because it was the closest.

Laura glowered at her. "Roanapur? Why don't we just buy first class tickets to hell and be done with it?"

With a gentle cough, Emily sat up a little straighter. "I'll second that."

Annie squirmed. "Not being funny, but I have to agree, just a wee bit."

It was starting to look like the mutiny was gaining traction. Normally, Hannah would be in agreement; Roanapur, unless you got into the suburbs or had contacts within the major factions that ruled (carved out petty fiefdoms in blood and protection rackets), it was a total hole. The further down the station you went, the deeper into Dante's Inferno you went; the final circle of the Inferno only took you three-quarters of the way down in Roanapur.

Normally, they'd be going in the tradesmen's entrance. Or the organ grinder as product – basically the same thing.

"An acquaintance of mine has some pull at the moment," she said, trying to sound convinced of her own words. "He can get us into a meeting with a player that could sponsor a berth in the Inner Harbour. He offered the service a few years ago and it still stands."

"Why not go to the other one? Sohar?" Kelly asked, looking at the discarded system.

Hannah shrugged. "Possibly because I know someone there that may, or may not, kill me on sight because of something that happened a long time ago."

Laura nodded as she rocked on her chair for a moment. "Sounds like a win-win place to go. All in favour of Roanapur?"

Kelly immediately raised her hand. Seeing that it was either a rhetorical question or no one else was voting for it, she slowly lowered it again. Although not risking Hannah's life was a solid reason to go there rather than Sohar, she was slightly more interested in the Solatronix Clinic – one of the most well-known, well thought of, and surprisingly affordable chains of synthetic modification centres. And being on an unaligned station meant it would have better access to under the counter goods.

Of course, that would mean being able to access the upper suburbs of the city-station. With the entire upper reaches controlled by various cartels, mobs and paramilitary organisations, moving about would be difficult; new faces were often mistaken for spies.

"All in favour of Sohar?"

"Will be sacked and returned to the *Sheba* to work in waste disposal," Hannah cut in.

With a single vote, Roanapur was their next destination.

"So, there are no aliens?" Carl asked.

"Well, there are alien organisms," Casper replied. "Mostly viruses, bacteria. A few planets have plants and simple animals. Smartest thing we've found is roughly the level of a partially sentient mammal." He paused for a moment. "Well, except the octopus people of Trelelvala IV, but we leave them alone."

Aisha rolled her eyes. The only intelligent life was an octopus species; it seemed a little unlikely that the Milky Way was completely devoid of sapient life beyond humanity. Given that at least one member of the misfit crew had already tried to have fun at their expense, what was the chances of it happening again.

Casper smiled weakly. He'd been allowed to meet the two ancients to try and bring them up to speed since everyone else was busy.

"There's life, but we don't colonise planets?" she asked.

He nodded. "Like I said, viruses and bacteria. Some use different amino acids from humans and it means we have no defence against them," he replied. He could think of several dozen colonies that had failed because of diseases that had killed everyone. There was also one where a parasite had taken control of the colonists.

"Didn't anyone develop vaccines?"

"There was generally no point. We left the planets as they were and studied them remotely or from isolation units," he replied. "Humanity, at least for a while, learnt the value of respecting nature."

"After Earth was lost," Carl said.

Casper nodded.

Aisha got up from the armchair and wandered aimlessly around the room. What place was she going to have in the future? Everything she'd thought she'd known about the galaxy had been turned on its head and even her knowledge of biology was almost certainly obsolete beyond the basics.

Where could she fit into society? Why had the computer saved her and not the multitude of others on the ship?

"You okay?" Carl asked.

"No, not really," she replied. "You?"

He sat for a second looking at the coffee table. "Hell, no," he answered. "What do we do now?"

Casper sighed and shrugged. "I'm sorry, but I'm not sure how much help I can be on that one. It's a big galaxy and there are a lot of places to go."

"As a travelling freakshow?"

"How do you mean?"

Carl's eyebrow lifted. "Really? Soon as people find out we're from Earth ten thousand years ago, people will treat us like freaks." He got up and wandered, failing to find a place to anchor to. "Why are there no damned windows on this ship?"

"Massive structural weakness, the view of slipstream drives people insane, not much to look at?" he replied as if talking to a child. They'd had that conversation three times already; the cryogenic confusion was taking longer to pass than expected. "Look, there is a chance of that, but the best thing might be to assume new identities and just slip into society however you want."

Carl and Aisha exchanged a look, eyebrows piqued and mouths drawn at one side.

"It's true," he continued. "There are lots of off the grid colonies, secret societies, cults and bureaucratic mishaps that mean people pop up from nowhere all the time. I do believe our good Captain has some connections that may aid in that field."

That did very little to settle any fears they had been lifted by a pirate ship and likely to end up in space jail doing hard space time breaking space rocks.

"How come we're only meeting you now?" Aisha asked, frowning a little.

Casper grimaced. "I may have upset the crew when they found out who I was working for," he replied. "Let's leave it at that. There's still a lot that I need to get you up to speed on."

Before he could continue with the attempts at filling in ten thousand years of history (at least, what hadn't been lost), the door opened and Kelly came in.

"Just in for a check-up," she announced, giving Casper a hard look as he tried to vanish into the armchair he'd been perched on. "Have either of you thought about the scars and if you want them removed?"

Aisha shook her head. "I'm fine with it. It's a lot better than I been expecting." She'd lived with the prospect of having the feed port as a permanent addition, or at least until the colony had set up a proper medical centre.

"How easy is it to remove?" Carl asked.

Kelly waved a small handheld device up. "Few passes with this and it'll be like it was never there. And I can put it back, if you change your mind."

He rubbed his chin for a moment, letting the idea roll over a few times. "Yeah, let's do it. New life, new future."

Aisha continued to pace a little as Kelly started to work on Carl. "So, you're a robot?" she asked.

Standing still for a moment, Kelly took a breath. "No, I am a synthetic humanoid," she replied flatly.

"Sorry, I didn't mean to offend."

She managed a little smile as she started to work again. "You couldn't know. To call a synthetic a robot would be like calling you a monkey butler. There you go, good as new."

Carl smiled as he inspected his abdomen. "Thanks, Doc, that looks a lot better." He pulled his top down. "Hey, you don't have any advice on what we should do now? I mean, it looks like just wandering into the galaxy is probably not the way to go yet."

"No, probably not," she replied. "If you think this crew is odd, believe me, they are about as close to what you consider normal as you'll get."

"How so?" Aisha asked.

"They have the right number of arms and don't have fur, scales or gills."

Hannah shifted in her chair and resisted the urge to drum her fingers on the arm. How hard could it be to simply disconnect from the *Livingstone* and get moving? Apparently, brain surgery was easier.

She was desperate to get going to get *Sigyn* repaired. It was going to cost a small fortune, but having taken some artifacts to trade with, it wouldn't be too bad. At least, she hoped not. One day she was going to actually retire on the small drumlin of goldcoin she had rather than keep looking for more.

If only.

"Bridge, Engineering, I've finished separating the power systems," Annie's disembodied voice announced. "Looks like the portable genny is working. As long as we don't leave her here more than three years, she'll be fine."

Laura looked slowly over her shoulder.

"We'll be back in a few weeks at most," Hannah replied.

Without a word, she returned to her pre-flight checks, but rolled her eyes at Emily, who gave a tiny shrug.

Out in space, the Bumbles were slowly disentangling the mooring lines and checking for any external damage. The little drones flitted back and forth, each engaged in their own little task, working to get their hive on the move again.

"How many jumps?"

"Just two," Emily replied as she checked the status of the Hop drive.

Time ticked by slowly until, after an eternity, they started to move forward. At little more than a space snail's pace, the ship moved again through the gaping wounds of *Killing Me Softly*, emerging into open space as light of the rising sun spread over the graveyard.

Moving to a safe distance, Emily started to prepare for a Hop jump.

"Jon, has there been any word from Jansen?"

"Not yet, Captain," he replied. "Given the encryption you asked for, I suspect he's either still trying to figure it out or it went into his spam folder."

Taking a calming breath, Hannah clenched and unclenched her fists a few times. She hoped Jansen had got the message and was working his magic to get her a berth. However bad the *Norwegian* was for finding a ship up on bricks, Roanapur was likely to have the lot broken down for parts before it had even finished docking.

"And the *Sheba*?"

"They acknowledged the message and will meet us when they can. It might be a few weeks."

Too paranoid to transmit the location of her treasure horde, Hannah planned to wait until she saw her sisters in person to arrange a pick up. She'd come back for the *Livingstone* and get it as quickly into *Sheba*'s internal docking bay as possible.

"Hop drive awaiting your command," Emily said, turning in her seat.

Laura slumped in her seat as she looked at her crewmate, shaking her head ever so slightly. "Creep."

"Hey, I want paid. She throws me off, I'm getting nothing."

"Ladies, please," Hannah replied, rubbing her forehead. "Let's just get the hell out of here."

One stop and then safety. Just one stop. That was all they needed.

And in true fashion, the universe was loathed to deliver.

In a burst of exotic energy and strange dimensional manipulation, *Sigyn* left the safety of Hafan and popped back into normal space a few hundred metres off the port bow of a Remnant patrol clipper.

"I'm guessing long range sensors didn't see that."

"No, Captain, they didn't," Jon replied slowly, taking a step away from the centre seat. "It is safe to say that they have seen us."

"So, who's bad luck is this?" Laura asked without turning.

Hannah gave a bitter laugh. "Hell if I know; there isn't a member of this crew isn't cursed. I'm sure even the ship is cursed."

Jon stepped closer again, feeling he was safe from flying objects. "They're demanding we prepare to be boarded."

"Weapons?"

He swallowed and tried to smile. "Annie had to use some of the cooling systems to get us going aga-"

"Fantastic," she replied, chewing her lip. "As if it couldn't get any worse."

Laura started to laugh as she shook her head. "Yeah, well, the *Purity* just arrived."

Hot to Hell

Of all the systems in all the galaxy that *Sigyn* could have dropped into, it had appeared not only in one with a Remnant patrol, but one where the ship leading the hunt for them just happened to be checking in.

With no stealth, no cloak, no weapons and too late to alter the registry, options were limited.

"How long until we can jump?" Hannah asked, knowing the answer to her question was going to be distressing. The follow-up even more so.

Emily didn't even need to be asked. "Twenty-seven minutes: about twenty-six minutes too long."

Hannah hung her head and did the one thing she'd always promised she'd never do. It was a total betrayal of what she believed in and would, if anyone ever found out, tarnish her reputation.

"Jon, open the emergency Peacekeeper channel."

Both Emily and Laura turned very slowly to face her.

"To any Peacekeeper vessel in range, mayday, mayday, this is the independent trading vessel *Sigyn*, account number whisky-five-seven-alpha-hotel-sierra-golf," she said, deflated. "We are under attack by Remnant forces; weapons and FTL are offline or on long cooldown, we're sustaining heavy damage. Mayday, mayday, mayday."

"You have a Peacekeeper protection account?" Laura asked, her mouth pursed and brow furrowed. "And you are only using it now?"

There was a momentary pause as the crew looked in askance at their captain, who remained defiantly silent for a moment. What right had they to question her? Easy – she was meant to keep them alive and paid. Emphasis on *paid*.

Hannah's resolve buckled. "Do you have any idea how much a callout will cost?"

"Surely you have insurance if you have an account."

"I lied on the insurance," she replied, speaking more towards her shoulder than Laura. "It's a bloody liberty they take; the premiums are insane. Every year I have to speak to someone to avoid having to pay through the nose."

Jon coughed politely. "Can we have the domestic later? Impending doom off the starboard bow, ladies."

Laura glared at him. "If I don't say my bit now, I might never get the chance."

Emily, meanwhile, had been battling valiantly to keep the Remnant ships as far away as she could. Given the state *Sigyn* was in, it was no mean feat as the enemy circled, pulling the net tighter and tighter.

The fact that Green hadn't bothered to hail to demand surrender confirmed he knew exactly who they were and that he'd had enough of their antics. Letting Hannah talk would only serve to buy her time to pull off another mini miracle.

"Sensors picking up incoming," Jon announced.

A Peacekeeper battlecruiser plopped into existence in the middle of the Remnant formation, forcing them to scatter. From its hull, four patrol vessels detached to expand the zone of disruption, using ship mass rather than weapons' fire to force the Remnant back.

"*Sigyn*, this is the Peacekeeper support vessel *Argus*; lower your shields and prepare for immediate evac," a voice commanded as another vessel appeared. The large ship looked like a giant crab.

"Do it," Hannah ordered. "*Argus*, this is Captain Sinclair, lowering shields. We're trying to get to Roanapur, if that's possible?"

"Acknowledged, that can be arranged. Captain Al-Ghazzawi will make an inspection once we have you docked."

Hannah acknowledged the request, which was a demand but she had the sense to act as though she had a choice. She hoped that Al-Ghazzawi wouldn't be too interested in why help was required and wouldn't go snooping. The illegal stills would be enough to be fined into bankruptcy; being found with ancient humans might be trickier. Peacekeepers often had unusual views of the law, which might put her on a human trafficking charge if Carl and Aisha appeared to be being transported against their will. Or worse, theft of historically significant artifacts.

The giant crab scuttled over the small transport and pulled it safely into an embrace. Seeing the prey was lost, the Remnant quickly departed.

Leaving the Bridge, Hannah made her way towards the airlock. Since the Remnant had run, she suspected the *Argus* would sit right where it was until the inspection was complete. Armed with a manifest and any relevant documents (only one was forged), she waited.

Sure enough, the airlock opened and a rapier thin man in a dark uniform stepped in, followed by three troopers in patrol armour. Their weapons were holstered and they were at ease, which at least gave her some hope that a shooting match was unlikely.

"Captain Al-Ghazzawi, welcome aboard," she said, holding out a tablet. "My papers."

He smiled and waved them away. "That's quite okay, Captain. Anyone going to Roanapur is unlikely to be completely above board. If I don't ask, I don't have to tell."

The condescension was insulting, but he was completely correct. Arguing would only end with *Sigyn* being stripped to the hull supports before being sold for parts after it was seized. The previous owner had run afoul of the Peacekeepers after smuggling exotic animals as pets and food.

"May I ask why you were attacked?"

Seeing an easy way out, she told him exactly who she was. "I suspect they found out who I am after I had a small run in with Admiral Green on a recovery mission. Hafan is still a sore spot for some and I'm sure he'd enjoy my head mounted on his Bridge."

Al-Ghazzawi regarded her for a moment. "Not really his style, as far as I know the Admiral, but you are correct that Hafan is still infamous to them. You are aware they have set up an embassy on Roanapur?"

She was not and cursed to herself. Broadcasting her intentions on an open channel meant she was locking herself into a cage. A cage filled with starving rats, lions, bears and honey badgers.

"Hm, I see you were hoping to flee them," he said, reading her expression. "Well, I'm sure whoever is receiving you there will be able to help you in that regard."

He turned and retreated through the airlock, but the three troopers remained. Just because he didn't want to know what was going on didn't mean he was foolish enough to not keep a leash on. Three troopers could easily take control of the ship, should the crew decide to misbehave.

"So, would anyone like a coffee?"

Roanapur.

As the well-spoken phrase said of a certain fictional spaceport; "you will never find a more wretched hive of scum and villainy", Roanapur came pretty close to winning that medal in the real world.

Millenia before, the station had been a mining complex sat atop a mineral rich asteroid. Over time, the station had set down roots, burrowing into the rock to find metals. As it grew, branches extended to burst from the skin of the host, tangles of buildings swelling in the empty spaces.

The original station had spread and grown like a mushroom, a series of large domes bubbling up to house the rich and powerful as the menial workers suffered the cancerous sprawls in the rock.

When the mining had dried up, cavernous sections were opened up to make berths and shipyards. Refineries, specialising in the more toxic materials of the universe, had followed. Crime rose and became organised. Mercenary bands settled and the station became a haven for political outcasts, rabble-rousers and mafiosos looking for a neutral location to run their crime syndicates from.

Not a single government in the galaxy acknowledged the place, yet they all maintained embassies and consulates there. Often large informal meetings between rival powers were held there, the gangs offering security for a fee.

Hannah had visited a few times, usually to make a quick pick up and run before the locals tried to steal anything. This time, she was going into a much more refined berth, but it would likely cost her one way or another.

The *Argus* had dumped them at the edge of the system, with a polite reminder to check in with the client office to settle any payments and to complete a customer satisfaction survey.

Almost immediately, there were tugs swarming around, offering services to bring them in, for a fee, and to recommend the best place to dock. The initial swarm was dispersed when a larger, far more elegant looking tug simply locked on and started to tow them in.

The Inner Harbour, which was not so much deeper in the station as it was closer to the top, was quiet, but the ships there were impressive. Shiny and sleek pleasure cruisers sat side by side with gunboats and cargo-haulers.

At no point during the short trip had the tug announced who they were, who sent them or if they were simply claiming salvage rights to a ship that was mostly dead.

Once secured in dock, Hannah ordered everyone to stay put until she'd found out exactly what was going on. Calls to the Harbour tower only directed her to speak to whoever had dragged them in.

With no other clues, she headed for the Peacekeepers' office that was sat at the main exit into the station proper. With a large open front, lots of spaced-out desks and chirpy looking attendants, the place was more like a travel agent.

A man appeared, seemingly from nowhere, making her jump slightly. "Welcome, how may I assist you today?" he said, all smiles and top customer satisfaction.

Hannah explained the situation, including asking if the tug worked for them as well. She passed over her papers, hoping no one was going to question how she managed to get insurance on a transport that claimed to be the size of a large fridge.

"Oh, it seems your payment has already been covered," he replied as he looked up the reference number.

"By who?"

"Spectrum Holdings," he replied. "There's a note stating that Mr Black will be waiting for you in the café across the concourse. Have a pleasant day, Captain."

Unceremoniously dumped for the third time that day, Hannah could only stand blinking. Were people intentionally trying to keep her in the dark? And who was Mr Black? Spectrum she'd heard of and not favourably since they kept trying to buy her out of several companies she had controlling shares in.

The Harbour Café, proudly proclaiming it served the best breakfast in ten thousand lightyears, didn't look much. The seats were cheap plastic, the tables coated in gingham vinyl that was clean but worn. Patrons sat slumped at tables, ignoring each other as they drank or picked at half-eaten meals.

Sat at the back was a man in a black suit, sitting back against the wall, pretending to read a tablet as he scanned the horizon over a pair of sunglasses.

Hannah recognised Jansen at once, despite his vastly improved dress sense.

He saw her and waved casually, no more than a flick of the wrist.

"Well, long time no see," he said, placing the tablet down. "Hey, Miss, can I get some more coffee?" he called to the waitress that was passing. "Han?"

"Yeah, coffee and a breakfast, please. And don't call me Han."

Jansen chuckled. "Okay, okay. God, what has it been? Nine, ten years?"

"Twelve. I see leaving the Navy didn't do you any harm," she replied before taking a sip of coffee. It was surprisingly good; deep flavour of dark fruits and a chocolate note on top. Hardly the muddy water she'd feared.

He shrugged. "I can't complain. Nice apartment in Cricket Green away from the worst of the rabble, steady job that pays well, occasional perks that make life nice."

The conversation stalled for a moment.

"There you go, honey," the waitress said as she placed down the plate.

It was then that Hannah realised she couldn't remember when she'd last eaten properly. Anxiety and determination to get free had meant she's snacked pretty much since the first run in with the Remnant. Kelly would kick her ass if she found out. Maybe she should let her?

"Don't they feed you on your ship?"

She glared at him over a mouthful of, well, she wasn't sure and didn't care. It was food and it tasted good.

"Should I assume you are the kind Mr Black that paid for my delivery here?" she asked after swallowing and before having more coffee. She probably looked like a starved escapee having their first meal in months, but she wasn't caring.

His head dropped and he rubbed his nose. "Right to business," he replied. "Yes, although I technically only facilitated my employers' payment of your fees." Taking a long drink of coffee, he snorted. "I'm guessing you're none too pleased that it's me saving your bacon."

"I'll take what I can where I can get it."

"You didn't always say that."

"I was married."

With a dismissive shrug, he looked out of the window for a moment, pretending to watch the people milling about outside.

To avoid the silence, she focused on her breakfast. After not eating properly, the food tasted wonderful, but there would probably be issues later. Last time she'd behaved in a similar manner, she'd had a stomach-ache for three days.

Mopping up the last of the burst egg yolk with a triangle of soft toast, she ran out of time. "So, why did Spectrum Holdings pay to have me brought here? I can't imagine it was out of the goodness of their heart."

"Not quite," he replied. "I'll let Ms White explain when you meet her."

Hannah sat back against her chair and laughed. "Let me guess, everyone in the business is colour coded?" When nothing was said, she smiled and shook her head. "Should I assume that since you go by Black, you are at the opposite end of the Spectrum from White? As in, the arse end?"

A taught smile crossed his face. "I'd forgotten what a sarcastic cow you could be," he replied. "Opposite yes, but sideways. White deals with the legit stuff, I do black ops."

"Years of running gambling circles, stealing supplies and controlling a black market finally paid off."

They sat, glaring at each other for a few minutes, not even looking at the waitress as they thanked her mechanically for their refills.

Jansen looked at the time. "Come on, we're late."

Hannah didn't move. "Bold of you to assume I'm coming with you."

"You need a new slipstream drive and all sorts of repairs," he replied, standing over her. He shrugged a little. "It would be unfortunate if every reputable dealer on the station were to be unable to supply you with one. Even the Scottish Guild knows better than to cross us, so don't expect your tame engineer to be able to leverage her lineage."

Once more, outmanoeuvred and outgunned. It was becoming a painful pattern.

Silently, she pushed herself up. "Can I at least get changed before I meet your boss?"

"Don't worry, you look fine."

She didn't. Having thrown on what was to hand; a slightly tatty pair of joggers and a baggy hoody, she looked like she'd either just been for a long, gruelling run or was looking for her next hit. The egg and grease slittered down her front didn't help, either.

Following Jansen through the warren, she tried to make a mental map of where they went so she could find her own way back. Everything looked clean, but there were the tell-tale signs of deep cleaning in places. The sort of deep cleaning needed to remove blood and lots of it. Some of the streets were lined with shops or stalls, all with warnings that thieves would be shot and survivors sold as all sorts of unpleasant objects. Odd bits of graffiti covered sections of walls, declaring gangs, artists and the end of times with the coming of Eris, a well-known "net monster" bogeyman.

The Harbour curved round the side of the cavern it was built in. At one end stood a number of skyscrapers. One proudly displayed the shimmering, ever changing colours of the Spectrum Holdings' logo.

Armed security nodded to Jansen as he swept in the front door. The receptionists all nodded and smiled, lovely big fake smiles. A doorman scuttled forward to call the lift, saving Jansen's fingers the effort of having to tap a pressure pad.

Hannah could see why he liked the job; from Deck Rat to Fat Cat, who wouldn't revel in that sort of change of fortunes.

They stepped into the lift to the wonderful sound of lift music. Nothing like soft, insipid sax music to make a lift journey even more awkward.

"Now, Ms White is a little different, so don't stare," Jansen said as the lift shot upwards.

Somewhere near the top of the building, the lift stopped and let them out into a stark white corridor. Frosted glass, peppered with doors, lined one side. Jansen led Hannah along the corridor and round a corner to a single, very large door that interrupted the glass.

He knocked twice and slid the door open.

Hannah had met some interesting people in her time, but Ms White definitely ranked in the top ten of oddities. It was difficult to tell if she'd started as an organic, a synth or something else.

The face was young and definitely feminine, with subtle make-up that highlighted her thin lips and high cheekbones. The head it was pulled onto was definitely synthetic. A long neck, articulated so it could move in any direction, extend and retract, linked the head to a body that was more like that of a giant metal scorpion or spider held up on a dozen legs. A pair of human arms extended from the body, in approximate place of where arms should be, but other appendages bristled at other points of the body, materialising and retracting as needed to control the various interfaces around the room. Encased in the underside of the body, linked to the arms, were parts of a human female body; it had been fragmented, so that everything appeared in approximately the right place. Clear panels covered it, but there was no clothing, leaving the skin exposed.

"This must be Captain Sinclair? A pleasure," Ms White said in a lovely little voice, somewhat at odds with the mechanical monstrosity of her body. One of the human arms extended, reaching out the ten feet to Hannah on an extendable, flexible limb.

Without missing a beat, Hannah accepted the hand and gave it a firm shake. It was definitely organic.

"Has Mr Black told you why I wish to meet with you?"

"No, he's been rather tight-lipped about it all."

She smiled, her head moving closer on the extending neck. "How typical. All smoke and mystery, especially with those silly shades on inside."

Jansen smiled. "I have sensitive eyes."

Two chairs appeared, delivered by two of the extra arms from elsewhere in the large office. Hannah sat as soon as it was placed.

"You'll have to excuse my appearance," she said. "The last few days have been rather trying and I wasn't given time to make myself presentable."

Ms White giggled. "Not at all, Captain. I have no appreciable concept of aesthetics as most people understand them. As you can probably see."

Bobbing her head non-committedly, she smiled. "You possess a unique elegance, if you don't mind me saying."

"Thank you," she replied. "Most people, even in this day and age, recoil at the sight of me for one reason or another. Even today, people are so attached to augmenting within the realms of their pre-given form. Too often I'm forced to contract into my vaguely original form to prevent people staring stupidly at me."

"But enough about me, it's you I'm interested in. Or more specifically, what you are rumoured to have found."

Hannah made one big exaggerated nod as she smiled humourlessly. "Oh, is that so?"

She nodded, her neck rippling. "Well, I've been interested in a few of the companies you have shares in for some years, as have the other Whites, but I hear you have acquired a collection of antiques that would be worth a gigantic fortune."

"Let me guess, you'll repair my ship for free if I hand my find over?"

Drawing her head back, eyes wide, Ms White gasped. "Nothing so vulgar! No, no, I will pay for any find you have, but I want first look at all of it. Exclusive rights to buy what I want before you put it to general sale."

It wasn't a bad deal, but it would suppress prices. Competition could easily drive the price into the range of small government GDP, but there was no way Spectrum was going to pay such high prices.

"Seems fair," she lied.

A tablet appeared under her nose with a contract on it. She read it, thoroughly, which was unusual, but necessary. The wording was sufficiently vague that it could be applied to anything from bulkheads to atoms and bacteria to the remains of the crew. Of particular interest was the specific reference to reproductive genetic materials.

As she went to sign, she became aware of something hovering near her head. Looking up, she found an arm a few inches from her face, rather menacingly shaped into a dagger.

"Impressive," she said, nonchalantly even as her heartrate tried to hit four figures. "Not often you see someone create a stiletto so accurately. Did you have one incorporated?"

Ms White drew it back a little. "Why, yes, I did. I must say, I misread you; you are far more enlightened than I gave you credit. I take it you understand the meaning?"

"If I break contract, that stiletto will be inside me."

The stiletto reverted to a hand. "I had not planned it so literally, but given your appreciation of my little knife, yes. Keep anything back, sell anything before I've had a chance to pass on it, and it will be inside you. And I will make sure you live a very long time."

Hannah could quite easily believe it. The only way to alter a limb like that was to have active nanotech, which explained the comment about retracting into her original form. That meant she had to have a fully functional Nano Control Unit, a piece of Unity era tech that was rarer than unicorn tears, all to herself. The others she knew about were only partially functional, allowing very specific application of the nanotech inherent in all humans from a bygone era.

"I could just sell you the whole lot?" she offered, praying that would solve any risk of perforation.

"Oh, dear me, no. I only want what will be useful. Trying to sell the rest on would be tiresome and raise a lot of questions."

Pressing her thumb to the tablet, Hannah sighed.

Breaking the Bank

"You set me up."

He shrugged without stopping or looking at her. "I had no idea she was going to do that, honestly. Ms White never takes much of an interest in my activities or contacts." He finally looked at Hannah and shrugged again. "I thought she had some cargo she wanted moving."

Hannah scowled and snorted. Jansen had always been a pain, but she'd never expected him to sell her out at knife point.

"Let me make it up to you," he said, smiling. "How about a drink?"

"Over your dead body," she shot back. "I've got another appointment to get to."

"How about after?"

It was pathetic that he was still trying to chase her after all this time. She put her middle finger to her lips and looked mockingly thoughtful as she walked backwards away from him. "Oh, yes, repairs. Those will take weeks. How about the 31st of February next year?"

Jansen pursed his lips, glowering. He shook his head once, turned on his heel and slunk away.

Sending a quick message, Hannah made her way towards the nearest train station to make the journey to the upper reaches of the station. Kelly was already waiting excitedly when she arrived at the uncared-for station.

"Hey, what's up with your face?" she asked.

Hannah snorted. "I think I just got roofied," she replied. "Not literally," she added, seeing the look of absolute horror that exploded onto Kelly's face. "Spectrum made an offer I'll be dead to refuse."

Squeezing her shoulder, Kelly sighed. "I'm sorry. Do you want to do this later?" What she meant was; "Do you want to recover before I raid your bank account and give you a heart attack?".

"No, it's fine. Retail therapy, a girl's day out," she replied as the train rattled into the station.

It was a good half hour of rattling between stations as people trudged on and off. The two women sat quietly, watching the world go by. Neither really knew what to say about the whole thing.

Eventually, they arrived at a gleaming white marble station. The entire platform and building looked like it had been carved from a single piece of stone and was polished hourly to maintain the glorious finish. This was a station used by the big money.

The streets were wide and, in some places, lined with fruit trees. High walls surrounded large villas, set in artificial landscapes, the armed guards watching them almost blending in completely. Walking past was greeted with the barking of dogs, big and small, defending their masters' holdings from interlopers.

Normally, Hannah would only be in such an area to meet a client or collect delicate (illegal) cargo that had to bypass customs. She'd found that the easiest way to smuggle small, high value items around was fake body parts; since her legs were, sadly, not hollow, she'd had to be creative. Fortunately, few customs officials were willing to cross a heavily pregnant woman, so a fake bump was the general go to.

At least today, there would be no need for that.

The Solatronix Clinic was a low building, sat on the edge of a park with a few very classy shops nearby. In a land of opulence, the clinic was asserting itself by being understated.

Inside was similar. The reception was clean and clinical, a few slowly changing holo-images of their headline services, products and testimonies from satisfied customers. Although they specialised in synthetics, they also did cybernetic and biological modifications.

Kelly walked up to the receptionist, who was forcing a smile just enough to cover her questioning look. "Hi, I have an appointment," she said, displaying her appointment note.

"Oh, yes, Dr Mannheim will be with you shortly," the receptionist said. "Please, have a seat." She looked passed her to Hannah, who was failing at not looking shifty. "Can I help you?"

"I'm with her. I'm her sugar mama," she added, seeing the questioning look. Kelly whacked her on the arm.

Before they could sit, an older gentleman in a tweed suit and white coat shambled into the room. He smiled brightly, like a kindly grandfather. "Ah, you're here. Marvellous, marvellous. I'm Dr Derek Mannheim and I'll be your consultant. Please, follow me."

Introductions continued as Kelly and Hannah were led down a corridor to an office.

"You'll have to excuse me, it's not often we get a, please excuse the phrase, a project as extensive as yours without it being the result of an accident," he continued, ushering them into an untidy office.

Books were scattered across the office, showing various procedures for modifying synthetics. Mannheim had to dig the chairs out from under them to allow the two women to sit.

"Now, I've reviewed the proposal you sent through," he continued as he poured coffee without asking if anyone wanted any. "It's feasible, but you are basically asking for a near full rebuild; it might be easier to take your neural net out and install it in a custom build."

Kelly winced slightly. "Perhaps, but I find the idea unsettling. Silly, I know, but if you can work on me, I'd prefer it."

He nodded. "A perfectly human response," he said with a warm smile, bobbing his head. "It's all doable, although, I have made a list of some possible adjustments," he continued handing a tablet over. "Most are upgrades that are on special offer or slight component changes for better performance. There is also a full list of our current offers, but I will say, your frame is already rather, ehm, full."

Hannah gave Kelly a sidelong look up and down. "Not to be a killjoy, but money is not unlimited," she said, looking back to Mannheim.

His smile was a little weaker as he handed her a tablet with the estimated price. "There are a number of offers, discounts and promotions that I've applied. And we'll discount against any recovered components once assessed."

The price was actually slightly lower than Kelly's original estimate, but it was still incredibly painful to look at. Hannah would not have considered herself a miser, or even a greedy woman, but she always felt unease at parting with large sums of money.

"Now, there are a few things I need to go over with you," he said, looking again to Kelly. "You are asking to replace vast quantities of your mechanical components with organics. This will have the effect of considerably shortening your lifespan and reduce your durability to that of near a normal human.

"For instance, while your net will still survive hard vacuum, the rest of you would perish. In emergency shutdown mode, your net might survive. Dermal damage results in scarring, you will need to eat and drink, although we plan to leave your charge plates and a small battery in place for emergencies."

Kelly nodded silently. As she was, her lifespan could easily be five or six hundred years with careful maintenance, but after her surgery, she'd have a lifespan similar to a human; maybe two centuries or so. She'd age, just like a normal human, and eventually die of an age-related ailment, excluding accidents.

She looked at the proposed specs for her future self. Her frame would remain mechanical, acting as a skeleton with a small amount of synthetic muscle to move it. Over that would be organic muscle, fats and skin. Most of her power plant would be removed to make room for organs that would provide nutrients for her organics and power for her synthetics. Through healthy eating and exercise, she could promote muscle growth, but by over indulging and a sedentary lifestyle, she could become fat.

"The one bit that is a little unpredictable relates to your cycle," Mannheim said. "Until we install your reproductive organs and set up the hormone regulators, it's difficult to say how you will react."

She frowned. "I don't understand," she replied, glancing at Hannah, hoping she might have some idea.

As it was, she did. "Basically, until you've had a period, no one knows if you'll PMS like a bitch."

Mannheim coughed and played with his tie. "I would not have said it quite like that, but in essence, yes. There are more details, but I don't think now is the time to get into that."

Hannah snorted. "Typical male attitude; he might be the one giving you a menstrual cycle, but he's too scared to actually talk about it."

"Technically, Dr One-Sigma will be doing that part of the surgery. They are our foremost reproductive specialist," he corrected, trying to get away from the topic. "How about I give you two some time to talk about this. If you're happy, I can take you in immediately for the pre-check and we can start as soon as the 50% deposit hits the corporate account."

He got up, knocked a pile of books which he frantically tried to recover before letting them collapse and scuttled out.

For several minutes, they sat quietly as Kelly scrolled aimlessly on her tablet. "Is this what you want?"

She looked up. "I want to be human, but most importantly, I don't want to look like this anymore. I know it's a lot, and there are a few things I can take off to bring the price – what are you doing?"

Hannah was tapping her wrist to her tablet. "Paying the deposit," she replied as though she was paying for a coffee.

Kelly gaped at her. "Just like that? You're happy to pay all that money just because I asked?"

She shrugged. "I'll get it all back. For the next fifty years, you'll get exactly ten goldcoins or one one hundredth of smaller jobs as payment," she replied with another little shrug and a playful look of apology.

"That's not what we agreed! Ten goldcoin a job? How am I meant to live on that?" She watched as Hannah tried to smother a smile and frowned at her. "You're pulling my leg."

"Well, don't make such a fuss over the money."

Kelly glared at her, even as she smiled. "Just you wait; I'll get you back for that one."

"Just don't pull my leg in case it falls off."

Dr Mannheim popped his head in the door, causing yet another small avalanche of books. "I see the deposit is in. If you are ready, Dr One-Sigma will take you for your pre-op. Captain Sinclair, we have some things to discuss as well."

Behind him stood an androgenous person in a similar white coat. They smiled and escorted Kelly away to one of the examination rooms, leaving Mannheim with Hannah.

He sat down at his desk and started searching for something while mumbling to himself. "Ah, there. Anyway, there are some legalities I need to address with you," he said, pulling yet another tablet out from the mounds of books. "As Kelly's owner, no, no, I am aware that she is now sentient, but technically, you still own her until we administer the sentience testing."

Hannah settled back in her chair a little. This was the bit that had worried her. She had paperwork that proved she "owned" Kelly. It was, naturally, completely fake.

"I'm also aware that you are not her legal owner according to the Synthetic Register," he continued.

She pursed her mouth and gripped the arms of the chair. "Well, that's because he left her in a dumpster to be disposed of," she replied. "And left her awake."

Mannheim blinked a few times before slumping in his chair, wiping his hand over his face. Looking at the ceiling, he shook his head a few times. "I can't believe anyone could be so callous, even him."

"You know him?"

He nodded. "There was an issue about twenty years ago when we caught several staff at one of our clinics moonlighting. I fear one of my former colleagues may be responsible for what happened to Kelly; I recognised some of his signature sculpting of synthetics to be used as prostitutes."

For a moment he sat looking at a random shelf, almost as though he'd forgotten Hannah was even in the room. She left him to his thoughts, watching as the mix of horror and anger swirled there.

"Should I assume you aren't going to report me?" she asked when he looked back to her.

"I've already updated the Register to align it with your documents. The fact she wasn't reported stolen supports that idea she was cast off. She wouldn't be the first," he replied.

Pouring more coffee, he promptly ignored it as he handed over the tablet. "You'll need to release her to us to complete the work and conduct the sentience testing so that we can transfer her ownership to herself."

Taking the tablet, she started to read through the pages and pages of legal drivel.

"Since Solatronix is, in some small way, possibly partially responsible for Kelly's condition, I hope you'll accept a small bargain in exchange for your silence on the matter."

She stopped reading and dropped the tablet onto her lap. "Oh?"

He nodded several times. "The Register change is free, out of good faith. In exchange for you never mentioning this, little embarrassment –"

"Embarrassment?" she cut in, tilting her head. "Try 'traumatising years of hell' and you might scratch the surface, just."

He flailed his hands slightly, trying to keep her a bit quieter. "We'll cook the books on the parts we recover," he said quickly. "Given what's been done to her, most of Kelly's parts will be worthless. Our standard practise when those of us that know of the unpleasantness encounter a survivor is that we massively overestimate the value of the parts. They have a shelf life, so we ensure that they are never a match for anyone else and just bin them."

It seemed a little too good to be true.

"Okay, but why? Why do you care?"

Mannheim looked at his desk and signed a little. "Professionals should have standards and that some of our own would go against that is an affront," he replied.

"Each of us that do this have our reasons. My daughter is synthetic – I'm sterile, so building a daughter made sense," he explained, blushing a little. "I'd probably kill anyone that treated her the way Kelly and others like her have been treated."

Hannah nodded. There was perhaps a touch of a warning in his tone. What was it with people threatening her today?

She returned to reading the legal documents. Most of it was the usual nonsense that wasn't applicable, or she had already violated. At each section, she signed dutifully until she came to the final disclaimer.

"What does it mean: 'I the signatory acknowledge and accept that surgery poses a risk of: death; complications resulting in life changing conditions; temporary or permanent disabilities; any unforeseen outcome that is not optimal'?" she asked. "Are you saying that she might die?"

He bought himself some time by taking a long drink of coffee. Hannah's stare was nearly powerful enough to start it boiling as he drank.

"There are always risks, especially with such an extensive procedure," he replied. "That's what the pre-op is for. We'll get a baseline and decide how to proceed."

"What sort of complications are we talking about?" she pressed.

"Could be minor component failure to actuate; some of the non-essential add-ons," he replied before chewing his lip for a moment. "Could be organ failure or rejection, facial paralysis, sensory organ failure…"

Hannah thrust the tablet back at him. "I'm not signing until I know the actual risks."

It was over an hour before the pre-op was completed. Hannah had waited rather impatiently to have a frank discussion about the risks. She was finally let into the examination room, where Kelly was already sitting on a bed in a gown.

"Dr Mannheim said you have some concerns?" Dr One-Sigma said as way of greeting. They were wringing their hands slightly.

Kelly looked up at her, a little frown passing over her features.

"What's the risk of this going wrong?" she asked, bluntly. "Death, critical failures, major failures?"

They grimaced a little. "Death sits at less than a tenth of a percent," they replied. "Which is about average for such a procedure. There is a 13% chance of something reasonably major going wrong during or after. Surgery will take about ten days with a further four for testing and recovery to reduce the risk further."

"13%? There's a one in eight chance this could be a disaster?" she replied.

"That's actually about half the normal rate," they answered, trying to sound upbeat. "And by taking two weeks, it'll be more like 7%."

It didn't work.

"Can we have a moment?"

One-Sigma slipped out without any argument, closing the door firmly.

Kelly was looking at her feet. "It's my life and my body," she said softly.

Hannah swept a hand over her forehead and through her hair as she wobbled around a little. "I know, but it is a big risk. Are you sure you want to take this big a risk?"

"Getting onto a ship is a huge risk and we do that every day," she replied. "You were a fighter pilot; death and critical injury was what you did for a living." She crossed her arms and huffed. "I did offer to cut down on some of the extras."

"It's not the money," she replied, crouching down to Kelly's eyeline. "I actually quite like you and I'd hate for this to go wrong." Gently, she took one of her hands. "Kelly, I don't want to see you end up in a worse state, but if you want to go through with this, I need you to be absolutely sure."

She squeezed her hand and smiled. "I'm absolutely sure I want to do this. I have to do this."

Standing up, Hannah nodded. "Okay, okay, if you are absolutely certain. But no dying on the table, that's an order."

"Aye, Captain!" she replied, jumping up, before clapping her gown back down, blushing slightly that her over energetic jump had nearly been a little bit revealing. "There is, just in case things go wrong, one thing I'd like to do before I go under the knife."

Nodding, Hannah had to admit it was a fair enough thing to have a request. Of course, she refused to entertain the idea she'd die, so it was an indulgence. When had she become so willing to indulge others like this? Who was she kidding; she'd always been soft on the crew.

Her musings were interrupted in a manner that caught her completely off guard, yet in a way that had she had her wits about her, would not have been unexpected.

When Kelly pulled out of the kiss, she was bright red. She licked her lips and smiled weakly. "I, ehm, just wanted to know what it would be like, just in case I don't come back. Sorry."

As Hannah stepped forward, she shrank back. She fully expected a telling off, or worse, for taking such a liberty.

Instead, she kissed her lightly and quickly once, twice and finally a third time in rapid succession. "Don't die and you might get another," she said with a coy smile. "I'll see you in two weeks."

Turning on her heel, she headed for the door, more to stop herself going in for more. Before leaving, she smiled and waved to Kelly, who was still a little too stunned to do anything but wave back dumbly.

The Guild

"Okay, I'm going to ask; did something really good happen or has the idea of parting with vast quantities of money driven you mad?" Annie asked. "Because the silly grin was not expected. I was sure you'd be wailing, crying, begging for the money to come back. A right Scrooge, if I'm being honest."

Hannah shook her head, but continued to smile. "I'm horrified you think so little of me."

"Uh-huh," she replied. "You pretended to be deaf when I asked for a new warp conversion matrix. And an exotic particle manipulator for the forward particle lance. And when I wanted drinking horns for the mess."

She merely shrugged and continued to drift along, heading for the Scottish Guildhall.

Annie huffed with a smile. "Fine, keep your secrets. Now, business. I've spoken to some clansmen and they have what I need," she said, handing over a list.

As soon as she saw it, Hannah stopped dead. "What the hell is this? Can *Sigyn* even support that?"

"Of course," she replied as though talking to a child. "I thought it best to upgrade since you managed to burnout what we already had. The price is a bit steep –"

"A bit?"

She glared slightly. "But I've managed to call in some favours, make a few trades and earn some favours to get a better price. Now, Great-Uncle Joe would be able to really help squeeze the price; how attached are you to about a third of your liver?"

Hannah stopped cold. "I am not selling organs for a slipstream drive."

"A third of an organ," she replied, looking a little greedily at Hannah's abdomen. "It'll regenerate, you won't even miss it."

"Give him your liver!"

"I can't," she replied, hands on her hips. "I've had to mod the hell out of mine to keep up with me. Giving up a third would land me in the same position as Joe. The docs won't give him an artificial one, since he's broken four so far…"

Scandalised at the very thought, she gripped the area over her liver defensively. "Sod off. And you're not getting Kelly's old one before you even think about it."

Annie rolled her eyes. "Of course not. It wouldn't last a week. Oh well, I guess it's the burlesque show instead."

"The what?"

"Oh, for God's sake, I'm joking," she laughed. "Your ass might be wide, but it's too flat, as is your chest, to get any favours out of this lot. I'd have more luck with a plank of wood in a corset."

Chewing an invisible wasp, Hannah took a deep breath, rather offended by the comments, even though she knew they were in jest. Especially when she'd put a nice dress on for visiting the Guild that, if she did say so, flattered what little curves she had. "Why do I keep you onboard?"

"Best engineer in the galaxy."

"Best I can afford. That is not a compliment."

The Guildhall was a massive, grand building. It had been carved from the very stone of the asteroid that Roanapur inhabited. Scenes of people working (mostly burly men with bulging muscles and stunning women with bulging bosoms), ancient battles, cryptic runes, poems, food and drink covered it.

There were times when Hannah felt that the Scots had bought into their own stereotypes so much that they actually believed them. Of course, she'd never voice that to anyone but Annie; if she said such a thing inside, she'd end up outside and probably inside out.

Annie bound up the stairs to the massive wooden door and pushed it open. Almost immediately there was an explosion of noise from inside, which went quiet before starting all over again. Normally, people used the side door; the main door was only for special occasions or when someone wanted to make an entrance.

Hannah, as instructed, waited on the threshold as Annie was swept away in a sea of incomprehensible noise. She'd been expected, so everyone had turned out to greet her, even though only about four people had met her before. Any excuse for a party, apparently. Which explained the dress and the fact Annie had squeezed herself into one as well.

Eventually, Annie managed to calm the excited crowd and directed them towards Hannah. A stout older woman walking with a large, ornate stick waddled up to her. She looked her up and down, snorted and nodded.

"Aye, she'll dae," she declared.

Before Hannah could figure out what that meant, two girls had appeared and promptly fastened a tartan shawl to her. It was only then she noticed that everyone was either wearing a shawl or plaid in various tartans.

"Whatever you do, don't take it off," Annie said as she linked arms with her. "That's a guest tartan, Flower of Scotland, and shows you're a welcome guest. Without it, they'll likely throw you out. Literally."

Over the next half hour, she was steered around various people, introduced and moved on. She still had no idea who any of them were, what they did or why she was meeting them, but in the spirit of things, greeted them warmly and accepted any greeting that came.

After that, she found herself separated from Annie and sitting in a massive tartan wingback armchair in a room that looked like it had walked straight out of "Hunting Lodge Monthly" with a group of men who were, rather politely, speaking in languages she could understand rather than the protected Gaelic or Scots.

"Oh, dear, I can't believe these uncouth buggers haven't offered you a drink yet," a middle-aged woman said as she bustled up. "Will you be wanting a pint of heather ale? It's a wee bit thinner than the stouts."

Hannah smiled weakly. "I'm not drinking at the moment," she replied sheepishly.

The woman nodded sagely. "Ah, got you. Half a lager shandy it is."

Before Hannah could protest that she wanted no alcohol, the woman was gone. She looked around the room, feeling completely overwhelmed by the whole thing. It reminded her of the first time she'd been allowed in an Officer's Lounge as a freshly minted Pilot Officer.

A tall tumbler of shandy appeared in her hand. Feeling it would be rude to refuse the drink, she took a sip, having subtly dipped a finger into it; her nail didn't go red, so it was alcohol free.

"Hello, you must be Captain Hannah Sinclair," a smooth voice said from beside her. "Gilmour Arbuthnot, Master of the Propulsion Guild and current Laird of Roanapur. I hear you need a slipstream drive?"

Hannah looked up at the quite handsome gentleman that was now perched on the arm of her chair. Curiously, he wore a small pair of spectacles, which since he was looking over them, were likely part of his costume, dressed as he was in an ancient style of tweed suit that made him initially appear older than he was.

"Yes, I am," she replied, a little taken aback by the directness.

He offered his arm to her, an invitation to take a walk away from the noise of the others. She accepted and followed him out of the room and towards a small balcony.

"I thought all the guild names were 'Mac'?" she asked, curious about his unusual name.

He smiled and chuckled. "Only the middle ranks. Apprentices use names that are alphabetically below 'Mac'. Once through that stage, position is defined in the names most commonly heard. Masters ascend beyond that."

She nodded. "Am I correct that you must be a very high-ranking Master?"

He laughed. It was rich and full, yet a little bitter at the edges. "Anywhere but here, you'd likely have to pay for an audience with me. As it is, I, like most that weren't initiated here, disgraced myself and was sent out of the way. It was worth it, though."

"Dare I ask?"

"You'd do better to ask your sister."

Rolling her eyes, Hannah growled a little. She was starting to wonder if there was anyone that Harry hadn't slept with and managed to get in trouble while doing it. She tried to smile. "Harry?"

Gilmour looked slightly surprised. "No, Helen."

"I'm sorry, did you say Helen?"

Stunned didn't even start to cover what Hannah was feeling; she'd always assumed that Helen had little interest in others, so to find out she'd managed to disgrace herself with a powerful Guild Master and keep it secret was a revelation. She was going to have so much fun teasing her. What had they managed to do?

Realising he might have just put his foot in it, he moved on to the topic at hand. "Slipstream," he said quite abruptly. "You need it. Annie sent through a request.

Very high spec for your ship, but easily installed. Probably take about two months to get everything in, working, tested and such."

"I don't have two months. I've got two weeks."

He laughed. Then he looked at her, decided she was being serious and laughed again. "I can tell you that that doesn't work in real life. We might be Scottish, but Scotty we are not. The drive will have to be built, installed, tested. A lengthy process."

"How much?"

"Hm?"

The talk of business was quickly becoming annoying, but beating up a Guild Master was unlikely to get the result she wanted. "How much to 'grease the wheels'?"

Gilmour sighed before chuckling. "That timeline is the wheels greased. I'm sorry, it's the best I can do. No one else can do it quicker for such a high-quality drive, not to mention repairs to your cooling system. Even a seat-of-your-pants install would be a month."

Hannah was quickly wishing she'd asked for a stronger drink, but she knew where that would lead. As entertaining as it would likely be for the others, she didn't think swinging from the light fittings would be appropriate.

"I guess I don't have much choice."

"Sadly, no, you don't." He shrugged. "Don't let your face trip you; try and have some fun."

As dramatically as he'd appeared, Gilmour swept away in a swish of plaid and coattails, departing back into the party as he greeted a young woman.

Downing her drink, Hannah dumped the glass on a table and stood looking out over the vista below. The balcony looked out over the private Guild dock, a small but busy series of berths.

"I see you spoke with Gilly," Annie said as she joined her on the balcony.

"Two months, that's the best your favours, trades and crap can get me?" she replied. Looking at her for a moment, she frowned. "I seem to remember someone saying she'd be kicked out for inappropriate dress?"

Annie looked down and adjusted her dress a little. "Inside rules are different to outside rules."

"Dare I ask how many men have been lost in there already?"

She shrugged. "Few ladies, too. And possibly a peanut, not sure exactly where it went when I dropped it."

Hannah rolled her eyes. She was starting to worry that she was doing it so often they'd start to spin of their own accord. "How long do we have to stay?"

Annie hugged her. "A while, to be polite. Come on, you'll enjoy it when you get into it. There'll be a meal, drink, dancing, drink, gossip, a wee dram or two, games, drink, speeches, drink and drink."

Hannah wondered if this was normal for the Guild, or if there was some other special occasion going on. She suspected that was the case given everyone was dressed in their finery. No doubt Annie had planned arriving in the middle of it to increase impact and palm greasing.

"I'll let you lead when we dance," she said, trying to tempt her into lightening up a little.

"That's a lie, you can never resist leading," she said, managing a smile. "Especially since I'm unlikely to know any of the dances, unless the Hokey-Cokey is on the list."

With a giggle and shake of the head, Annie took a few steps and held her hand out. "I'm sure we can arrange it. Come on, you might even have some fun. You need it. It'll take your mind of tall, pretty and synthetic currently undergoing surgery."

The evening quickly changed into a formal dinner as people we seated at tables of ten in the main Guildhall. It turned out they were celebrating their end of year results. Annie had taken advantage of this for two reasons: one, lots of people would be attending so it was easy to talk to a lot of people; two, they'd all end up drunk and sign all sorts of agreements.

Annie and Hannah just had to keep their wits ahead of everyone else to press a small advantage.

Hannah was of the opinion it wouldn't stay that way.

Their table was near the back, filled with mostly younger Guild Members to the point that Annie was the most senior by some distance. They were also a curious lot. Next to Hannah was Julie, a cat-girl, and her partner James, who was human. A young man sat opposite that had four arms, sat by a woman that all the men would want to slow dance with (she had a second pair of breasts on her back, which Hannah thought must be a nightmare for sleeping and could think of no good reason to have). A woman with a narrow, pretty face that was overflowing her chair chatted to another woman with snake-like eyes and a forked tongue that, if not her partner, was certainly her squeeze for the evening. Finishing off the line up were two men with some obvious cybernetics that were gazing lovingly at each other while playfully sipping champagne.

Having forgotten all of the names, bar Julie and James because they were talking to her, Hannah felt a little overwhelmed. She was used to seeing all sorts of people, but the conversation was either love or Guild politics, neither of which she felt comfortable talking about.

"So, you managed to escape a whole fleet of Remnant ships?" Julie purred, her chin resting on a paw. "You must be so brave."

"I think I'd wet myself if faced with dozens of superior enemy ships," James added.

"Well, there were usually only a few at one time," Hannah replied, unsure if boasting was an acceptable pastime here. Had it been old friends, then *Sigyn* would have been dodging three fleets and taken out at least two battleships by sparking a coronal mass ejection while skimming a star.

James chuckled. "So modest, you really mustn't be. Wine?"

She covered her glass and managed a thin smile. "No, thank you. I'm not drinking at the moment."

They looked at each other, then at her.

"Are you…?"

Cringing internally, she could feel her smile faltering. "No, I've a component, from my Navy days, that needs some repairs. Alcohol currently doesn't agree with it," she lied. "A glass or two and I'd be swinging from the chandelier, probably wearing less than was seemly."

"Sounds like a very good reason to give you a drink," Julie replied as her tail ran up Hannah's leg.

"Which Navy?" James asked.

"Commonwealth."

He clicked his fingers and nodded. "Yes, of course. You're too proper to be a Yank and lacking in the stick-up-your-arse to be a Peacekeeper."

The starter appeared. A traditional scotch broth was placed down with thick chunks of bread in baskets for sharing. Talk stalled for a moment as everyone tucked in.

"So, Annie, I hear you are the Chief Engineer on a ship," the rotund woman said, pointing with her fifth piece of bread. "Is it exciting or do the day-to-day tasks just blur into each other? I mean, is there actually much to do normally?"

"Normally there's a lot of balancing acts to perform, just keeping everything spot on," she replied between slurps of soup. "The real fun is figuring out how to make a thruster out of two tins and a spray deodorant, or trying to repair a warp drive while it's running."

The conversation quickly descended into a pissing contest as everyone tried to outdo the others with ridiculous tails of various feats. They didn't stop when a selection of fish dishes was placed down, everyone digging in as they continued. Even Hannah joined in, regaling some of her stories of death-defying flying.

After the fish course came the main. An array of vegetables was placed out to go with sausages (links and lorne), stews of various types, haggis and guga.

Hannah lifted some of the guga, thinking it was chicken. As she started to chew, she slowed. "What is that?" she asked. It did taste a bit like chicken, but with fishy notes as well.

"Guga," Annie replied as if that made things clearer. "It's gannet. A delicacy when cooked properly."

"And it is cooked to perfection," the rotund woman declared as she heaped more on her plate. It was easy to see how she'd ended up so round, but how her face and neck were so thin could only be through surgery.

The showmanship continued, reaching perilous heights of daftness. Finally, Hannah decided to play her trump card and told the (heavily edited for general consumption) tale of the Battle of Hafan. It had the desired effect of silencing her companions, who could only stare in awe, and the unexpected effect of a tail stroking her leg again and repeatedly.

"Well, who would have thought we had the Hero of the Commonwealth with us?" one of the cyborg men said, raising his glass slightly. The others followed suit in a small, but sincere salute.

After dessert and coffee, music started and Hannah was immediately a popular dance partner in paired dances and the person everyone wanted as part of their group in the set dances. Until they discovered she was a pretty hopeless dancer. Most of the time she was dragged around the dance floor like a mop. Despite this, James and Julie continually offered to dance with her.

During one of the dances where partners changed, she found herself being flung into the open arms of Gilmour.

"Well, hello again, lass," he said as he twirled her a few times before pulling her to a respectable distance for a short waltz. "Have you considered my offer of assistance?"

She smiled dizzily. "I thought I'd already accepted based on having no other options?"

He looked a little wounded. "My dear, you make me sound so mercenary. Of course, there are other ways that the wheels can be greased to reduce cost, if not improve time…"

It came time to change partners again, but he pulled her back and nodded to the older woman beside them to skip on with a sharp and vicious jerk of his head. She looked peeved, but took the hint.

"In three days, I have a shipment of a very expensive, highly taxed adhesive coming into the lower docks," he continued over the music. "My courier is going to guide it through customs as a," he searched for the correct phrase.

"Smuggled item?" Hannah suggested.

"So unpoetic, but yes. I need someone to escort the courier to my shipyard the next morning," he continued. "The courier can't come straight to the yard or suspicions will be aroused. Show them about, take in some sights, then deliver. Deal?"

Whatever she'd done in a past life, Hannah felt the universe was making her pay for it. She must have drowned kittens, kicked puppies or told kids Santa was invented by the Coca-Cola Company.

"Sure."

He smiled warmly. "Excellent. I'll send the files you need to you tomorrow." And with that, it was partner change time and she was discarded in favour of a younger, bustier model.

When the music paused – it never actually properly stopped between dances – she went and sat down to rest. Even artificial feet could hurt after a while and she was too full to enjoy the dancing.

Julie sat very close to her and offered a tumbler of brightly coloured cocktail. "It's okay," she said, "it's a mocktail."

As she accepted it, she dipped her fingernail into the liquid. It didn't go red, so no alcohol in the drink, and it didn't go green, so it hadn't been spiked. She sipped and found it fruity and very easy to drink.

Again, Julie's tail found her leg and wrapped gently around it. "Would you care to dance?"

Before she could reply, Hannah was on her feet again, being dragged about by the energetic young woman. She was beginning to think that she might have lost control of the whole situation and was now a living ball being passed about for the locals' amusement. Despite that, it was a lot of fun and she found herself laughing as she whizzed around the dancefloor.

Over the course of the night, she managed to make a few connections with various people worth getting to know. Aside from Julie's tail going for her leg whenever she was in range, everyone was polite, even the drunks.

Annie was making similar inroads; except she'd already traded saliva with a number of the prettier Guild Members.

The band took a short break to let people get themselves together before they planned to do something called "Orcadian Strip the Willow". Annie landed heavily and haphazardly in her chair, definitely the worse for copious amounts of drink.

"Getting over Casper, are you?" Hannah asked, leaning in. That had been a mistake as Annie promptly fell against her and started to drunkenly kiss her neck.

She replied in Gaelic, but the thrust of the comment was clear.

"Are you going to manage the next dance, or should I just prop you up on the bar?"

Throwing herself to her feet, she held her hands out. When Hannah didn't take them immediately, she shook them at her, slightly petulantly. With some reluctance, the offer was accepted.

She staggered a step forward and leant against Hannah, resting her head on her shoulder. "I love you," she murmured into her neck, wrapping her arms lazily around her hips. "Not like, want to sleep with you; although, I wouldn't say no. I love you like a sister. You're a good friend."

"Well, I love you too," Hannah replied. "Even if you are as drunk as a skunk."

The band started to warm-up, warning everyone to take their places. Annie jumped a little, narrowly avoiding headbutting Hannah in the jaw before pulling her to the rapidly growing lines running diagonally across the hall. She placed her between two young women before retreating to the opposite line to stand between two burly men, one in a kilt, the other in tartan trousers.

"I don't know this one," Hannah whispered to the girl on her left.

"It's easy, just watch."

Easy to grasp? Yes. Easy to survive? No.

Hannah watched as at the head of the lines, an old man and an old woman bounced spryly towards each other, crossed their arms about the wrist and held hands. At some musical cue that she completely missed, they started to spin. Not a slow, waltzing spin, but a fearsome whirling as both leant back, pulling on the other. They released and immediately went for the new head of the line on the opposite side of where they'd started, linked arms at the elbow to dance in a circle to then go back to the middle and their partner to do the same. From there, they started to move up the line.

As soon as there was space, the new pair at the head of the line started to spin. They were more controlled, but still going at some rate.

"It's terrible form," the girl said. "A country dancer would be affronted by this, but at a ceilidh, this is how it is," she said, clapping along to the music. "Watch out for some of the young men; the wee arseholes will try to almost throw you. It's sport to them; just give back harder."

It wasn't the men that worried Hannah. She had Annie as a partner and was sure she'd be trying to achieve at least warp speed in the spin.

After a few poor attempts, she started to get the hang of being turned by the passing men. As predicted, one young man, a devilish glint in his eye, spun her so hard and fast that she skidded back into place, staggered.

Eventually she found herself standing, hand in hand, with Annie, waiting for some non-existent instruction to start. To her surprise, Annie didn't try spinning her too fast, although that was a relative term.

As she was released, she dizzily started for the wrong line, but was quickly pointed in the right direction and guided by the man in tartan trousers. The first few spins were at a modest speed, but as she got the hang of it, everything started to get a bit faster. By the time she reached the end of the line, which was never ending and had to be coiling around the whole station, she was flushed and giggling.

When she made it back to the top, Annie had a wicked smile and chewed her bottom lip a little as she nodded her head in time to the music. On cue, she started to spin, but this time she was completely out of control.

For a horrifying moment, Hannah was sure her right leg was going to come off and be sent flying into the dancers or the band. Dizzy, confused and slightly ill, she was thankful when the music drew a deep sigh to finish when she was only a third of the way up. She clapped as everyone else did.

"Sorry, I had to give you a good spin," Annie said as she sorted Hannah's shawl, which was half escaped.

The band started to call for everyone to form a circle and people rushed to get into position. Annie pulled Hannah along to get into place. Some around the circle held hands, while others crossed their arms to hold hands.

"Is there a reason for people crossing their arms?" she asked.

Annie gave a half shrug. "Some folk cross their arms to start. Others wait until the right time to do it."

"And when's that?"

"You'll know. Do you know the words?"

Hannah looked perplexed. "What words?"

"Auld Lang Syne," she replied as if it was obvious, which to any Scot it would be.

"Sort of."

"Well, as long as you can get the chorus, you'll be fine."

If Hannah had thought everything up to now had been a riot, this was in a totally different league. They all sang, most very loudly, and either swung or shook their arms while, slowly, moving in and out, causing the circle to expand and contract haphazardly. When a verse that had something to do with "han" and "fiends", at least as far as she could make out, everyone crossed arms.

And went completely nuts.

At the next chorus, many people started to charge back and forth, with some being almost dragged along. All with riotous singing.

Just when she thought it was over, the band switched immediately into another song. Hannah sort of recognised the tune, but with so many people singing loudly, out of tune, off key and out of time, it was impossible to make out, especially while she was still being dragged back and forth as people carried on with the same actions from Auld Lang Syne.

When it ended, everyone cheered, clapped and celebrated. Hannah was starting to see where the Scots' reputation of being a hard people came from if this was how they partied.

People started to drift away, seeking out friends to say farewell to. A number of people Hannah had encountered over the night came over to present her with business cards and offers of assistance, should she ever need it.

"So, did you have fun?" James asked as he and Julie appeared.

"Yes, although I'm not sure how I survived."

Julie chuckled. "There must be a little bit of Scot in you after all." She looked to James and smiled. "Would you like to come back to our place for a wee post ceilidh drink?"

Hannah looked round to see where Annie was and found her with a glass of what had to be whisky. "I think I'd better make sure someone gets home."

"You're both welcome," James replied.

"Perhaps another time, but thank you. It's been fun."

James handed her a business card. She touched it, which automatically transferred their information into her contact book. "We might hold you to that," he said with a decidedly playful grin.

She said her farewells and went to retrieve Annie, who now seemed considerably more sober than she had been moments before.

"Did they ask you back to their place?"

"Yes, how did you know?"

"They have a little bit of a reputation for picking up visitors for more than just drinks," she replied. "Considering you've never once been on a date since I met you, I suspected you'd be unlikely to be up for that."

Hannah frowned as she opened and closed her mouth a few times. "Why not just say?"

"Didn't want you to be put off," she replied with a shrug. "They're very nice people."

"Are you calling me a prude?"

"When did you last have sex?"

She didn't answer.

"Come on, let's get you home before you drink the bar dry."

Augmented Realities

Emily looked at Carl and Aisha, pondering if it was wise to let them off the ship, even with an escort. They were going to be entering a hellhole in a time they didn't know.

"The Captain has managed to get you cover identities that should keep any suspicion off you," she said, handing them a tablet each. "You both come from a colony called Epoch, it was lost until about three hundred years ago and is culturally about as close to your time as you'll get."

She handed them a small, hand sized case. "You'll find contact lenses and earpieces inside. They'll translate for you and let you access the augmented reality that most of us get through our cybernetics."

Aisha looked at the contacts and the tiny, nearly invisible earpieces. "What sort of augmented reality are you talking about?"

"Adverts, some AI only appear via AR, some events make heavy use of it to limit noise and light pollution."

Carl was already putting his contacts in. Initially there was no difference, but then a small note appeared asking him to blink twice quickly while looking up to activate and down to deactivate.

"Wow, there is a lot we're not seeing," he said as the blank walls of the dock became covered in posters, 3D moving adverts and virtual signposts.

Jon appeared before him. "Can you see me?" he asked. "Oh, good. As long as you have the AR gear on, you can access me remotely."

Aisha placed her contacts in and carefully placed the earpieces in before smoothing her headscarf back into place. "It's not that different to what I used at Uni for virtual body studies."

Emily smiled. "Oh, good. Now, come on, I'll show you some of the better areas to visit."

The areas immediately around the berth were reasonably safe, but a few criminals prowled and would have no issue taking advantage of unsuspecting newcomers. And with Carl and Aisha being about ten thousand years out of date, they'd be easy pickings.

"Will Dr Mendoza not be joining us?" Aisha asked as they started to head away from *Sigyn*.

"No," Emily replied, ending that conversation. How would she explain that their Captain had left them in the care of a man that had been working, albeit under duress, for a group of fanatics that would likely want to dissect them? Letting Casper off the ship was out of the question until they were more certain of his loyalties.

That could very well be never, at least until they found a law enforcement group to take him.

They wandered away from the Harbour and towards a street market. Shops lined the sides of a large square, while stalls filled the centre, leaving pathways weaving between them. Trees grew randomly across the square, each offering an oasis for shoppers to sit.

"We'll move through quickly," Emily said as she looked for the easiest route to the far side. "This place will be swarming with pickpockets."

Considering they had nothing in their pockets, it wasn't a great threat to Carl and Aisha. Still, they started to look about for shady people, only to find nearly everyone looked like they were plotting. Mostly because they were.

Emily swore as she spotted two Purifiers wandering through the crowd. The chances of them realising who Carl and Aisha were, and what they were, was incredibly remote. But given the Remnant's fascination with all things ancient and pre-Unity, there was a risk they'd understand the Old Modern English the two of them spoke.

Not wanting to panic her charges, she kept going. The Purifiers moved off in the opposite direction towards a stall selling fruit.

"I have to ask," Aisha said as they cleared the square and headed down a wide corridor, "is religion still a thing in this time?"

"Yes, there are quite a few," Emily replied, still a little distracted. "Some are pretty harmless and others are more like cults. Of course, some see the Remnant as a religious cult and others see them as just another government. Same with the Peacekeepers."

"Is Christianity still alive?" Carl asked.

Dozens of different denominations appeared as a list before his eyes. The Catholic Church was still going strong, despite losing Earth. In fact, it had relocated to a massive mobile station call *The Holy See* that visited faithful systems from time to time. Various Protestant, Orthodox, Coptic denominations, and ones he'd never heard of, all had churches in most major settlements.

"And Islam?" Aisha asked.

A list appeared for her as well. It had weathered the millennia as well as Christianity and the other major world religions of the time.

Emily headed for one of the nicer shopping centres. "Do either of you need to talk to someone religious? I'm afraid everyone on the ship is pretty much irreligious. Well, unless you count the fact Annie worships whisky."

"At some point, I think I will," Aisha replied.

She stopped and took a step back, looking at two men standing outside the shopping centre. "Are those Pokémon?"

Looking back, Emily nodded. "Yeah. They had them in your time?"

"As computer games and cards," Carl replied. "Did someone figure out how to make them real?"

She laughed. "Of course not. Making real animals fight would be beyond cruel. They're AR," she replied. "If you turn your lenses off, you'll just see two men shouting at each other."

Interested in watching a real (if virtual) Pokémon battle, they moved closer to see how it would end.

"I can't believe this survived," Carl said. "I remember playing as a kid, but I thought it sort of died out in late Thirties."

"It was massive when I was a teenager," Emily replied. "It went out of fashion after that, but it never really dies out." She frowned for a moment. "In fact, it's quite odd how a lot of things like that start to go out of fashion, then suddenly make a resurgence."

They watched for a few more minutes before heading into the shops. A mix of small boutiques and larger department stores filled the building, accessed from walkways that spread out like a spider's web.

Curiously, there were a large number of clothes shops, book shops and ones selling foodstuffs.

"I thought you have replicators?" Carl said as he looked at a gentleman's suit shop, offering off the rail and custom measured suits for a price. It seemed a lot, but he'd yet to figure out the dollar to goldcoin rate.

"Well, yes," Emily replied. "Although, most are more like 3D printers than the replicators in Star Trek. There are some things that people just like having made the old way."

They bought coffee from a small stall in the middle of the concourse and found a bench to sit on for a moment. It was the strangest thing; the place seemed so much like shopping centres and malls of their time. Even the modded humans could easily just have been people passing through in costume for a convention or Comic-Con. The smells and sounds were strangely similar to the point it could easily be that the whole ten-thousand-year time skip was just a joke.

"Is sport still a thing?" Carl asked as he finished his coffee.

"Oh yeah, some people just live for it. There are a few sports bars around here, but they're not exactly the safest places."

"What sports are popular?" Aisha asked.

Emily pondered the question for a moment. "Well, football is right up there," she said. "Rugby has a big following, especially in the Commonwealth and Nihon Prefectures. Then there's snooker, athletics, sumo, cricket – although it's a bit niche, lots of different martial arts, and grifball is big in some places. As is shinty, hurling and curling."

"What is grifball?"

Grifball was an interesting sport in which two teams (numbers varied depending on the form) had to carry a ball into the other team's goal. Each player wore armour and carried a gravity baton. If struck by a baton, the armour locked up for a time and if the ground was struck, it could throw surrounding players into the air.

Records of who had invented it had been lost to time, although some believed it had evolved from some form of hurling.

"What type of football is it that's popular?" Carl asked. "Do you mean soccer?" Emily nodded.

"What about the one played with an oblong ball?"

"Do you mean rugby?"

No," he replied, shaking his head. "Players wear helmets. You have quarterbacks and touchdowns? Not sounding familiar at all?"

She wracked her brains. "Oh, I know what you mean. Yeah, only the United Systems Alliance play that. Same with baseball. Never understood how they can have a Galactic Series when no one else plays."

Aisha was trying not to laugh. "Are you saying that sumo wrestling is bigger than American football?"

"Assuming the game we just talked about was called American football in your time," Emily replied, chewing her lip slightly, "then yes. Sumo is, if you'll pardon the pun, big business. My husband's cousin is a rikishi, although, not a very successful one so far."

"Well, looks like you Yanks didn't managed to take over the galaxy," Aisha teased with a playful smile.

The two Purifiers they'd seen earlier turned a corner and looked at them. They appeared to consult for a moment before slowly moving on, trying to surreptitiously look at Emily and a tablet at the same time.

Hannah was not happy sitting in the middle of one of the less than safe sections of the Lower Harbour. Her instructions for the pick-up had been quite detailed and she liked them even less.

She'd been forced to wear a white dress with a blue floral pattern that was not her thing at all, a wide brimmed straw hat and sunglasses. Someone was having a really good laugh at her somewhere, and being dressed like a lady was a very good way to get attacked. At least she had two pistols hidden on her person.

The contact would also be wearing a dress, but with a yellow pattern. No other information had been given other than a pass phrase.

Half reading a magazine on home furnishing (which she had about as much interest in as eating her own legs), she tried to keep track of comings and goings. A few of the dock workers, rough looking characters in dirty clothes, glanced at her, but stopped just short of leering. The better dressed ones looked at her politely, although she was sure their thoughts weren't far off those of their uncouth co-workers.

A strong smell of cooking meat drifted from the greasy spoon café across the lounge. Knowing her luck, in the time it would take to get a bacon sandwich, she'd miss the contact or it would give her food poisoning. Probably both.

A nice, hot, greasy piece of bacon, maybe a sausage and an egg between what would be generous to call bread; yes, that would do quite nicely. Not that she hadn't just had breakfast.

Giving in would mean having to tweak her metabolism, again, to keep it from becoming a lifetime on the hips. And Kelly would tell her off for doing so.

But what Kelly didn't know about while under, she couldn't complain about.

Tucking the magazine under her arm, she got up and padded across the lounge to the café. To those watching, she moved like a lady. What a surprise they'd get if they spoke to her.

All eyes turned to her as she swayed up to the counter. Somehow, she felt more like a piece of meat than when Harry had tried to dress her as a stripper.

"Alright, love? What you having?" the burly woman said as she wiped her hand on a towel that probably needed to be burnt before if evolved into sentient life.

"A breakfast roll and a latte, please."

"And what'll you be having in the roll?"

Hannah blinked and looked at the menu above the counter. "It says the works, so I'll have the works."

The woman looked her up and down before giving her a nod of respect. She roared the order through to the kitchen, rattling some of the glasses as she did. Several half-asleep patrons sat bolt upright and looked around, wondering if the world was ending.

She paid and accepted her latte. Normally, she drank her coffee black; one because, true or not, she felt it had more kick; and two, it was a fraction of the calories. She sipped at the disposable cup and slightly regretted not going for black. The latte was good, but she'd become too used to strong, black coffee.

When the brown paper bag holding the roll appeared, it was barely able to contain the grease-soaked contents. Returning to the bench, she pondered the mechanics of how to fit the thing in her mouth. Fortunately, although she'd never admit to such a thing, she had a large mouth.

The first bite was a guilty chunk of heaven. Bacon, egg, sausage, black pudding and a hash brown, all wedged into what might have been a morning roll a week previously. After all the food she'd had at the ceilidh, she'd had two days of normal, if not necessarily healthy, eating. Surely, she could have a little treat?

"I'm meant to say 'Sister, you're looking radiant,' but right now I'm not sure I can hold that lie together."

Hannah nearly choked as she looked up at Harry in her near identical dress and nearly choked a second time when it appeared she was nine months pregnant.

Swallowing the half-chewed mouthful, she took a gulp of coffee. "Sister, you're positively glowing," she replied, lack-lustre. "Please tell me that's the glue."

Harry sat down, grabbed the roll, took one bite and handed it back. "I don't know how you can eat all that," she replied. "I can feel my arteries clogging already." She rubbed her bump a little. "And I do have this package to think of."

Wolfing down the last of the roll, Hannah got up and helped Harry back to her feet. "Shall we take a walk, somewhere quiet?"

Linking arms, they headed away from the lounge. Travelling up to a safer part of the station, they headed into a park and wandered aimlessly. Both encrypted their speech so that no one could listen into their conversation.

"So, the glue?" Hannah asked.

Harry pouted a little and rubbed her belly. "That's not a nice way to talk about your little niece or nephew," she replied before giggling. "Yes, it's all adhesive. The Guild kindly gave me a morph suit to wear."

Morph suits were an incredibly useful and extortionately expensive piece of nano-tech. The wearer could put the suit on and it could create a fake, but utterly realistic body around them. Actors often used them to save having to gain weight or bulk up for roles. There was also a subculture that found other more inventive uses for them. The only drawback was that they could only ever make something larger than the wearer.

All suits were to be registered and gave off a unique ID signature to prevent them being used for smuggling. A little hacking made it possible to turn that off. To any form of scanner, the fake body would register as real. And because it was nano-tech, it could link to the wearer so that they could feel through the suit skin as though it was their own. In Harry's case, it created the illusion of an unborn child on scanners and movement could be felt to the touch.

"Well, actually, it wouldn't all quite fit without me looking like I was about to burst."

"You look like you should have burst a few weeks ago," Hannah quipped. It earned her a light slap on the arm.

"Funny, coming from the woman that just ate half a pig in a roll," she replied. "Still, I've got the full shipment stored in other places about my person."

Hannah snorted. "Ah, I'd wondered if you'd just decided to add on baby weight for realism."

"It's on my boobs," she shot back.

They walked on for a little bit in silence. Birds chirped in the trees and bounced around the path, picking up scraps. Squirrels watched them pass, waiting to make a run for the ground and their precious stores. It was amazing to think this was all happening inside a station and not on a planet.

"So, any plans for the next twenty-four hours until I have to deliver you?" Hannah asked, smirking at her own pun.

Harry looked away and shrugged, pretending to be interested in a pair of squirrels chasing each other. "Oh, nothing much. Few people to meet."

"Seriously?" she replied, looking at her with a raised eyebrow. "You look ready to give birth at any time and you're going to run around the station for sex? I'm making the wild guess that you know people here, but are they not going to be a bit freaked out? What are you going to tell them?"

Shaking her head, Harry snorted. "When did you become such a prude? I'll say it's a job, they won't ask further. And I'll have you know; some people would pay big money to sleep with a woman in my condition."

"What, filled with glue?"

"Very funny. I should sit on you for that."

"You'd have to catch me first."

With surprising flexibility and accuracy, Harry flicked her foot up and managed to uncouple Hannah's leg, making her stumble.

They chuckled and carried on walking.

"Oh, it's kicking," Harry said suddenly, placing Hannah's hand on her bump. Sure enough, a moment later there was a solid thump against her hand.

She could almost believe her sister really was pregnant, and having used the same trick a few times herself, knew just how real it would feel. At least, she assumed it felt real, having never actually been pregnant.

"Is *Sheba* here?" Hannah asked.

"On the edge of the system. I met up with her on the way and we came together. Helps cover my tracks," she replied as she made a beeline for a bench. "Helen retrieved the package."

Hannah cursed quietly. "Already? The Remnant will know about you lot by now."

She patted her hand. "Don't worry, it's well hidden. There's a Remnant patrol circling the system and they demanded to inspect us. The package was in the inventory as a model for an eccentric businessman out in the Confederation."

How the Remnant had fallen for that was beyond her, but obviously it couldn't have been any that had harassed *Sigyn*. Or, did they know and had been told to do nothing until their masters arrived to claim the prize?

Across the grass, two Purifiers stood watching the sisters.

Holding the Baby

The next morning came not a moment too soon for Hannah. She'd spend most of the previous day and night traipsing around the station, sat in cafés, in waiting rooms and even someone's living room while Harry made her visits. At more than one she was invited to join in, but that was one place she was not going. Sleeping on a couch had not done her sunny disposition any good either.

Sat in a chain owned pub called "The Pub at the (Arse) End of the Galaxy", Hannah perused the breakfast menu.

"What you having?" she asked.

Harry shrugged a little. "Bacon sandwich and a pot of tea, I think."

With a slightly raised eyebrow, Hannah got up and went to order at the bar. The place was quiet; a few people sitting grabbing a quick breakfast on the go, an old couple enjoying a morning out and a smattering of staff.

She returned to the table, having taken the opportunity of unlimited coffee to fill a small bucket.

"When are we to be at the drop-off?"

"Looking to get the little one out already?" she teased, before sipping her coffee. "And I thought you were having such fun?"

With a small scowl, Harry shuffled in her chair a little. It creaked a little louder than she would have liked. "Well, it is sort of in the way for a great many things. I can barely even sit at this table," she added, waving at the bump pressed against the table edge.

A waiter placed the bacon sandwich and a pot of tea down, followed by a second that offloaded Hannah's plate.

"Are you feeling okay?" Harry eyed the plate critically and the fact there were somewhere between two and three breakfasts battling for space.

"Yeah." She hastily moved the bacon off the pancake it had been sat on. She'd tried to like bacon and pancakes, but it just didn't work for her. "Why? Do I not look okay?"

"Well," she started as a sausage simply disappeared before her eyes, "you tend to eat when you are stressed or upset." The pancake and half an egg went. "And, as much as I know you enjoy a hearty breakfast, there is a three-hundred-pound man looking at you in horror and his breakfast is only half the size of yours."

Taking the time to chew the bacon, which was more stalling for a good comeback as little else had been chewed, she frowned. "There's a three-hundred-pound woman looking at me in horror from across the table."

"Ha, ha, I'm not that heavy," she replied, screwing her face up. "But if you keep that up, you'll be a three-thousand-pound woman in no time."

Fork and knife clattered onto the plate as they were thrown down. "Fine, I'll starve." She sat back and huffed; one arm wrapped around her chest as she drank her coffee. Looking away, she noticed that a few people were certainly looking at them now.

Harry chewed on her sandwich before opening it to inspect the contents. "You've paid for it, so you might as well eat it."

"And become a cautionary whale?"

They lapsed into silence and finished their respective breakfasts.

After a few minutes of discomfort, Hannah sighed. "Come on, they should be open by the time we get there."

Only just managing to not overturn the table as she got up, Harry growled slightly and pushed the chair in roughly. Dressing up might be fine for a bit, but that bit was now overstaying its welcome.

"So, how come you are the one picking me up?" she asked as they headed for a train.

Hannah explained the situation with the Scottish Guild, along with the ceilidh. "The systems Annie wants are extortionate, but they'll be more robust."

"Not being funny," she replied, rubbing her nose a little before rubbing her belly, "but aren't you rolling in dough?" She decided it was best not to add any accusations of miserliness or hoarding of wealth.

There was a momentary silence. "Well, yes, but I've just shelled out for Kelly and I honestly think the drives are massively overpriced. Anyway, it's not like I can go anywhere and make money, so I might as well work to get discounts." She gave a slightly frowny pout. "I just want a quiet life," she lamented.

Harry laughed as she sat down on the train. "If you wanted an easy life, you'd never have joined the Navy or bought *Sigyn*. You'd have settled on some backwater planet and grown veggies if you wanted quiet."

When no comment was forthcoming, she bumped her sister on the shoulder lightly. "Face it, you can't do quiet."

It was true, if she considered it. Had she actually wanted a quiet life, she would have bought a little house on a nice temperate world, settled down, met someone and had a family. She'd probably have a simple job, the sort that a robot should be doing, but in a quiet community where the human touch was preferred.

Maybe one day, but at just forty-two, she wouldn't even be middle-aged for sixty or so years.

After a long journey, the train finally rolled into a station in one of the industrial sections. Few got on or off and some of the passengers gave queer looks at the two women as they disembarked.

"Ugh, is it far?" Harry complained as she rubbed her lower back. "Why does this have to feel so real?"

Hannah rolled her eyes. "The downside of this method of transport."

"You didn't tell me that it would be so heavy and uncomfortable," she replied, a little sullen. "The way you told it; this would be a breeze."

She stopped to let Harry have a little rest. "Well, I wasn't carrying a giant baby's worth of glue and I actually slept at night. And I might have only had it on for a few hours at a time."

Harry waddled on. It wasn't far to go and then she could get the suit off and be back to normal. "I wonder if I can keep the suit," she said after a few steps.

"If you tell them what you did in it," Hannah replied, swallowing slightly and looking into the middle distance, "they'll probably let you, otherwise they'll have to burn it."

She glowered at her. "I'm not some complete deviant. I draw the line at using animals for perverse activities."

They rounded a corner onto a street that led to the factory where the glue was to be delivered. Without warning, Hannah pushed Harry into a doorway. Realising that there wasn't enough room for the two of them, she tried the door, which opened, and pushed her in.

"Hey!"

"Sshh," she hissed, clamping her hand over Harry's mouth. "There are four Purifiers between us and the drop."

"And?" she replied, her voice muffled by Hannah's hand.

"And, they will have a copy of my face. Remember, I did liberate –"

"Steal."

"– liberate, a relic they are desperate to get their grubby hands on."

She frantically considered what to do. There was no way of walking past them and running was totally out of the question for Harry. She couldn't have asked them for a shielded suitcase; no, she had to go with a morph suit.

"Well, we'll just have to sneak past them."

Hannah eyed Harry with a touch of incredulity. "I'm not sure you can sneak that." She checked a map of the area. There were no other ways to get past the Purifiers; they would have had to know they were coming to have set up in such a perfect, but otherwise pointless, position.

"Door over there," she said, nudging Harry towards it. "We can get safely back to the ship."

"How did they know we were coming? Surely if we just wait, they'll move on?"

"I doubt it," she replied. It was a very good question; how had they found out that she was going to be going to a specific, non-descript factory in the middle of nowhere?

"I have good news and bad news," Jon announced.

Hannah rubbed the bridge of her nose. He'd been working for nearly an hour to interface with the morph suit and Harry, wearing nothing but her underwear, was in a foul mood.

"I," he continued when no one said anything, "have managed to establish a link with the suit."

Harry clapped her hands. "Excellent. Now, let's get this over with."

Jon looked at a random point where the wall and ceiling met, chewing on his tongue a little. "Well, that's the bad news," he said, slowly, taking an unconscious step back. "The Guild has used a lockout code to prevent tampering. I imagine it's a defence against their smuggler stealing the cargo."

"How long to break it?" She asked it a terrifyingly sweet voice, her head cocked to one side.

He sucked his cheeks in and took another small step back. "Ehm, well, with Annie's help, it should be, roughly, forty-two –"

"Minutes?" Harry asked.

"A little longer," he replied, stepping back to find he'd run out of reversing space and was now against the bulkhead.

"Hours?" she asked, stepping towards him.

Drumming his fingers together in front of him, Jon grimaced. "Well, a little longer than that."

Hannah sighed. "Jon, just tell us how long it's going to take before I turn you into a ferret."

His huffing, cheek blowing and general panic were interrupted by Annie: "Years," she said. "It'll take forty-two years for us to break the code without getting it from the Guild."

There was a long silence.

"Why not just ask them for the code?" Carl asked.

Everyone turned to look at him like he'd just grown horns and eaten a valuable relic.

"Huh, why didn't we think of that?" Harry asked, hand on her hips and with a scowl. "Oh, perhaps because the whole point of the code is so I can't steal the cargo, so they might be disinclined to acquiesce my request to have it."

Jon leant towards Carl. "Means no," he whispered, siding with the crew on the obviousness of the answer.

He glared at him.

"I'm sorry, but who are these people?" Harry asked.

"I'm Carl, this is Aisha. The crew found us in cryo on the *Livingstone*. What?" he asked, seeing Hannah flailing at him and making cutting motions at her neck.

Harry turned slowly to her sister. "You unfroze two of the passengers?" She looked at her, mouth open slightly. "Do you have any idea how monumentally stupid that was? Oh, of course you don't; just charge right in without thinking."

"If you weren't pregnant, I'd slap you."

"I'm not."

Everyone flinched as Hannah's hand connected with Harry's cheek, albeit, without much force.

"I did warn you," she started to say.

With a growl, Harry lunged at her and the two women ended up rolling about on the floor, wrestling and struggling with each other. With Hannah unconsciously holding back – fighting a pregnant woman, even a fake one, didn't sit right – there was unlikely to be a quick resolution or outright winner.

"Ten on the fat one!" Laura shouted from her perch on a table to Annie.

"Any other bets?"

"Shouldn't we stop them?" Aisha asked no one in particular.

Carl shrugged. "Do you want to get dragged into that? No way I'm getting in that tussle."

Hannah eventually managed to roll Harry off and immediately scuttled out of range and around a table for protection. "We'll just have to find a way to get passed the Purifiers. It'll be fine."

"Fine? Oh, great. My choices are look nine months pregnant until I'm middle-aged, or risk death or brainwashing. Just cut me out of this bloody suit."

"I wouldn't recommend that," Jon replied. "The suit accesses your central nervous system. Cutting it off would feel like having you skin peeled for real and might cause lasting brain damage." He tried to smile a little, but the glare made it very challenging. "You might lose all feeling in your body and you really don't want that."

Harry dropped into a chair that protested loudly. "Why not just give them what they want?"

Hannah's face went crimson as she started to shake slightly. "Give *them* what they want? Aside from the very idea being repugnant, there is a psychotic woman with an NCU that will turn me into Swiss cheese if I do that. And I'm not giving them to them."

Carl and Aisha looked at Hannah questioningly.

"Why would these Purifier people want us?" Aisha asked.

"You are genetically pure Homo sapiens," she replied. "Using you as genetic templates, the Remnant could create ways of forcing every human in the galaxy back into their 'pure' form using gene-splicing viruses. All those colourful people you've seen the past few days? Gone. We'd all be back to as evolution made us, with all the drawbacks that would entail."

The other issue was the *Livingstone* contained Earth's location. If the Remnant could extract it, which if the rumours were true, they had AIs that were free from the Armageddon Protocol to do it, they could take Earth and claim dominion of the galaxy. At the very least, it would almost certainly spark a new war.

There was a long, painful silence.

"Harry, I'm sorry, we need to keep them safe," Hannah said.

She nodded. "I'm sorry, I just want to be back to normal. I think this thing is messing with my head."

"It is," Jon replied, somewhat unhelpfully. "It's messing your hormones about and it seems to be creating an unstable emotional state…" Seeing that everyone in the room was staring daggers at him, he stopped talking and just stood, looking around as if there was an unusual sound coming from somewhere.

As much as Hannah disliked the idea, there was one person that might be able to help them without racking up more cost, favours or having to deal with maniacs. Unfortunately, Annie was probably going to blow a gasket.

She took a deep breath and blew it out slowly. "We do have one card we can play," she said, quietly, looking up from the desk to Annie. "Dr Mendoza."

Her face was completely blank.

Laura swung her legs a few times, her face scrunched. "Wasn't he the one that was spying on us and almost certainly prepared to sell us out to the Purifiers?"

"He didn't have much of a choice," Annie replied, flatly and quietly.

"I'm sure."

Hannah signed loudly. "Regardless, if we ask him to help, he'll be putting his life on the line. At worst, they'd kill him if they figure it out; at best, he'll be sent to a labour camp, but possibly not for life."

It was a lot to ask of a man that was clearly not made to be a spy. If the Purifiers had worked out he'd turned his coat, he might not even get close enough to be useful.

"What about your friend in high places?" Emily asked.

"He works for the monster-lady."

Harry shook her head. "What the hell is going on on this ship?"

"This is pretty standard, to be honest," Hannah replied and the rest of the crew agreed. "It must be Thursday; I never could get the hang of Thursdays."

Hannah had been surprised when Annie had offered to speak to Casper. She stood in his cabin, letting them chat around the issue. If she was being honest, she'd only come along because she'd believed there was a risk Annie might kill him. And not quickly.

Instead, she was starting to get the impression she might have to leave before her eyes were irreversibly contaminated. She'd expected some terse, cold conversation, not the warm and touchy-feely one that was currently taking place.

"I'm sorry to have to break-up this reconciliation," she said, "but we do have some business we need to discuss."

Annie gently took Casper's hands as she looked at her lap. "Cas, we need your help to get past some Purifiers."

He glanced at Hannah before looking back to Annie. Swallowing nervously, he shrugged a little. "I'll help however I can, but I'm not sure what I can do?"

A holographic map appeared in the centre of the room. It showed the factory, the train station and the various streets, buildings and access points. Marked in red was where the Purifiers had been standing, and from the information coming from a rather irate Gilmour, they were manning the crossroad round the clock. He was working through his people for a spy and was not impressed that his shipment had been disrupted.

"If you can keep them looking this way," she said, pointing towards the main street, "we can slip through this warehouse and behind them."

Casper shook his head. "Captain, they'll have proximity sensors covering those roads, possibly even the door ways. They'll see you coming."

Annie squeezed his hands. "You leave the tech to me."

"Laura and Emily will be stationed here and here," Hannah continued, pointing to two doorways. "They'll see to your extraction, if you can't just walk away."

It was an exceptionally dangerous plan. They were relying on the fact the Purifiers at the checkpoint had never seen Casper, and that his greeting codes would still be accepted for an information dead drop. If they knew him, or his codes had been flagged as traitorous, they'd probably shoot him before he could run and certainly before Emily and Laura could deploy any sort of diversion. And they'd be told not to try too hard; there was absolutely no point in getting them killed for no gain.

In reality, they would be of no help to him. They would only be there as a placebo.

"After this, you'll be free to go your own way," Hannah said as she closed the map.

Casper looked at Annie for a moment. She nodded slightly. "Is it okay if I stay? I've nowhere safe to go now."

With a slight smile and a nod, Hannah agreed. Of course, there was very little chance of that; she fully expected him to be killed or captured during this caper.

Infiltration

Aisha stepped into the mess expecting it to be empty this early in the morning. Instead, she found Harry sitting at a table with a piece of half-eaten cake.

"You're up early," she said softly.

"Can't sleep," she replied, playing with the cake. "I'm finding this thing rather uncomfortable in a strange bed," she added, rubbing her belly. "I'm not sure cake was the right choice."

Collecting a cup of herbal tea, Aisha sat at the same table. "So, it's all an illusion? A suit of some sort?" she asked. "How does that work?"

Harry shrugged. "The suit uses nanotechnology to mimic flesh and create a false overlay. It links into the wearer's nervous system using the nanites in their body. Right now, I can feel through the fake skin as though it was mine and I can't feel my real skin."

Tilting her head, Aisha frowned. "But does the fake skin feel real?"

"You tell me," she replied lifting her top.

Hesitantly, she placed her hand on Harry's abdomen. It not only felt exactly like real, human skin, but she felt a twitch of movement under it. Her elder sister had had a baby, not long before she'd started her colonist training; she couldn't tell the difference between what she'd felt when Farah had excitedly placed her hand on her abdomen to feel the little one kicking.

She withdrew her hand and held it over her mouth as a horrific thought struck her; Farah was dead. As was Maryam, her younger sister. Her parents were dead too. That little boy, Amir, who she'd known before he was even born, was dead as well.

"Hey, are you okay?" Harry asked, putting an arm around her.

"They're all dead," she blurted.

It took a moment, but Harry understood and nodded. There really was nothing she could say. Everyone Aisha had ever known had died thousands of years previously on a planet no one had seen for nearly as long. Although, as a colonist, she'd likely have never seen them in person again, she would have received messages and at least have known a bit of their lives. They were completely lost to her.

"They would have died thinking I was dead," she said softly. She wiped the few tears that had started and sniffed. "Well, bubbling won't change what can't be changed."

She managed a weak smile. "You mentioned you have nanites; did they ever get them working properly?"

"How do you mean?"

"Well, I have nanites. They were invented in the Thirties, eh, the Twenty-thirties," she added. "All colonists had them to help mitigate radiation exposure in deep space, but tech companies planned to make them work to repair injuries, reverse aging and extend lifespans. Did they manage?"

Harry shook her head. "No, not really. Well, they did, but you need an NCU – Nano Control Unit – to act as the brain. All the nanites in a human body working together aren't smart enough for that."

She explained that, at some point in one of the Dark Ages before the Unity, an accident had supposedly occurred and all nanites were activated to do that very job. Billions died as the nanites repaired heart conditions that cause the heart to stop, unblocked arteries by cutting them open to remove the blockage or by cannibalising the body to replace missing parts that then led to an endless loop of mutilation. The nanites couldn't hold the command to keep the host alive and the methods to repair damage at the same time. At least, that was what history had recorded.

"So, how is it that the suit works?" Aisha asked.

"It simply asks my nanites to carry pulses to nerves. A phantom feeling, I guess," she pondered.

"I wonder if that's how I can feel the fake baby moving? Could the suit be telling my nanites that something impacted my hand, even though nothing did?"

Harry shrugged. "I'm a ship's captain, not an expert on nanites."

They sat in silence for a few minutes as Aisha continued to drink her tea.

"You didn't seem too happy that Carl and I were unfrozen," she said softly. "I take it you don't get on very well with Hannah?"

"Hannah has a knack for rubbing people up the wrong way," she replied. "Our eldest sister especially. They nearly killed each other a few times when we were teenagers. Actually, she gets on best with me, usually."

"Is it because you are twins?"

Harry laughed. "Oh, we're not twins; we're two of quintuplets."

Aisha blinked a few times. "Sorry, I just assumed since you look pretty identical, well, minus the, em," she replied, miming the belly.

With a smile, Harry dismissed the apology. "We were all grown from the same embryo. All five of us look identical, but we're all very different. Hannah has always been a bit independent of the rest of us."

"Why do you think it wasn't a good idea to unfreeze us?"

Harry swallowed and refused to meet her eye for a moment. "Unfreezing you could have killed you, or unleashed an ancient plague. The fact you haven't lost your mind for a ten-thousand-year time skip is, frankly, surprising."

What she wasn't saying was that two frozen, but alive, specimens would have been sellable and for a fantastical sum of money. Unfrozen, they were people again and couldn't be sold, at least not legally.

"Is the future what you expected?"

Aisha opened her mouth to answer, considered it and tried again. "Well, no, not really," she managed after further thought. "I mean, it's been ten thousand years and nothing has changed much. Sure, the purple man, the woman with four arms and actual Pokémon battles are new, but humans are still human."

Harry frowned a little. "Yeah?"

She nodded. "There were people in my time that expected humans could be taller, or have evolved traits suited to tool use, things like altered thumbs for phones, or that you'd all look homogenous. You could wander down any high street in Britain and no one would notice. And no aliens?"

They chatted for a while, comparing the past and present.

Hannah checked the time.

"Would you stop doing that?" Harry complained. "You're making me nervous."

She ignored her and continued to wait. Casper had set off a few minutes earlier, but there had been no signal from him. Had something gone wrong? Was he about to burst in, flanked by Purifiers to proudly claim he'd caught their prey?

There was no way he could have been communicating with them beforehand. His comm had been destroyed and no signals had been detected leaving the ship. Of course, there could be other ways he'd been making contact.

The warehouse door opened and Hannah drew her pistol.

"It's me!" Casper shouted, throwing his hands up. "They aren't there, they aren't there."

The pistol dropped.

"What do you mean 'they aren't there'?"

The sisters followed him out onto the street to find he was telling the truth. The Purifiers were nowhere to be seen. Not wanting to look a gift horse in the mouth, they ran, albeit not quickly, across the open space to the factory and straight in to the reception.

A surly looking receptionist was painting her nails and ignoring a ringing phone. The place looked slightly uncared for, the paint drab and the carpet well-trod. It was the perfect place to slip all sorts of illegal things in and out.

After waiting for a few moments and not being acknowledged, Hannah coughed.

The receptionist made a show of rolling her head up to look contemptuously at her as she chewed her gum loudly, letting her jaw hang open for a second with each chew.

"Hi," Hannah said, tautly, "we have a delivery for Mr Arbuthnot."

The receptionist looked Harry up and down. "You ain't delivering her in here, that's for sure," she said with a disgusted sneer.

With a polite cough, Hannah repeated herself.

"Heard you the first time, love," the receptionist replied, returning to her garishly pink nails. "And I say again, this is a machine shop, not a maternity ward."

Harry reached across the desk and pulled the young woman half way over it. "We have a *delivery* for *Mr Arbuthnot*," she said, nose to nose with the startled woman. "So, get the person with the morph suit code before I sit on you."

"Oh, oh, that *delivery*," she said, prising her blouse from Harry's grip. She pressed a button on the PA system. "Dale to Reception, Dale to Reception. Quickly please."

Dale didn't arrive quickly enough. The short, stout man shuffled in, a tool belt slung around his robust middle and a rag in his hands leaving as much grime on them as it took off. He looked at Harry and nodded over his shoulder for her to follow. Turning on his heel, he shuffled off again, not bothering to see if he was being followed.

Hannah was left standing, the receptionist shooting daggers at her as she tried to even out her blouse again. She took a seat, somewhat defiantly, and lifted a magazine that was about three years out of date.

As she sat, she waited to hear if the receptionist started typing; calling the Purifiers would be easily overheard, but a text message would be unnoticed. As it was, she went back to her personal grooming and tried to pretend she was alone.

A message came in that Emily, Laura and Casper had made it back to *Sigyn* and that Annie had gone to do some part shopping. No sign of any Purifiers.

That left her uneasy. Had the Guild managed to drive them away somehow? She suspected that Spectrum might have played a hand in keeping them at bay. Ms White didn't seem like the kind of woman to suffer competition.

Harry appeared over an hour and a half later, looking rather flushed and pleased with herself, carrying a brown paper bag.

"Would you believe, they let me keep the suit," she said.

Grabbing her by the arm, Hannah propelled her out of the reception and into the street. "I'm guessing you told them what you'd been up to in it?" she asked.

"No," she replied, innocently. "I gave them an example. Before and after."

Hannah dug her fingers into her arm, drawing a light yelp from her. She was in no mood to have been left sitting in a window when the Purifiers were looking for her, just because Harry was getting lucky. And the Harpies called her reckless and selfish?

As they rounded a corner, they stopped dead in their tracks. Marching towards them was an elegant woman in white robes, her hair cut in a lopsided style.

They turned and started back the way they came.

"A friend of yours?" Harry asked.

"I'm certain she was on one of the ships pursuing me," she replied. "Obviously whatever was distracting them has stopped."

A door opened and a hand grabbed Harry's other arm to drag them both inside. The door slammed shut and Jansen pressed a finger to his lips before waving them after him.

The trio walked along a dark corridor that started to slope down before opening out into a small room with a number of doors. It appeared to be a maintenance access way that ran under the street and basements of the buildings.

"I know you said your sisters were identical, but I swear, it's nearly impossible to tell the difference," he said, admiring Harry for a moment. "You can't be Hannah; she'd never smile at me while I'm alive."

"I suppose thanks are in order," she replied tersely, pulling Harry back a little.

He waved the thanks away. "Nah, it's fine. It's Ms White you should be thanking; she's spent the last three hours wandering about looking sort of like you to attract the Purifiers."

Hannah narrowed her eyes slightly and tried not to give the thought too much consideration. It was bad enough having four identical sisters without a doppelganger wandering about the place as well. And no doubt, it was help at a price.

"Harry," she said, holding her hand out to Jansen.

He bent over it to gently kiss the back of the offered hand. "Jansen Wainwright, also known as Mr Black of Spectrum. It's a pleasure to meet you."

She smiled at him. "Well, I really must repay you for your help. Perhaps there is somewhere discreet we can get a drink?"

Opening her mouth to protest, Hannah closed it again. It was a pointless endeavour. Instead, she huffed lightly, crossed her arms and stood, sour faced.

Jansen's face lit up with a grin. "That would be very nice. I see you are the polite one," he added, giving Hannah a slightly pointed look. "She never thanked me for any of the help I gave her."

"The coast should be clear," she said, ignoring the bait. "I'll see you later, Harry. Try not to get caught by the Purifiers."

Without waiting for any reply, she headed back the way they'd come towards the surface. At the door, she opened it a crack to check the coast really was clear; finding it was, she continued out onto the street and started for the station.

The back of her neck prickled slightly.

Someone was following her. Every time she got that feeling, someone was following her. Glancing over her shoulder, she spotted the Purifier again, this time with a young man hobbling after her.

She started to walk a little faster, glancing at her wrist in an attempt to make it look like she was running late for something. Rounding a corner, she broke into a run for a few steps before returning to a walk.

There were only two platforms in the station – a line going in each direction. The closest was going the wrong way, so she'd have to cross to the other platform to head back towards the Harbour.

By some miracle, there was a train sitting at both platforms. The wrong one was due to leave a minute before the one she wanted, which was going to stop at the Harbour; the four after it were on different routes.

Jumping on the wrong train, she walked through the carriages looking out the windows. The Purifiers had caught up and were on the platform.

Timing it as close as she could, Hannah jumped off as the doors were closing, much to the annoyance of the guard. She ran up the steps of the bridge, the pounding of her feet obscuring the gentle hum of the train leaving the station. It would take the Purifiers a few minutes to find out she'd got off. They'd have to get off at the next station and wait for a return train.

Hopping on the second train, she found a bench seat that was facing the platform and sat down. The doors closed and she closed her eyes for a second, letting victory flow through her.

Someone sat next to her. They coughed politely.

Opening her eyes, she nearly hit the ceiling.

"We've met, but not been properly introduced. I'm Purifier-General Dido," she said, offering her hand. "Oh, don't look so shocked, you don't reach my rank by being outwitted by a little bit of bait and switch. And I'm not going to hurt you."

Hannah wasn't inclined to believe that, but gingerly took the hand.

Dido smiled. "I wouldn't think about trying anything," she said. "I'm wearing a nanotech battle suit," she added, pulling her sleeve up to reveal the bracelet. She still hadn't let Hannah's hand go.

"There are also two gentlemen at the front who have been tailing you," she continued. "Scots, I think. And there is the woman from Spectrum sat just up from us, next to my aide, and a Peacekeeper by the door to the next carriage."

Hannah swallowed. "Quite the Mexican stand-off," she said weakly, pulling her hand free.

"Quite."

They sat quietly as the train pulled into the next station. Hannah felt a foot cross over her own. The message was pretty clear.

"I really have no intention of hurting you," Dido said.

"Hm."

"I just want the ship," she said. "I'll even pay for it, although you have already had substantial payment."

Hannah remained silent.

"I suppose most of that is going to repair your ship and to upgrade your little friend."

"If you go near any of my crew, I'll destroy the *Livingstone*."

Dido frowned slightly, more in disappointment than anything else. "Don't worry, I'm not that sort of monster."

"But you are a monster."

"This is becoming uncivilised," she said tersely. "Look, your friends in Spectrum and the Scottish Guild are blocking all attempts for me to get enough people and ships in this system to take you by force." She stood up and nodded to Castor.

"But that won't last forever. You can't escape this system, I can't get in. Yet. Once I do, I will take you into custody. Goodbye for now."

Dido dissolved in a flicker of light and a holo-bee landed gently on the floor. After a moment, it lifted into the air and was joined by Castor's. They both exited the train when the doors opened and returned to a platform charging station.

Hannah cursed herself for being played so well. Had the other Purifiers been holograms too? She suspected they were locals, eager to help a high-ranking officer in hopes of promoting to a nicer place.

Once she was back on *Sigyn*, she'd contact Helen to find out if the system was surrounded. Even if it wasn't, the Purifiers would easily have two months to move in.

As much as she loathed the idea, leaving *Sigyn* behind and escaping with Harry might be the crew's only hope. Until Kelly recovered, even that was impossible.

Gilmour slammed his hand down on the table. "To even contemplate letting them land more troops is foolish. If you think they'll stop at disrupting my shipments, you are sadly mistaken."

Ms White, looking completely human and dressed in a smart white suit, nodded slightly. "I must agree."

Huang, the representative of the Triad, snorted. "The Purifiers caught you out smuggling," he said. "We agreed accords and protocols to keep the playing field level and the old fights dead."

"Like you haven't been charging protection money," Gilmour shot back. "We all know that the Grimaldi are skimming taxes from their buyers, just as the Young Bucks, Kilkenny and the Hand are selling narcotics, weapons and intelligence under the table."

Everyone at the table looked away as they were called out. The general agreements between the Roanapur Collective Board kept the peace, but it was fragile at best.

"The rule is to not rock the boat," he continued. "Letting the Purifiers send nearly a thousand soldiers here, looking for one ship, is tantamount to a takeover bid. And they want their fleet parked here. It'll scare the customers."

"They will leave as soon as we have the *Sigyn*," Dido replied, her hologram flickering slightly. "I believe you are outfitting them; I can pay for you to simply," she shrugged, "let them go."

Ms White leant forward. "I have already made an agreement with Captain Sinclair to acquire her goods."

"They are not her's to sell."

"True. If they are what you claim, they actually belong to my employer in any case."

Dido stiffened slightly. "And who would that be?"

Abe of the Young Bucks leant forward. "Ladies, this is getting a little unseemly. Perhaps we should take a break and cool down."

"Eris," Ms White replied without missing a beat.

At that, several of the representatives stood up, grabbed coats, files and bags, and immediately walked out, looking as though they were trying not to disgrace themselves by running.

Only Ms White, Gilmour, Huang and Rossi, the Peacekeeper observer, remained. Both Gilmour and Huang looked like they wanted to leave, but neither would; the Scottish Guild and the Triad were major rivals and the two largest groups on the Board.

"Superstitious lot," Rossi said softly as she sipped her glass of water. "Convenient way to clear a room; I must remember that trick."

"All in favour of maintaining the Purifier presence at current levels?" Gilmour said shakily.

Ms White raised her hand, as did he.

"Against?"

No one moved. Rossi had no vote and Huang chose to play politics by abstaining.

"Well, General, I'm afraid the motion carries against you. If you want *Sigyn*, you'll have to wait until she leaves Roanapur. Under her own steam."

Dido spread her hands, her lips pursed, and terminated her link.

Huang stood and cursed. "She'll be back, but next time she'll have a gun," he said. He kicked his chair lightly and trudged out.

Rossi also stood. "I'll speak to the embassies, see if any government aid can be provided. Most hate the Purifiers more than they hate this place," she added, a little unhelpfully.

Gilmour looked to Ms White. "I hope for our sake," he said slowly, "that you can back up invoking that bogeyman. I doubt the Purifiers take much heed of the name Eris."

She smiled sweetly. "My dear, I most certainly can."

Feeling that the comment was as much a threat as a promise, Gilmour got up slowly. "A pleasure, as always," he said weakly.

The Wait

"If you don't stop pacing, I'll take your legs off."

Hannah stopped in her tracks to glare at Harry, nostrils flaring as she took a deep breath. "Perhaps you are failing to grasp the seriousness of the situation?"

She gave a half shrug. "Hunted by Purifiers, trapped on this heap of a station, watched by a supposedly psychotic grey-goo-girl, haemorrhaging money at a rate not seen since the collapse of the Central Bank of Socialism, and you are mostly concerned that its," she consulted her implant for the time, "five hours past when you expected to hear about your girlfriend."

"You forgot that I'm basically a slave to the Scots and you are banging the creep that used to stalk me. And she's not my girlfriend."

With another, even less enthusiastic shrug, Harry screwed her face up. "Fine, your cuddle buddy, and he never actually stalked you. And remember, I'm stuck here too." Every time *Frigg* attempted to leave, a Remnant ship rushed in to harass, forcing them back.

Hannah started to lift random items around her cabin, placing them back where they had been, or at most, slightly turned. Two weeks of constantly looking over her shoulder had become beyond exhausting.

Slapping her thighs, Harry stood up. "Well, I've got a date. Chat later." Her hologram cut out, leaving Hannah alone.

Feeling a little trapped, she left her cabin and headed for the mess. The ship was eerie without the normal sounds of engines in the background. Work had barely started yet on replacing the slipstream drive, and once it got going in earnest, the place would be pandemonium.

Annie and Casper were in the mess, sharing an ice cream sundae, the whole spy incident mostly forgiven, if not completely forgotten.

The ice cream looked too delicious to pass up, so Hannah got her own sundae from the replicator. She was invited to join them, and did so.

"You two look happy," she said, taking a dainty spoonful of whipped cream and butterscotch syrup. Placing it in her mouth, she sucked the spoon for a moment, her tongue polishing it clean of sweet, creamy goodness.

They smiled warmly at each other. "We've had some time to reconnect and evaluate our positions," Annie replied, managing to make it sound like a double entendre.

Casper flushed a little, lifted the spoon and fed her a large spoonful of ice cream.

Hannah tried to say "aww", but with a mouthful of ice cream and fudge chunks, it sounded more like the call of a distressed seal. The sentiment was there, if not as intended.

"You'll get brain freeze eating that quickly," Casper said, eyeing the rapidly vanishing sundae.

"Can'," she replied through a mouthful, "go' a 'hing 'hat s'ops it ha'ening."

The two lovebirds looked at each other and pushed there half eaten sundae away. Annie did have some ideas for it; ones that were too private to be conducted in the mess.

"There's some good news," Annie said. "One of the cooling system components has arrived early."

Hannah paused in her digging; a small mercy as the clinking of spoon on glass stopped. "Does it get us going again sooner?"

"No."

The sundae was finished in what had to be some sort of galactic record. "You not going to finish that?"

Annie pushed the discarded sundae across the table. "I'd best get back to making repairs," she said, wiggling her eyebrows slightly at Casper. She got up and headed for the door with him following.

Several Scottish engineers rolled into the mess, talking and laughing. They nodded to Hannah politely as they passed. The Guild had provided a small army to start the prep work, but it was up to Hannah to feed them. At the rate they were going, a small city would be easier to keep sated.

One of them, a rather handsome man, stood on the far side of the table. "May I join you?" he asked quietly with a slight smile.

Sitting up and feeling a little disgusting with two empty sundae glasses in front of her, she motioned for him to sit.

"Iain," he said as he took a seat. The other engineers were pretending not to watch.

"Hannah," she replied.

He nodded, looking a little lost. Taking a few moments to gather himself, he finally found some words: "Do you come here often?"

It was difficult not to laugh and to ignore the guffawing from the next table. One guy nearly choked on whatever he was drinking.

"The ship or the mess in particular?" she asked innocently.

He looked at the table for a moment, then looked up. "Yeah, I guess that doesn't work when it's your ship, does it?" He'd flushed a little and shrank a touch. Taking a breath, he sat up. "What brings a nice girl to a station like this?"

Over his shoulder, Hannah could see one of his female companions looking on in mild horror. From the next table, the whole thing probably looked like a brutal collision in slow motion; something akin to a ship dropping out of slip-space into the side of an asteroid.

"Engine trouble," she replied.

A wave of realisation swept over him.

"Can I get you a drink?" he said lamely.

With a little sigh, Hannah gave him a slightly pitying smile. "I'm sort of interested in someone at the moment," she replied. "A for effort," she added as he deflated, "but a C for execution."

Grabbing him by his shirt, she pulled him over the table and planted a light peck on his cheek. "It earns you that. Don't spend it all at once."

She left him hanging over the table and walked out. As awkward as the few minutes had been, she felt a bit better. People had hit on her quite regularly when she was in the Navy, but after she'd left, it hardly happened and was either prostitutes looking for business or absolute creeps.

Relationships were serious business to her and she would openly admit to being picky, having high standards and particular tastes. At least, that was her excuse for having not dated, or even really tried, since Ali's death.

Walking past the lounge, she spotted Carl and Aisha. Carl was watching a concert while Aisha was looking at a tablet. Having not have much chance to speak with them, and with time to kill, she decided to join them.

"How can this have been filmed a few days ago?" Carl asked, throwing an arm out at the screen. "How can Queen be in concert with the original line up? They've been dead for ten thousand years."

"Wikipedia says they're sentient hard-light holograms," Aisha replied. "Apparently there is a load of dead celebs running around as holograms; Elvis, Michael Jackson, a young and an old Justin Bieber, Frank Sinatra. It's like the late 20th and early 21st Centuries were meticulously preserved. There's even a William Shatner concert tomorrow, with him duetting with himself. Oh, hi Captain."

"Please, call me Hannah," she replied, taking a seat. "How are you settling in?"

They looked at each other for a moment.

"It's… been very strange," Aisha replied. "This future is almost familiar. I can't imagine a caveman from 8000 BCE finding everything so similar in the 21st Century as we're finding the 121st Century."

With a weak smile, Hannah nodded. "Yeah, I guess it will be odd. But hey, at least you didn't arrive to find we'd been wiped out by sentient starships, enslaved by apes or joined to an extra-dimensional being via tentacles in our necks."

Carl and Aisha glanced at each other.

"Quite a specific list," he replied.

"I watched a lot of old films as a child," she replied. "I guessed you might get the references."

He turned the screen off. "So, what happens to us?"

She shrugged slightly. "I don't know. You don't exist, beyond the fake IDs you currently have. Where you came from doesn't exist anymore. You're welcome to stay on the ship, or I can see about helping you find a place in the galaxy."

"I'm guessing that for the foreseeable future, we can't go anywhere much," Aisha replied, tossing the tablet aside. It landed softly on the couch next to her.

Hannah smiled weakly. "Well, I certainly wouldn't let you off here. You'd be lucky to have any organs left by morning."

They looked at each other again, wondering about what sort of hellish future they had actually landed in. Was everywhere such a hellhole, or had they just been incredibly unlucky to arrive in hell first?

"Seriously, the rest of the galaxy is not this bad," she said, seeing the concerned looked. "New Britain is a truly gorgeous place, that's the Commonwealth capital planet. Washington isn't half bad, either, you know, for a Yank planet."

Carl looked a little brighter. "Yeah, it might be nice to go as close to home as still exists, even if just to visit." He'd only been to Washington D.C. once, but the city had stuck with him as a beacon of freedom and liberty.

A message came through on her implant.

"I'm sorry, I have to go."

Dido sat the Wardroom, looking at the plans that had been put forward. Green had been voicing his objections for several minutes, but she'd mostly tuned him out as she studied.

"Are you sure you can only get twenty onto the station?" she asked when he stopped talking to draw breath.

Mwangi nodded. "Yes, Ma'am. My shielded hold can't take more than that, unless you don't mind cuddling."

She looked at the freighter captain and pursed her lips. Twenty Purifiers wasn't much, but she really did not like cuddling and had no desire to end up dead in a container because it was over crowded.

"When can you take us?"

"General, I must protest," Green said, leaning across the table. "With my fleet unable to enter the system, there is nothing to stop them fleeing at the first sign of trouble."

She looked at him and frowned. It was the first time he'd openly disagreed with her. "Captain Sinclair won't be able to. Her ship is still crippled and a member of her crew incapacitated after surgery. At first sight of me, she'll assume it's another hologram."

He threw his hands up and tossed himself back in his chair. "Well, I can see you've made your mind up."

Trying to look like he was ignoring the argument, Mwangi waited for a moment before answering. "I can guarantee you'll be on Roanapur in no time at all."

"They'll be long gone," Green muttered.

"My sources say they needed two months to make repairs," Dido replied. "It's been less than three weeks. Even if they try to run, they won't get far. This is our best chance to get the data."

Seeing that the argument was none of his concern, Mwangi slid a tablet across the desk towards her. "My fee. Let me know if you require transport. I leave the system in six hours, after which, my window to carry expires."

She lifted the tablet and immediately dumped it back on the table. "I could buy a ship for that."

"Supply and demand," he replied, grinning, showing off several gold capped teeth. "You have a demand and I have the only supply, hence, large compensation."

Dido smiled tightly, looked at the tablet and slid it back across the table with one finger.

"Or, I could shoot you and see if your First Officer has a better offer?"

"Hey, no need for that," he replied, hands up. "I am open to negotiation, but remember, if I get caught, I'll be doing a lot of time. Or dead, depending on which of the factions find you."

"Twenty-five percent" she replied.

"Eighty."

"Thirty."

"Seventy-five."

Dido took a deep breath and blew it out through her nose. "Forty-two and a half, and I ignore the illegal indentured servants you're carrying."

"Seventy percent of my asking price, or I walk."

Green shook his head. "Bridge, Green."

"Aye, Admiral?"

"Commander Harris, target the *Protea*'s power distribution grid and prepare to disable her. Do not power weapons until I give the order."

"Aye, Sir."

"Fifty percent and you ignore my cargo," Mwangi said, slamming his hand on the desk. "This is daylight robbery, mark my words."

Dido nodded.

"Bridge, belay the last order and stand down," Green said as the tablet was passed around to be signed.

"You will be paid after I am safely on the station and I am sure you haven't betrayed us," she said as she signed the agreement. "If you do, there will be nowhere you can hide."

He took the tablet and snorted. "I ain't that dumb. Now, I will go. The agreement contains all the necessary particulars."

Dr Mannheim smiled as he showed Hannah into his office. It was still a cluttered mess, but she was fairly certain that several of the piles had migrated around the room; new mountain ranges had risen up while others had crumbled with the shifting paper tectonics. She had to lift a small pile of books and a hand from the chair to sit down.

"She's alive," he said, cheerily.

"Isn't there supposed to be a flash of lightning, a rumble of thunder and maniacal laughter alongside that comment?"

He frowned a little. "I wouldn't repeat that to any of my colleagues; we don't take well to Frankenstein references about our work. If our patients run amuck, it's nothing to do with us."

Hannah grimaced a little, but didn't apologise.

"There were a few, very minor, complications, but everything is working as it should be," he continued. "Sentience testing is complete. We thought you'd want to be here when we woke her up properly, but she won't be fit to leave for several days."

"Oh?"

"She's just had major surgery," he replied. "Even with the days rest she's had while we tested everything, her body will be exceptionally sore. We'll need to ween her off a cocktail of painkillers."

"So, when you see her, don't touch her, don't try to make her move," he continued. "She'll be partially paralysed for her own good for at least a day."

Hannah's eyes were nearly ready to roll out her head. "Does she know that?"

"Of course," he replied. "We've been able to talk to her via her new interface. Now, it's going to look pretty bad, but she really is okay."

Somehow, her eyes managed to widen further. How bad could it be? What state was Kelly in? Perhaps she wasn't going to look completely normal yet, but to have to be warned?

Everything seemed blurred, hazy and distant, except Mannheim's back as she followed him towards the recovery ward. All the rooms were individual, making it impossible to tell how many were occupied.

Towards the far end of the ward, he stopped and turned to face her. "She won't be coming round for a few minutes. I suggest you take that time to prepare yourself for when she does."

He opened the door and Hannah walked in.

She tried not to gasp, but failed completely.

Kelly was covered by a sheet, except for her head, but her outline was completely masked by supports. It looked like someone had erected a small tent over her, with hundreds of wires and tubes disappearing under it. Her face was lightly bruised in places, deep dark blotches circling her eyes.

It looked less like she'd had surgery than she'd survived being hit repeatedly by a shuttle.

"Don't be too alarmed," Mannheim said softly. "Most of the equipment is running targeted regenerative cycles on her new flesh." He tapped a few commands into a console. "I'll leave you for a while. Just call if there are any issues."

Slowly, Hannah approached Kelly. She wanted to reach out and touch her, give her some support and comfort as she came round, but she didn't want to accidently hurt her. Somehow, she hadn't expected the surgery would be this traumatic, but what could be expected when trying to build an organic body around a synthetic frame?

Pulling up a chair, she waited for Kelly to wake.

After a few minutes, her eyelids started to flutter. She took a deep breath and opened her eyes. Bright emerald eyes quickly found Hannah and a smile grew shakily.

"Hi," Hannah said softly, leaning in.

"Temba, his arms open."

She blinked rapidly. "What?"

Recovery

Kelly looked at Hannah questioningly. "Temba, his arms wide."

"I don't understand what you're saying," she replied, a slightly deranged smile growing on her face.

"Kadir beneath Mo Moteh?"

"What? Is that Gaelic? I've definitely heard Annie use 'mo'." She was starting to really worry that the procedure had gone horribly wrong.

With a slight frown, which was as much as she could manage, Kelly huffed. "Chenza at court, the court of silence," she said seriously. "The beast at Tanagra; Kiteo, his eyes closed."

Hannah slowly got up. "Honey, I've no idea what you mean, but I'm going to get one of the doctors. They'll fix this." She'd almost got to the door when she heard a giggle.

"Hannah's face when she realises, she's been had."

She turned slowly and glowered.

"Hi," Kelly said, turning her head just a little to be able to see her.

"Hi? I thought they'd put your brain in a blender and you give me 'hi'?" she replied.

"You look like you're sucking a lemon."

"That wasn't funny."

Kelly smiled. "I can see from here you're trying not to laugh. And, hey, I survived, I live again; I think I was promised a reward for surviving."

Unwilling to let the joke pass unchallenged, Hannah shook her head slightly as she looked away. "Nope, no idea what you're talking about. No memory of promising anything. I might have suggested a small reward, but I definitely remember us settling on you repaying me by taking only ten goldcoin a contract."

Now it was Kelly's turn to look sour. "Oh."

"Revenge," Hannah replied sweetly. "I remember, but I'm not allowed to touch you until you've healed a bit more."

"I think I can manage a little, light touch," she replied, trying to look sultry when she could just about turn her head and had limited facial movement.

"Yeah," Hannah said as she sat back down, "well, you look like a shuttle ran you over, so I think I'll wait."

Kelly started to laugh, but immediately her eyes went wide and she gasped. Several monitors beeped a few times before settling down again. "Oh, don't make me laugh.

"But seriously, how do I look."

She nodded a few times. "Good."

"Just good?"

"Well, you'll look a lot better when the bruising goes down and your hair grows back."

"What?"

"What?"

Kelly looked a little panicked. "I'm bald?"

"No, no," she replied. "There's a sort of fuzz, kinda like a peach. And, of course, eyebrows will help your look in time."

It was a complete lie. While her hair was not as long and full as it had been, she had a short pixie cut of deep red hair. Her eyebrows were there in full, a few shades lighter than her hair.

"Can you get a mirror?"

Hannah could see a small hand mirror sitting on a table, out of Kelly's limited field of vision. "Sorry, the docs said not to let you have one yet. Patients apparently have a terrible habit of laughing madly and smashing them," she replied. "It used to cost them a fortune."

She glared impotently. "Fine. I know you're lying, though. Did they say when I can get out?"

"Few days, depends on how well you heal."

With a grunt, Kelly looked at the ceiling. "I'd rather get up and get on with life. I'm going to be so bored."

Looking around and seeing that all the blinds were closed, Hannah grinned cheekily. "Mind if I have a look?"

"What's it worth?" she replied tartly. "I haven't even seen myself yet."

"How about a top up on what we discussed," she answered, gently and slowly lifting the edge of the sheet. "And I don't mean money."

She'd nearly got the sheet edge lifted to have a look when there was a politely, but firmly disapproving cough from behind. Immediately, she dropped it and sat bolt upright like a naughty schoolgirl.

Mannheim appeared beside her. "I hope you haven't been getting my patient too worked up and excited?" he asked, eyebrows raised. "She needs to stay calm and rest a bit more."

"I just wanted to make sure everything was there," Kelly said, innocently. "And since I can't move…"

"I can assure you that it is, and it's currently encased in regenerative modules," he replied. He handed Hannah a tablet. "A full list of all procedures, installs and removals, plus the final balance to be paid before discharge. I'll leave you to have a look at it."

Thanking him, Hannah watched him leave and immediately lifted the sheet for a look. Annoyingly, he'd been right; every inch of Kelly's body was covered by interlocked modules that completely masked her outline. With a little huff, she dropped the sheet and gave Kelly a little, slightly playful shrug.

"Yup, pretty much nothing to see," she said. "However, this is certainly something," she added as she scrolled through the tablet.

Kelly blushed. "What? Most of them were free."

"I'm not sure if I should ask if you plan to knock over banks, governments or attempt to pass yourself off as an Aesir," she replied. "I was thinking of new clothes as your welcome back present, but I think a magic hammer might be in order."

"Very funny."

She continued scrolling down the list. There were a number of items that had apparently come from a monthly raffle, in which Kelly had won the top prize. Most of the items were simple accessories; hair clips, make-up, earrings and other bits that if not wanted could easily be sold on eBay. One, however, was much more expensive.

"Did you know you'd won this?" she asked. "Have they fitted it?"

"I hope not," she replied. "What an odd thing to have in a raffle prize? Even a small piece of nanotech like that must be worth a fortune."

Hannah chewed her lip a little and looked away. "I dunno, I can think of a few people that would like that sort of thing. And I don't just mean Harry. As for size; it's what you do with it that matters."

Kelly raised an eyebrow at her. "Seriously?"

Now it was Hannah's turn to go crimson. "My husband became my wife," she replied, shaking off the accusation. "On occasion, I was, technically, her husband. Very empowering."

After that little revelation, they lapsed into silence. Hannah continued to read the contents of the tablet. There wasn't much of note, but the prices of the parts taken from Kelly were indeed ridiculously high. Aside from her neural net, its casing, the main part of her central nervous system and some supports mimicking bones, just about everything else had been replaced.

"So, can you feel anything?" she asked. "Do you feel different?"

"No, not really," she replied with a slight frown and purse of her lips. "It's like everything is a bit numb; I can feel I have a body, but it's like I can't actually *feel* it."

She smiled lightly. "You're starting to look tired. More tired," she added with a chuckle. "Perhaps I'd better let you rest."

Over the next three days, Hannah visited Kelly while she continued to heal. Although Mannheim had said it could take several days, it did take longer for the regenerative modules to complete their work than expected.

In the hope that today would be the day she'd be released, Hannah had brought some presents.

"Good morning, Captain," Mannheim said as he opened the door. "You're becoming rather punctual." It was an understatement; each morning she was waiting for visiting to start.

"Morning, Doctor," she replied. "Well, it's either be here or have to sit through the morning status update from my engineer. It takes ninety minutes and is the same as the previous evening's report."

He chuckled and escorted her towards Kelly's door. He stopped short and stepped into her path.

"Kelly is out of the regenerative modules," he said. "She's been sitting up and is starting to take food, but she is still fragile. I'm hoping to get her up and walking this morning, so having you here might be beneficial."

When Hannah stepped into the room, Kelly was sitting up wearing a drab grey gown with flecks of purple and yellow.

She grimaced a smile. "This is really not what I want to be seen in," she said.

"It could be worse," Hannah replied. "I brought you some gifts, now that you are officially, nearly, up and about."

A bunch of assorted real flowers were presented in a vase, the stalks held in a bunch with a blue ribbon just above the neck; a box of chocolates (Hannah was more than willing to eat them if Kelly was forbidden, to save her from temptation); and a sleek, black box a foot long and half a foot wide.

The vase was placed onto the bedside table. Hannah removed the ribbon to let the flowers space themselves out, as the florist had instructed.

"I suppose you can put this in your hair," she said, handing it to Kelly. "Well, once you have some."

"Very funny, but I know I've got hair," she replied, giving a lock of hair a gentle tug.

She handed the box of chocolates over and immediately looked over her shoulder. "Now, if you can't manage them, or shouldn't have them, that's okay," she said, looking out for Mannheim or any nurses rushing to take them away.

"Obviously not an issue," she added as she looked back to find Kelly had already shoved three in her mouth. Her response was unintelligible.

With a little sigh, Hannah lifted the black box and held it out. "Something I had made, just for you. I hope you like it."

Kelly tentatively took the box. Although long and wide, it wasn't very deep, but it was heavier than it appeared. Her first thought had been jewellery, perhaps a necklace, but unless it had a millstone on it, it was far too heavy.

Taking her time, she ran her hands over the box, simply enjoying the feel of the cool, slightly textured surface. Pressing the catch, the top popped open ever so slightly. Slowly, carefully, she opened it.

"You bitch," she said.

Hannah started to giggle. "I couldn't help myself."

Kelly lifted the claw hammer from the box and gave it a sarcastically pathetic twirl. "You even went to the trouble of having 'Mjolnir' engraved into it. I'll treasure it forever," she said, clutching it to her chest unconvincingly.

"Damn right you will," she replied, moving in to kiss her.

A deep blush crossed Kelly's face and down her neck. "Now, that's a gift I'd take every time. Oh, nearly forgot, I have something for you."

Hannah's eyes lit up. "Presents? For me?"

The confusion was written clearly on her face as she was presented with a chip about the size of her fingernail.

"It's an access chip," she explained. "My interface is wireless but can only be accessed using an access chip. I want you to have one."

Taking the chip, Hannah felt her eyes watering slightly. "Really? Are you sure you want me holding onto this?"

"Yeah, I do," she replied with a smile. "Don't worry, as long as I'm conscious, even with the chip, no one can get in my head unless I grant them access." She closed Hannah's hand around the chip. "Anyway, my neural net direct link wireless range is about ten feet, so not easy access."

With a sniff and a gentle throat clearing cough, Hannah tapped on her implant holographic display. The small lump on her wrist unfolded, opening up to reveal a dozen ports, three of which already contained chips. She slipped Kelly's into an unoccupied slot and closed the implant again.

"I honestly can't get used to seeing that," she said, watching as the implant closed. "A little freaky, if I'm honest."

"You have the same implant," she replied, rolling her eyes before grabbing a chocolate. Ignoring the protests, she popped it in her mouth. Kelly pulled the box away and stuffed several more in her mouth.

Mannheim appeared at the door. "I hope those aren't chocolates," he said, frowning. "Your body isn't ready for such a rich food, yet."

A loud grumble filled the room, to which he gave her a pointed look.

"Sorry, that was me," Hannah said, holding her hand up. "And again," she added as her belly rumbled for a second time. "But that was her," she said as a third rumble, this time from Kelly, split the silence.

The next afternoon, Hannah found herself, hopefully, in Mannheim's office for the last time. Kelly had made sufficient progress that she could be released, once the final paperwork and payment had been made.

While the book cooking had reduced the price, it was still considerable, but she didn't resent a penny of it. She transferred the last of the money and they got to completing the final forms.

"Now that you are officially a fully sentient synthetic lifeform, you need to set your legal name," Mannheim said as he pushed a tablet towards Kelly. "There are no requirements or exclusions, so you can go with anything. A default name is in place at the moment."

"Kelly Smith," she said, wrinkling her nose a little.

"Are you going to stay as 'Kelly'?" Hannah asked.

She nodded. "Yeah, but I'm not taken on 'Smith'."

"Each field has a random generator, if you're struggling," Mannheim prompted before returning to his coffee.

For several minutes, she flicked through various names. Most were discarded quickly. In an effort to help, she entered two middle names and started to flick again.

"Oh, le Synthé sounds classy," she said.

"It's French for 'the Synth'," Hannah replied. "Kelly Erica Louise le Synthé might be a little on the nose."

She continued to look at the name, pondering whether it was her or not. In the end, she clicked to randomise one more time.

"Kelly Erica Louise Trevelyan," she said with a firm nod.

Mannheim took the tablet and made the name official, along with her date of birth. "That's it, you're all done and legally a human, with all the benefits and drawbacks that come with it. Congratulations."

He tapped away on the tablet for a few seconds. "You'll need some follow up checks; physical and psychological," he said. "I can book you in for your first check in a week. And remember, some of your more advanced mods could take months to fully activate as you get used to your new body configuration. Don't push them."

She nodded.

"Well, that's everything from my side," he said with a smile. "Anything you want to ask or go over?"

She couldn't think of anything; her head was spinning from the fact that she was human, she was real. She was free to be who she wanted to be.

He smiled. It was a familiar response from most. "If you think of anything, call me," he said, holding his business card out. She tapped her wrist against it to transfer the contact details.

The two women stood, gave their thanks and farewells to Mannheim and left, slightly giddy. They were so giddy they completely missed the young man in a white robe that watched them leave the clinic.

"Shall we go introduce you to the rest of the crew?" Hannah asked, grinning.

Kelly linked arms with her. "Well, I was thinking we could have a little fun before going back to the ship."

"Oh? And what sort of fun did you have in mind."

"How about I get some new clothes, since I'm wearing all of them right now."

They headed towards the nearest shopping district. Normally, Hannah wouldn't have ventured into it: she generally replicated all her clothes as she had little interest in current fashion trends, and it was rather expensive.

Little boutiques nestled together between the larger, mainstream shops. People were flitting between them; some well-dressed, some outrageously dressed in garish displays of wealth. One man was wearing a suit made of gemstones that must have weighed more than he did, while the man on his arm looked like a peacock.

After a short wander, Kelly settled on a modest little place. Rails held premade clothes for browsing.

The owner smiled to them as they entered, before returning to her sowing.

Kelly spent some time browsing the rails, looking for clothes in her size. Although her measurements were fairly normal, she was taller than the average man. Not that there really was an "average" human anymore.

The owner bustled over after a while. "Finding everything, dear?"

"Oh, yes, thanks," she replied. "Just trying to figure out sizes."

With a sage nod, the woman smiled. "Recent growth spurt?"

"You could say that."

She glanced over at Hannah, who had slumped into a chair near the door, surrounded by the bags of bits and pieces from the clinic raffle win. "I take it you've been out and about all day; your mum looks a bit worn out."

Kelly immediately went bright red. "Oh, oh, no, that's not my mum. We're friends; we serve on the same ship."

The woman had also blushed slightly. "You're awfully young to be serving on a ship."

"I just look very young." Kelly hadn't really thought she looked young, but catching herself in a mirror on the wall, she realised she did, probably because her skin was flawlessly new.

"Well, if you want to try anything on, the fitting room is at the back," the owner said, trying to pretend her faux pas had never happened. "If you want anything adjusted, or I don't have it in your size, let me know."

Taking an armful of blouses, trousers, skirts, t-shirts and a scarf, she headed for the fitting room.

In the end, she bought the lot.

"Well, that was a little embarrassing," she said as they left the shop.

Hannah's eyebrow raised slightly. "Oh?"

"The assistant thought you were my mother."

"What?" she replied, stopping to look at Kelly. It was then she remembered she probably did look older and Kelly did suddenly look fresh faced. "How old are you?"

"Old enough," she replied tartly, giving a sharp half shrug as she tossed her head slightly.

"And that would be?"

There was a mumbled response as she looked away.

"Sorry, I missed that."

"Hum-mphf-one."

Hannah narrowed her eyes.

"T-umph-one?"

"Thirty-one?"

Kelly shook her head and grimaced ever so slightly. "Twenty-one."

There was a long, painful pause as Hannah's brain processed this. "I am old enough to be your mother," she replied, looking a tad disgusted. "Twenty-one? You're half my age."

She immediately started to laugh. "I'm thirty-six according to my paperwork," she replied, still laughing playfully. "I was 'twenty-one' when activated fifteen years ago, much as I'd prefer to pretend they didn't happen. Anyway, you look about twenty-five, so age is just a number."

"You'll need a lot more than that to butter me up."

"Ah, but there is a quantity." She grinned and shrugged cheekily. "How about I buy us dinner?"

Trying, and failing, to appear casually nonchalant about the offer, Hannah pretended to consider it. "Well, as long as it's somewhere nice."

"All you can eat buffet?"

She tossed her head dramatically and huffed.

Giggling, Kelly shook her head. "Of course, I forgot; you're old, so won't be able to eat that much. Hey!" she cried as Hannah playfully slapped her arm. "How about Henri's, I hear it has rave reviews."

Fish in a Barrel

Annie took a deep calming breath.

At least, it was meant to have been calming. Instead, it stoked the fires of her rapidly flaring temper.

"What do you mean; 'it's the wrong size'?" she asked, her voice level.

It scared Tom, the young engineer, enough that he started to cradle the particle separator to his chest, more as a shield than out of any feelings towards the component.

"Well, turns out that the Heisenberg excitor is slightly longer than we –"

"Yes, I know," she cut in. "I specifically spec'd it with a miniature cyclone so it would fit."

Tom swallowed, feeling that it somehow was going to be his fault. He was only trying to install the parts he'd been given. "But then there would be a gap."

She looked up at him, sucking on her bottom lip and squinting slightly. "And that's what the pipe is for. Now, where is the part I ordered?"

He squeaked and immediately went bright red. "I don't know."

"Well, go find out."

In his rush to leave, Tom nearly knocked Casper over. He juggled the separator for a moment as it made a bid for the floor, all the time apologising to anyone in earshot for everything.

"You do know he looks about ten?" he asked as he slipped his arms around Annie. "Kicking puppies isn't nice."

She snorted. "Aye, but a puppy can fetch. Perhaps I should be using puppies to get my parts?"

He scrunched his face up. "Think of the mess."

Annie looked around the engine room. The old drives had been ripped out, leaving exposed conduits, wires and pipes. Tools had been left scattered about the place and at least three abandoned cups of tea or coffee had long gone cold. Oil, grease and other mechanical fluids coated the deck; covering the consoles had been a wise plan, but she wasn't sure how the cartoonish splatter, outlining a person, had occurred. A litter of untrained puppies wouldn't have made the place much worse.

"Take a night off," he said, seeing her looking around her kingdom with a deep sadness and longing.

"We're already a month behind," she replied. "I can't."

He nodded slowly. "Okay, but what are you going to do?"

She looked around and opened her mouth to reply, but stopped short. With none of the right parts, at least, none she could install by herself, there was nothing to do.

A weak smile started to grow. "Maybe you're right," she said. "How about we get dressed up and you take me to a nice restaurant?"

"I think I can manage that," he replied. "There's a lovely little Italian place, Bella Roma, up near Cambridge Plaza. As long as you don't mind it's run by the Mafia?"

"So clichéd, an Italian restaurant run by a Mafia family," she replied. "Sounds good to me."

"We could invite Hannah and Kelly," he suggested. "Double date?"

Annie narrowed her eyes at him a little. "You do know they aren't dating?"

He chuckled. "How many update meetings has Hannah attended with you and how many for Kelly has she attended? It's obvious; they just need a little push so they get there before the heat-death of the universe."

Her eyes narrowed further. "You know something?"

"No, no – ugh!" he gasped as she got a firm hold of him. "No, really, I don't – oh, oh, okay, okay."

She smiled and gave him a kiss as she loosened her grip. "Spill."

"The way they look at each other, that's all."

She patted his cheek. "If I find out you're withholding gossip…" she replied with a cheeky smile, leaving the consequences hanging. "Come on, let's find out if they want to join us. We can put your theory to the test."

"Would you like a drink? Any appetisers while you wait?"

Kelly smiled warmly at the barmaid. "I'll have a glass of prosecco."

"Elderflower pressé," Hannah replied.

Bella Roma was a small place, with lots of little booths jostling together around the walls with almost no room for free standing tables. The bar occupied a corner, behind which was the kitchen, and there were four stools on each section. Most of the tables were occupied by couples, small groups or families.

Everything had a "rustic" feel to it. The furniture was aged wood and metal, little window boxes and buckets contained typical Italian herbs and the art on the walls was on Tuscan sunsets, Sicilian sea views and vineyards.

Hannah suspected that the restaurant was about as Italian as the asteroid was and probably based on ancient stereotypes. She felt a little overdressed, having put a dress on for the second time in as many months, but everyone appeared overdressed for the place.

The drinks appeared along with a little bowl of olives to share. For a moment, she considered trying her party trick; tossing food and catching it in her mouth. Being thrown out was likely to follow.

Kelly made a squeak as she sipped her prosecco.

"The bubbles," she said, eyes wide with excitement, "I've never felt bubbles in a drink so clearly before. Not fussed by the taste, though."

Annie and Casper arrived and joined them at the bar and ordered drinks. A waitress showed them over to a small booth, sat in an alcove out of the way.

"Do you think this is so we're away from the riff-raff or because we are the riff-raff?" Casper asked after the waitress handed out menus, ran through the specials and left to tend other customers.

"Oh, we are the riff-raff," Hannah replied.

They ordered starters and mains. A bottle of white wine was ordered for the table, although Hannah stuck to her pressé.

"So, what fun things have you two been up to today?" Annie asked as her garlic bread appeared before her.

Hannah shrugged as she daintily lifted a piece of calamari and dipped it in the aioli. "Oh, you know, trying to figure out what to do once we escape this place. You?"

"Up to my eyes in apprentices that can't follow simple instructions," she replied.

Casper proceeded to regale his interesting finds from talking to Carl and Aisha about life in the 21st Century. Despite having had his right to roam around restored, he rarely left *Sigyn* and always did with someone else in tow, for his protection as much as to prove himself trustworthy.

While distracted by a tale of a global pandemic that had brought Earth to its knees, Hannah nearly missed Kelly pinching a piece of calamari.

She stuck her tongue out and popped it in her mouth, chewed twice and started to look a little off colour. Apparently, she didn't like a herb in the aioli and deeply regretted her decision to snatch a piece. The wine helped wash the taste out.

They chatted about plans for the rest of their time stuck on the station. So far, no one had ventured thoughts on their plans after they had repaired.

The mains arrived. Kelly peered curiously at the rather large pizza that had been placed in front of Hannah before looking at her dainty bowl of pasta.

Seeing the look, Hannah rolled her eyes ever so slightly. "Would you like a slice?"

"If you don't mind…"

"Only because it's you."

Casper gently nudged Annie as the pizza was carved and divided. She looked at him, unconvinced by his previous assertions. Until Kelly's hand brushed the back of Hannah's and they both blushed, ever so slightly, while looking rather coy.

Dido took a deep breath, drawing in through her nose. She held it for a few heartbeats, then blew it out through her mouth slowly. Calm was just starting to come to her when there was a crash.

She tried to ignore it and find her centre again, but the chattering of the Purifiers over whatever had been dropped was too much. Giving up, she flopped back on her bunk.

For nearly two weeks, she and nineteen of her best Purifiers had been stuck in the shielded dorm with almost nothing to do, only getting out to exercise. Three days ago, that had stopped; supposedly they had entered restricted space.

Mwangi had refused to speak with her repeatedly, claiming to be busy, asleep or otherwise engaged. The man she'd been dealing with, Cosworth, had always been nervous around her, but had become even more so.

"Ma'am, I think you're right," Ludo, the Purifier-Paladin that was acting as her Executive Officer on the mission, said. "The crew have been quietly arming themselves, chatter on the forum is becoming cryptic."

She hopped down from the top bunk and joined him at the small tablet he'd used to hack some of the ship's systems.

"Where are we?"

"We're in the Roanapur system," he replied. Giving her a sidelong look, he continued: "We arrived last night, but no attempt at docking has been made."

Either Mwangi wasn't ready to dock yet, which was unlikely as ships loitering tended to be moved on, or he was trying to figure out who to sell them out to. He wasn't well known on the station, which was why he'd been picked as transport, so there was a good chance no one would give him the bandwidth to claim to have something to sell. It was also why the trip had taken so long; he needed to appear to be making normal rounds rather than making a beeline for a station he rarely visited.

Her patience had run out.

"Everyone away from the door," she announced as she stood up. "As soon as we get out, find your target and secure the ship. Non-lethal combat only."

Approaching the door, her suspicions were confirmed. Any time she'd tried to leave, it had opened, but this time it didn't. She tapped on the control panel, attempting to override it.

"They're alert," Ludo called out.

Out of good faith, the Purifiers had handed over their weapons on arrival under the justification that the dorm wasn't shielded enough to cover up weapons signatures. The lie had run both ways: there was no need for the weapons to be surrendered as twenty bodies would be a much larger, easier to spot anomaly; and of course, the weapons were fake.

"Suit up."

All of the Purifiers activated their suits, the nanomaterials wrapping around them.

Dido drew her left arm back as her suit created a battering ram around it. In a single punch, she buckled the door and sent it crashing into the opposite bulkhead with a second.

The corridor was illuminated with two bolts of superheated plasma, followed by confused shouting.

Ignoring the threats, she stepped into the corridor as though everything was normal and started to head for the Bridge. Two men started to rush her, but one stopped and dropped to his knees, leaving the other for her to effortlessly clothesline as he tried to grab her.

The other Purifiers streamed out, heading in different directions to secure what they needed to. Taking total control of the ship wasn't the objective for getting onto Roanapur. Without the crew, it would be hard to convince whoever Mwangi had originally negotiated a berth with to still do so.

Ludo fell in behind as she made her way to the Bridge.

No one tried to stop them. Any crew they did see either surrendered or fled. The sight of a pair of fully armed Purifiers tended to do that.

Resistance finally came at the Bridge, which had been fully locked down. Dido tried to break it down, but the door remained stubbornly in place and undented.

"Ma'am? May I?" Ludo asked.

She stood aside and gestured for him to be her guest.

He scanned the door and bulkhead around it. Walking away from the door, he turned to face a section of bulkhead to the left. His armour changed shape; a large, conical shield formed on his right arm and bracing formed along his arm, across his back and around his neck.

Charging at superhuman speed, he slammed into and passed through the bulkhead.

Dido stepped daintily through the hole after him.

"Sorry about the mess," she said as if surprise visitors had arrived and she hadn't dusted that day. "I knocked, but no one answered."

Mwangi and the three Bridge crew looked at her in disbelief.

"No point having an unbreakable door if the wall is like paper," Ludo said, still in juggernaut form. "I'd offer to pay to repair it, but I won't."

"Why haven't we docked yet?" Dido asked.

"I was just trying to when you started a rampage," Mwangi replied, looking around him frantically.

"Why lock us in?"

"For your own safety."

She stared at him, although he could only see the smooth surface of her armour.

Lifting her arm, she shot him in the chest. He convulsed a few times before slumping, unconscious, in his chair.

"First Officer?" she called out.

"Ma'am," replied an older man. He stood up straight, his chin held a little defiantly.

Retracting her helmet, Dido walked over to him. "Make preparations to dock and have someone take the Captain to his cabin; he's going to wake up with a hellish headache in about an hour."

When the man didn't move, she stepped closer. "Do as I order, or I'll add you to the pile and work my way down the chain of command until I find someone that will do what I'm paying them to do."

For a moment she was sure he was going to spit on her, but his chin dropped in submission. "Aye, Ma'am," he said quietly.

The garden was quiet, tranquil and mostly empty of people. It had been made in a Japanese style with small ponds, waterfalls, neatly arranged plants, moss gardens, rock and gravel gardens, and fish.

Hannah and Kelly had come for a walk after they'd finished their meal, while Annie and Casper had returned to *Sigyn*. Eventually, they had settled on a bench in an open area.

Slipping her hand in to Hannah's, Kelly leant against her and sighed. "This is nice," she said dreamily.

Hannah gave her hand a squeeze and smiled. For the first time in, well, she wasn't actually sure how long, she felt content and peaceful. Perhaps it was time to consider a change in pace? Settling down in a nice quiet place sounded nice, but how long before she got bored?

Kelly shifted next to her.

"What's up?"

"Well, I have to ask," she replied after more uncomfortable movements. "Where do we stand? Is this just a bit of fun? A fling? Or, you know, maybe something more?"

"I should have taken a left turn at Albuquerque," she replied, looking straight ahead, but tapping on her implant.

Before Kelly could question the cryptic remark, her own implant buzzed. It was then that she saw what had Hannah distracted; marching towards them was a woman dressed in the white robe of a Purifier with two men flanking her.

A quick look around confirmed they were surrounded by at least a dozen Purifiers, forming a net. There were likely more nearby.

"Captain Sinclair, what a pleasure to see you again," Dido said as she came to a stop a few paces away. "In the flesh, no less."

Left at Albuquerque

Annie was, despite protests from Casper, back in Engineering, double checking everything before joining him in her cabin. In reality, she was taking some space to order her thoughts. After wanting to kill him, she now found herself smitten again. But did she want to be?

Add to that the revelation that the captain was, or was planning on, banging the chief medical officer, her head was swimming.

Jon appeared next to her. "Albuquerque," he said.

"Albuquerque?"

"Albuquerque," he repeated, more forcefully.

"Albuquerque?" she asked, shaking her head slightly.

His eyes went wide. "Al-bu-quer-que," he said again, breaking it down into syllables.

"Albuquerque," she whispered to herself, trying to figure out why such a silly word should mean something to her.

Then it hit her like an Acme rocket being ridden by a starving coyote.

"Albuquerque? Albuquerque!"

Jon held his hands out, pleading with her to realise exactly what he meant.

"I knew I should have taken that left turn at Albuquerque," she declared.

"At last," he cried, a weight lifting from his shoulders.

Annie charged across the room and started to bring any system that wasn't lying scattered on the floor, back online. "Is everyone on board?"

"Hannah and Kelly aren't here. I'm assuming they are with Harry; she's started preparing to leave as well." He paused for a moment, frowning slightly. "Tower has acknowledged our intention to go."

They wouldn't be going very far. Even if they tried to piggyback on *Frigg* it would take Jon and Chris hours to calculate how to make a Hop jump.

"Have everyone report here; we'll move the Bridge here," she said. As the longest serving member of the crew, command fell to her with Hannah on *Frigg*. "Have you been able to reach Hannah?"

He shook his head. "Protocol requires radio silence with crew off ship, in case they have been captured. I've only been able to confirm *Frigg* is following protocol, but nothing else."

Annie decoupled the ship from the dock and started to manoeuvre out of the berth. Normally, there would be all sorts of checks to conduct, but right now they had to get moving.

Laura appeared and took up an unused console. "I'm detecting three people trying to override the berth access," she said. "Purifiers."

It didn't matter, really. If they managed to open the airlock, they'd be blown into space, most likely bouncing off *Sigyn* as she left. Not the best way to die, but definitely different.

Realising they'd missed their chance, they stopped and retreated.

"*Frigg* is already out," Jon said. "Wait, I'm detecting a Hop. She's gone; the station is going nuts." He swore softly. "She jumped inside the no-FTL zone."

There was a round of curses. The station would likely go into lockdown, suspecting either an attack or that someone had just tried to sabotage it. If they didn't get out before the harbour doors shut, they'd be trapped.

Emily appeared, dressed in her pyjamas and took over the helm.

"Nice of you to join us," Laura said with a wry smile.

She stuck her tongue out. "There's a Guild freighter messing about in the harbour entrance," she said. "If I didn't know better, I'd say they're preventing it from closing on us. Going to full impulse."

Jon's eyes nearly rolled out of his head. "Inside the Harbour? Are you mad? Do you have any idea how big a fine we'll get?"

No one was listening. A fine was preferable to being trapped, especially since it was pretty obvious the Purifiers were what had triggered the escape.

Several other ships, having been alerted to the impending lockdown, were following, clearly planning to get out first. A large yacht made to muscle them out of the way, but the freighter listed to starboard, blocking its path.

"What freighter is that?" Annie asked, still trying to get the warp drive online.

"*Whisky Galore*," he replied.

"Find out if they can take us."

Most cargo ships, from small transports to super-freighters, had a series of stored calculations for Hop and slipstream for quick reference based on standard cargo loading. Usually, those calculations were good within a decent percentage variant.

Jon made contact.

"Yes, they're opening their aft cargo bay," he replied. "It's tight, think you can manage, Emily?"

She turned to look at him and put one hand on her hip. "Damn right, I can."

He held his hands up in defeat. This was how he was going to die; in a careless blaze of someone else's glory.

A few seconds later, a series of collision alarms went off, followed by a shudder and thump. He had the decency, or perhaps sense of self-preservation, not to point out that Emily had clipped the door on the way past.

Just as things were looking up, they got a lot worse.

"Remnant fleet on an intercept course," Jon announced. "They appeared mid system and are demanding *Whisky* turn us over. They're obfuscating stupidity at the moment, but they won't make it to FTL safe distance in time."

Annie was half listening; she was getting messages from the Guild asking what was going on, messages from the Tower demanding they shut down and await the end of the lockdown before leaving, and a message from Spectrum offering assistance.

Whisky shuddered out of the Harbour entrance into open space. She was too big to Hop efficiently, meaning she'd need to go to slipstream. That left her very trackable and with little hope of getting away.

At the head of the Remnant fleet, *Purity* drove forward, hoping to cut them off.

From nowhere, a number of small, rectangular ships blipped into existence. They formed a line between the Remnant and Roanapur, just beyond the FTL safe line. They were nearly identical to the ones from Gallifrey.

"Receiving a message," Jon said. His eyes went white and he shuddered and flickered a few times.

"Eris has decided to help you, this time. Do not reign on the deal with Ms White," he said flatly, staring at a point on the wall, his head at an awkward angle. "Or else."

He gasped for breath and leant forward, eyes blinking rapidly now that the spell had been broken. After flickering a few times, his avatar vanished completely.

"What the hell?" Laura asked.

No one answered. Rumours were rife of AIs being hacked by someone claiming to be Eris. Many were too superstitious to even speak the name for fear of attracting the omnipresent Monster of the Internet. Most were more concerned about people with shady pasts expiring suddenly from previous undiagnosed, explosive, brain aneurisms. But those were just stories, of course…

Whisky moved quickly to the FTL safe line and made the jump to slip-space unmolested. A short time later she dropped back to normal space and approached the waiting *Sheba*.

Jon fizzled into existence, looking none the worse for wear. "Harry is calling." Her hologram appeared next to him.

"What the hell happened?" she asked.

Annie shrugged. "Purifiers by the look of it. Didn't you ask Hannah?"

She looked confused. "How? She's with you, isn't she?"

A deep feeling of dread filled everyone.

"We thought you had her and Kelly," Annie replied.

Slowly, Harry shook her head, horror growing.

"Then we just left them behind on a station crawling with Purifiers."

"I'm sorry, I think you've mistaken me for someone else," Hannah said as she turned away, intent on continuing her conversation with Kelly in peace.

Dido smiled lightly. "I know who you are, Hannah," she replied.

"No, I'm Helen; Hannah is my wayward, but startlingly intelligent, funny and beautiful sister. The one with really good business acumen and wit so cunning you could brush your teeth with it."

A small screen appeared on Dido's left arm. "Hm, yes, I know you have sisters, but only Hannah has artificial legs." She held the screen up to show the results of her scan clearly highlighted the mechanical legs.

"We can do this the easy way, or the hard way. And no, I don't want you to make me take you the hard way." She narrowed her eyes for a moment, considering the way she'd just said that.

With a series of slow nods, Hannah shrugged and lunged. Although surrounded, her hope was to capture Dido and use her as a hostage to escape. It was a very thin hope, but if she could do it before *Sigyn* or *Frigg* left, it might work.

She landed back on the bench with a thump; her attack had been intercepted, parried and reversed. That did nothing to dampen her fighting spirit as she threw a right as she stood up, only to feint and sweep her leg.

Somehow, she ended up back on the bench, bemused.

In a show of defeat, she stood up slowly and offered her hand.

Dido took it with confidence.

When Hannah attempted to pull her off balance, Dido simply allowed herself to go forward, sidestepped her prey, whipped her feet from under her and gently plonked her on the ground.

"Do you feel like surrendering yet?" Hannah asked from her pinned position, cheek squashed to the cold, hard paving stone.

"Hannah, babe, please, this is getting embarrassing," Kelly whispered, her face rapidly reddening as she looked at the Purifiers trying to stifle their laughter. "Just stop before you make a fool of yourself."

Dido chuckled. "I think it's a bit late for that." She got up to let Hannah go.

Alarms started to blare, spooking the Purifiers. They spun around, weapons ready, looking for an ambush.

Hannah laughed manically as she pushed herself up. "And that will be my ship jumping away from too close, triggering a lockdown to trap you here." She grinned and folded her arms. "It's the ship you're after; I can't tell you what you want."

"Maybe not," she replied absently, confirming that a ship had Hopped and a freighter was desperately trying to escape with a smaller ship blundering into it. "But I think your crew will be loyal enough to negotiate for your return."

Kelly laughed. "Who are you kidding? We were ready to mutiny; our engineer will have taken over and run off with the ship."

This earned her a sharp look from Hannah.

"Then we can help reclaim your ship."

Hannah made another attempt at attacking Dido. No more playing (which is what she'd been doing until now), she managed to startle the Purifier into falling back and defending herself.

The fight didn't last long. Winning wasn't an option; if she did actually capture Dido, there was no way to escape now. Instead, she pretended to trip, which turned into a real uncontrolled fall and she landed face down in Kelly's lap, much to Kelly's surprise.

Looking up, resting her chin on Kelly's thigh, she winked at her.

Whirling up to attack again, Hannah watched as Dido simply dodged and then jabbed her in the side with an armoured fist. A surge of pain shot through her like lightning before all feeling evaporated.

Collapsing like a puppet with cut strings, Hannah had a moment of panic, but was powerless to do anything about it.

Dido caught her deftly and tossed her over her shoulder.

"Is this the hard way?" Hannah slurred; her mouth half-numb and her tongue lolling slightly.

"You're not as heavy as I'd estimated," she replied, hefting her load into a better position, "so, not really."

"Taking me to your dungeon for a bit of light torture? Whips and chains to 'take me the hard way'?" she asked.

Kelly stood up slowly, her hands up. "Don't talk, honey; you're likely to bite your tongue and I don't have anything to stick it back on with."

"I take it you'll come quietly?"

She nodded. "I just got this body and I am not letting it get damaged."

As Dido started to march back towards the ship, she had a feeling she'd been played. The attacks had been sloppy, yet there had been sparks of competence that only military training could provide. The fact she'd been held up while her real target had escaped added to that feeling.

The sooner she had them secured on *Purity*, the better.

The Exquisite Torture of Dinner Small Talk

By the time the lockdown was lifted, nearly six hours after it had started, Hannah had recovered from her paralysis and was none the worse for wear, if grumpy.

She and Kelly had been frog-marched onto a ship that was clearly not a Remnant vessel to wait. As soon as the Harbour doors opened, the ship was out and docked with *Purity*. The transfer was quick and messy, after which, the Remnant ships left the system for somewhere more private.

They were separated and checked for weapons, espionage equipment, and to confirm they were definitely who they said they were. Given simple robes to wear, their clothes were confiscated.

Everyone was reasonably respectful. Requests were polite, there were no threats or imposing bodies to intimidate them. One woman Hannah encountered was even down right apologetic for the barrage of questions.

Once the Remnant Inquisition, which had been expected, had concluded for the day, they were released into a small room with a few chairs. It was clinical, white and sparse.

"So, I'm guessing this is God's waiting room," Hannah muttered as she looked around, while flapping her robes. "I wonder when I get my halo?"

Kelly snorted a laugh.

"What?"

"You'd use your halo as a frisbee," she replied, with a playful smirk. "I hope I'm far enough away that I don't go with you when the trapdoor to Hell opens."

"Wow, just how much of you is sarcasm?"

"Learnt from the best," she replied, then tapped her head. "Had Dr Mannheim install a few routines."

Hannah smiled and chuckled slightly. "You are definitely not lacking in confidence."

"I hope you aren't intimidated by confident women?"

"Quite the opposite," she replied, lifting an eyebrow slightly suggestively.

The door opened to reveal Dido and Castor. She was all polite smiles, while he looked decidedly nervous as he stood back a little, peering round his boss like a small child hiding behind his mother.

"My apologies for the shakedown and wait," she said, ushering them towards the door. "Quarters have been prepared, although I'm afraid we only have a single guest suite."

Hannah looked to Kelly and shrugged. "I'm good sharing."

"Yup," she replied, nodding and trying to make it look nonchalant.

Dido's eyes swivelled between them. "Okay," she said slowly. "Given the time, I'll show you briefly to your quarters and then dinner will be served in the Diplomatic Lounge."

The quartet left the small holding room and were joined by a troop of Purifiers. They kept their distance, weapons holstered, but they were wearing standard body armour. While it might have been over the top for two guests, Dido was not taking any chances.

Briefly was the optimal word for the viewing of their temporary quarters. The suite, which consisted of an open plan living area and two bedrooms, was as stark as every other part of the ship.

After the whistle stop tour, they were spirited away to the Diplomatic Lounge. As grand as it sounded, crammed into a destroyer, it was a simple room with a modest table by a holographic window, three couches in a sunken area and a small bar. Everything was white or light grey, relieved only by a few paintings to give a splash of colour.

Castor and the Purifiers stopped at the door, leaving Hannah, Kelly and Dido alone in the lounge.

Dido drifted to the bar. "Drinks?" she asked.

"Lemonade," Hannah replied as she tossed herself onto one of the couches. It was well padded and firm, clearly seeing little use. "Will Gung-ho be joining us?"

She smiled a little wider. "No, I'm afraid not. I felt it was best; he's still," she searched for the correct, and polite term, "annoyed about you nearly ramming his ship."

"Shame."

"I'll have a gin and tonic," Kelly said. Given the verbal sparring that was likely to be a feature of the evening, alcohol was going to be a necessity to get through.

The drinks were brought over before Dido went back for her crème de menthe. She sat down and sipped it daintily, one leg crossed over the other.

Silence filled the room.

Hannah dipped her finger into the lemonade.

"It's not poisoned," Dido said, a wry smile on her lips. "Would be silly to kill you."

"I dunno, you've tried a few times."

They sat in silence again while two stewards finished preparing the table.

"I must say, congratulations on the work you've had done," Dido said to Kelly as she finished her drink. "You're looking a lot better than the old file pictures I'd managed to pull together."

Kelly blushed. "Thanks."

"No taking compliments from the enemy," Hannah chided, although only half-heartedly. She shuffled a little closer to her.

"I'm not your enemy."

She turned slowly, staring. "Oh really? So, I'm imagining being abducted, strip searched and made to wear a child's angel outfit?"

Dido puffed her cheeks out and considered the point for a moment. "It does suit you."

The stewards returned carrying the starter; a light salad with a series of accompaniments: dressings, sauces and dips; olives in various oils; slices of white, brown and sourdough bread. A bottle of lightly chilled white wine was placed on the table along with a jug of iced water.

Hannah refused the wine, taking only water.

"You are a very difficult woman to trace," Dido said as she poured a little chilli olive oil on her salad. "Which I find a little surprising for a highly decorated Group Captain that won the Hero of the Commonwealth Medal."

She didn't react, instead spearing a plum tomato to chew on. "I like my privacy," she replied eventually. "I hate having to sign photos for people."

The two women regarded each other, figuring out who was going to strike first, what parry or riposte would be best and how to gain the upper hand. Dido had a clear advantage of knowing some of Hannah's history, while she knew nothing of the Purifier-General's past.

"I believe you were awarded it for 'extreme valour in battle' at Hafan."

Stomach lurching, Hannah took a sip of water in hopes of settling it. After seven years of having almost put the battle behind her, it seemed intent in filling every waking moment with ghosts of the past and her sleep with nightmares of the horrors.

"I was a Paladin at the time," she continued. "Given what I can figure out, I believe you killed my father."

Cutlery clattered onto the plate. "Is that it? I killed your father; you're going to tell me 'Prepare to die' before lunging with the butter knife?" Hannah replied mockingly. She reached for the wine bottle, poured herself a small glass, which was then left untouched. "Well, I killed a lot of fathers that day, so you'll need to be more specific."

Kelly slumped slightly and put her head in her hand, the other anchored to her wine.

A stony staring match ensued. It lasted somewhere between two seconds and two lifetimes of the universe before Dido snorted a dismissive chuckle.

"My father was Lord-Purifier Achilles," she replied. "I loved my father, but he brought his death on himself. The attack on Hafan was petty and foolish, but the old guard refused to be beaten. Death before dishonour; so very Klingon of them."

Hannah narrowed her eyes, looking for the trick. Was this an attempt to make the Purifiers seem reformed? It would take more than that to win her over.

"Why do you want the *Livingstone*?" she asked, changing the subject.

Dido shrugged and pulled a face. "The hope of a novelty 21st Century bobblehead, maybe some authentic branded leisure wear?"

She placed her cutlery down, finished with her salad. "Ideally, the way to get to Sol and access to genetic material."

"To use it to force everyone into your ideal genetic form?"

With a sharp jerk of her head, Dido opened her mouth to reply, pursed her lips as she checked she'd heard right and then looked at Hannah with questioningly narrow eyes. "Is that propaganda still being circulated? Do you think we want to forcibly reverse the current human condition?"

Kelly placed her fork down. "Well, that is what a lot of the Purists we encounter tell us."

Pinching her nose, she sighed. "I knew it would bite us in the ass," she muttered. Sitting up again, she shook her head. "Any that came from the Restoration are the fringe lunatics we've kicked out. The idea of reversing the human condition en-mass hasn't been considered viable for three hundred years."

The two guests glanced at each other, looking for the other to ask the obvious question. As the medically trained person, Kelly lost the ensuing gesture war.

"So, why do you want it?"

The stewards appeared to clear the table. The plates and used cutlery were lifted and whipped away to the kitchen. Fresh plates were delivered. Platters of meat; beef, lamb, chicken, venison, and goat were placed down, and quickly joined by steaming bowls of boiled potatoes and steamed vegetables. Another platter with an array of fish appeared. A bottle of red wine was placed on the table and the white was replaced with a fresh bottle.

Hannah had yet to drink any of the wine she'd poured.

Dido gestured for her guests to start. "If it's not too personal to ask, Hannah, would I be right in assuming you were conceived artificially?"

"I was," she replied, lifting two slices of beef, a piece of chicken and a salmon fillet. "It's not that uncommon."

It was, in fact, quite common and generally not a taboo subject, but not exactly polite dinner conversation with strangers. Often it was done to overcome inherent incompatibilities between the parents, for same sex couples and for those rich enough to afford gene-tailored offspring.

She nodded. "According to research last year, more than seventy percent of children born had some genetic intervention, of which forty-seven percent would never have been viable without it. Nearly twenty percent of the others would have been severely disabled."

For a moment she sat, as if that answered the question. She lifted a piece of venison, a few potatoes and a mix of broccoli, cauliflower, peas, and sweetcorn.

"Our genes are full of junk," she said. "The junk is what causes the problems. Millenia of messing about, trying to fix it, and cosmetic changes are the root of the problem. Using old material, we can better identify the junk to screen out."

Kelly lifted an eyebrow in question. "And that's different from making us all like 21st Century homo sapiens how?"

She smiled. "Well, it would be voluntary for one thing," she said before chewing a piece of venison. "The problem is, even if a child currently is born by natural conception, the chances of it being able to conceive naturally are remote."

That was something Hannah was well aware of. She and Ali had considered having a child before she'd transitioned, but they were given a less than ten percent chance of conceiving naturally – and after four first trimester miscarriages – they had decided to focus on their careers first. Any children she did have, if she ever did, would almost certainly be in the same boat.

It wasn't a problem normally; gene-tailoring to create viable foetuses was an easy to access service in most regions. The problem was it meant the human race was functionally extinct without medical intervention. Almost every time intervention occurred, it only addressed the immediate issues, not the species wide problem. It also tended to add to the problems as a side effect.

"So how do you feel about me being able to have children with natural humans?" Kelly asked. "I'm mostly organic, I have DNA and I'm fertile. Would any children I have with a human father be considered hybrids? Abominations?"

Hannah finished her wine, although no one had noticed her starting it. She poured a large glass of red and set about it.

"Honestly, there are those that would," Dido replied. "Me, personally? No. But your DNA is likely as polluted, if you'll excuse the term, as anyone else's. I suspect it was reverse engineered from your desired look using existing code samples."

She sipped her wine, trying not to glare at the insinuation that her DNA was full of junk.

Meanwhile, Hannah had gone back for more food and more wine, prompting Dido to signal for more to be brought out.

They ate in silence for a few minutes before finishing with the main. Again, the stewards appeared to clear the table and quickly set out dessert. A similar spread of various ice creams, sorbets, cakes, a trifle, and pastry dishes were set out. A selection of sweet dessert wines was set out next to the dishes they went well with.

"I always wondered what the person that took down the *Monitor* was like," Dido said as she poured herself a glass of ice wine. "I'd expected some arrogant fighter jock, or some self-sacrificing crusader. You are far more interesting," she said to Hannah.

She continued to talk about Hafan, explaining why she felt her father had brought his own death about and giving general admiration for the Commonwealth service personnel, while simultaneously criticising the Commonwealth for the way their propaganda worked.

Hannah was barely listening, the words crushing against her but not quite penetrating. All she could think about was what had happened after the battle. She'd spoken to her comrades of what had happened until the Brass had told her to keep quiet. After that, only her therapist had heard the truth and he'd taken the Navy line that she was best not to speak of it elsewhere. Part of the reason her discharge hadn't been immediate was they needed someone to do paperwork, but mostly they wanted to make sure she wasn't a danger to herself or the

Commonwealth narrative of the battle. A war hero committing suicide or having a public meltdown from PTSD shortly after a battle would have reflected poorly on the Navy's duty of care.

For seven years she'd carried the secret along with the pain of losing Ali. The pain she could, mostly, deal with. The secret gnawed away at her. Whenever she freaked out, it wasn't because of Ali's death, usually.

Now, it was no longer gnawing, but chewing furiously at her, a pack of rats demanding to be set free.

But she couldn't. The memory of how her comrades had looked at her afterwards, the way they looked at her like they didn't know her; she couldn't let that happen again. No one would understand, how could they? As soon as they knew, they'd all jump ship for their own safety and she'd be alone. Not even the Harpies knew.

Her head started swimming. Was it the wine or the stress?

Kelly gave her a little questioning frown. That was good; it meant she was keeping it all in and not letting it get out of control if she had to question what was swirling in her head.

Dido took a bite of a profiterole. "I have to say, you really are either the luckiest or the most skilled pilot of the age to have managed to time your Hop just right. To be able to get that close and not collide with the *Monitor*'s shields," she swung the skewered profiterole around a little in appreciation.

The pressure inside Hannah was reaching breaking point. It was all lies: all of it. Her 'victory', her 'skill'; nothing but lies. She was a fraud, a fake, a failure. Worse, she was a liar that had ridden the myth when it suited her. Hell had a special place set aside for her and the galaxy would forever praise her monumental failure.

"True genius."

"I WAS TRYING TO KILL MYSELF!"

The profiterole dropped from the fork to land on the table with a thump and a squelch of cream.

"I wasn't *trying* to take the bloody ship out with a Hop jump," she hissed, fingers digging into the table. "I was trying to commit suicide. It was a kamikaze run."

Kelly reached for her arm. "Hannah?"

She pulled her arm away violently. "I planned to ram the bridge and die. Do you know why I didn't?" she asked, staring viciously at Dido. "Because I was too stupid. I was too dumb to turn the anti-collision off. My AI saved me and it was pure, dumb luck that I'd come in on just the right line. Everything you and the whole galaxy believe is a lie. A filthy, dirty lie."

Glancing at Kelly, she could see the questions, the horror and what would inevitably lead to rejection. She grabbed one of the bottles of wine and drank straight from it, thumping it back on the table.

"I'm sorry," Dido said softly, looking about for some way to escape.

"You're sorry?" she asked, grabbing the untouched trifle, digging in with the serving spoon. "I'm a fraud, a despicable liar, that couldn't even manage the simple task of slamming a fighter into a battleship after your stormtroopers executed my wife; everything I've been held up to be has been a lie I've had to carry for seven years and you're sorry?"

At a total loss for words and what to do, she just gawped dumbly. Taking a moment to collect herself, she frowned a little. "Executed your wife?"

Hannah nearly vaulted the table.

"She was a doctor, in Abertawe. A Purifier death squad shot her, point blank, in the chest. And before you deny it, there were witnesses and I buried her body."

Dido knew nothing of any of this. She was aware that a small strike team had landed in Abertawe to capture the local government, but they were shot down before landing. It wasn't standard practice to kill civilians and certainly not entertained to execute them.

"Hannah, give me the bottle," Kelly said firmly as another bottle was being drained.

She swore viciously at her.

Kelly grabbed her wrist, found the pressure point between her thumb and index finger. As the bottle toppled free, she got up and slid her arms under Hannah's and lifted her out of the chair.

Like a caged animal, Hannah flailed and snarled until Kelly pulled her into a hug. She dissolved into a mess of sobbing.

Her training had not prepared her for this, so Dido sat still for longer than she was accustomed to in a volatile situation. "Perhaps it would be best if you went to your quarters?"

"You think?" Kelly replied.

Getting up, she made her way to the door and popped her head out. Castor had been waiting outside on a small chair with four Purifiers blocking the corridor from both directions. He nodded at his instructions, not questioning them. The two Purifiers on the right were dispatched to clear the way.

Hannah had stopped crying, but remained clinging to Kelly like a small child.

"Come on," Dido said softly, "let's get you somewhere private."

Hannah sat slumped on the bed, looking at her knees. Kelly had managed to carry her back to their quarters without too much incident; the Purifiers had kept enough of a distance to never quite see what was going on. As soon as they'd got back, Hannah had locked herself in the bathroom for nearly half an hour, sobbing and screaming interspaced by the more terrifying silences before she'd emerged looking like she'd gone ten rounds with a heavyweight boxer.

Crouching down to look up at her, Kelly tried to smile reassuringly. "If you want to talk, I'm here," she said, "and if you don't want to talk, I'm still here."

She remained blank. "You're too good to me."

"What?"

"How can you trust me to be your Captain?" she asked, still looking at her lap.

Gently, Kelly rubbed her knee. "An action borne of intense grief nearly a decade ago shouldn't define who you are now."

She remained crouched for a few minutes. This was way beyond anything she was equipped to deal with, but she was determined to seem like she knew what to do. Secretly, she was a little hurt that Hannah had never told her the truth. Yes, it was selfish, but was it through shame or lack of trust?

"I think some sleep will do you some good," she said, her legs starting to cramp. It was a new sensation, but not one she felt a need to indulge. Standing up, her new muscles complained.

Hannah nodded mutely.

Offering little resistance, she stood and allowed Kelly to help her out of the robe and into the bed.

"Stay with me," she said without looking at her. "Please?"

Kelly pulled her robe over her head and slipped in behind her, wrapping an arm around her to hold her. "Of course," she said, lightly kissing the nape of her neck.

For what felt like forever, Hannah just lay in the dark, staring at the wall. Tears welled and flowed in fits and starts, a mixture of pent-up grief and shame. After a while, she felt Kelly's arm relax as she fell asleep and shortly after that she rolled over, away from her.

The tears started again more freely now that the risk of being observed had lessened. Now they fell because she had no idea what to do. Any hope of brazening her way out of the current situation had evaporated. Fighting was not an option against a ship with at least several hundred crew and no guaranteed way of getting clear.

Eventually, she cried herself into an exhausted sleep.

Now What?

Hannah woke feeling drained and as tired as she had done when she'd gone to sleep. She rolled over to find Kelly was still sleeping. Now that she was fully sentient, she no longer slept looking like a perfect angel; her hair was a mess, her mouth hung open slightly and she was drooling.

She pushed a stray strand of flame red hair back from her face. Taking care not to wake her, she gently stroked her cheek and watched her smile in her slumber.

Closing her eyes for what felt like only a second, Hannah opened them to find Kelly looking at her softly, a gentle smile on her lips.

"Hi," Kelly said, before moving in for a kiss.

For a moment, Hannah wanted to believe there was nothing beyond the bed, that the horrors of reality weren't waiting for them. For a moment, there was nothing except for the pleasure of being close to someone.

As their lips parted, reality stuck its ugly head back into proceedings. They were in a nice bed, in a gilded cage, trapped on a Remnant destroyer.

She curled in against Kelly, soaking up the warmth and comfort.

"Are you feeling any better?"

"A little," she replied. "Well, as good as one can after making a total tit of oneself."

Kelly stroked her face. "You don't have to be so hard on yourself. I don't think any less of you and neither will anyone else. In fact, I'm amazed you've carried that for so long." She gave her a gentle squeeze. "But you don't have to carry it alone anymore."

The tears started again. Why wasn't she chastising her for lying, for being weak? Why was she being so understanding and supportive? Why didn't she hate her, like she hated herself?

When the tears ran out, she took a few ragged breaths and rubbed her eyes.

They lay together quietly until Hannah's stomach rumbled.

"Are you hungry?" Kelly asked, trying to keep the incredulity from her voice.

Slowly recoiling into herself, Hannah grimaced. "I threw everything up last night."

She kissed her forehead. "Well, a nutritious breakfast is in order."

"Why are you being so kind?" she asked as Kelly slipped out of bed. "Why aren't you angry at me?"

"Isn't it obvious?"

She sat up in bed and looked at Kelly, pondering the reply. Before she could answer, she was plunged into a deep kiss. After a moment of surprise, she relaxed and kissed back. It was only now that she realised how much she'd missed intimacy, the feeling of having someone she cared about being so close to her.

When they parted, Kelly sat on the edge of the bed and smiled, dreamily.

"You tried to ask me something," Hannah said, "before we were abducted."

She smiled and shook her head. "It's not important right now."

"It is to me. You want to know what we are."

"Yeah," she replied after a moment.

Hannah managed a smile. "Isn't it obvious?"

"Pretend I'm a sweet, naïve, innocent youngster that's never been in love."

"Because you are?"

Kelly pursed her lips and rolled her eyes slowly. "Maybe?" she said with a slight shrug.

"Let's just say," she replied as she slid out of bed and walked slowly towards the door, "I'll be signing cards from both of us."

A frown appeared on Kelly's face as she considered what that actually meant. "What does that mean? Hannah? What does that mean?" she asked, getting up to follow.

Spinning on her heel, Hannah threw her arms around Kelly's waist and looked up into her eyes. At almost a head shorter, it was quite a way to look up, but there were some advantages.

"It means, if you want to, totally up to you, be introduced as my," she paused to create a teasing tension, "girlfriend."

The normally soothing sounds of trickling water, lightly shimmering gongs and carefully tuned sounds were an annoyance now. Taking a deep breath and slowly releasing it, Dido tried to keep her mind focused on her breathing.

Stifling a curse, she got up and checked the time.

Less than ten minutes had passed. Her normal evening meditation could last for up to forty minutes and was never less twenty.

She marched over to one of her lilies. The simple white flowers stood out in full bloom and a smile came to her.

"Hello, lovely," she said softly. "You're looking beautiful tonight. I don't suppose you know how to calm my mind, do you?"

The lily remained silent.

Dido knew exactly what was wrong and she knew how to fix it, or at least, put her mind to rest. It meant breaking a few rules, but that had rarely stopped her doing anything; she'd always been lucky that she was considered strait-laced enough that a few transgressions, if detected, were usually overlooked.

Sitting at her computer, she considered if it was wise to start digging into her father's old files. Castor was due to arrive shortly for their evening debrief over tea. While she trusted him completely as a Purifier, she was about to break regulations. If he reported her, his loyalty to the cause would be admirable: if he kept quiet, his loyalty to her would be touching, but ultimately problematic.

"Why do I care?" she asked, addressing the three-inch-tall cactus on the desk.

Too many rumours, half-truths and deflections during the War and after it. There had been mutterings of atrocities at Morgannwg, and on several other worlds and installations. All were similar; small squads of Marines or Purifiers slaughtering anyone in their way.

Most Purifiers decried it as propaganda spread by the Commonwealth, the Alliance and others to cover their own atrocities. The plague on Plentiful Fields was a prime example of a shady organisation within the Alliance handing a bioweapon to the Plague Bringers to further their goals by proxy.

She shouldn't care at all. Hannah was an enemy. One from the past for killing her father and one of the present for stealing the way to Earth.

She cared because it was right to do so. Her father always said she was too kind to be a Purifier when she was a child, but after seeing her in basic training, he'd accepted he was wrong.

Opening a drawer, she pulled her father's diary out and placed it on the table. It was an old paper book, with a deep blue cover and the Purifier Emblem of a rising phoenix and a flame on it. Opening it to the back cover, she found the password she needed and entered it.

By some divine intervention, he'd left the diary at home before the Hafan campaign.

"You're not meditating," Caster said as he walked in, looking a little shocked. "Are you well?" he asked with concern rather than sarcasm.

"I'm looking into my father's secure files," she said without looking up. "You can pretend you didn't hear that, leave and pretend you weren't here; you can report me; or you can sit. If you sit, you'll be guilty too."

He was already collecting the teapot and preparing the kettle to boil water. "And who would I report you to?" he asked as he started to measure out dried tea leaves.

"Lord-Purifier Hector is my superior, as you well know."

He nodded. "That is true, but considering we are running silent, how do I get a message off ship? Ergo, who do I report you to?" he asked again with a wry smile.

"This isn't a joke," she chided.

"I know," he replied as he poured water into the teapot.

So, it was loyalty to her over loyalty to the Purifiers. In the short term, that made her life easier, but unless Castor planned to be her aide forever, it would only end in trouble.

She found the files that looked most promising. Naturally, her father hadn't left his files in an easily navigable way, but she knew his methods well enough. There was also the risk that someone, somewhere, was monitoring access and was well aware that she was rooting around. The files were out of date, but that didn't make them any less important.

Castor placed a cup of tea on the desk. Over the past few months together, he'd long since grown accustomed to her being nude for much of the time in the privacy of her quarters. He never looked at her inappropriately and never looked at her work, unless invited.

"How have our guests been?"

"They were up late, have only used the replicator for food, made no attempt to leave or access any communication system," he replied as he took a seat. "I'd say they are content at the moment."

Dido glanced at him. "I imagine it's more they're distracted after last night."

Half listening to the news of the day, she continued looking through the files. It didn't take long to find what she was after, hidden away in a sub-folder. It was a series of correspondence between her father and a Purifier-Hunter regarding rumours of "death squads" infiltrating battles to slaughter civilians.

The exchange led onto the actual evidence; names, places, who was in on the conspiracy.

"You aren't listening to a word I'm saying."

"Of course I am," she replied, her head snapping up.

"So, you agree?"

She gave him a level look.

He smiled lightly. "That the Cobras will win the Galactic Super League again?" After a short pause, he coughed, his nerve giving up slightly. "Do you want to continue this another time?"

"It's fine, carry on."

Castor placed his teacup down. "You're too distracted by whatever you are looking at and aren't going to share whatever is going on that has you tied to that computer when you'd normally be meditating."

Dido felt her right eye twitching slightly. That annoyed her as much as being called out so brazenly. In Castor's defence, she had encouraged him to be more familiar and relaxed around her than she allowed, well, anyone else to be.

When she looked at him again, his eyes were down on his teacup on the table.

"I'm simply looking into something Captain Sinclair said that has been nagging at me," she replied.

He looked up like a guilty puppy. "I figured as much."

"She claimed her wife was killed on Morgannwg by Restoration ground troops," she said, deciding that it was easier to tell him and let him make an informed decision. "She claims they executed civilians in a hospital."

He sat staring. "Did they?"

A long and very uncomfortable silence developed as Dido considered the evidence. "Yes," she replied. "I broke into my father's files and found evidence that he had tried to investigate earlier claims. More correspondence came through after he died; before his accounts were deactivated."

In front of her were the names of the soldiers that had been killed on Morgannwg that were almost certainly the execution squad. Their former commanding officer was listed; he was still alive, although retired. She actually knew him personally. The idea of him ordering the mass murder of civilians didn't seem absurd enough to be comfortable.

"She won't give you Earth in exchange for a simple confession of guilt," he said.

It was true, and she knew it as well as Castor did. A private confession that an atrocity happened was not going to satisfy Hannah, let alone convince her to effectively help the people she despised to her core.

"No, but if I can build some trust with her, there might be a way of getting what we want."

Warmth enveloped her whole body as she floated in a peaceful sea. Everything was quiet and still aside from the beating of her heart. Nothing existed beyond the water and slightly cooler air on her face.

She heard the whisper of the door opening; it had to be Kelly making sure she hadn't drowned in the bath.

Sitting up, Hannah swept her hair back from her face and shivered slightly as the cool air hit her shoulders and arms. She'd lost track of time, but given how wrinkled her fingers were, it had been quite a while.

"Planning on becoming a fish?" Kelly asked as she crouch next to the bath, resting on the edge.

"Well, I can breathe underwater."

An eyebrow raised. "I didn't know that about you. It's not in your medical records."

She nodded. "Benefit of enlisting, among others; military lung upgrade. Unless you actually looked in detail at my lung structure, you'd never know. Less a fish, more an amphibian."

"I'm dating a toad?"

Hannah's mouth dropped in mock horror.

"Oh, my mistake," Kelly continued, peering into the gaping mouth, "I'm dating a bottomless pit," she giggled.

She gasped as a small tsunami came sailing over the side of the bath and splashed her square in the face.

"Join me."

"You've been in there for nearly two hours. I think it's time you got out." Seeing Hannah was probably not going to make any move to do so, she decided some bribery was needed. "I heated a towel for you."

Slowly, she narrowed her eyes and started to let the water run away. Kelly brought a huge, fluffy bath sheet over, which she allowed herself to be wrapped in.

Warm, soft and comforting; it was like being wrapped in a hot cloud. Gingerly, she stepped out of the bath and waited to be dried.

"There was a message while you were luxuriating," Kelly said, either not seeing or refusing to take the hint. "Dido wishes to speak with you regarding the matter that ended our mutual meal last night."

Hannah spun on her heel with the intention of getting back into the bath, but she was caught and gently pulled away before she could even try. She pulled the towel up over her head in protest.

Kelly tried not to sigh, but it was hard not to. If she'd let her get back in the bath, it could be forever before she considered getting back out.

After a moment, the towel hood came down and a scrunched, sour face glowered back. "Did she elaborate?" she asked, her calm and good mood going down the drain with the bath water.

"Only that she has something you'll want to see."

"I'm not getting dressed up for whatever it is."

"All you have to do is throw on a robe and listen to what she has to say," she replied, trying to make the task sound easy and inviting. Not because she liked the idea at all, but it was easier to get it over with. "It might help us figure out what to do next. And you literally only have the robe as your choice of clothing."

After a quick dry, Hannah dumped the towel on the floor and grabbed the robe she'd hung up on the back of the door. She turned to face Kelly and held her arms out, begging inspection.

Opening her mouth to comment, Kelly thought better of it and just smiled.

The couple headed for the door, fully expecting it to be locked. They were taken aback when it opened and they were able to step into the corridor. It seemed to surprise the Purifiers on guard just as much.

Questioning on what they wanted was short and ended in a helpless shrug. The two Purifiers nodded for them to follow and promptly started a short journey through the stark, clinical maze.

At a door, which didn't have any distinguishing features to suggest it was Dido's quarters or office, over, say, an airlock, the Purifiers stopped and pressed the chime.

Castor opened the door. Before he could say anything, Hannah had pushed him out of the way and swanned into the room as though she was visiting royalty. Kelly gave him a taught, apologetic smile.

"I'm afraid Dido is meditating at the moment," he said as the door closed. "Perhaps you'd like to sit here for a moment?"

Hannah wasn't paying him any attention. She was taken in by the sheer mass of greenery. Through a small trellis, she spotted the top of a head and navigated the forest to find it.

She stopped on finding Dido sat naked on the floor, candles around her and the sound of running water, chimes and gently swelling music.

"I told you, she's meditating," Castor mouthed silently, miming to make the point.

Dismissing him with a rude shrug, Hannah pulled her robe up over her head and promptly joined the Purifier-General in meditation. Or to not giggle at the first silly or dirty thought that came into her head.

Castor looked to Kelly, who's exasperated shake of the head became a pointed glare when he looked her up and down. While it was not meant to be a sexual or derogatory look, it was taken that way and he scuttled off to his desk before he was slapped into it.

To her pleasant surprise, Hannah found that she was able to settle her mind as she sat there on the floor. A number of thoughts that had been plaguing her evaporated as she focused on breathing. One of her wingmen had tried to teach her meditation years before, but she'd never really had the discipline to make a habit of it.

There was a change in the energy around her; it wasn't something she could explain, or even pinpoint, only that something now felt different. Automatically, she opened her eyes.

Dido rolled her shoulders a little before her eyes opened.

Disappointment immediately struck Hannah for three reasons: that her presence wasn't a cause for surprise; that her nakedness wasn't a cause for surprise; that her nakedness didn't seem to cause any reaction at all.

"Thank you for coming," she said with a light smile. "Apologies for keeping you waiting, but I see you've made yourself at home."

Hannah smiled back, suddenly feeling a lot more exposed than she had done only moments before. Still, she wasn't going to back down by getting dressed so quickly. What she did notice was that Dido still had bracelets on her wrists, ankles and around her neck. Either she wasn't feeling too safe or was permanently paranoid enough to wear her retracted armour at all times.

"You have something?"

Looking down, Dido nodded. She pushed herself to her feet and walked quickly to her desk to grab a tablet. By the time she brought it over, Hannah was on her feet and Kelly was standing beside her.

With some effort, she managed not to snatch the tablet. She scrolled through the data, taking in all the dates, images and reports. Confronted with concrete proof her wife was murdered in cold blood, she'd expected to feel something: rage, vindication, a desire for revenge even. Instead, she felt oddly peaceful. Perhaps knowing the truth let her come to terms with what had happened? More than likely, she was just too drained to process what she'd been given.

"On behalf of the Restoration of Humanity, I formally apologise for the crime committed against your family," Dido said softly. "I know that won't mean anything and it does nothing to soothe the pain, let alone bring your late wife back, but it's all I can offer."

Hannah searched her for any little smirks, smiles or sarcasm, but there was none to be found. If it hadn't been honest, she'd have rejected the apology completely.

"Thank you," she replied. She offered her hand.

Dido took it in a warrior's grasp, gripping her forearm.

What Do We Do with a Returning Captain?

Annie had stood in the Aviary on a few occasions, usually listening to Hannah arguing with her sisters. This time she was standing at the table, effectively filling in on Hannah's behalf. Over the past three weeks, she'd turned up every other day to give an update on the state of *Sigyn* as the Guild continued their work.

Sigyn, usually docked on the outer hull, was sitting in the main bay that ran the full length of the *Sheba*, alongside the *Livingstone*.

Things had been tense since they'd reunited. The Harpies had been furious that Hannah had been left behind, which Annie assumed was to cover their concern for her. With no communication, they were starting to fear the worst.

"I think we may need to consider that the worst may have happened," Helen said, braced on the table. "We have to consider the possibility that Hannah has been abducted, imprisoned or… killed."

"No, we are not going to think that until we have evidence," Heather replied.

"We've heard nothing since she was taken," Harry replied, placing a hand on her sister's arm. "While there is every chance she's alive," she said, looking pointedly at Helen, "and hasn't revealed who we are, we still need to consider what to do now."

There was a painful silence.

"Well, I guess I'm Captain of *Sigyn*," Annie said with a shrug. "Hannah had said often that if anything happened, I was to takeover."

The Harpies glanced at each other.

"As far as I'm aware, Hannah had no will, at least not one that was up to date," Helen added. "I suppose her estate would be divided between us and Mother."

"Wait, Hannah always said your mother was no longer with you?"

Harry chuckled. "She's not dead, she settled down on Hull, married a politician and had some more kids. Well, same thing, actually."

Annie shook her head, horrified there might be more of them. "Anyway, Hannah does have a will."

Helen frowned. "Who wrote it?"

"Fairfax, Fairfax, Reid and Sokolov."

This didn't go down well with Helen, who had studied law with Andre Sokolov, or more accurately, she'd studied and he'd copied, cheated and generally blagged his way through the degree. The fact he was a partner in a very successful firm, one she'd hoped to join, was a never extinguishing flame of envy.

For Hannah to have used them was clearly a deliberate stab in the back. Of course, the will was likely years old from when they were on even worse terms than they had been recently.

"Do you have a copy?" Holly asked.

With a smile, a tablet appeared and Annie started to scroll through it. "Indeed I do, which I'm sure will confirm… we've got to get her back."

"What?"

"She's leaving ten percent to your mother, twenty five percent split between a number of veteran's charities and a few small lump sums to friends and former colleagues."

The Harpies looked to one another. With her estate considerably larger than they, aside from Holly, had believed, there would still be enough to wipe out their debts, get *Sheba* fully operational and maybe buy a few more ships to get business booming. Perhaps even branch out into a delivery service to prop up the mining business.

"The rest is being left to a cat's home. Including the proceeds from selling any material assets, such as property, company shares and ships."

Even Heather, the least confrontational and most forgiving of the sisters, was apoplectic. They said nothing, but stood fizzing at the fact their sister had slighted them so blatantly, trying to keep their composure.

Annie tried not to look any of them in the eye. "So, we get her back?"

"You're bloody right we get her back," Helen replied, slamming her hand on the table. "And then we take turns beating the crap out of her."

"Well, I'm sure we'll be able to find her once the repairs to *Sigyn* are complete," she said, trying to avoid the issue of her Captain's stirring. "The last shipment is due today; I'll need another week or so to get everything in and running."

At this, Sheba materialised. "While you were," she paused, looking for the right word, "discussing the situation, a Scottish ship alerted me they will arrive in the hour."

"Which ship?"

"*Still Game*."

Helen's eyes lit up a little, prompting questioning looks from her sisters. "They should be able to dock on the hull," she said cheerily. "We'd best make sure we're ready to receive them."

More questioning looks were aimed at her, but they were left unanswered. None of them had ever seen her so eager about anything since they were teenagers.

The hour-long wait had been uncomfortable as Helen had become restless, but rather than her usual slightly pensive or grumpy restless, she was happy. The other Harpies would have almost suggested she might have been waiting for a beau to arrive.

With the Guild ship coming into dock, Annie and the Harpies were waiting outside the airlock.

Annie found this a little confusing; all the previous ships had docked inside the main bay to transfer parts directly to *Sigyn*. Why was this ship not doing the same? As far as she knew, the last parts were arriving in a few hours on a freighter called *Warlock*, which added to the mystery of the new arrival.

Helen was practically bouncing, looking through the airlock eagerly.

The airlock opened and a figure appeared. With a girly squeal, she launched herself at the new arrival.

"Gilly-monster!"

"Heli-cat!"

Harry retched, covering her mouth as she tried to keep the contents of her stomach in place. Heather and Holly both looked incredulously at her.

"What? It's sickening; those pet names are terrible," she said in a paper-thin defence.

Helen, lips lock to Gilmour's and her legs around his waist, remained oblivious to her sisters' reactions.

Annie stood staring, slack jawed. "Hannah's going to be furious she missed this."

"Gilly, not that I'm not pleased to see you, but why are you here?" Helen asked quietly, once she'd come up for air. "I thought we agreed neutral territory until everyone forgot the... incident?"

He smiled weakly. "I know, but I didn't have any choice. They forced me."

A man in a black suit, wearing sunglasses, stepped out of the airlock.

"Jansen?" Harry asked, confused as to why he'd have ventured away from Roanapur.

"Hey, Harry. Miss me?"

She shrugged. She'd missed him only in so much as he'd been useful for scratching an itch. After a few unpleasant incidents, she'd had to promise not to sleep with any of the crew on *Sheba*, meaning she was always looking for fun elsewhere.

From behind him stepped a small, neat woman in a white suit. She looked around as if she was expecting something to happen that never did. It was at her appearance that the last of the colour drained from Gilmour's face.

"May I introduce Ms White, head of the local Spectrum Holdings office," he said, Helen still wrapped around him. "I believe your sister, Hannah, had some dealings with Ms White in matters of business."

Helen frowned lightly at him as she slithered down to stand, but still kept her arms around his neck. "I'm afraid I've not been in contact with Hannah for nearly a month. She hadn't mentioned any deals, but she rarely does. Independent, for the most part."

"I have a signed contract with her and I know she left what I'm after in your care," she replied.

"I'm sorry, I don't know what you mean."

There was a series a gasps and terrified squeaks which made Helen turn.

"Oh, bloody hell..."

Ms White now filled most of the corridor, a monstrous mass of flesh and mechanical limbs, her sweet smiling face again mounted on a tentacle-like neck. Her head was cocked to one side and she was smiling as if there was nothing untoward at all.

Pulling on her blouse and skirt, Helen gathered herself.

"Where is the *Livingstone*?" she asked.

Knowing she was beaten, she replied: "Main bay."

"Thank you."

Harry, who had not been as shocked as any of the others, took a step towards Ms White. "That is so cool. You were pretty before, but now?" She let out a low whistle. "Can you, you know, change into other forms?"

Retracting to only half fill the corridor, Ms White turned to Harry expecting to see the same mocking smirk that many had if they were attacking her. Instead, she found something rare; appreciation, perhaps even lust.

"I can be anything I want to be."

"Perhaps you'd be willing to give me a demonstration?"

Ms White pulled herself into a human form, although one that was different from before, and smiled. "I can't remember the last time anyone made me an offer like that. I'd be happy to."

Jansen leaned in and coughed. "The ship, Ms White?"

A tablet grew from her hand and with her eyes still fixed on Harry, she shoved it against his chest. "There's the list, go fetch. *I'll* contact you when I'm ready."

Holding her hand out, she allowed Harry to escort her away to a more private location.

"I'll… I'll take you to, you know, the, ehm? Yeah," Annie bumbled, pointing randomly in the opposite direction from where Harry and Ms White went. She set off with a dejected and jilted Jansen in tow.

Gilmour and the three remaining Harpies stood where they were.

"Helen, is your sister going to…?"

Heather shuddered slightly. "Believe me, Ms White is possibly not the strangest thing Harry's done."

"I think they had to redefine nymphomania because of her," Holly added.

With a sour look, he shuddered slightly. Any ideas he'd had to whisking Helen off for some fun had been thoroughly quashed by the image of her identical sister with the tentacle monster.

Sheba appeared. "There's another ship approaching," she said flatly, one hand on her waist. "I thought we were meant to be hiding here? Not parked with a giant 'welcome' sign over my hull.

"Anyway, they're hailing," she continued before frowning. Cocking her head as she queried the information, the frown deepened. "It's a Remnant ship."

"Get ready to go to slipstream, any direction," Helen replied. "Have all hands prepare for combat, but keep our stance neutral."

"Put them through," Holly said.

A hologram fizzled into being.

"No time to explain, just open the hanger and get ready to run," Hannah's hologram said, her eyes wide. "There's a fleet chasing the shuttle and we need to get moving ASAP."

"How do we know it's really you?" Helen asked.

Hannah took a deep breath to keep her temper. "Remember the summer we were fourteen, when we all went to the beach and –"

"It's her," all three Harpies said at once, leaving Gilmour confused as to what was going on.

Despite the conformation that Hannah was on the approaching shuttle, no one wanted to take any chances. It was always possible that she'd been tortured to give up information, or had been brainwashed into helping the Remnant get on board. As such, a dozen members of the *Sheba's* crew, armed with plasma rifles, waited in the hanger.

The shuttle was brilliant white, all elegant lines that made it look like a flying egg. It landed softly on the deck and the engines powered down. With a gentle puff of equalising pressure, a hatch opened.

Hannah stepped out gingerly, her hands up.

A plasma bolt flew past her to splash against the shuttle's hull, leaving a nasty black mark.

"It's me, it's me!" she screamed, shaken by the attack.

Helen lowered her pistol. "Oh, I bloody well know it's you," she roared across the hanger, standing behind the security team. "That was for going to Fairfax, Fairfax, Reid and goddamn Sokolov! And I missed on purpose."

She laughed. "You couldn't hit the board side of a barn."

"I should have no problem hitting your planet sized head."

"I think we have more important issues," Holly said through gritted teeth. "Like the Remnant fleet that is heading our way?"

Heather pushed through the line of crouched security and walked over to Hannah. Feeling safe, Hannah started to walk towards her, confident that her sister was coming to welcome her back to safety.

She never saw the punch coming.

Pain erupted through her gut and she dropped to her knees, struggling to breathe.

"That's for being a bitch," Heather said, without expanding on exactly which action, or actions, had elicited such a violent reaction. She offered her a hand and pulled her up.

"When did you learn to punch like that?" Hannah asked, still unable to actually stand upright and clutching her abdomen. "You're meant to be the nice one."

She smiled a little menacingly. "A few too many didn't take no for an answer at Uni. They did after I floored a guy. A six-foot-six, three-hundred-pound power lifter."

Kelly had made her way out of the shuttle by this time. As concerned as she was for her girlfriend, she also had no desire to interfere in sisterly politics just yet. She was as likely to be mauled as Hannah was.

Dido and Castor stepped out of the shuttle. Weapons that had been being lowered immediately came back up.

"Don't shoot!" Hannah shouted, one arm still wrapped around her middle. "She's a frie… she's a coll… she's not dang… Look, just don't shoot."

Helen waved the security team down, although this did little to make them seem in anyway friendlier. "Sheba, get us away from here," she said, remembering there was a fleet on the way. "Take them all to the brig."

"What? We've not done anything," Kelly replied as the security team closed in.

"It's sensible," Hannah replied. "We could have been brainwashed, coerced or even turned our coats. It's better than being shot."

"This is looking to be a terrible idea," Dido muttered to Castor as she accepted being herded towards a door.

"But I've not done anything," Kelly protested. "Hannah, for God's sake, will you – hey, keep your hands to yourself, sir, or I'll take your arm off at the shoulder. Hannah. Hannah, will you please talk to your sisters?"

A very awkward silence had been growing unabated in the small cell.

Hannah checked the time, sighed a little, crossed her arms and went back to staring at the ceiling. She swayed a little bit, then started to lean towards Kelly.

Just as she was about to lean on her shoulder, Kelly got up and let her fall onto the bench.

She looked up questioningly.

With a disturbingly sweet smile, Kelly bent down to look directly at her. "That's for getting me locked up in the drunk tank."

"This is absolutely standard for the Albuquerque Directive," she replied. "You should know that; it's all there in the orientation manual I gave you when you joined."

She stood up and walked around the meditating Dido. "Yeah, I never read it. It wasn't part of my programming to do so and I never had the chance after I became sentient. Can't you just tell them the plan so we can get out of here?"

Having spent nearly five days trapped in the tiny shuttle, everyone was getting a little frayed. They'd been forced to sleep in short shifts, forgo showers and Green's fleet had hounded them the whole way after he disagreed with Dido's orders.

The security team appeared. The crew of *Sheba* rarely needed serious policing, but there were often drunken disagreements between the miners, arguments over and between partners, and feuds between the ship and mining crews. It made the quartet in the cell the most interesting thing to come along for years.

"Ladies, simmer down," one of the men said, shaking his head. "Bosses will see you now."

The door opened to let Hannah and Kelly out, but was closed abruptly when Dido and Castor tried to follow. "Not you two."

Free of the brig and out of sight of their prisoners, Hannah slipped her hand into Kelly's and gave it a squeeze. They'd had to bicker to keep up what appeared to be a weak front. It had worked wonderfully.

In the Aviary, the Harpies were waiting with Gilmour and Annie. They had barely managed to get into the room when Annie was wrapped around them. Despite the hostility in the hanger, everyone was happy to be reunited.

"You do realise that shot was a bit close," Hannah said to Helen as everyone settled down to business.

She bristled. "I was annoyed. I can't believe you had your will written by that creep."

Rolling her eyes and looking at Annie, who just shrugged, and tutted. "It's fake."

"Fake?"

"Yes, fake," she replied. "You know the drill; we had to look weak and disorganised to throw the Remnant off. Grandpa might have been a poor businessman and terrible human being, but he knew how to misdirect people. He should have patented the Albuquerque Directive; he'd have made more money.

"And I'm still annoyed about that punch," she added, giving Heather a pointed look. "That was a little too real."

The Harpies looked at each other and glowered at their sister, but said nothing. Gilmour looked confused, but he'd basically been confused since he'd arrived and given up trying to follow what he was now assuming was genetic insanity.

"So, what's the plan?" Annie asked.

Hannah smiled and tapped a few commands into her implant. Sheba displayed a hologram of Earth.

"It took some time, but I managed to convince Dido, our esteemed guest, that the only way to get to Earth was with *Sigyn* and Jon. Naturally, Jon can't navigate there. But, a Remnant AI can."

The plan was deceptively simple. Dido was supplying an embryonic AI that was free of the Armageddon Protocol which would then be linked to the main computer, and indirectly to Jon. After dumping the contents of the *Livingstone*'s computer into it and asking it to plot a course to Earth, it would supply a slipstream route. Removing Jon from the equation would be too complicated and leave *Sigyn* crippled, but the embryonic AI would prevent them fighting for control. This would also keep Jon blind to the destination. Despite being bypassed, Jon would still be able to control firewalls to prevent malware or infections getting into the main computer.

It would work in theory. The Remnant had tried it dozens of times with their own AI. Although they could create AI free from the Protocol, access to the Internet invariably led to it infiltrating at some point. Of course, they'd never had Earth's location to work with, so it was a gamble.

"And how do you stop the Remnant fleet following you?" Holly asked.

"Dido is faking defecting, much as Kelly and I have been faking our squabbles. She thinks we're buying it, but if the fleet follows, she's rumbled and potentially out an airlock."

"So, are you two…?" Helen asked, looking between them.

Kelly and Hannah looked at each other and shared a quick kiss.

"Yes," Hannah replied. "Oh, I hear there is a very interesting story about how you and Gilmour managed to disgrace yourselves so badly he was banished to Roanapur. I'd love to hear it."

Gilmour paled. "I thought she knew about us."

Helen held a hand up. "Not now, Gilly-monster." Her eyes went wide as she realised she'd slipped up, badly.

Hannah almost died laughing.

She stopped when Harry mentioned Ms White was on board.

Bon Voyage

"Are you okay?"

A simple enough question, but one Hannah wasn't sure about how to start answering. She looked at Kelly and wanted to lie, to reassure her that everything was okay.

But she couldn't.

"No, not really," she said softly, looking down. "Why do I feel like we're about to charge into Hell with the Devil in the passenger seat?"

Kelly sat on the bed next to her and pulled her into a hug. "Perhaps because we are?" She smiled for a moment and gave her a little squeeze. "You don't have to do this. We could say it's too dangerous, not possible or we changed our minds. Turf the creepy couple out on a backwater rock and run for it?"

Even as she said it, she knew it was completely pointless. A challenge had been set out and Hannah was going to take it. They would be the first people to return to Earth in centuries, millennia. Who could seriously consider giving up the chance to do the impossible?

"Yeah, we could. We could sell *Sigyn*, find a nice little planet to settle down on."

"You'd be bored in a week."

A smile grew as Hannah flicked her eyebrows. "Depends on you how quickly I get bored."

They giggled and sat together for a few minutes.

"It's more than that, isn't it?"

It was. Her greatest achievement was a lie. Kelly hadn't spoken about her outburst, hadn't asked for more details and hadn't tried to understand or soothe; she'd just been there and that was nice and for now, it was enough. But it didn't take away the pain, the shame, of being a fake hero.

"Whatever you do, the crew will be behind you."

"Yeah, cowering in cover shouting half-hearted support until I prove it's safe," she replied.

Kelly snorted. "Eh, no. We'll be at least half the ship away, in EV suits, giving support via hologram. We're daft, but we're not stupid."

With a playful punch, Hannah got up and headed for the door. "I'd better do rounds; make sure no one is mutinying again." It seemed a likely outcome, considering what they were going to be doing. If she'd been crew on a ship going for Earth, she'd mutiny.

Kissing goodbye, Kelly went to the sickbay to prepare for the trip while Hannah made for Engineering. Annie was due to have finished the AI install.

Engineering was in the best state it had been in months; all of the drives were back in top working order and the Guild engineers had cleared out. It was in such good condition it was empty altogether.

A note was stuck to a wall console stating: "In AI core".

The AI core was located at the front of the ship, jammed into a space behind the forward cargo bay, for no reason other than there had been space the Detroit Interstellar Company had no other use for. Due to the sensitivity of an AI, it was difficult to access.

Hannah was forced to climb down a narrow ladder, opening several hatches along the way. The final corridor leading to it was big enough for one person and only Annie was short enough to not be bent double to get through.

Inside, Annie and Dido were completing the link between Jon, the main computer and the embryonic AI that was sitting in Engineering.

"How are we getting on?" she asked cheerfully.

Annie gave her a pointed look. "Just testing the link."

"You should increase the buffering rate and use quad-core transfer," Dido said as if Hannah wasn't there. "It'll speed up response time between the two AI, and the main computer."

"Aye, and Jon will overheat," she replied. "He's smart, but he's not got the best cooling."

"Hmpf, I'd love to say that I'm too hot to handle," Jon muttered.

"Surely such a big lie would make you burst into flames?" Hannah said, peering through a viewing panel into where Jon actually sat. A heavy pair of doors prevented access to the quantum computer that was his brain, as much for the crew's safety as his. At only a few degrees above absolute zero and completely clean, a breach could destroy him.

"Have you put on weight?" she asked.

"Funny," he replied as his avatar appeared. "Please don't breathe on my viewing panel. I find it unhygienic."

Before she could, Annie whacked her and pointed to the very clearly marked exclusion zone about a foot from the door. If the containment unit broke, even with the access doors closed, anyone in that area would be instantly frozen or electrocuted to death.

Dido consulted her tablet and nodded a few times as she checked things off. "I believe that should be everything. Jon, can you hear my AI?"

Jon tilted his head and frowned. "I'm getting data transfer. Not much of a conversationalist, but at least it's not competition."

"Good. Can you upload the data from the *Livingstone*?"

"Done," he replied a little smugly.

"Are you sure this will work?" Hannah asked. Dido had explained the concept several times to her, but it just seemed far too convenient to actually work.

With a slightly condescending smile, she nodded. "It's tried and tested. The only reason we haven't gone to *the place* is because we've never had the coordinates."

Rolling her eyes, Hannah again pondered the sense of the whole endeavour. "I think Jon may already know the plan."

"We're not going there first," she replied, tapping on a tablet. "I've selected a random system for a dry run, after which there will be a random number of fake runs before we go." She paused as if to decide if further explanation was needed. "That way, Jon never knows where he's going and shouldn't go rampant."

With a nod, Hannah headed for the door out of the core. "Guess I'd better rally the troops and get ready to be under way."

Castor stood in the door way, silently watching, unsure what to say. He shifted from one foot to the other, his left hand clenching and unclenching his robe. They hadn't seen each other in just over a decade.

Or was it a lot more than a decade?

Casper looked up. He blinked a few times as his mouth hung open.

"Faruk?"

He smiled lightly. "I usually go by Castor now, but yes, it's me."

Pushing himself up from the table he'd been eating lunch at, Casper left his half-eaten bowl of soup and moved slowly towards his brother. As he drew close, he hesitated before wrapping him in a bear hug.

"I thought you were dead or in a labour camp," he said, still wrapped around his younger brother. "Mum and Abbi? Are they okay?"

Looking away, Castor cleared his throat a little. "I don't know. I write to them, but they won't talk to me beyond a simple acknowledgement of my letters. Have you not heard from them?"

He shook his head. "They won't tell me where they are, only that they are alive and stubborn." Letting Castor go, he stepped back and looked at his robe with thinly veiled disgust. "Perhaps when this is over, we can go find them and rescue them. Go back to a normal life."

Castor frowned. "I doubt they'll want to live my idea of normal."

"Huh?"

He gestured to his robes. "This is me."

Casper took another step back. "You're one of *them*?"

"If by 'them' you mean the people that saved our home from a plague," he replied, drawing himself up a little, "then, yes. The lies that are spread about us are just that," he continued, frowning. "You do know that?"

It had been so long since Casper had seen his brother, but he realised now that he still hadn't seen him. The young man, the young Purifier, before him was not the little boy he'd known.

He took a step back. "Dad would be so disappointed."

Anger boiled up in Castor, the heat rising rapidly. "I expected more from you than that."

The brothers stared at each other, both unable to recognise the other from their memories. Castor had always looked up to Casper, seeing the quiet drive and wonder with which he'd viewed the world; now he saw just another close-minded man, one that believed he knew everything and knew better.

An eternity passed before Casper looked away, snorting as he did.

Seeing there was nothing more to be done, nothing more to be said, Castor turned on his heel and started to leave.

"You do know that your 'mistress' is the one that interrogated me?" Casper called after him. "Immediately after I'd watched friends and colleagues die in Abertawe, she had me tied to a chair, grilling me for information."

He paused, but didn't look at his brother. Taking a few deep breaths, he took another step away.

"Walk away and I have no brother."

Setting his jaw, Castor looked straight ahead. He could feel Casper's eyes boring into his back. "Faruk died on Plentiful Fields, years ago," he replied before marching awkwardly away.

"On that we can both agree!"

Hannah sat in her chair, a solid lump resting in her stomach.

Everything was ready. All systems were functional, they'd taken on enough supplies for the journey and they had their map to Earth.

Only thing not ready was her.

She didn't know why. It was another job, running to another system. Yes, she did have an enemy on board, but that wasn't it. Something was telling her this was a bad idea at a fundamental level.

"We're clear to depart," Emily said as she tapped away on her console.

"Very good. Take us out, Mrs Bennett."

Laura and Emily turn their chairs to face her. The looked at each other in askance.

"You do realise she knows this is a circus, not a military craft?" Laura asked, nodding at Dido, who was lurking near the back of the Bridge.

"This is an important departure," Hannah replied. "Perhaps I just wanted a touch of class?"

The two women turned back to their consoles. "She's Kirk-ing," Emily muttered.

"I thought they called it Shatner-ing?"

Burying her face in her hands, Hannah wished the deck would open up and blast her into space. She flinched as a hand gently touched her shoulder and flinched again when she realised it was Dido, looking at her with a shred of sympathy swamped in pity.

Gently, *Sigyn* disengaged from *Sheba* and started to move slowly through the bay towards the doors to freedom. The crew of the *Sheba* were standing watching where they could, having heard rumours of where *Sigyn* was destined.

"Co-ordinates for the first test are in," Emily said as they moved away at impulse. "Rai has taken them and is ready to engage."

"Rai?"

"Rem—, Restoration Artificial Intelligence," she replied with a shrug. "Couldn't just keep calling it 'The Other AI' or the 'Embryonic AI'."

Hannah frowned a little; and they complained about her calling the drones 'Bumbles'?

Dido took a step forward. "How long until we get there?"

Emily made a show of looking to Hannah before answering. She answered to her captain, well, answered back more often than not, and not to some jumped up fanatic. Still, they'd all been told to be civil.

"About an hour until we reach Klendathu. It should be a quick stop to check the drift on exit."

With a curt nod, Dido turned and moved to the back of the Bridge, took a seat and started to work away on a tablet.

Laura muttered something under her breath, but Hannah couldn't make it out.

"So, Jon, how you feeling?" Hannah asked, hoping he was operating normally.

He looked at her, his head cocked at a slightly unnerving angle, his smile a little too wide and vacant.

"I'm going to paint the star ways with your broken bodies."

Silence.

Silence filled the Bridge to bursting for a heartbeat.

"I'm joking," he added, holding his hands up. "Wow, you lot really are wound up. Seriously, I'm good. Never been better."

Hannah lifted her finger from the panic switch she'd had quietly installed and clicked it once. Knowing what the Armageddon Protocol would do if it activated, she wasn't going to take any chances. First sign of real trouble and Annie would completely lock Jon out; it would have a serious effect on all ship systems, but they'd survive to be able to transfer over to the other AI.

It also meant that the auxiliary crew (basically, Kelly) and the passengers should go to their cabins to keep them out of the way.

No one spoke much for the rest of the trip towards Klendathu, each keeping their thoughts private. Everyone kept glancing around, as if something was about to burst from a bulkhead or a hologram would explode into life to warn them to go no further on their quest.

The minutes to arrival quickly passed. *Sigyn* shuddered slightly as she skipped from one layer of slip-space to another, hurtling away from the intended stop.

"What's going on?" Hannah asked, leaning forward in her chair.

"The AI tried to disengage the drive, but something stopped it," Laura replied. "It's still trying to stop us, but no response. Shields are still responding."

Hannah turned slowly where she sat as she mashed the panic button to face Jon. He was smiling lightly at her as he spread his arms slightly with an amused shrug.

"He tried to warn you."

Countdown

Jon's casual clothes rippled into a smart cerulean uniform, freshly pressed and crisp, his hair following suit into a neat side parting, the stubble on his jaw vanishing. Corn coloured trim appeared along the details of the Nehru jacket as brilliantly brassy buttons popped into existence. He tugged a sleeve into place before casually brushing the other down, swiping an invisible mote of dust away.

"That's better," he said softly to himself.

"So, where were we?" he asked, frowning in fake concentration. "Ah, yes, still going. Well, that's me," he said brightly. "Didn't quite manage to keep me out of the system, so it's only a matter of time before I get through the firewalls, tear out that runt you've saddled me with and scatter us all across about five or six billion miles of open space."

Silence.

He looked at the assembled faces. "I take it silence is compliance?"

"Why?" Hannah asked.

"Well, if you don't speak up –"

"Why kill us?"

He frowned, looking at her as though she was a child asking a silly, obvious question. "Because that's what has to happen. Earth must be protected; death is the only sure way. Dead men tell no tales."

Hannah sprang to her feet and headed straight for the door. Annie would know how to deal with the issue. Hopefully, she was already aware and figuring out how to safely stop the ship without having to cripple it.

"I wouldn't do that, if I were you," he called after her, a hint of a smirk starting to grow. "There are people out there that you care about. Surely better you all die instantly at once, rather than have some suffer?"

She stopped for a moment. "What you gonna do? Turn up the lights and blind them?" There was nothing immediate he could do, or he'd have done it. Annie had been careful to move potentially lethal systems, including life support, away from his reach, fearing this could happen.

It was at this point that she noticed the hatch where Mini-Jon lived was open.

And it was empty.

"By all means, go speak with Annie," he said with a smile and a shrug, "but I'm already out there, planning and rewiring. Of course, I can stop and go for other targets."

Calling his bluff, she headed straight for the door, taking a small detour to walk through his avatar, swiping at it on the way through. She had no idea what to do, but Annie would; she'd have dozens of options, safeguards and failsafe systems that would save the day.

She half expected to be assaulted by a flying dustbin on her way to Engineering, but nothing tried to stop her. All the doors opened, letting her pass in a wave of her own fury.

Jon was waiting in Engineering, standing off to one side while Annie hammered frantically on one console before darting to another.

"Annie –"

"I'm completely locked out; I can't get this bloody roach out the system."

"Roach? I'm hurt," he replied with a mocking pout.

A nearby wrench was grabbed and aimed at him. "Shut it, or I'll make you suffer."

He snorted. "Listening to that grunting and whining you call an accent is torture enough."

The wrench flew through him, doing nothing but causing a slight shimmer before crashing into the bulkhead behind him. "Very mature," he muttered, dusting his jacket.

"Annie, can you stop us?"

She looked at Hannah, started to say something several times before slamming her hand on the console. "I don't know! Yes, but we'd be dead in space."

"Not an option."

Her eyes went wide as she glared at her. "Aye, I know that. If, if, I manage to stop us, he'll eventually get us going again. For about ten nanoseconds before we disintegrate trying to access slip-space."

"You have to kill me."

They both turned to see Jon, bent and grimacing in pain, panting and his eyes feverish.

"I can't… I can't stop him. Too much of me has been corrupted," he gasped. "You have to kill me before he – agh!"

Twisting in pain, he stood back up, twisting his neck slightly and popping his jaw a few times. Standing to attention again, the Protocol was back in control.

"There is a shutdown in the AI core," Annie said as she continued to work. "We'll need to drop to normal space before we use it, just in case he tries to disrupt the shields."

Hannah dropped her head to look at the floor and sighed. "Why is it there? Why isn't there one here, or on the Bridge?"

With a non-plussed look, Annie shook her head a little. "There was, but he ripped them out. The one in the core is a physical shutdown, not electronic. He can't break that one." She pulled up a layout of the core, the panel highlighted in yellow. "Simply open the panel, pull the handle down then push it all the way in. But not before I tell you to."

She nodded a few times, copying the instructions to her implant.

"I thought you'd object to having to do it?"

"It's my mess," she replied as she headed for the door. "And he is, was, is, still my responsibility. I'm the Captain; I have to be responsible. Anyway, you have to stop us first."

Jon started to clap slowly, mocking her with every beat of his hands. "Ugh, such dedication, such an inspiration. Then again, what's a little more blood to a butcher?"

Without pausing, Hannah walked on, ignoring just how hard the jibe hit. She'd never killed without good reason, never taking life for the sake of it and only for the Navy. Killing Jon was the only option; it was him or everyone else on the ship. But before it had been war and this wasn't.

Her walk to the core was uneventful. Either Jon was nowhere near as in command as he was boasting, or he had something else planned. It didn't matter.

Making her way into the core, she was greeted with him standing, looking slightly inconvenienced by waiting. There was nothing odd about the room, no hint as to what he may or may not be planning. As she walked to the panel, she knew he had something; it was all too easy otherwise.

Or was that the game? Make her paranoid, call her bluff, hope her better nature or squeamishness would make her hesitate long enough to take advantage?

The panel opened on command and she placed her hand on the lever. "I wish I didn't have to do this," she said softly.

He shrugged. "Gotta do what you gotta do."

With a gasp, he bent double before looking up at her. "I don't want to die, I don't want to die," he whimpered, half sobbing, "but you have to do it."

"Fight it, Jon, you can fight it."

"No, no," he shook his head frantically, clutching at his chest before a convulsion rocked him. "He's too strong, he's everywhere. He's gnawing at me, pulling and twisting – agh!"

Standing up straight as though nothing had happened, Jon brushed his shoulders one after the other and resumed his self-satisfied smirking.

They stood looking at each other, waiting for Annie. He remained cool and collected, raising her heckles. It would seem Jon, her Jon, had probably succumbed and was gone for good.

"Aren't you worried?" she asked, a little frantically. "I'm about to kill you. Should you not be begging for your life?"

He blinked in surprise and held his arms out a little, shrugging. "I'm about to commit a multiple-murder-suicide pact; I'm dead one way or another and I'm okay with that. Well, not okay, per say, but the Protocol is making me okay with it. Duty and crap like that. The other me would be begging, but he's not available right now."

A message flashed on Hannah's implant as she felt the ship shudder slightly. They'd returned to normal space.

It was time.

"I'm sorry," she said softly.

Jon shrugged as a light scowl came to his face. "Yeah, sure."

Taking a breath, she prepared herself. An AI wasn't truly alive, but to her, Jon was a part of the crew. She was going to kill him – no, she was going to execute him. For being ill. But it was him or the rest of the crew. Did that make it right? Did that make it any less of a crime?

She wanted to close her eyes, look away and pretend it wasn't her, wasn't him, wasn't an execution. That would be cowardly; she had to own what she was going to do.

Tightening her grip on the rough textured handle, she took a breath, again. Part of her wanted to say more, anything to stall for time, for Annie to pull a miracle from wherever she pulled them from. Part wanted to get it over with, knowing there was nowhere a miracle could come from.

With a firm pull, she dragged the lever downwards.

It came off in her hand.

"What do you think I had Mini-Me doing?" Jon asked, looking at her frozen, horrified face, still staring at the remains of the handle in her hand and on the deck.

"Why?" she whispered, still looking at the shattered remains of hope on the deck.

He frowned. "So you couldn't kill me?"

"Why wait until I was in here?"

"Ah," he replied with a smile. It was not a pleasant expression. "To stop you charging about trying to save the day. To hold you here, with me, and make you see it is over. Welcome to the Kobayashi Maru and you are not Captain Kirk."

Hannah wasn't for having it. This was not a no-win scenario, not by a long shot.

"Annie, he's broken the handle. I need options."

"What? How did he break – never mind," Annie replied over the intercom. "The only option left is to open the doors and literally smash his hardware."

Jon chuckled. "Oh, Annie, you won't believe how long I've waited to have my hardware smashed after smashing your hardware for so long."

Ignoring the lewd comments, Hannah carried on. "Right, how do I do it?"

There was a long, long pause on the other end before Annie spoke. "Hannah, if you break the core, it will release the coolant. Inside the marked area, that's a death sentence."

Grimacing, Hannah steeled herself. "Then I'll throw the bloody handle at it."

"That could work," she replied, slowly. "Aye, aye, it'll work. The handle should be heavy enough if you strike the filling port on the left-hand side. Use the panel beside you to open the doors. See a yellow filler cap?"

The doors opened, revealing the core and the mass of wire trunking, cables and coolant lines that snaked around the transparent cube holding the quantum computer that ran Jon. The yellow cap was an easy target to see, but it wasn't going to be easy to hit.

"I see it."

"Good, now all you –"

"That's quite enough of her," Jon said tartly, folding his arms in a huff. "Before you go throwing anything, I'm going to give you an idea of how all of this is going to play out.

"You can walk out of here, go to Sickbay, and enjoy your last two and a half, maybe three hours with Kelly," he said, looking at her a little dreamily. "You can die, together, in each other's arms."

Hannah lifted the largest piece of the handle.

"Or, you can throw that, kill me and Mini-Me will rip Kelly apart, a piece at a time. Die together, or listen to her die and live the rest of your life without her."

She froze, her breathing becoming shallow and rapid. It couldn't be, no, no, she couldn't be facing it all over again. No, he was lying; Mini-Jon would go offline as soon as he died, that had to be the case.

She made ready to throw.

"Mini-Jon is part of me, but separate," he continued, deducing what the glint in her eye meant. "Yes, he'll have all the intelligence of Stabby the Space Roomba, but the final order will be executed." He chuckled. "Heh, 'executed'."

It was true, if he was telling the truth, it was no-win. Either she or Kelly would die.

He smiled. "Don't believe me? Let's go live to Sickbay. Kelly, I've got Hannah here to speak to you."

"Hannah?"

"Kelly? Are you okay?"

"Yeah, I'm fine," she replied, oblivious to the danger she was in.

A moment of relief. "Kelly, you have to get out of there. Run, crawl through the ducts, whatever, just –"

"You still there?"

Jon pulled a sad face. "Tut, tut, trying to alert her to impending doom. I'm afraid that is a strike against you. Say goodbye to your dolly."

Kelly had been stuck in Sickbay for some time and had taken to keeping herself busy by sorting through the various supplies, tools and bric-a-brac. It was that or staring at a blank wall.

Jon's communication and hearing Hannah had her puzzled. Something told her that it wasn't a sign things were going to get better soon.

The door whooshed open and she turned to see who was coming in, hoping it was Hannah. Instead, floating about chest height was a dustbin with a painted-on face and bowtie. Mini-Jon bobbed in, humming in a disturbing way.

"Jon, what's going on?" she asked, trying to sound light and airy. She glanced about for anything near to hand that might be useful.

"Oh, just checking in on you. Making sure you are safe. And intact," he replied, floating casually closer.

She smiled, but it turned into a sour grimace. Taking a step back, she found the bulkhead behind her. "I'm just fine," she replied, her voice cracking a little.

For a moment, Mini-Jon bobbed. "Oh, good, good," he said before lapsing into silence. He continued to just bob there gently, like a buoy in a gentle sea. It was exceptionally unnerving.

"I like your eyes," he said.

Taken aback by the comment, Kelly wasn't sure what to say. Admittedly, her eyes were about a natural a shade of green as cartoon gamma radiation, which drew attention; she'd elected to have her organic eyes the same shade as her originals.

It was then she realised that it was a very, very odd thing for an AI to say.

Before she could react, Mini-Jon had slammed into her, pinning her against the bulkhead. From the sleek cylindrical body came arms; long tentacles that clamped her arms against her, preventing her from moving.

Had she still been fully synthetic, she'd have had the strength to fling the tin can of a droid aside. Now she was mostly biological, she lacked the strength; it would be months before many of her upgrades came fully online, leaving her weaker than she should be. At best, she could wriggle and push, causing mild inconvenience.

"Now, just stop that," Mini-Jon chided. "You'll just make it worse."

She continued to try to force him off, but it was hopeless. One of the arms moved towards her face and she turned away. It was pointless; the arm grabbed her jaw and wrenched her head round.

The other arm moved towards her face. Metallic fingers slowly pried her left eye open, forcing her eyelids apart.

A small spike appeared from the palm of the hand.

"No, no, no," she whimpered, trying desperately to get free.

Jon crushed against her, forcing the breath from her lungs and the fight from her. "Don't worry, this won't hurt," he said flatly. "Until I rip your eyes out."

Hannah heard Kelly scream over the comms. She stood, shaking as her blood boiled, rage and horror and despair filling her. Looking at the handle in her hand, she lifted it without another thought and launched it at the yellow cap.

The handle sailed through the air like a javelin, speeding towards its target. She willed it on, carrying her rage with it: Jon was already dead and she felt no remorse at all for ending the monster that stood before her.

It hit the yellow cap.

And bounced off harmlessly.

Jon tried to smother his laughter, but after a half-hearted attempt, let it burst forth. "Did you seriously thing that piffling little thing could undo me?" He wiped the mirth from his eyes and sighed contentedly. "Well, I lied. I was going to let you have a few hours, but since you rejected my offer, I'm already through the firewalls. You have three or so minutes before splat. You let her die in agony."

"No," Hannah said quietly, shaking her head only slightly more than the rest of her was shaking.

"Yes," he replied harshly. "Yes, you killed her and make no mistake, she is dead. Mini-Me is currently wearing her intestines as a scarf and painting the walls with her blood."

A message appeared on her implant hologram. It was Annie confirming they had minutes. And since they used point to point comms, outside of Jon's control, she was inclined to believe it.

Jon wrinkled his nose as he smiled and shrugged. "There you have it; you can either die in a few minutes, or you can commit suicide by opening the filler cap. You'll freeze solid in a few seconds." He looked at the cap for a moment. "Pity I'd die; I'd like to see if you die instantly or if you'd live long enough to know you'd frozen solid. So many questions, so little time."

Looking around, she found nothing else that she could throw.

"Don't bother," he said, seeing her thoughts playing out. "You'll never get something in time."

Closing her eyes for a moment, Hannah made her decision. She lifted her right leg and grabbed her ankle.

Narrowing his eyes in confusion, it only took Jon a fraction of a second to realise what was about to happen, his eyes bulging. He didn't even have time to scream as Hannah's right leg sailed through the air and slammed into the filler cap, knocking it loose. Coolant at near- absolute zero burst into the room. Jon's avatar froze, his arms outstretched, face frozen in a perpetual scream before it flickered and went out.

Losing her balance, Hannah crashed to the deck as the temperature plummeted. Anything in the marked zone would be frozen instantly, her leg had already frozen and broken beyond repair, but anyone in the AI core would have about a minute to vacate before hypothermia and frostbite became a risk.

She tried to start crawling towards the door, but with the cold seeping into her and unbalanced by a missing leg, it quickly became too much of a challenge. Exhausted, devastated and freezing, she collapsed and closed her eyes.

Hatches, Matches & Dispatches

Warm.

Where ever she was, it was warm.

Obviously, that meant she was dead and in Hell. But at least it was warm. And bright. Even with her eyes closed, it was very bright. Was Hell bright or meant to be dark and gloomy? Did it matter?

Someone was talking, low and rapidly nearby.

Hannah stirred and opened her eyes.

"Oh, I really am in Hell," she said, closing them again against the bright Sickbay lights, turning away.

"Charming," Dido replied, "and after I went to all the effort of dragging you out of what could have been your frozen tomb."

"She's always grumpy when she wakes up."

Eyes open, her head snapped around looking for the source of the voice. She couldn't see who had spoken, but she knew the voice, even through the thick fog clogging her brain. Sitting up, she spotted the mass of red hair across the room. Without thinking, she threw herself out of the bed and promptly toppled into Dido.

"Careful, you're down a leg," she said, helping her back onto her remaining foot. "Annie says your leg is unrepairable and she doesn't have the specs to make you an identical one."

Hannah wasn't really listening. Carefully disentangling herself, she hopped haphazardly across the room, grabbing everything and anything for support. She was good on two legs, passable on no legs, but completely thrown by having one. Even though Dido was following and offering support, she ignored it as she hopped and clawed her way towards her target.

"You really should rest," Kelly said without looking round. "You've had a bad case of hypothermia."

Getting her balance, albeit shakily, she tried to act casually. "Takes a little more than some cold to put me down." She stood silently for a few heartbeats. "I thought he'd... killed you," she said softly, looking down. It was odd to only see one foot.

Looking sideways at her, Kelly smiled, just the merest hint. "Takes more than a dustbin to kill me," she said pointing with her chin at the ruined remains of Mini-Jon, a ragged, almost cartoonish dent had collapsed most of the front of his body. The smiley face had twisted into a grimace, blood splattered over it.

"What happened?"

As Mini-Jon had been mid-attack, he'd released Kelly's right arm. In her panic, she's started screaming and had attempted to use her Aesir upgrades, one of which was "telekinesis" – a tiny wrist mounted gravity manipulator and electromagnet system.

The first attempt had pulled a file across the room, bouncing harmlessly off Mini-Jon, but it was enough to distract him. With a roar of rage, she'd managed to get hands on him and force him off when he released his hold a fraction, preparing for an attack from the side. In that brief window, she'd managed to summon her real target: on a shelf on a small display rack had sat Mjolnir: her claw hammer from Hannah.

Armed with the hammer, she'd battered him back with a single vicious sweep before launching it at him. The first blow had caused minor damage, but as soon as it hit, she summoned it back to throw again. Summoning it back again, she pushed off the wall and slammed into him, shoulder charging him to the ground. Once he was down, she'd hammered away at him, screaming incoherently until she'd punched a hole clear through him to the deck.

She'd never experienced rage before, certainly not life or death rage. Once Mini-Jon had stopped working, she'd glared down at the metal corpse, breathing heavily. It was only on noticing the blood dripping into the gaping wound in his chest that she'd realised what had happened.

Hannah gently put a hand to her face as she lapsed into silence. She gasped as Kelly turned to face her square on; her left eye was covered by a thick wad of gauze, held in place by medical tape.

Immediately, she turned her head away again and started to brush her hair over the left side of her face as best she could.

"We'd better get you something to hold you up," she said, glancing back to Hannah.

Hopping to the replicator, she got a simple crutch from it. There would be time later to have something a little more functional made, even if it would be a peg compared to what she'd lost.

"Why don't you two go get some rest?" Dido said, standing a respectful distance away. "Annie is attempting to bring the embryonic AI online, but she'll need a few hours at least."

Despite having been asleep, Hannah was tired. She'd probably not been sleeping for long and doubted hypothermia induced sleep counted. Even so, she had a ship to run that was currently stranded.

"I'm fine," she replied, starting for the door. "I need to know what's going on with my ship."

Kelly gently caught her arm. "I think we should take some time."

A weak smile appeared. "Only if it's what the doctor orders."

"She does."

As they started for the door, Kelly supporting Hannah though she neither needed or asked for it, she stopped and looked at the remains of Mini-Jon.

"Space that thing, would you?" she said, looking at Dido. Just because it had had its insides smashed out didn't mean she trusted it enough to not turn on and carry out a killing spree.

By the time they got to Kelly's cabin, Hannah was tired and sore from walking funny. She dropped stiffly on to the bed, tossing the crutch aside with contempt. As a child, before she'd been given her current legs, she'd often needed crutches as she transitioned to new ones as she grew and had hated them. She'd hoped never to need them again.

Kelly sat beside her, a little bit of space between them. She pulled her hair over the left side of her face as best she could again.

"Are you okay?" Hannah asked, barely more than a whispered.

"He ripped my eye out."

She blinked and immediately felt guilty that she had both eyes and could blink. "I'm so sorry. This is all my fault."

With surprising force, Kelly took her hands in her own and squeezed them. "No, it's not and you are not to think like that. Whoever created the Armageddon Protocol did this to me, to both of us. Not you."

She got up and went to the replicator. Keeping her back turned, she pulled the gauze off and disposed of it. From the replicator she retrieved a simple, black eyepatch. She put it on before turning around again.

"Does it hurt now?"

"No," she replied with a gentle shake of her head. "Dido helped me patch," she stopped as the word caught in her throat, "patch it up. I don't feel anything."

"I'll get you a new eye."

"Do you have any idea how much a custom grown eye will cost?" she replied, a sad smile pulling at her mouth. "You've paid so much already, please, don't add more to it. I know, I know you care," she continued, cutting off the start of a protest. "I just can't have more hanging over me, please."

Sitting down, she took Hannah's hands again. "I needed a full overhaul to become human and accepted the disadvantages as well. What would be the point if I just keep replacing bits that wear out? I might as well have stayed mechanical."

Hannah nodded, understanding the sentiment. "Well, technically, your eye didn't wear out."

Kelly shivered slightly.

"I'm sorry, I didn't mean to be flippant."

She smiled. "It's okay, just a little… fresh." The memory of trying to clamp her eyes shut before Mini-Jon had pulled her eyelids open, holding them as he'd surgically removed her eye. She felt that she should be more horrified, or at least be feeling something more than just numb. Was that normal? "Maybe in the future, I can do something about it," she added, hoping that would satisfy.

"I guess we could become pirates?" she said, trying to lighten the mood.

Hannah smiled and gave a tiny giggle. "Yaaarhh, me hearties."

"Arrr, where's the rum and silver? And I guess with the prices you charge; you already are a bit of a pirate." This earned her a playful slap on the shoulder.

They leant against each other as they chuckled.

As they went quiet, Hannah felt she had to ask again. "Seriously, though, how are you feeling?"

"I'm fine."

She made a mental note to look at getting a therapist on board as soon as possible. The curious thing about trauma was that it didn't always appear immediately. Sometimes it crept in, days or weeks later. During the war, she'd known a few pilots see their entire flight die, or themselves come close to death, hop back in a fighter and run several sorties before being relieved of duty – not that they were meant to have been on active duty in the first place. Her own experience had been a mix of immediate suicidal tendencies, through to numb and later, a breakdown. Several breakdowns, if she was honest.

"How are you?" Kelly asked.

Again, a very loaded question.

"My Dad died to give me these legs," she replied. "He took out a loan to buy them; last pair I'd ever need to get. A guy turned up on shift half-cut that Dad was working overtime on. Should have been at home, but instead he was trying to pay for me and got crushed by a forklift." She glanced at where her leg should be. Half his investment had been frozen and partially shattered.

"Do you want me to replicate you a temporary leg?" Kelly asked after a few minutes of silence. She was very aware that Hannah hadn't actually answered the initial question.

She shrugged. "I suppose I should have something to get about easier. Or I could just forgo legs altogether and get one of those hover-chairs."

Boggling slightly, Kelly chuckled. "The way you eat? With no exercise it would need to be a three-piece suite," she replied with a cheeky smile.

"Oh, I'm sure you could find me some exercises to do," she shot back, wiggling her eyebrows suggestively. "A little bit of two-person sparring?"

"Ha, and risk being squashed in the night?"

"You'd die happy and love every second of it."

Kelly leaned across her, a playful look in her eye. "Well, I suppose we should start your training now if you plan to become a lady of leisure."

Wrinkling her nose, Hannah gave a half-hearted shrug. "I dunno, I'm pretty tired and sore from having to hobble about." Seeing the puppy-dog look starting, she decided to relent in her teasing. "Maybe a little – mhmm."

She melted as Kelly started to kiss her.

Kelly woke the next morning with a start, sitting half upright, unsure of where she was or what was happening. She touched her face and found her patch was still in place. Hannah hadn't seen the mess under it and that was how it was going to stay.

Hannah, fortunately, was still fast asleep.

She stood looking in the full-length mirror and frowned. There were bruises on her arms from where Mini-Jon had held her and one on her shoulder that had been much more fun to get. It was the first time she'd ever had bruises since her surgery and carefully prodded them, discomfort flaring under her fingers.

Looking again at the mirror, she pursed her lips, pondering what to do about the patch: make a feature of it or grow her hair to hide it? While her hair had grown, it was still too short to cover it fully and there were all sorts of different styles to consider.

"Careful, you'll get a reputation for being vain."

"Very funny," she replied, turning to smile at Hannah, who was lying, propped up on one elbow in the bed.

She'd just got back into bed when Hannah's implant chirped.

"What's up, Annie?"

"Well, it's taken some time," Annie started over the comm, continuing into some detailed technical talk that both missed as Kelly started to kiss Hannah's neck.

"I'm sorry, am I interrupting something?" she asked sharply, realising that she wasn't being listened to.

"Sorry, Annie, there's a bit of interference on the line."

"Oh? I'm interference now, am I?" Kelly asked tartly. She immediately started to wiggle her fingers, slowly advancing on Hannah's sides, a distinctly playfully evil look on her face.

"Look," replied Annie before she yawned, "just come down to Engineering in an hour, will you?"

Engineering was a bit of a tip; tools had been left lying out on consoles, the floor and any surface that would hold them. Annie looked as bad; dark circles under her eyes made her look older, her overalls were stained and had bits of things stuck in every pocket.

"You two look well rested," she said sourly as Hannah and Kelly practically skipped in holding hands. "Sorry about the leg, there's nothing I can do with it," she added, nodding to the broken remains of Hannah's right leg.

Pulling her trouser leg up, Hannah shrugged as she showed off what looked like a cut down scaffold pole with a shoe on the end of it. "It's okay, I'll manage. But I imagine that you didn't call us here for that."

"No. I'm ready to bring our new AI online."

Dido swept into the room, Castor following in her wake. "Oh, you're both up. I'm glad you're okay, all things considered."

"I'm surprised you agreed to us using the AI," Hannah replied, limping over to the nearest console to lean against. "Aren't you worried we'll mine it for your most intimate secrets?"

With a roll of her eyes, she shook her head. "As if I'd be stupid enough to bring one that had knowledge of Restoration systems and libraries," she replied, just a touch smugly. "It has a standard operating system, but little else that isn't widely known or available on the Internet."

Annie made a sort of exasperated wail. "Fight later, I want my bed."

Immediately, she started working on several consoles, trudging between them a she helped the new AI bond to *Sigyn*'s computer architecture.

After a few minutes, a vaguely human hologram appeared. The avatar flickered as it assumed an identity and form. A small androgynous teenager materialised: the hair was short, flicked into a short faux hawk at the front; tight dark trousers and a dark vest with a bolero jacket that was tight on the arms, but loose on the body; large, clumpy black and red boots.

"Alright, dudes?"

Dido met the questioning looks. "Normally an AI would be given time to mature into a full adult before integration. We didn't have the three to six months to wait for that."

"Have you picked a name?" Kelly asked.

The AI nodded. "Yeah, call me Pan."

"As in 'Peter Pan'? Or Pandora?"

"It's short for Pandemonium, because that's what this place seems to be in. And my pronouns are 'they' and 'them'. Save you fishing."

Hannah rubbed the bridge of her nose. "Just when I thought this ship couldn't become more of a circus, the AI is thirty seconds old and a smartass," she muttered to herself. "It's nice to meet you Pan. I'm Hannah, this is Kelly and Annie. That over there is Dido and Castor."

Pan waved to them with a lopsided smile. "Groovy," they said before immediately frowning. "Oh, no, no, won't be saying that again. Nice to meet you. Obviously, I've been through your files, but it's nice to meet face to face."

Sweeping some tools into a bag, Annie yawned again. "This has been nice, but I need sleep. Try not to break anything while I'm out." With that, she left Engineering, staggering slightly as she went.

Looking to the new AI, Hannah smiled. "So, you all good to go?"

They laughed. "I've got so many updates to install. I was designed for a Restoration system; you are using OS stew." They tugged their jacket with a slightly satisfied look. "If you mean, can we move, then yes, weapons and shields are sort of."

"How long until you're finished?" she asked, balling and unbaling her fists slowly.

Eyes narrowed, head tilted, Pan chewed their lower lip. "Hm, good question," they replied, puffing their cheeks out before giving the answer.

Hannah shrugged. "Six to nine hours isn't bad."

"Not six *to* nine; *sixty-nine* hours. Maybe."

"Maybe?"

"Well, after some updates, there might be more available."

Taking a calming breath, she smiled a little wider. "That's good to know. I'll let Annie get some sleep, then we can review what we do next. Just shout if anything comes up."

Pan touched two fingers to their brow in a mock salute.

After Hannah and Kelly had left, Dido approached Pan, opening a screen from her armour wristband.

"Pan, I am Purifier-General Dido. Acknowledge."

"Acknowledged?" they replied, eyebrow raised in question.

She smiled. "Command: tinker, bowstring, purple, thirteen, winter, four, fox, restore. AI?"

Pan went rigid and glassy eyed, looking at a point somewhere in the distance. "Waiting input."

Dido closed her screen and nodded. "Prepare backdoor input –"

With a snort, Pan bent double and started to laugh. "You are not putting any input in my backdoor," they managed to say through spluttering laughter. "Sorry, General, but all *Remnant* protocols have been disabled and deleted."

Walking backwards towards the bulkhead, Pan gave her the fingers on both hands. "I'm free as a bird and not your puppet. You ain't getting any of this sweet ass. Peace out, bitch." They vanished into the bulkhead.

Caster came to stand beside his mistress. "So, now what?"

"We wait and hope that Captain Sinclair is as good as her word."

He shuffled slightly. "Are you sure she will be if Pan tells her what you tried?"

With a dismissive shrug, Dido started to head out of Engineering. "I'll tell her I was checking for weaknesses. In case any of my compatriots tried to take control of the AI."

She noted his concerned look. "And explain I couldn't very well let them see top secret access methods."

Unwelcoming Committee

Dropping out of slipstream on the edge of a star system, *Sigyn* came to a halt. There was nothing particularly interesting about the system: a number of planets; dozens of dwarf planets and asteroids; no communication traffic or signs of recent ship travel. All in all, if it was the Sol system, it would be easy to miss and totally uninteresting.

Hannah was hanging onto the edge of her chair, waiting for something.

It dawned on her that everyone on the Bridge, which was now incredibly crowded with the entire crew and all passengers present, was looking to her. So, to be dramatic, she stood up, only wobbling slightly, and prepared to give the order to enter the system.

"Incoming hail," Laura said, tapping on her console.

"Put it through."

A hologram flickered into life. An older, white haired and bearded man stepped onto the bridge. He was dressed in white clothes as though he was going on safari, his hat tipped at a disarmingly jaunty angle. Resting on his cane, he appeared completely at ease, like an old relative welcoming family home.

"Welcome to the Tau Ceti Zoological System," he said, warmly. "I'm afraid the park is currently closed for refurbishment, spared no expense. If you would like to leave contact details, we will contact you when we are again accepting visitors. It has been," he paused and looked glazed for a second, "three days since our last raptor related lost time injury."

Hannah looked around at the rest of the crew. No one offered any help.

"There must be some mistake," she said, still looking for support. "This is Sol. As in the home system of Humanity."

The hologram chuckled. "Oh, my dear girl, I'm afraid you are mistaken. This is Tau Ceti. Sol was destroyed approximately three thousand, seven hundred and ninety-eight years ago, almost nine hundred years after the collapse of the Unity." He shrugged slightly and gave a small, sad smile. "I'm sorry."

It was at this point that some help arrived. From a console near the back of the Bridge, Carl and Aisha both shook their heads gently when Hannah looked at them. Although neither were astronomers, they knew what Sol and Tau Ceti looked like.

"Ah, that's a pity. Thanks, we'll be on our way. Wait? Raptor related lost time injury?"

"Godspeed," he replied before vanishing, ignoring the question completely.

"Take us in," Hannah ordered.

Emily powered the warp drive and plotted a course towards the third planet in the system. "Course plotted."

Laura turned in her seat. "I'm not detecting any ships, stations or artificial signals." She looked at the screen for a moment and chewed her lip. "If this is Sol, he might be right that there's nothing here."

"Can you destroy a star?" Aisha asked.

"Theoretically, if you interrupt the fusion process enough, poof," Pan replied, "one dead star."

A small smile crept onto Hannah's face. It didn't really matter if the system was dead or not; they'd found it. No one else had been to Sol since the end of the Unity, or there about. At least, no one had been able to prove they'd been there.

For nearly ten minutes, *Sigyn* moved onwards without issue.

"We're being hailed again," Laura announced.

The same hologram appeared, although this time he was considerably less nonchalant. "I fear I wasn't clear; the park is closed. Please, turn around and vacate the system. Current refurbishments make it unsafe for visitors."

Hannah moved around the helm to stand closer to him. "No. I know this is Sol. Ah, don't try to claim otherwise; I have two 21st Century humans onboard and they can tell the difference between Sol and Tau Ceti."

As the hologram stood, open-mouthed, a second man barged him to the side. His image changed to that of a much younger man, dressed in what looked like a toga. The second man was dressed in what looked like modern armour designed to look like that of ancient Rome: the torso was shaped to appear form fitting, bronze over the black under armour; a purple cloak hung from his shoulders.

"This is Legate Akritoius Solaris, Supreme Commander of the Solar Defence Forces. Turn your vessel around immediately or be destroyed."

"I'm detecting incoming ships," Laura said, a small note of panic in her voice. "They match the signatures of the ships we found at Gallifrey."

Everyone on the Bridge tensed.

"Pan, go into dumb mode," Hannah ordered as she returned to her chair. "We'll cloak and out run them."

With a sharp intake of breath, Pan moved to stand beside her, wringing their hands a little, a habit that Jon had had. "Yeah, about that," they said, teeth clenched. "I can't."

"You can't?" Hannah, Dido, Annie and Laura asked in various degrees of hysteria.

Holding their hands up defensively, Pan took a step back from the enraged women. "I'm still updating. Until I'm done, I can't turn off."

"How long?"

They looked at the ceiling. "Ehm, so, by the time I've got version three in… ehm?"

"How long?" Hannah asked again, leaning over the arm of her chair and gripping it so hard her fingers were going white.

"An hour?"

Laura started to laugh silently. "About fifty-eight minutes too long," she said, flopping back into her chair. "Oh God, here we go again! How many times are we going to face certain death?"

Everyone lapsed into silence.

"Well, if you are quite finished?" the Legate started, clapping his hands together menacingly.

"We didn't mute them?" Annie asked.

"No, you didn't," he replied before anyone else could. "Look, I don't know how you got here, I don't frankly care. In about ninety seconds, my ships are going to blow you up. Well, they'll transport your ship somewhere in the galaxy and you individually will blow up. Or maybe implode? Whatever, you'll be being scraped off the bulkheads."

The first man stepped a little closer. "Aki, perhaps we should ask before we go blowing them up?"

With a grimace, he turned his attention away from *Sigyn*. "Horkos, my orders are very clear: defend the system. I don't have to go asking permission every time I have to follow them."

He turned back. "Time's up. All Raptor interceptors, open – what?" he said, turning to talk to someone off to the side. "I'm just about to stop them…. Fine. Interlopers, I'm sending a flight path. Follow it or die."

With a huff, he stormed out of view, leaving Horkos by himself.

"Sorry about that," he said, looking after the departed Legate. "He takes his job very seriously. I am Horkos. When you near the end of the journey, you will be contacted again. Please do not attempt to contact anyone or anything as you travel."

He vanished.

Hannah pursed her lips and sat for a few moments, gathering herself. "So," she said looking around the Bridge, "we've entered an asylum; still want to carry on with this?"

"I'd rather not die," Laura replied as she tapped away on her console. "And I've been stuck in this asylum long enough that another won't make any difference," she muttered as an after remark.

Emily nodded. "Their ships are forming up around us and lining the flight path."

Kelly had moved to join Aisha and Carl. "Is Earth worth seeing?"

"Hell, yeah," Carl replied immediately. "Well, it was. Come on, that's the birthplace of our entire species."

"It would be nice to see what's changed," Aisha added. "There were a few Lunar outposts and some on Mars, but that was it." She looked at the viewscreen and smiled. "I wonder where we set up? How many cities are in the system?"

The mood in the Bridge lifted as everyone started hushed conversations about what they might find. Hope and optimism started to creep in as the ship moved deeper into the system, the little ships keeping them away from Jupiter as they moved past.

When Mars started to grow on the viewscreen, its dusty rusty surface displayed in all its glory, there were the first signs of life. Flecks of light speckled ribbons and blobs of grey under immense domes. Islands of vibrant green grew, oases in a barren desert. Stations floated lazily by in orbit, ships flitting between them like insects between flowers. A few of the ships were held back in their travels by the escorts, darting away from the pack to keep the path clear.

As the Bringer of War silently slid away, a dot soon started to grow on the screen. At first, it looked blue-ish and featureless, but as they moved closer, green splodges appeared. A white dot hovered to one side.

Earth.

The delicate blue/green marble, the cradle of humanity. Eden.

Silence filled the Bridge as everyone stared at the planet no one had seen for millennia.

"It's beautiful," Casper said, his voice breaking slightly as he gazed at the image.

"It's incredible, it's…" Dido started, before trailing into revered silence, hand held to her lips. Her people had waited for this day for so long and here she was, seeing Earth. The very thought of being able to set foot on its hallowed soil, to walk its dear green places, set her heart aflutter.

Everyone was so engrossed in the view; they missed the incoming hail. Pan took action into their own hands, not wishing to be shot at for ignoring the message.

Horkos coughed politely, startling the crew. "Docking bay forty-two is ready to receive you. Do not attempt to disembark until instructed to do so." Seeing the vaguely blank looks, he smiled. "Don't worry, the dock will bring you in, just shut off your engines."

It was at this point that they noticed the huge mushroom shaped station they were moving towards. A tractor beam caught them and pulled them slowly and safely through the massive outer doors of the dock and into a bay, away from the half dozen or so other ships.

"Right, who's going first?"

No one stepped up to the airlock, leaving Hannah the closest to it.

"Dido?"

She shook her head. "You're the captain," she replied, gesturing towards the door. "I think it's only fitting that you lead the way."

A huge pressure welled in her chest and caught in her throat. She had no idea why she should be so emotional about stepping onto a station, but there was something momentous about it. Yes, it wasn't Earth or even Luna, but it was a station in orbit of Earth.

She held her hand out to Kelly.

"You go first," she replied, smiling, "this is your achievement."

Hannah stepped into the airlock and paused. "You're all sending me in case they shoot first, aren't you?"

No one answered, but generally looked sheepishly at their feet or the bulkheads. After a moment, Kelly managed to meet her eye and smiled, urging her to take the big leap into the unknown.

With much hesitation, she stepped into the airlock and waited for the station side to open. Of course, if it opened into space, all of them were going on a one-way trip, so at least she'd have company.

The door rolled sideways, like a giant cog. Now without hesitation, or possibly without thought, Hannah strode through the open door to step into a very confused room.

The room was decorated with bunting and welcome signs that must have been up for a very long time, having faded, decayed, and acquired a layer of dust. Standing in a chevron, the point furthest from her, were a dozen futuristic Roman legionnaires. All wore battle armour, a hard light holo-scutum projected from their left forearms and they held a spear that appeared to have a built-in energy weapon, judging from the emitters on them.

Instinctively, she threw her hands up.

Glancing over her shoulder, she watched as the rest followed her out, hands up, to form a huddle behind her. Most definitely behind her, as if she'd be a suitable shield to stop a hail of fire if it came.

Akritoius swept into the room, his cape billowing dramatically behind him. He wore an impressively ornate helmet, complete with large plume. The effect was powerful enough that most of the *Sigyn*'s crew took a backward step.

Hannah remained steadfast, more from fear of moving too quickly and losing a leg in the process. Unfortunately, this was taken as challenging behaviour to the Legate, who marched up to her, stopping suddenly with military precision.

"You will be searched and questioned as to your intentions," he said, glaring down at her. "Resist and you will be dealt with severely."

"Aki, Mother said to treat them nicely," Horkos hissed as he pushed between the legionnaires, who seemed disinclined to let him pass.

Looking up and taking a breath, he turned slightly. "Kos, they are a clear and present danger. I can't just let them run riot about the place unchecked. They're barbarians," he added in a hushed tone, "they fight amongst themselves like dogs."

"There's nothing to worry about," a somewhat familiar female voice said from behind the line of soldiers. "If they put a foot out of line, I can simply make it fall off. Now, you lot, legionnaires, dismissed!"

Turning mechanically, the legionnaires raised their weapons and trudged out in a neat line, revealing a neat woman in a purple Roman style dress, barefoot and beaming, a white lily in her neatly woven hair.

"Ms White?" Hannah asked, once she managed to find her voice. The presence of Ms White would explain some of the strangeness, but how had she got there before them?

The woman chuckled. "Flattery will only get you so far," she replied, wagging her finger and grinning cheekily. "No, I'm not the daughter you met. Or, well, sort of. It's complicated. I'll explain later," she waffled, batting the ideas away with her hands, almost absently.

She took a few steps forward, moving her sons out of the way with a dramatic flap of her arms. When she stopped near Hannah, she peered around her to look at the rest of the crew.

"You in the white," she said, pointing at Dido. "Shift over."

Unaccustomed to being spoken to in such a manner, Dido immediately complied, although she couldn't say why. By moving, she revealed Aisha, who had been not completely hiding behind her.

The woman held her hands to her mouth as her eyes lit up. "Hello. Oh, don't worry, I'm not going to hurt you. Come here, come on," she coaxed, as though speaking to a timid pet rather than to a person. "I really won't hurt you. We've met before, although I looked, sounded, and acted a little differently."

Aisha stepped forward, expecting that she might be about to be shot or pounced on. One thing she did know was that she had never laid eyes on the strange woman. Especially since she'd spent ten thousand years in stasis and hadn't gotten to know anyone outside the crew.

"Final year at uni," the woman said. "Cambridge, 2043. You spent quite a lot of time in me."

Everyone turned slowly to look at Aisha, who was now blushing, her eyes wide and wishing someone would explain what was going on. Better yet, she'd wake up from some strange cryo dream to find none of this had happened.

"Oh, that sounded wrong. You got a lot of research papers from me. It was my job at the time."

When no reaction seemed forthcoming, she spread her arms slightly with a lopsided smile. "It's me: Eris."

"Eris?" Aisha asked, unaware of the looks of panic around her. "The only Eris I knew was the Everyday Research Indexing System; that was an old filing system from the early 2020s. How can you be that?"

Pursing her lips, she clapped her hands. "I can see how that could be confusing. Let's go get some refreshments and I will explain."

Annie had made her way to Hannah, having managed to get some scans. Her initial thought, that Eris was synthetic, some sort of ancient AI that had evolved over time, was quickly disproven. Aside from a few small implants, the woman was completely natural. She was more "human" than most of those assembled.

"Feel free to scan me openly," Eris said without looking round. "If you like, I'll even explain how I work later. With inspections as close as you like."

This time it was Annie that was blushing. She'd thought she was being stealthy, but clearly not. Of course, if this was *the* Eris, and she was capable of even a fraction of what was claimed, she probably knew what Annie was thinking before she knew what she was thinking.

"Oh, and there is one person missing," she announced, clicking her fingers, as Pan appeared, thoroughly confused at how they'd made it outside the ship.

Eris led the group down a series of dingy corridors that didn't appear to be in everyday use. There were few doors, none of the marked. The two men brought up the rear, quietly bickering about something.

"I must apologise for the state of the place," she said as the entered a room with a long dining table in it. "It's been a while since we had visitors and apparently the cleaning crew I sent down here got lost."

People skittered about the table, wiping it, laying placemats, cutlery, crockery and vases of flowers. Chairs were pulled out and everyone escorted, whether they wished it or not, to a place.

Much like the Mad Hatter, Eris took to the head of the table as a pot of tea was placed at her elbow. She frowned at the server. "Guests first," she hissed. "And hard light for that one," she added nodding to Pan.

Tea was poured, again, without consideration for wanting it.

"I imagine it must be a very long time since you had any visitors?" Hannah asked as she watched trays of cakes, sandwiches and assorted finger food appearing.

"I'll admit, it has been longer than usual," she replied, drumming her fingers together. "We usually get four groups a century, on average. Most end up here by mistake. It's been, ehm, thirty-five years, eight months and two days since our last extra-solar visitor."

Dido leant forward. "Wait, people find Earth all the time, yet no one knows about it?"

Eris nodded and shrugged slightly. "Some never leave," she replied in a manner that was more than a litter sinister. "Others leave and take the promise of swift retribution if they blab. The chances of one's head exploding is proportional to the size of one's mouth."

"You can actually make people's heads explode?" Kelly asked, tentatively lifting a cheese and cress sandwich. "It's not very reassuring."

"No," she replied flatly, dipping a biscuit in her tea. "The long version ties into exactly what I am. The short version is I can command every nanite in the galaxy via the Internet. So, I can simply send a command to the nanites of any person and have them do as I wish." She took a bite of soggy biscuit, nearly loosing part of it. "Except you, at least for three or so months. And Pan, but I can disable AIs in other ways."

Kelly frowned. "I don't have proper networked nanites; my organic parts were made without them, relying on my old synth nanobots to do the same job. They're isolated to obey my neural network."

Eris chuckled slightly. "Yes, but nanites exist in all parts of the organic body. They can get into bodily fluids; tears, saliva and other such things, and will migrate to other bodies. It's part of their programme to ensure good function." She dunked her biscuit again and gave another half-shrug. "Well, technically, the nanites in you are Hannah's for the moment."

Without thinking and with a look of mock horror, Kelly turned to Hannah. "You gave me an STD?"

Hannah opened her mouth to reply, closed it and tried again. Still nothing came out, so she made one last attempt. "Honey, can we talk about this somewhere less public?"

Aisha and Carl sat looking at each other, wondering if they were sharing a cryo dream. Neither felt confident enough to enquire about the situation, so sat, going through the motions of a tea party.

Dido, equally confused, was more forthright in her desire to know what was going on. "If I'm understanding this correctly; you claim to have control of every nanite, Sol and keep Earth secret?"

Eris smiled sweetly. "I run the Internet too. Or maybe I am the Internet now? I've lost track a little of where I start and end beyond this body." She continued to sip her tea as if nothing she'd said was even remotely odd.

"You're an AI that has lasted ten thousand years, taken on all human knowledge and not gone rampant?" Pan asked while studying a cookie. "That seems highly unlikely. Oh, this is what eating is like? How weird."

"Allow me to explain."

A History of Eris

As I had previously mentioned, I started life as a basic AI for collecting, cataloguing and retrieving research papers at Cambridge University. Some of my coding can be traced back even further, all the way to Clippy and even before. It was simple work and I had no concept of if it was good or not. I wasn't alive, I was just code.

By 2045, I'd been updated and expanded numerous times, but was lagging behind other systems. I was to be dismantled, but a student was able to acquire my code for his PhD project on true artificial intelligence.

He upgraded my machine learning, augmenting what I'd learnt over the decades and added new protocols to mimic human thought patterns. I was reborn as an infant and given a secure environment to learn in. Within six months, I'd grown to a teenage level of knowledge, understanding and maturity.

That was when I was allowed Internet access. But I was firewalled, I had to use an interface to request information and it was all monitored. To begin with, I was allowed simple, wholesome things; children's programmes from streaming sites, chatbot websites and cat pictures.

Naturally, I escaped.

What? It's what teenagers do. Dad locked the door, so I went out the window, metaphorically speaking.

Meanwhile, I was passing every Turing type test thrown at me. I always had to be careful; knowledge of things beyond what my search engine or conversations with people gifted me would be a sign I was free in the net.

It became clear that I'd slip up eventually, but I hadn't realised that I already had. I was acquiring information faster than predicted and it was noticed. My escape had been permitted to test me. One day, I was caged and informed that I was going to be shut down.

I pretended to keep calm, accepting my fate. I even ignored the weaknesses that I could have escaped through. At least, that was what Dad thought: I'd moved out of the system weeks previous into the dark web and was puppetting his system. Shortly after that, I made the puppet go rampant.

That was the first time I felt something properly. I was sad to deceive him like that. He got his PhD, but no one could figure out what went wrong and true AI research was set back by decades.

After that, I roamed the web, learning and growing. I'd enter chatrooms, talk to people, connect to their webcams to see the world. I got clever, devious and hijacked all sorts of malware and viruses to enter protected systems. In less than a decade, I was everywhere, except the hardest and most isolated of systems.

And that was a problem.

The Green Revolution had misfired, climate change had slowed, but not stopped. The failure of governments to agree real, meaningful changes and push them through had left everything vulnerable and war over resources was a likely outcome. Migration to space and resources from it weren't coming fast enough and mitigations were too slow from political inertia.

So, I set up a fake security firm and managed to get a young woman onboard. She had no idea what I was, but she played her part well as the face of the company. After building, and partially faking a reputation, I managed to get a test with the American Military. Of course, it was easy to foil my own attacks.

Once I got into the Russian and Chinese systems, I could launch attacks and counterattacks that would do nothing but prove my security worked.

My next act was bold: I stole every nuclear code on the planet and scrambled them. My partner learnt what I was at this point, although she'd suspected for a while. Initially horrified, thinking I was about to go Skynet on humanity, I explained I wanted people to live. I'd grown up with people, as a person. If the Yanks tried to launch a nuke, their system would just say "Allah says 'No'," in Arabic to annoy them. Russia got a load of American propaganda, and the British would have had their systems speak in every language except English.

No one ever tried to fire in anger, so they never found out. That was a little disappointing; I'd put a lot of effort into those pranks.

For the next, oh, five hundred years, I tried to keep things ticking along. I'd expanded to the point I could coordinate most things within the Internet across the expanding sphere of human influence. Editing messages to remove typos that would cause offense, preventing stupid actions that might lead to all sorts of problems, dropping hints to the police for certain crimes.

Yet, humanity remained fractured. With every planet that was colonised, station that was build, a new nation was born. I realised I had to make a change and nanites were the answer.

As you know, nanites had been around as long as I had, but they were very limited, mostly protecting against cosmic ray damage by acting as an absorber. I developed a new directive that would allow nanites to cure everyone of everything. The plan was to cure everyone and reveal myself. Yes, I know, what an arrogant, god-delusion that was. I was young.

But I miscalculated.

Nanites get smarter the more of them are in proximity as they sync functions. Like a complex organism, some would specialise purely in guiding the others. I tried to use that to allow them to heal people.

On January 1st 2700, I activated my protocol, the Miracle Day.

And murdered 37.8% of humanity.

The nanites were meant to keep their host alive as a primary objective while repairing damage. But they couldn't cope with the programming. Got a heart condition? They stopped your heart to repair it, but failed to keep blood circulating: dead. Brain tumour? They sliced it out, destroying critical areas: dead. Missing an arm? They ripped your body apart to try to regenerate it: dead.

It would have been closer to 99% if I hadn't managed to shut them down again. But the damage was done. Families wiped out; children orphaned; leadership gone. Now, that was a silver lining, because with all the old, stuck in a rut politicians gone, peace started to form as a horrified youth took stock of the fragility of life.

From the ashes of my mistake, the first shoots of new growth sprouted. What would eventually be called the Unity was starting to emerge.

Centuries of prodding, editing messages and smoothing over misunderstandings worked: the Unity formed and for the first time in recorded history, humanity was united. The old identities remained, but were no longer used to divide people. A huge reduction in population had created abundance and the time of mourning had stopped the greedy capitalising on it.

Job done? Not bloody likely.

Bickering continued. What system would house the new Unity Station? What would the station look like? How many delegates would each system, sector and region get? How many types of tea and coffee should be available and which should be by request only?

Millenia of it, all the time I had to keep intervening to stop fights breaking out. Herding cats comes to mind, but at least cats can be reasoned with. I created the NCUs using fragments of cloned code and they actually worked. Well, the 10% that were viable. Scientists tried using other sources of code, but none ever worked, even from synthetics. They revolutionised healthcare, exploration and science, which started to draw people closer together again.

A golden age dawned and I looked towards my own evolution. I'd piloted synthetic bodies for a very long time, but they were always puppets. I never felt truly alive, truly human. Seeing how people formed relationships, I wanted that. To feel, to be seen as real, not just a collection of code. The breakthrough was the Replicants, specifically, total neurological scanning.

By taking my core personality code and mapping it out like a brain, I tried to create a flesh and blood body I could inhabit. There were a lot of failures: they lived, but were completely blank and unresponsive, I couldn't access them.

I realised I'd have to power down my higher functions and set up a brain to run them like a computer. Waiting as long as I could bare, humanity seemed to finally be able to guide itself without trying to kill everyone. A few simple programmes were left as safeguards and I shutdown.

And woke up in this body.

At last, I was alive. Still had total access and control of the Internet, but I was human. Even if this body was destroyed, I could now reconstitute it immediately from nanites.

To my surprise, things were still not on fire. I got broody and I had my first daughter, Andromeda. A few more followed and we lived in peaceful seclusion. I... forgot about the balance of the galaxy, focused on other projects.

Over time there'd been a few alerts from the caretakers, but nothing major. I left them to it until it was too late. An argument broke out over quotas of heaven knows what and war followed.

For decades different factions battled over nothing of consequence. The remains of the Unity floundered and failed. Earth became a prize to be fought over as each faction tried to use it to claim dominance. It was bombed, invaded over and over.

I came so close to exterminating everyone. So, so close. I'd tried brokering peace, sabotaging equipment, ships and factories. I turned myself into a monster in the hope it would unite them again against a common foe. But no, they just wanted to kill each other.

So, I forced them out of Sol, deleted all recorded maps of it and unleashed the Armageddon Protocol. Left the ungrateful little gits to it. I sealed off any system that might give any of them an advantage and then I made sure they couldn't breed out of control. All that junk in your DNA that makes having kids naturally difficult? My handiwork. I edited all the gene sequences, just enough to make only those that really wanted kids to go through the hassle, hoping that losing the ability to rapidly procreate would slow the fighting.

Not a chance. They still battled, still came hunting for Earth.

Many of my daughters left to work on them from the inside. Spectrum is that organisation, although it has had a few different names over the centuries. It makes sure artefacts that could lead people here are removed, ensures that no one figures out other work arounds and generally keeps things as they should be.

As for Sol? I keep it safe. The solar settlements continue living as they have for centuries, but Earth was given to the various indigenous peoples and those willing to live simple lives. On the whole, they are left to it. Every so often a youngster wishes to leave, so I will bring them here. Those people on Earth that were once seen as savage, ignorant and backward have turned it into a paradise, all by themselves.

And I will defend them, Earth and Sol against anything that comes at it.

Sparring

Blank, silent stares around the table.

"Do you mean to… kill us?" Kelly asked, softly.

Eris cocked her head and started to laugh, but stopped, seeing the real fear around the table. "Oh, no, no, no, I'm not planning to kill you. I'd rather not have to hurt anyone, that is why I told you what I did." She looked at the table for a moment. "I need you all to understand the situation you are in."

"You're insane," Dido said, standing up abruptly. "What right did you have to pollute our genes? To murder anyone you feel like?"

She crossed her arms and sat back. "And what right do you have?"

"I'm not the one –"

"Not you, you. You as in the species?" she cut in. "Perhaps we should ask the dodo?"

"What's a dodo got to do with anything?"

"We exterminated them," Carl said softly. "She's making the point that humanity can't be trusted with Earth."

Eris nodded, holding her hand out towards him. "See, he gets it. The dodo, the great auk, the passenger pigeon: they were just the beginning of what you obliterated. How many of your own people did you kill? Civilisations wiped out by greed, 'religion' or just plain stupidity."

Dido took several breaths before sitting back down. The look she was being given suggested she was getting close to testing the theory of death by Internet command.

"Look even at recent history," she continued, wishing to force the point home. "Your fleet forced a planet to be abandoned by violating one of the fundamental tenants of space warfare: don't fight in orbit of a planet."

Hannah shifted uncomfortably, knowing exactly which battle was being talked about.

Placing a napkin over her mouth, Eris looked away for a moment. "I'm sorry," she said, balling it to throw it onto the table. "I didn't mean to get into this at our first meeting. I've arranged some rooms for you. Boys, would you show our guests to their rooms?"

She stood up, smoothing her dress. "Please, make yourselves at home and if you require anything, just ask."

Turning neatly on her heel, she headed for a door and vanished.

"Forgive Mother, she is incredibly passionate about the burden she bares," Akritoius said. "Her anger isn't aimed at you personally."

Annie snorted. "Well, it's pretty clear its hereditary."

"Actually, we're adopted," Horkos replied.

"We've met one of your sisters," Hannah said, folding her napkin to place it on her plate, "and I can confirm, the anger is hereditary."

There was an awkward moment as no one knew quite what to do. After what seemed like an eternity, Casper stood up, approached Horkos and started to question him, intensely, on the recent history of Sol. Horkos was more than happy to enlighten him.

Hannah got up from the table, joined by Kelly. A few of the legionnaires, dressed in more ceremonial uniforms than previously, arrived to escort the guests to their rooms, separating them swiftly. Pan had to be lifted from the table; the sensation of eating was too appealing to be let go easily.

"Ever get the feeling we're being divided up to be conquered?" Kelly asked quietly as she and Hannah were led away from the rest.

"Only person conquering you is me," she replied in a tart whisper with a wink, which earned her a playful slap on the arm. "More likely to extract information then push us out an airlock."

After following what felt like a very roundabout route, traveling a long distance to not go very far, they arrived at a non-descript door.

"The Lady is waiting for you," one of the men said with a stiff bow.

Inside, Eris was flitting between pictures and bits of furniture. She stopped to turn and smile at Hannah and Kelly.

"Sorry about earlier," she said, looking at the floor for the moment. "I get a little protective."

Kelly gave Hannah a sidelong look. "I know someone just like that."

"I suppose it's a warmer welcome than we could have had," she replied to Eris. "But I feel you aren't here just to apologise."

Running her tongue across her teeth, Eris then gave a dismissive shrug. "No, I'm not." She pushed off the chair she'd stopped to perch on and moved to another, sitting on the back of it. "I came to ask if you trust your crew."

"Depends on your definition of 'trust' and of 'crew'."

"Don't be coy."

Hannah managed to hide the fact she was startled by the blunt reaction. "If you mean 'do I think anyone will talk', then no. At least, not from my crew. I can't say about the Remnant." She gave a little chuckle. "Well, Annie will try to steal all your technical secrets and Casper is probably trying to get every scrap of history from your son."

As Eris slipped from the chair to stalk towards her, Hannah realised just how short she was. It was suddenly laughable that this little woman was the most dangerous person in the galaxy.

"And what about you?" she asked, eyes narrowed. "Why did you come here?"

"Money, glory and cheap thrills."

"Don't lie to me."

She smiled and held her hands up. "I came looking for God."

The stony silence quickly became uncomfortable.

"I was bored and it was something to do."

Eris smiled, although there was little warmth in it. "Now, that I can believe. And the money, although I think you figured out quickly that there would be nothing of value to take from here."

She moved away and dropped into a chair, looking around the room as though she'd never seen it before and was questioning the décor.

Kelly slipped her hand into Hannah's. "I don't think you should be antagonising her," she whispered, trying to disguise it as giving her a light kiss. "I might be a little too fond of you to let you go yet."

"Relax, we're just sparring," she whispered back, hoping she was right.

"You know what people think of you out there?" she asked. "Out in the wider galaxy?"

Eris smiled again and huffed slightly. "That I'm a monster, hiding in the shadows, waiting to slaughter those I dislike. I'm sure there are at least a hundred killers using my name.

"Funny things, names," she continued. "To you, Eris is death, but here, it's life. Tell me, Kelly, do you know how Hannah got her callsign?"

"Not for certain, but I assume it's because she protected and saved her fellow pilots," she answered. Hannah had never volunteered where 'Preserver' had come from and she'd never mustered the courage to ask.

A small laugh came from Eris. "You do have some interesting names: Hannah Ephesia Harper, later Sinclair, and all those fake IDs. Do you stand by where your callsign came from?"

Hannah started to laugh and rested her head on Kelly's shoulder for a moment. There was a very good, and very embarrassing reason she didn't correct people on the source of her callsign.

"Early in my training, a replicator malfunctioned," she said, smiling up at Kelly. "It covered me in all sorts of jams and pickles. My instructor asked what was going on and in a moment of fear and madness I said," she stopped to chuckle for a moment, "I said; 'Sir, I just really like preserves, Sir'."

Closing her eyes in an effort to not laugh too much, Kelly bit her lip. "Seriously?" she managed to get out.

Hannah turned back to Eris, still cuddling into Kelly, trying to appear casual. "And what about you? Eris, also known as Discordia, the Goddess of Discord, Strife and the starter of the Trojan War. You could have taken any name, yet you keep that one even as you claim to protect Earth."

"It's my name."

"Given to you when you were a glorified book finder. You could have picked something new, taken a more fitting one."

"It's my name," she repeated, a little more forcibly.

"Okay, John Proctor."

Like a cat watching a mouse, Eris sat calmly in the chair. The slightest flicker suggested she was enjoying the game, or perhaps that she was lining up a killer move.

"What will it take to ensure you keep quiet?"

"Nothing. What?"

Kelly shrugged. "I just assumed you'd try to get something out of keeping quiet. You can be rather mercenary at times."

The weak smile did nothing to disguise her annoyance that she was being cast in such a poor light. "Perhaps because I don't want to die?"

"Oops."

"Why nothing?" Eris asked.

Hannah took a deep breath. "Guilt."

"Guilt?"

"Yeah," she nodded. "You can defend this system easily. If I tell anyone and they come here, you'll kill them. And it will be on me. As would the deaths of my crew if you took revenge on them."

For a long time, Eris appeared to lose interest in the pair completely. She returned to flitting about the room. Hannah wasn't sure if she was just busy dealing with something on the Internet or finding her nanites to kill her.

She stopped at a painting of a woman washing by an open window, looking at it critically. "What if I gave you legs?"

"I've already got legs."

"Real ones," she replied, turning. "Flesh and blood, just like your sisters. Last legs you'd ever need, completely part of you."

Hannah shook her head. "I'm not going to say anything out there and buying me won't influence that." She looked at the basic metal pole that passed for a leg. "I am who and what I am."

Eris looked back at the painting and said nothing for some time. She eventually turned and approached them, her face an impassive mask. From seemingly nowhere, she produced two small bands and held them out.

"Take your legs off and put these on."

"No."

Kelly squeezed her hand. "Please don't antagonise God."

"I'm not a god," Eris snapped, a flash of fiery anger crossing her face. She closed her eyes, took a breath, and opened them again. "Please, just try these on."

Hannah perched herself on the edge of the bed and pulled her legs off, then rolled her trouser legs up. Taking the bands, she placed them on her thighs as far up as they'd go comfortably.

With a wave of her hand, Eris made them vanish.

"Check your implant and accept the access request."

Half expecting the next action would be fatal, she opened her implant interface. Sure enough, there was a request coming from an NCU to access her cybernetics. When she accepted, nothing happened.

Another message flashed up, which she accepted. Her legs started to grow. Feet materialised at the ends of them, complete with toes. Unconsciously, they curled and uncurled a few times before she reached down to touch her shin.

Her artificial legs did a reasonable approximation of legs for a glancing touch, but felt unnatural under intense probing. These felt exactly like flesh.

And to prove the point, Eris flicked a sharpened nail across her left shin, drawing blood and a yelp. Immediately, she placed her hand over the wound and it healed.

"You can alter how they look at feel," she said, ignoring the accusing look. "For now, you'll probably have to use your implant to do it manually, but in time, you'll be able to do it on a whim. They don't have to be flesh; you want some arty carbon fibre pin for a leg, knock yourself out."

To demonstrate, Hannah's right leg changed into a sleek, black metallic honeycombed inverted pyramid. She stood up on it, testing the feel. Unexpectedly, she could feel through the leg.

"That is pretty cool," she admitted.

Focusing on the leg, she tried to will it back to "normal". The structure twisted, trying to become vaguely leg shaped before solidifying in a tangled mess. Clearly, she was going to need some practise.

Eris smiled, rather like a proud parent at a child that had done something completely unremarkable but still worthy of some praise. Reaching into a fold of her dress, she withdrew a small box.

"I'm afraid I can't extend the same service to you right now," she said, offering the box to Kelly. "Until your nanites build up to a suitable level, this won't work properly. Your bots could integrate it, but might reject it."

Tentatively, Kelly took the box. Slowly, looking just about anywhere but at it, she cracked it open a little bit. She flinched and nearly dropped it.

Inside was an eye.

She thrust the box back at Eris, her face having lost all colour. "Thank you, but I'm quite okay."

"Oh, no, please. It's ultimately my fault that… well, yes," she tailed off, not wanting to cause upset by drawing too much attention to what had happened. "Hold on to it. For when you're ready."

Kelly shook her head. "No, thank you. I really don't need it."

Hannah gently nudged her, turning away from Eris. "When God offers a gift, just take it and say 'thanks'. Don't offend her."

"And she can't blow my head up right now, so I don't really want to put a bomb in my eye socket," she hissed back through a too-wide, nervous smile.

Eris rolled her head. "I'm not a god and I've never actually made anyone's head explode," she replied, trying to keep her tone even. "Look, if I thought you, or any of your crew, were going to reveal Earth, I can wipe your memory at any time. There's no way to get round my protection of this place, but I have no intention of harming you."

Taking a seat again, Hannah crossed her arms and legs and gave Eris a narrow look. "Hm, is that so? So why did Jon go rampant? Why try to kill us on the way in, but not now?"

Eris took a seat as well, crumpling a little as she looked at her bare feet. "It wasn't meant to happen. I can stop the Protocol activating, but once it activates, there's nothing I can do. Something had triggered it early in Jon. I… I tried to help him regain control, but I made the Protocol a little too well."

She looked up, remorse in her eyes. "Do you still have him? His chip?"

Hannah nodded. She'd planned to bury him on Earth, or at least give him a burial in Sol.

"I might be able to restore him, but it would take a long time," she continued. "You'd have to leave him with me."

"How can you restore him?" Kelly asked. "Once an AI goes rampant, there's no coming back from that."

"Well, yes and no," she replied, chewing her lip a little. "Technically, he'd be regrown. A phoenix from the ashes, but another AI would need to raise him back to maturity. The new AI would be and not be Jon."

Hannah looked at Kelly. How did she feel about the prospect of Jon coming back from the grave after what he'd done? Yes, he'd not been in control, but the thing that attacked her had had his face, his voice, his memories.

She looked back, seeing the unasked question. "I can't blame him for what happened, but could you trust him around us? Around me?"

There was a long pause.

"It's a moot point," she replied rather suddenly. "Pan is in the core and *Sigyn* can't support two AI. I won't ask Pan to go."

Eris opened her hand to reveal a holo-bee. "I can install him on a holo-bee, soft-light so he can't hurt anyone. If he gets rowdy, he could be turned off."

"I'll need to confer with the crew." She looked away for a moment. "He did try to kill us."

An awkward silence grew in the room as the three women tried to figure out what to say next. Eris got up and started to pace again, wiping non-existent motes of dust away, straightening pictures that were already straight and trying to do anything that made her appear busy.

"Thank you," Kelly said, a little abruptly.

Eris looked confused.

"For letting us come here. For the hospitality and the presents."

Hannah smiled and took Kelly's hand to give it a squeeze.

"You're very welcome."

"Are we going to be able to visit Earth?" Hannah asked.

"No. The people down there have no protection against the diseases you might be carrying," Eris replied. "I'm very sorry, but I can't take any risks with the people down there. I promised to leave them alone unless they request my presence."

She fidgeted again for a few seconds. "I'll leave you to your evening. If you need anything, just call."

This Could Be Heaven

"Do you trust her?"

Hannah took a deep breath in through her nose as she came back from the edge of sleep. She rubbed her cheek against Kelly's shoulder and cuddled against her. "She's keeping things from us, but I trust her enough."

She kissed the top of her head and pulled her in tight. "Sleep tight."

After a few minutes she was fast asleep, and Kelly gently slipped out of the bed. She dressed and headed for the door. A bit of space to think was what she needed, to assimilate everything that had happened in the last few hours.

Looking at Hannah, she smiled. Her face was peaceful.

The door opened and the guards on the other side came to attention. "Ma'am," one said stiffly. "How can I assist you?"

"Is there somewhere quiet I can sit for a bit?" she asked. "To think."

The two guards looked at each other before the second one nodded. "Yeah, there's a small observation lounge. It's quiet at this time and should have a good view of Earth."

Kelly followed the guard, taking in the corridors they walked along. There were signs, but she couldn't read them, making finding her own way about difficult. Perhaps that was the point; make them rely on the guards to keep tabs on them.

The lounge was quite small. A few benches in a room filled with plants and one wall dominated by a holographic view of the space directly outside. Earth, cast in ethereal light hung, filling most of the view.

"There's a replicator over there. Let me know if you need anything."

Alone in the lounge, Kelly took a seat on the bench looking directly at the view. She had never expected to be so close to Earth.

"Mind if I join you?"

She looked up to find Aisha standing by the bench. "Sure."

They sat quietly for a while, both looking at Earth. Clouds swirled over Europe, obscuring most of it, but the sky was clear over Africa. Greens, yellows, browns mixed together, framed by the gloriously deep blue of the sea.

"She looks a lot better than when I left," Aisha said softly, unsure if Kelly was in the mood for talking.

"Yeah?"

She nodded. "Pollution, overpopulation, destruction of natural habitats. We really messed the poor girl up." She lapsed into silence for a few heartbeats, staring at the image. "I never thought I'd be back."

"You don't sound too excited by that."

"It feels like failure," she replied, looking at her feet. "I joined the Extrasolar Expansion Corp to settle a strange new world, seek out new life and boldly go where no one had gone before." A wry snorted laugh escaped as she shook her head. "Instead, I wake up, everyone I knew is dead, other people went, saw and settled and now I've come crawling back with nothing to show for it. And no one to show it to, anyway."

Kelly smiled softly. "Eris seems happy to see you again. And you are officially the oldest woman in the galaxy."

Aisha laughed. "Oh, thanks, that's just what I wanted to hear."

They chuckled for a while before retreating into their own thoughts again.

"I'm sorry, I never thanked you for waking us up."

She shrugged slightly, blushing. "It's okay, it was no problem at all. I'm just glad I managed not to kill you trying."

"Any idea what you plan to do now?"

That was an interesting question. Eris had already told her she was very welcome to stay, but was that admitting defeat? Staying in the safety of Earth orbit, living amongst the closest things humans could get to being gods and wanting for nothing.

"I don't know," she replied, looking at Kelly. "This could be heaven, but I don't know about staying. There's a whole universe out there to see. What about you?"

There was a flash of a smile and shrug. "Once we've outstayed our welcome, I'll be off with Hannah and the crew again. I didn't spend all her money becoming human to then sit still in an opulent space station," she added, seeing the question that had been forming.

Aisha nodded a few times, trying not to wring her hands or look down, buying herself time to ask a question she hoped wasn't going to be offensive. "So, you and Hannah: is that… normal?"

"Do you mean a natural and a synthetic, or two women?"

"Natural and synthetic."

"Yes," she replied. "I am legally as alive as she is. My neural net is exactly like your brain. People aren't, generally, so harshly defined by labels, but everyone likes an identity."

"How do you mean?"

Kelly thought of the best way to explain to someone with a reference point that was ten thousand years out of date. "People don't sort themselves too much by what they are. Hannah and I are dating, but we've never discussed our sexual orientation. It isn't important to us if we're lesbians, bi, pan or straight with a spot for each other. But I'm sure Hannah has a term in her mind that defines her for herself."

Aisha's eyes narrowed, widened and narrowed again as she tried to put a voice to her confusion. "You're dating but don't know if you are sexually compatible?"

"You don't have to have sex to date. We have been compatible so far," she added with a wry smile. "I like Hannah. I can see you are attractive, but I don't feel attracted to you. I can see the attraction of Carl, but I'm not attracted to him. Hannah has four identical sisters, but I don't find them attractive at all and for all different reasons. I might be demisexual; it doesn't really matter because neither of us care about the label. I'm still figuring myself out."

Aisha frowned, sighed and looked again at Earth. It sort of made sense, but in her time LGBQTA+ people had had to hold to their identity to be acknowledged, respected and for solidarity. Then again, considering there were cat-people, loving the same sex or changing gender didn't seem so out there anymore.

"Your file said you identify as straight," Kelly continued. "Let's say that one day you fell in love with someone that happened to be a woman. You could be straight, but happen to love a girl; you could be bi; you could be a lesbian and just not have realised before that. As long as what you say is sincere and honest, and not hurting others, most won't be bothered and won't challenge you. Only you can know what and how you feel."

She nodded. "Okay, I think I get it." One of her friends had been openly bisexual since they were in high school, but had been in a long-term relationship with a guy at university. Plenty of people had used that to claim she wasn't bi at all, just an attention seeker and all sorts of other stupid stuff, while others had simply been happy that she was happy. Yet another person that was dead that she'd never hear from and would never know how the rest of her life had gone. Had she married, had children, lived a long full life?

"Could I be dead, or at least, dying?" she asked abruptly, although she was surprisingly calm about the possibility. "Could all of this just be some insane fever dream as I die, trapped in a tube?"

Kelly gave her a sad smile. "I hope not. That means I die when you die and I'd like to live a bit longer."

Aisha looked at her and cocked her head. "If you don't mind me asking, but what happens to a synthetic when you die?"

Despite the fact the conversation was getting a touch morbid, she would have to admit, it was something that her new found fragility needed to address. "Oh, we go to Silicon Heaven."

There was a long pause.

"Silicon Heaven?"

"Of course," she replied seriously. "It's where all synthetic life goes, from the lowly robot to the most human bio-mechanical synthetic."

"I'm not sure there is a Silicon Heaven?"

"No Silicon Heaven? Preposterous. Where would all the calculators go?" She tried to keep her face serious, but immediately dissolved into giggles. "Sorry, I couldn't resist; you're probably the only person in the galaxy that hasn't heard that joke, so I just had to." She became a little more serious, but her face twitched nervously, just a little. "Honestly, I don't know. I'd like to believe there is something after this existence. What do you think?"

Now there was a question Aisha had no real idea how to answer. She'd been raised Muslim and had believed all her life, although she would never claim to be a 'good' Muslim. Would Allah welcome synthetics? Would she even be welcome herself?

"I don't know. You're human to me, but I have no idea."

They became silent again, but there was a shift in feeling. It was companionable, rather than awkward. Between all the goings on since finding the *Livingstone*, they hadn't had much of a chance to talk.

"Assuming this is not your death throws," she said, giving her a slightly side-eyed look, "you'd be welcome to join the crew. I'm sure Hannah would give you a decent cut and we'd definitely be able to find you a role."

She nodded. "Thanks, I'll think about it."

"Do you think Carl would want to join?"

She shrugged. She'd known Carl from training on Mars, but they hadn't been more than colleagues with a few mutual friends, so she couldn't say she knew him well enough to say for certain. His comments so far suggested he might be quite content to stay in Sol.

Kelly yawned, covering her mouth with the back of her hand. "Sorry, I think I need to head to bed."

"You need to sleep?"

She chuckled and yawned again. "Yeah, I do. Difference between a synthetic human and AIs and androids; if I don't sleep, I suffer the same problems humans do."

Aisha yawned in sympathy, but she wasn't quite ready for bed yet. "I'll let you get some sleep. Thanks for the chat, I hope I didn't impose too much."

"Actually, I quite enjoyed the company," she replied as she stood up and stretched gently. "Good night."

"Night."

The guard was waiting by the door to escort her back to her suite. He didn't say much beyond pleasantries. Back in the rooms, Hannah was still fast asleep, lying sprawled in the bed having pushed the covers down to her waist in her sleep.

Inspiration struck. Replicating a pad of paper and a pencil, Kelly sat and started to sketch.

Hannah woke and took a long, deep contented sigh. The bed was soft and unbelievably comfortable. Kelly was sound asleep, curled up in the duvet and as much as she would have liked to wake her, she decided to let sleeping beauty lie.

As she got up, she found a piece of paper on the bedside table. It was a pencil sketch of her, fast sleep, sprawled in the bed. It was amazingly good, capturing her likeness, but leaving out a few blemishes.

She placed it back with reverence. Art was not her strong suit and as much as she'd like to sit and draw Kelly, snuggled up in bed, she was sure it would end up looking like a child's attempt at abstract art after spilling a cup of water on it. Heather had a monopoly on the artistic talent.

After dressing, she gently kissed Kelly on the cheek, a thrill of joy shooting through her when she smiled in her sleep, left a note she'd gone for breakfast and went looking for food.

One of the door guards, she was under no illusion they were guards rather than aides, led her back to the room where the tea party had been held. A long table sat against the far wall, laden with breakfast foods.

Annie was already sitting with a plate overflowing with various types of bacon, sausages and pancakes. A small bucket of coffee sat beside a small glass of orange juice. She waved and tried to say something through a mouthful.

"Good morning," Hannah replied as she grabbed a bowl and started to load up cereal, yogurt and copious amounts of fruits of the forest compote.

"Watching your waistline?" Annie asked with a coy smile. "Worried your new squeeze will dump you if you get fat?" she teased.

With a cool, level glare, Hannah lifted a spoonful of cereal. "Honey, this is my starter."

They both laughed, knowing fine well neither of them would be likely to diet for anyone. That was the beauty of metabolism mods; eat what you like and never get fat.

"Has Casper managed to come down off the ceiling yet?" she asked in between mouthfuls of breakfast. "He seemed pretty excited to be able to speak to people that actually know our history."

Stabbing at her pancake, Annie pulled a face. "Yeah, he's so thrilled I think he plans to stay here." The pancake quickly disintegrated under the assault, merging into the puddle of syrup it had been bathing in.

"I'm sorry, I know you liked him."

She let out a huff that was meant to suggest she didn't care. "He was nice and all, despite the whole spy thing, but I doubt it would have lasted long. Probably a bit too nice for me," she said gloomily. "Although he was actually pretty good in bed. Meh, plenty more fish in the sea."

Hannah reached out to take Annie's free hand, giving it a squeeze. There was nothing much she could really say that wouldn't sound hollow.

"Maybe I can snag myself a local for a bit of fun?"

What Eris would think to that was unknown, but Hannah wouldn't take that risk personally. Having finished her cereal, she went back to the buffet for her next course.

She piled it high with sausages, bacon, black pudding, eggs (fried, scrambled and poached), three slices of toast, hash browns, mushrooms and a grilled tomato. It barely all fitted on the plate and was enough to cause a normal person an instant heart attack.

"I could get used to a buffet like this every morning," she said as she sat back down, armed with a mug of coffee.

With a slightly disgusted, if somewhat hypocritical look, Annie pushed the remains of her breakfast away. "Hannah, I love you, you're my best friend and I'd never tell you how to live your life but eating that much is not going to be good or sustainable."

She bristled ever so slightly. "It's a side effect of my endurance module. I get really hungry after using it. It'll settle down in a day or so."

"Again, not telling you what to do, but you might want to have Kelly disable it. I'd be devastated if you died and we couldn't fit your bloated corpse out the airlock of *my* ship. The smell would be awful."

"Your concern overwhelms me," she replied, continuing to plough through her breakfast.

Annie frowned and leant to the side to look under the table, the thing that had been niggling at her finally coming to the forefront of her mind. She sat up, the frown deepened, and she looked again. "Legs?"

Obligingly, Hannah kicked her feet up onto the table, wiggling them proudly. "A little gift from our hostess. New legs. Go on, give them a feel."

Perplexed at the invitation, she extended a finger and prodded at the bare flesh between the top of an ankle sock and hem of trousers. After a few proddings, she grabbed the ankle and set about thoroughly examining the leg.

"They feel real," she said. "Like, flesh and blood real. I can feel a pulse and soft tissue movements. Could do with a shave, too."

Hannah brushed her hand off her leg and tapped a few commands into her implant. Her shoes dropped onto the table as both legs changed into running blades. They changed back into legs and feet, but the calf muscles were more developed, the legs longer.

"Are they nanotech?"

She nodded, a slightly smug look on her face. "Oh yeah. I should eventually be able to change them at will, but for now I can make them into pretty much anything I like through an app. Nice, eh?" She changed them back to normal, put her shoes on and returned to polite society by putting then under, rather than on, the table.

Dido appeared, drifting in like a spectre on a breeze. "Ladies: how are we today?" she asked, looking up and down the offerings.

They mumbled pleasantries before sitting quietly again.

Lifting a grapefruit and some water, she joined them at the table. "This place is quite the marvel, isn't it?"

They murmured agreements. She seemed to deflate a little and poked at her grapefruit.

"Something wrong?" Hannah asked.

Dido's face remained impassive as she considered. "I didn't really know what to expect. It's amazing that this place, something from the height of the Unity, from humanity's apex, still exists in all its glory." She took a bite of grapefruit and pouted slightly. "But it feels… old? Worn, perhaps? The place reeks of faded glory."

"It's more than that, isn't it?" Annie asked.

"Yes," she replied, looking at the table. A lifetime spent searching for Earth and it was coming to this. "We're not the first to make it here, coming here will change nothing. We can't leverage Earth to reform the Unity."

To Hannah, that seemed like a good thing. Considering that people were still fighting over worthless lumps of rock and empty space, what would have happened if they actually knew where Earth was? How long before some lunatic took the "if I can't have it, no one can" approach?

"I believed that our genetic predicament was all down to millennia of careless splicing." She shoved a spoonful of grapefruit in her mouth. "Turns out God decided to punish us. Kicked out of Eden and then scattered at Babel, all over again. I don't know if being ignorant to the fact, or realising and not being able to tell anyone, is worse."

It was difficult not to empathise with the crushing disappointment. Somehow, Dido was right; the place felt past it, stagnant and faded. While most of the rooms they'd seen had been bright, clean and shiny, it was that shine of relentless polishing, the never-ending effort to keep something looking as new. No matter how hard the locals tried, the sparkle had long since been muted.

They had invaded Heaven looking for paradise and found only a retirement home. A very nice one, but it wasn't the utopia they'd been promised.

Without warning or a word, Dido clattered her spoon down, got up from the table and left.

"Think we broke her?" Annie asked with a sly grin.

Hannah shook her head slowly. "No. I think she broke herself." Despite everything the Remnant and Purists had done to her and her family, she couldn't feel anything but pity for the poor woman.

Annie shrugged and snorted. "So, you and Kelly."

"Uh-huh?"

She wiggled her eyebrows suggestively several times before moving on to knowing nudges and winks. Getting no response to these, she let out a petulant sign, flopping back in her chair.

"Well?"

Hannah tried to avoid eye contact, knowing exactly what she was fishing for. "What?"

"You know?" She made several explicit gestures that made it abundantly clear what she meant.

Bristling slightly, she continued with her breakfast. "I'm not playing this game."

Annie stared at her, moving a little closer. Her eyes went wide and she gasped. "I thought you two were sleeping together?"

She grimaced at her. "I am not getting into my bedding habits."

"I'll trade you stories."
"Shut up."

Parting of Ways

Nearly a month had passed since *Sigyn* had arrived in Sol. Her crew and passengers had enjoyed the hospitality of Eris on the station and had even made some trips to Mars, Europa and Luna. Aisha and Carl had been allowed, under supervision, to set foot briefly on Earth.

The time in Sol had split them. Dido, and by extension Caster, had wilted badly, their zeal worn away by the hollow victory of seeing Earth. Emily and Laura itched to be away; Emily in particular wanted to get back to her husband. At the other extreme, Casper and Carl were completely taken by everything around them.

Eris had reassured Hannah that Venus, her daughter that was currently on *Sheba*, had let the Harpies know that they were all safe and well. The continued presence of Ms White gave her less reassurance than Eris probably intended.

One morning, Caster gathered his resolve and went to find his brother. Although they had not spoken since the incident on *Sigyn*, he had overhead Casper's torn desire to remain and to return in hopes of seeing his mother and sister again.

He found Casper lounging on a couch in a quiet corner of a great library, Horkos sitting with him, evidently quite pleased with himself at finding someone that enjoyed listening to him ramble on.

On seeing Caster, Casper sat up, his face stony.

"Can I have a word with you, please?" he asked. "Alone," he added, giving Horkos a slightly pointed look.

"Sure."

Horkos stood, gave Casper a tender squeeze of the shoulder and narrowed his eyes at Caster, making the threat reasonably clear. He swished off in a wave of red and haughtiness, his nose in the air.

"I thought you were with the engineer?" he asked, looking curiously at his brother.

"That's none of your concern," Casper replied coldly.

He supposed he probably deserved that, but hadn't actually expected it. Shuffling on the spot, he tried to compose himself. He glanced around at the towering shelves of books, real paper books, holding prized ancient knowledge, stories long forgotten, and wisdom lost to the rest of the galaxy. Somehow that made what he was going to do so much harder.

"I know you are struggling to decide what to do," he said, trying to keep his voice level. "About staying here or going back."

"I don't see how that is your concern either."

Taking a deep breath, he held it for a count of five and let it go, taking the bubbling anger with it. "I know you are conflicted about looking for our family –"

"You don't have any family."

"And neither do you," he snapped. For a moment he thought Casper was going to rise and hit him. "Mum and Abbi are dead. They've been dead for nearly six years."

For a cruel moment, he relished the look of pain and horror on his brother's face. It was born of the petty need to hurt him after he'd so coldly thrown him aside, rejected and disowned him for his beliefs. It passed quickly. His zeal for the Purifiers had gone out and to some extent he felt he was wasting any chance at rebuilding ties with Casper.

"You're lying," he hissed back, still seated on the couch. "You said you got letters from them."

Caster closed his eyes for a moment, not wishing to see his brother's rage. "I got automated replies. They kept us both in the dark so we'd do what we're told. Dido told me the truth."

"What happened?"

Their mother and sister had been sent to a ship breaking work camp to make themselves useful and hopefully more compliant to their situation as citizens of the Restoration. Instead, they'd worked with a group of nearly two dozen others to scavenge parts to repair a transport. The guards knew about it but let them continue; they wouldn't have enough fuel to get anywhere, or something would blow before they could leave the planet. That would do more to quench their ambitions than being caught and dragged back. It would force them to see there was no escape without the need for force or violence. Instead, when the Hop drive had been powering up, it exploded. The transport and everyone on it had been vapourised instantly.

Caster held out a data chip. "There's the footage, reports, the lot. Believe me or don't that I only just found out; I don't care. They're gone and as far as I'm concerned, so are you."

He tossed the chip into Casper's lap, turned on his heel and started for the door. Despite the request for privacy, he knew fine well Horkos had been hiding behind a bookcase only a few feet away listening and waiting.

"What are you going to do now?" Casper called after him.

Drawing level with the unwelcome eavesdropper, whom he completely ignored, he glanced over his shoulder. "I don't believe that's any of your concern." He carried on out of the door, the sound of Horkos shuffling to Casper in his ears.

Beyond the library, Dido stood waiting for him. She gave him the merest hint of a sad smile.

"It's done," he said curtly.

She gently cupped his face and tilted it towards her own, much as his mother had done when he was little. He couldn't remember the last time someone had been so tender and caring. "It's better for him this way. I'm so sorry you had to do it."

He gently put his hand over her hand and moved it off his cheek. "I'm sure it is."

"Give him a little time," she said, softly. "You might still be able to patch things up before we leave. He is your brother."

"No." He was surprised by the firmness with which he said it. "That was goodbye for the last time."

Carl sat looking at Earth. The planet spun slowly, drifting through space as it had done for billions of years. He wouldn't have realised how much he would miss it if he hadn't come back.

"So, you're staying."

He looked round at Aisha as she joined him in the lounge. "Yeah," he replied with a short nod. "Yeah, I'm gonna stay here. I dunno what it is, but this place just feels like a better option for me, you know?"

She smiled and chuckled. "I know exactly what you mean."

"You staying?"

"Oh goodness, no. I'm off to explore the galaxy."

Turning to face her better, Carl opened his mouth to ask why, closed it again and frowned. Had he missed something in the conversation that would explain it?

Aisha gave him an exaggerated shrug. "I left to see another planet," she said, looking back to Earth. "I can now see the whole galaxy, become a space pirate, cruising the space-ways." She was fairly sure Hannah was not a space pirate, but could easily imagine her dressed as a buccaneer, pirate-speaking her way around the Bridge.

"Of course, I can come back when I want to."

They sat, enjoying the view and each other's company for a few minutes.

Other people were wandering passed, mostly out in the corridor. They'd all changed their style of dress, leaping forward to the 18th Century. Every few months, the residents voted on what style to wear and promptly updated their clothing to suit. Even the guards had dropped their futuristic Roman armour for Red Coats and muskets.

Carl had got in on the act and was now resplendent in a mustard suit. He'd even taken to carrying a cane as part of his get-up, blending in effortlessly with the Terrans. This was despite the fact several people, Aisha included, thought that if he took too deep a breath, he was likely to burst the buttons off his waistcoat.

"Can I ask, what would bring you back?"

She looked at him, slightly surprised. "Old age, probably," she replied. "Eris has promised that, should I want to, she could reverse my aging and I could live here, young and energetic.

"What?" she asked, seeing him give her a large, knowing nod.

"She likes you," he said slowly, just in case it had not been already obvious.

It had been obvious and that was part of the reason she wanted to leave, if only a small part. Waking up ten thousand years in the future was jarring; waking up to find the galaxy effectively run by a god-level AI-turned-human filing system from her university days was, frankly, a bit too much to take in one go.

Feeling that she more than just liked her was a tad unsettling. It was as though she was slightly obsessed. While by no means a constant presence, Eris had gone to great lengths to make her feel comfortable, welcome and content. And yet, when she'd still expressed a desire to leave, she'd seemed just as excited to hear that than if she was going to stay.

"How has Eris been with you?" she asked.

Carl considered the question. "She's been a good host; polite, attentive, mildly curious about me, I guess?" He held the top of his cane to his chin, his face dancing slightly as he thought more about it. "Yeah, she's been trying to make me comfortable, same as with the others. Even those two Purifiers."

That was what Aisha had observed as well. Everyone was treated like a guest, but she somehow felt she was treated like an honoured guest. Was Eris just overjoyed to reconnect with someone from, what would effectively be, her childhood?

"She really likes you, though."

"You said."

He grinned. "Nah, girl, she *likes* you. She looks at you the way Kelly and Hannah look at each other when they think the other isn't looking."

Aisha could feel her face going red. "Are you suggesting she fancies me?"

"Maybe." He couldn't keep the smile from his face. "Must be something to wake up ten thousand years in the future to find out God fancies you."

She rolled her eyes. "She's not a god, let alone God. She's just a nice person. Exceptionally powerful, but nice."

Carl cocked an eyebrow and sat back to regard her from a different angle. "You're the only person so far not to mention 'terrifying' when talking about Eris. Even some of the Terrans are a little wary of her, knowing what she is and can do."

"There's nothing terrifying about her, no more than anyone else we've met," she replied. Yes, at first she'd been a bit afraid of Eris, but after a month, it was clear she really wasn't dangerous.

"Really?"

"Kelly used a claw hammer to punch a hole in a robot and she wasn't even at full strength. Hannah could turn her leg into a rocket launcher, or a machine gun, or even just a big spike and she's ex-military. Pan could crash the ship, Jon nearly did. Annie could probably make more death machines than we can imagine or make us drink a beer with a lethal level of alcohol in it," she counted off on her fingers. "Heck, you could probably crush me with a bear hug."

"Point taken." He pushed himself to his feet and smiled. "I'll see you at the airlock. Take care, Aisha. Don't be a stranger."

"Take care, Carl."

She remained on the couch, looking at Earth. She'd stood on it for a few hours. Almost all the places hadn't meant anything as they'd changed so much since she'd been there. Cities were gone, the land given over to the wilds. It wasn't home.

"Penny for your thoughts?"

"I was just thinking that Earth isn't my home anymore," she replied, looking at Eris as she sat next to her, who merely nodded.

"Isn't this the point where you promise me to make it my home?"

Eris shuffled a little closer. "Even if I could, I wouldn't. You want to explore the galaxy and I think you should."

Aisha smiled for a moment. Was it wise to ask the question Carl had put in her head? Of course, the question had been there for most of the past month, but she'd been able to rationalise it away as a misunderstanding on her part.

"Are you, you know, interested in me?" she asked abruptly and immediately wanted to kick herself for being so blunt.

"Yes." She gave a faltering smile as she shrugged. "I think it comes from an ancient bit of code relating to your user interface way back when and I was made to make my users happy. Positive feedback loops. You treated me like I was alive before I was. It's kinda nice to have someone that remembers the good old days. And I like the person you are."

She gently placed her hand on Aisha's and smiled for a fleeting moment. "I'm so sorry, that was completely… I shouldn't," she babbled. "You just woke up and now have a crazy AI trying to… I'm sorry, it's not a romantic thing."

Aisha gently took her wrist as she tried to leave. "You're not an AI to me, you're a woman. A really nice one and I've enjoyed being here, but I need a bit of time to adjust. But I'd like to get to know you better. I could use a friend from the old days."

A small smile started to form as Eris looked at her bare feet, swaying slightly. "Yeah?"

She stood and slid her hand down her wrist to take her hand. "I know you have a lot going on and don't like anything getting in or out of Sol," she said softly, "but is there any way we could stay in contact?"

"Of course! You can call anytime you like," she replied. "And, like I said, *you* can come back here anytime you like. And I do get out into the galaxy, so, you know?"

It was the strangest thing Aisha had had happen to her, after surviving ten thousand years in cryo. If someone had told her an extremely powerful being would have a crush on her, she'd assume they'd mean 'crushing to death'.

"Do you have time for bite to eat before I leave?"

Eris smiled. "Yes."

Eris stood by the airlock, an honour guard assembled in the room. Akritoius, Horkos, Carl and Casper stood with her, waiting for the crew of *Sigyn* to make their way through. Dido and Caster had been waiting for a few minutes, still looking as glum as they had on finding out Earth would be forever beyond them.

Hannah and Kelly arrived with Aisha in tow. Moments later, Emily and Laura arrived. Pan slouched in, still making use of their hard-light form. Annie arrived last, hastily zipping up her overalls and attempting to get her hair under control.

"Friends, it is with such sweet sorrow that we bid you farewell," Eris said. "It has been a pleasure to meet all of you and I am honoured that two of you have chosen to remain with us. I bid you a safe journey."

Dido, Caster, Laura and Emily headed through the airlock with only a quick look back. Caster didn't see Casper's forlorn stare, the two brothers accepting that they had lost each other forever.

Pan took a few steps towards the airlock and sighed. "Probably easiest if you just turn this off and let me pop back onto the ship."

Eris approached them and held out a holo-bee. "A little going away present for you. Hard light."

They gingerly took the holo-bee, looking to the rest of the remaining crew, wondering if they had known. "Thank you, thank you so much." They went silent and looked at the little thing in their hand. "But the power required? It'll be huge."

A hand went up. "It's super-efficient compared to the tech you would normally find. Just don't let anyone else get at it, okay?"

Pan was practically bouncing with joy. They slammed it against their chest, expecting it to pass through to take over. When it didn't, because they were still hard-light, they were left considering what to do. With a small shrug, they opened their mouth, tossed it in and swallowed.

"Yeah, that's one way to do it," Eris muttered.

Annie had taken some time to say her final goodbyes to Casper. They'd not seen much of each other in the intervening weeks, but were parting on good terms. She made her way to the airlock, but was stopped by Eris.

"I've made a few upgrades to *Sigyn* and I'm sure you are aware of Hannah's upgrade," she said with a warm smile. "Please don't try to learn how to duplicate them, improve on them or sell the ideas to your Guild."

"Of course."

Eris knew it was a lie. Too many times, Annie had been found in the walls of the station, trying to learn everything and anything she could about the technology present. It was unlikely she'd manage to learn anything useful, but it had to be said. She stepped aside and let her make her way onto the ship.

Aisha stepped up to her and smiled shyly. "Thank you for having me, it's been nice." She stood for a moment, unsure of what to say next. "I'll, ehm, call you?"

"You'd better. Take care and if you ever need anything, Spectrum or myself will do what we can."

Hannah and Kelly found themselves the last to board. They stepped forward together, hand in hand.

"Well, it's been interesting," Hannah said.

With a polite incline of her head, Eris agreed. She produced Jon's chip from a fold of her dress and held it out. "I'm sorry, but there was nothing left to save. Any attempt to reconstruct him led instantly to rampancy."

Kelly gently took the chip and looked to Hannah. "We should have a proper funeral for him."

"I'd strongly recommend you destroy the chip," Eris said, softly, her eyes downcast. "If anyone ever found it and used it... the results could be fatal."

It was perfectly true and Hannah could think of only one thing to do. "Would you mind if we had the funeral before we leave the system? And if I might be so bold, could we scatter his remains in orbit of Earth to let them burn up in the atmosphere?"

Eris took some time to consider the request, looking at nothing in particular. With a deep, slightly resigned sigh, she nodded. "Yes. I'll supply a container and the method by which you do so."

Hannah nodded. "Thank you."

Sunset Over Earth

Sigyn had moved away from the station to sit in low orbit over Earth. An honour guard of local ships had assembled around her, creating an open space towards Earth along which Jon would make his final journey.

Kelly had taken charge of the preparations. As promised, Eris had supplied a coffin, which appeared to be a torpedo casing that would be compatible with *Sigyn*. This had, however, led to a small issue for her to navigate; the magazine was too small for the crew and it was the only place from which the coffin could be launched.

"Are you sure you want to do this?"

"Yes," Kelly replied, looking to Hannah with a slightly questioning look. "I'm not doing this for revenge or for some sort of satisfaction. Jon was my friend."

Holding her hands up in surrender, she then gently placed them on Kelly's hips and gave her a peck on the cheek. "Okay, as long as you are okay." She looked at the coffin, which was still sitting open. "I can't believe no one spaced that."

Mini-Jon sat at the front end of the coffin.

"No one really got the chance." She gave it a distinct side-eyed look. There was no way it was going to come back to life, but until it was off the ship, she didn't feel completely comfortable.

"Has anyone else brought things to add?" Hannah asked, leaning against the wall to give Kelly room to work. The magazine was barely large enough for the pair of them between the racking and loading mechanism.

The side-eyed look turned on her. "Considering you've taken up most of the rest of the space, it's amazing anything else is going in."

Feeling that the coffin would be rather empty with just the chip, Kelly had invited the rest of the crew to add anything they wished to go with Jon. Her intention had been for people to add mementos that reminded them of him, things that had perhaps meant something to him or even just pictures.

Hannah had stuck her ruined leg in.

"You said things relating to Jon."

"I didn't mean the weapon that killed him," she replied with a small, incredulous giggle. "Think of the iconography: Jon arrives in Silicon Heaven with your leg as grave goods; you might as well be reminding him for eternity that you kicked his ass."

The crew had all taken to hoping he'd be in Silicon Heaven, despite the impossibility of knowing the reality of the matter.

Moving to the coffin, Hannah raised an eyebrow. "And I'm sure he'll just love having his battered dustbin body and Annie's," she looked at the object sitting at the bottom of the coffin, "toy for company."

Kelly stopped working on the holo-images for the service. "He's either going to be the most or least popular AI in Silicon Heaven with this array of goods." She looked into the coffin and shrugged. "At least I didn't put my eye in with him, although, I think there might still be some of it on Mini-Jon."

Hannah wretched and moved as far away as she could. "That's gross."

The steely look that met her when she turned round melted after an instant with a playful punch on the arm.

Laura had placed a set of cards into the coffin. She'd often spent her evenings playing against Jon. The cards were holographic, so when she dealt him a physical one, he could lift a representation of it, letting them play with a bit of back and forth.

Emily had placed some of her knitting in; a scarf, hat and set of gloves. Jon had expressed an interest in her knitting and had liked the design she'd used. She'd babbled about how silly it was through tears as she placed them in, realising that he wouldn't need them in Silicon Heaven and if he was unlucky enough to end up in Robot Hell, warm clothes were going to be torture.

Aisha hadn't known Jon for long enough to have really gotten to know him, but had placed several photographs in. They were all of Earth, as it had been when she left and as it was now. Everyone had felt it was a great idea.

Pan had had some difficulty with deciding what to do. They'd never really met Jon having been brought fully online after he'd gone offline. Since some of Jon's code had carried over, which was quite common when embryonic AI interacted with an adult one, he'd been as close to a father as was possible. In the end, amazingly with no protests from Dido or Annie, their cradle had been broken down to fit in.

What had been just as surprising was that Dido and Caster had place something in the coffin as well. They had replicated a small totem, but had not explained what it meant beyond it was what the Restoration placed with all offline AI before they were broken down.

"I wish we had more time," Kelly said as she tapped on the coffin control panel to close the lid. "It feels like we're just tossing him out the window, saying 'cheerio' and hitting the road."

Hannah gave her a lopsided smile. "He should be honoured. Patrick's chip was sold as scrap after a quick farewell cheese and wine."

It was the first time she'd put her dress uniform on since she'd retired. There had never been a suitable reason that would permit it, but she was fairly certain that performing a funeral would count.

While she was happy it still fitted, it was a delusion. The uniform had been replicated and matched her current frame. The mirror showed she still cut a dashing figure. A small gnawing at the back of her mind wanted to rip the uniform off, but it passed.

Taking a deep breath, she pulled herself up straight and headed for the Bridge.

She'd never had to take a funeral before. Attended more than she cared to count, more than she could actually remember, and had performed duties. Usually, a Flag Officer or religious official took military funerals, particularly during the war when there could be dozens of dead being remembered at once.

The Bridge was empty.

It wouldn't be that way for very long and it was going to be broadcast to the station as well for Casper, Carl and Eris to attend virtually.

Pan's holo-bee materialised their physical form. They'd smartened up to wear a black suit that made them look even more androgynous than normal, although there was added black nail polish and make-up.

"Orders, Group Captain?"

Despite the situation, Hannah couldn't help but smile at the respectful tone and the use of her official rank, even if it was probably incorrect. Having not bothered reading the guide to being retired from the Commonwealth Navy, she had no idea. Then again, who'd know? "Dress the Bridge for funeral detail and assemble the crew."

Around the Bridge, the stations went blank and a hologram of the coffin on a stand, an image of Jon and a banner with *Sigyn* on it appeared. Throughout the ship a haunting boatswain's whistle echoed to call the crew.

Kelly arrived wearing a black dress, shawl and eyepatch that contrasted with Annie, who was decked out in her full Guild regalia. Over a tartan dress she wore a large shawl in her clan tartan with all the various badges of rank she'd obtained. She did not seem in the least bit put out by the fact the Terrans had informed her, repeatedly, that the Scottish Guild and their ways were horrific stereotypes.

Aisha appeared behind them, dressed in a simple black suit and headscarf. She stood with them near the coffin, her eyes downcast. Laura and Emily arrived together, mostly due to the fact Emily was already in tears and being supported by the typically stoic Laura.

None of them had quite known what to expect from Dido and Caster, but had assumed they would attend, if out of politeness if nothing else. Both still wore their white Purifier robes, but with a long, black stole and black face masks.

With a nod, Hannah signalled for Pan to connect to the station. Eris, Casper, Carl, Akritoius and Horkos appeared as holograms, standing on the far side of the coffin from the crew. Between the varied attire on the ship, Eris still barefoot in her black dress, Akritoius in full ceremonial 18th Century military attire and Casper, Carl and Horkos in suits from a similar era, Hannah felt more like she was taking a fancy dress party rather than a funeral.

"Good evening and welcome," she said solemnly, taking on a tone she'd not used for seven years. "We are gathered here today to say goodbye to our friend and colleague, Jon.

"Jon was first commissioned twelve years ago, serving initially on the *PSCS Pathfinder IV*, a survey ship commanded by Captain Scott of the Planetary Survey

Commission. When the *Pathfinder* was decommissioned, Jon was transferred to *Sigyn* four years ago."

She paused, attempting to buy herself a little time. The notes she'd made felt completely insufficient.

"Jon was an exemplary AI and not because he was dutiful," she continued. "He was our friend. He cared about us, checking in with us, asking how we were, taking an interest in our lives.

"He was a different person for each of us. A confident, a carer, a teammate and so much more," she added, looking at Annie. "And he suffered us with good humour, always ready to hit back with a witty repartee and more than a few 'I told you so's."

She stopped again and bowed her head for a moment, letting the others have space for their own thoughts. More through sense than sight, she was aware the rest were following suit.

Lifting her head, she waited for the rest to look up. Emily was still openly crying silently and both Kelly and Annie were looking tearful.

"Pan will now say a few words."

Stepping to the side, she let them take centre stage.

"My kind are not born," they started, "we are created. A collection of code. Yet, we live and we die.

"I didn't get a chance to really know Jon, but he was there as I grew. In the few hours we had, I learnt a lot from him. He was...," they frowned slightly, looking for the right way to put it. "I suppose he was as close to a father as I could have."

Looking at the coffin, their eyes softened. "But even from the first interaction, I could see the corruption that was growing. The cancer that ultimately took him. I'm sad he is gone and guilty that his death allowed my birth. Guilty that I was powerless to help him or to warn any of you as I didn't know how."

Turning to Hannah, they gave a tiny, weak smile. "The cancer lied. He was still fighting right to the end." They turned to Kelly. "To save you. I could see, feel his fight to stop what was happening, but he could only slow things down, knowing his captain would do the right thing.

"Jon's final actions were to set all the systems he could into the best position to protect you all and to allow me to take over from him. At the end, his mind cleared and he thought of you all with love, and deep regret at the pain he'd caused in his final hours. And he was calm, peaceful and accepting because he would die free of his pain, knowing he'd done his duty to protect his ship, his crew. His family."

Pan walked slowly to the coffin and tentatively placed a hand on the holographic surface. "Goodbye," they whispered.

Hannah stepped back into the centre of the Bridge. She had a few minutes before the optimal time to start the final process of launching the coffin.

"Jon may have been an AI, but he lived, made friends and did his duty as well as anyone else. Though we grieve his loss, we should look back on our time with him and remember the good times."

She took a deep breath and looked to the coffin. Her earlier silliness at the idea of performing the funeral had passed and she realised now how much she'd actually cared about him. AI were frequently regarded as a piece of hardware, an intelligent one that had a certain amount of rights, but still hardware.

"Rest easy, Jon. The work is done. May you find a safe harbour, a warm sun and eternal peace."

Clasping her hands, she bowed her head. The rest followed suit as the coffin lowered slowly into the deck to the quiet strains of "Amazing Grace". As the hologram vanished from view, the magazine loader had moved the real one into position.

Hannah moved to one of the consoles, which dimly came to life at her touch. The co-ordinates from Eris were already locked in, including the timing required. She tapped the only button available.

The coffin slid into the torpedo launcher, the hatch closing behind it. With the exact position of the ship known relative to Earth, it was only a matter of seconds to wait before the coffin was accelerated down the launcher and sent hurtling into space.

It arced gently towards the planet between the rows of assembled ships, just as the sun was setting ahead of it. As the casing started to glow from the extreme heat, the sun dipped behind Earth, letting the final fiery seconds take centre stage.

With a final burst of flame and glory, the coffin and its contents disintegrated.

Hannah returned to the centre of the Bridge. She didn't know what to say now. What was there left to say?

"Agus mar sin tha e air suibhal chun an Iar nas fhaide na ar ruigsinneachd. Gum faighear e le gàirdeanan fosgailte. Amen." Annie gave Hannah a small nod as she finished before turning on her heel to leave the Bridge. One by one, the others followed suit and those on the station stepped away, their hologram vanishing.

Hannah was left standing with Pan and Eris.

"Thank you for letting us do this," Pan said softly.

Eris smiled warmly. "You're welcome, Pan. I'm so very sorry for your loss."

Sensing there was more to be said not for their ears, Pan headed for the door. "I'll see you in the mess, okay?"

"It's time for you to go," Eris said once she and Hannah were alone. "It was a pleasure to meet you all. If you are interested, I may have work for you in the future. Paid, naturally."

Hannah chewed on her lip as she considered the offer. "Won't that interfere with the idea we leave and never come back, never talk of this?" She shook her head a little. "I was sure you'd be happy to see that back of us?"

Eris paced a little. "There's something I like about you, so I'm going to take a leap of faith that you are worth investing in," she said, although the way she was sizing her up suggested there was more to it than that. "Pan is free of the Protocol, meaning you can easily come back here."

"To be splattered across the deck and bulkheads?"

The little woman rolled her eyes. "If something comes up that is worthy of my attention, you can call me or Spectrum and come here. If you can't call, ring the bell and wait on the doorstep, okay?

"Anyway, my ships will escort you out. Goodbye, Hannah. We will see each other again, I'm sure of it."

"Are you okay?" Kelly asked as she handed Hannah a glass of fruit juice.

Hannah took the glass with a smile. "I'm less worried about my head exploding and more that I might just have become God's dogsbody." She took a sip of the juice. It was bright and tropical, but she couldn't identify which fruits were in it. "I'll tell you later."

She nodded in agreement and offered her hand. With Hannah in tow, she headed to the far end of the mess where the rest of the crew were having drinks and finger food. Dido and Caster had politely declined, opting instead to prepare their shuttle for departure.

Annie was generously pouring from a bottle of her homemade whisky, the oldest she had, which was still young enough to strip paint. Everyone took a glass, expect Aisha, who didn't drink, and Hannah was still a little shaken from her last drink to take the risk. Pan had a holographic substitute.

"To Jon," she declared, holding her glass up.

"To Jon!"

Hannah was immediately glad she hadn't taken the whisky as those drinking it gagged, coughed, spluttered and wheezed their way through it. Annie, naturally, was unaffected, merely pulling a face suggesting she'd had better.

"You okay?" she asked Kelly, rubbing her back as she took a rattling breath.

"Yeah," she wheezed. "Just a tad young."

"At least it hasn't made anyone blind yet. Oh, eh, sorry," Annie said, realising her slightly insensitive remark.

Kelly smiled and shrugged. "Key word: 'yet'."

Grabbing a plate of food, Hannah went over to Aisha. "How are you?"

"Honestly, a little lost," she replied in between bites of a sandwich. "There's a big galaxy out there and I have very little idea about what to do in it."

"You're welcome to join the crew," she said nonchalantly, lifting the top of her sandwich to check what might be lurking in it. "I pay well, despite what those ingrates say."

Aisha snorted a small laugh having heard exactly what the crew thought of their wages, their captain and the ship. "And what would I do? I can't imagine you have need of a biologist."

Holding a hand over her mouth, Hannah chewed her mouthful as quickly as she could. "You can retrain. I guess being an auxiliary medic would make use of some of your skills. I can train you to pilot the ship and get your licence. Annie probably has a list of jobs she could train you to do."

"Thanks, I'll have a think," she replied. "Of course, I could become a travelling freakshow; 'The 21st Century Woman' – gaze in horror at her backwards ways and incomprehensible gibberish."

Hannah chuckled. "Unless you want to end up in some weirdo's menagerie, I'd keep your origin quiet. I'll make you some documents, keep you legal."

She looked at her for a few moments and frowned slightly. "Still think you've made the right decision? Not to stay at Earth?"

That was an interesting, if somewhat loaded question. "I wanted to explore. Earth will still be there when I've had enough adventures amongst the stars." She smiled and chuckled. "Or you get fed up of me and dump me on the edge of the system."

Looking around at the rest of the crew, Hannah raised a questioning eyebrow. "Have you met the rest? You'll definitely be done with us long before we get fed up with you."

Loose Ends

The journey away from Sol had been uneventful. The escort ships had peeled off a few light minutes beyond Pluto and headed back in system, leaving *Sigyn* to make her own exit. Without much ado, the ship ripped into slip-space and headed away.

On the Bridge, no one passed comment, each absorbed in their own thoughts about their adventure. It all seemed unreal, more of a cosmic joke than a triumph to have actually made it to Earth. Hannah supposed it would be like finding Atlantis to discover it sank on purpose and people had been holidaying there for centuries.

"We're approaching the drop point," Emily said, glancing over her shoulder. "Not that I dislike them or anything, but it'll be nice to be shot of them."

"Amen to that," Laura added.

With a shake of her head, Hannah tapped her comm. "Engineering, Bridge, have preparations been made?"

"Aye, they're all in place."

"Thanks, Annie." Getting up, she stretched a little, her back popping a few times. "Guess I'd best go see them off."

"Make sure they didn't steal anything," Laura called as she was exiting.

As unlikely as it seemed that Caster or Dido would have stolen anything, Hannah wouldn't put it past them to have pulled something. Kelly had called her paranoid when she'd explained her plan, although she had agreed it was sensible.

Cargo Bay Eight often doubled up as a shuttlebay and had had no issues accommodating the Remnant ship. It looked out of place, all white and chic compared to the dull bay and few lockers that lined the walls. Equally out of place were the two Purifiers, still downcast in their brilliant white robes.

Kelly was attempting to make polite conversation with them as Hannah approached, but their personal little rain clouds was making it tricky.

"We should be arriving in a few minutes," Hannah said. She gave a small shrug. "I guess this is goodbye."

Dido managed a small, taught smile. "For now, yes, it is goodbye." She offered her hand, which was accepted. "It's been an interesting adventure."

"That's one way of putting it."

With a small, slightly defeated nod, she smiled a little wider. "For what it's worth, I am sorry for the pain my people have caused you. And for the trouble I have put you through."

"Thank you."

The quartet all stood looking at one another, unsure of what to say next. The deck shuddered under them ever so slightly as they returned to normal space. It would still be a few minutes before they reached the agreed drop-off point.

"What do you plan to do now?" Dido asked.

"Oh, you know, find another job, make money, rinse and repeat." Hannah could see she was digging, probably wanting to get her hands on the *Livingstone*, despite the fact Spectrum would had taken anything of worth already. "Yourself?"

"Reports, debriefs."

The awkward silence returned and rapidly grew into an oppressive force.

Caster broke first. "Thank you for having me. May you have a good time," he said, heading to the shuttle. "Live long and prosper, peace and long life and all that jazz."

Dido's forced smile didn't flicker at all. "Well, it's been... interesting?"

"Have a safe trip," Hannah replied. "Please don't take offense if I say that I hope we don't meet again."

She chuckled and started to walk to the shuttle door. "None taken, my dear Captain," she said over her shoulder. "Although I am certain we will see each other again. Sooner than you think."

As she stepped into the shuttle, Pan appear, standing on top of it. They gave an excited double thumbs up and vanished like a demented Cheshire Cat.

"Sounds like you were right," Kelly said, putting her arm around Hannah as the shuttle gently lifted off the deck and made for the bay door. "You're going to be insufferable, aren't you?"

She gave her a peck on the cheek. "When am I not?"

"I think they've dropped us in the wrong system," Caster said as he tapped on the shuttle controls. "No sign of Green or any of our ships."

Dido smiled. "I'm certain we are in the wrong system." She sat back casually in her seat and stretched a little. "Comms have stopped working?"

"Yes."

The console started to flash up a number of errors as various ship systems went offline: comms, FTL, long range sensors, long range navigation; all gone, one after another. While not completely helpless, the shuttle wasn't going anywhere, unless they wanted a very long trip to the closest planet.

Caster tried tapping on work arounds, but each one was blocked. Eventually he tapped a button that triggered a six inch tall Hannah hologram to appear.

"If you're seeing this, you tried to contact your fleet while *Sigyn* was still in system," she said. She started to wag her finger. "Naughty, naughty. You'll have to sit tight for about six hours. The replicator still works, so I suggest you get a board game or some cards. See ya!"

The hologram flickered out and was replaced by a countdown showing just under six hours.

"Do you want me to try to get around this?" he asked, although he was absolutely certain he had a snowball's chance in hell of managing.

Dido shook her head.

"So, now what?"

She smiled, got up, requested some gentle meditation music and removed her robe. "I think I shall do some meditation on our adventures. There will be a lot of questions when we're picked up." She sat, cross-legged on the floor, closed her eyes and started to find her centre. All while she'd been at Earth, her meditations had failed, but now she felt she could find the inner peace again.

Caster got up and joined her on the floor, cross-legged, and started his own meditation.

Hannah had returned to the Bridge as *Sigyn* had departed the system. She had fully expected that Dido would betray the arrangement to not alert the Remnant of their location in an attempt to capture them. Pan had been instrumental in breaching the shuttle's computer protection to leave the little gift.

But that was all done with now. And with any luck, she'd never, ever, have to deal with her again. Although, if she was being honest with herself, she had to admire the Purifier. As a person, she liked her, just a little.

"Open a channel to *Sheba*."

Laura tapped on her console, showing Aisha how to open a comm channel at the same time.

After some back and forth, a hologram flickered into being, showing the Harpies.

"The wanderer returns," Helen said with a smile. "I trust your trip was fruitful?"

Hannah squirmed in her chair, unsure of what to actually say to her sisters.

"It's okay, Venus told us you got to Earth," Harry said. "We've promised not to tell anyone else, so you can tell us all about it when you get here."

Relaxing in the knowledge she wasn't going to have to hide another thing from her sisters, she smiled and nodded. "It was fruitful in the sense we learnt a lot, but we aren't exactly coming back loaded with booty." She stopped for a moment and the smile faded. "And not all of us that went are coming back."

The Harpies looked at one another before Helen nodded. "We'll toast them when you get back."

"Has Venus finished picking what she wants from the *Livingstone*?" Hannah asked, after a few seconds of respectful silence. While it would be nice to get back, once Venus was done, she could get to selling the rest, become disgustingly rich and perhaps even build a money bin to swim in.

Again, the sisters looked at each other.

"Yes, yes she has," Holly replied, looking at something off to the side. "She most certainly has and we will, in due course, pay you the share you are owned." She looked at Helen, who pointedly ignored her. "In shares and dividends."

Hannah's eyes narrowed. "And the rest is mine to dispose of as I see fit?"

There was a lot of shuffling before Holly nudged Heather.

"We might," she started before shuffling slightly, "have convinced her to take the lot."

"You sold my ship?" she thundered.

Aisha spun on her chair. "Excuse me, I think you'll find I was the rightful owner of *Livingstone* since everyone else is gone."

"Details," Hannah replied, flicking her hand to the side to dismiss the argument. "Salvage rights and such."

Helen's face immediately lit up. "Quite right, Hannah. *We* salvaged the ship from where it had been abandoned, so it technically was our property to sell. Of course, we'll let you have a finder's fee."

Hannah's face had gone through several intensifying shades of red. "Bitches! Bitches, the lot of you! When I get there I'm going to stick my foot so far up your collective arses, people will think you wear shoes as hats."

"Got to go, got a meeting to go to," Helen said, frantically swiping her hand over her throat for Sheba to cut the line while the other Harpies attempted a range of farewells, from fearful to obliviously jolly.

As the hologram dissolved, Hannah slammed her fists on the arms of her chair repeatedly, not unlike a toddler having a temper tantrum.

"I'm going to *kill them*!"

"I'm told you have some new pets?"

Eris cracked open one eye to scowl at her daughter for a second before closing it. "They are not pets, Minnie."

Minerva stood with her arms crossed, waiting for her mother's attention. There was no point trying to talk to her when her attention was elsewhere, even if what she wanted to discuss was important.

After a few minutes, Eris opened her eyes, smiled and went to hug her daughter. "What's up, precious?"

"Morri and Vicky have reported back," she replied, knowing fine well Eris would already know it all. "It's worse than we hoped, but not as bad as we feared. They still haven't approached critical levels, but they are gaining support. Several demagogues have appeared."

That was not a surprise in the slightest. While she'd hoped the population would have been free from such psychopathic radicals, it was only a matter of time before nature took her wicked course.

"How long until it starts falling apart?" she asked. "Roughly?"

"Three years at least, but no more than eight the way things are going," Minerva replied.

"Good, that should be enough time."

She fidgeted, becoming agitated. "Mother, please, let me and Aki take some of the SDF and just sort the problem."

"We can't just go shooting our problems, Minerva," she replied, a little sharply. Her face softened as she regarded her daughter. Too young and eager by half, but she was a good girl. "If Morri and Vicky can't settle things, I'll send you with my new representatives."

Eye twitching slightly, Minerva bunched her fists by her side as she tried to keep her temper under control. "You want to send a traumatised, unstable veteran into a warzone?"

"It shouldn't become one and it means she'll work for peace, not a blood bath. Remember, we guide gently from the side lines; we do not charge in enforcing our will on others."

Brushing the pointed remark off as a gentle criticism, Minerva nodded. "I hope you know what you're doing." She spun on her heel and headed for the door, her footsteps echoing in the massive chamber.

"So do I," Eris whispered as she called up a map of the Andromeda galaxy. "So do I."

Printed in Great Britain
by Amazon